AFTER WE BREAK

JILL HANNAH ANDERSON

After We Break
Red Adept Publishing, LLC
104 Bugenfield Court
Garner, NC 27529
https://RedAdeptPublishing.com/
Copyright © 2026 by Jill Hannah Anderson. All rights reserved.

Cover Art by Streetlight Graphics[1]

No part of this book may be reproduced, scanned, or distributed in any printed or electronic form without permission. Please do not participate in or encourage piracy of copyrighted materials in violation of the author's rights. Thank you for respecting the hard work of this author.

This is a work of fiction. Names, characters, places, and incidents either are the product of the author's imagination or are used fictitiously, and any resemblance to locales, events, business establishments, or actual persons—living or dead—is entirely coincidental.

---

1. http://StreetlightGraphics.com

In memory and honor of Vietnam POW

Colonel David Everson 1931–2024

Chapter 1
Eden
End of May 2022

The weight of his absence hit like a wrecking ball as I opened the screen door. Stepping from heavy early-morning humidity into my still-cool kitchen didn't lessen the instant nausea that had beckoned me home.

I had my answer as the air wept devastation in the silence. The birds quit chirping, the squirrels quit chattering, and the vocal cords of the whispering breeze had been ripped out. Wildlife and Mother Nature grieved with me as if knowing my pain couldn't bear noise.

How could you leave? My silent question would never be answered.

Then there he was—his shoulder-heaving chuckle, the hint of his woodsy soap, his hand patting my cheek as if everything would be fine. As warm tears bathed my cheeks, I was resolute about one thing. Although he'd left without saying goodbye, he would never be gone from my heart. Goosebumps formed on my skin as I stretched my arms to hug the air he'd recently breathed, to tuck it into my heart, where he would forever stay.

Eight years earlier
April 2014

I pressed a hand to my drumming chest and forced out a slow breath as I leaned back on my apartment door. Even the post–rush hour commute home hadn't lowered my heart rate.

"It's been a hell of a day," I said to the empty kitchen as if expecting the walls to offer a sympathetic response. Somewhere over the past few years, my I've-got-this attitude had turned against me like a fickle grade school frenemy. "Miss Eden Everson, you gave up control of your life the day you married." I yanked off my tennis shoes in front of the entryway closet and added, "You fool."

Two years after the divorce, Trent and I were still linked together because of our son. *Until Ryan graduates from high school in eight years, you're stuck.*

Hobbling on aching feet down the hall to my bedroom, I tossed my navy-blue blazer and skirt onto the bed before sitting down to tug off the constricting pantyhose I detested as much as my boss at Minneapolis Trust Corporation.

My shoulders slumped as I stared out the window at the setting sun. I'd missed another beautiful spring day, thanks to thirteen hours spent behind my desk. The excitement and challenge I'd once felt for my corporate job had slowly morphed over the years to feel more like wearing a full-body Spanx constricting the breath from my lungs, sucking the life out of me.

"You did this to yourself," I muttered, slipping into cotton shorts and a tank top. In two days, I would get a much-needed break from work, thanks to poor Ryan's upcoming appendectomy. We'd scheduled it for the Thursday before Easter break so that he wouldn't miss any school, not that it mattered too much. The kid was breezing through fourth grade. The timing would also give him a chance to heal before baseball practice began in a few weeks.

I had two more days until Ryan was back with me—less than forty-eight hours before I could smell his prepuberty sweat, feel his hair tickle my cheek when I leaned down to hug him, and look into his golden-brown eyes, one of the few traits he'd inherited from me. Meanwhile, Facetiming him at Trent's, like we did every night he was there, would have to do.

I had twelve minutes before our designated call time to eat and to splash cold water on my eyes, which had somehow swelled with unshed tears on the way home. I worried that Trent and I had destroyed Ryan's childhood when we divorced. I didn't need to make things worse by letting Ryan notice my unhappiness.

I swallowed the guilt of giving up on a marriage to a man who had never cheated on me, abused me, or gambled away our money. Trent had been the brave one to first utter the word "divorce." While chewing on that guilt, I also spooned in mouthfuls of leftover tuna salad after giving it the sniff test.

After dropping into the recliner and elevating my aching feet, I fed myself with one hand and rubbed my too-long-in-high-heels feet with the other until my twelve minutes were up. I pressed the FaceTime button for Trent's cell at eight o'clock and pasted a carefree smile on my face before Ryan answered.

"Hi there, favorite person of mine." My blood pressure dropped several digits when Ryan's face filled the screen. His blond hair, a shade lighter than Trent's, stuck up as if towel-dried without bothering with a comb, the style similar to my messy pixie cut. "All showered and ready for bed?"

"Yep. Dad promised we could play video games after I talked to you if I took a shower."

Video games bonded Trent and Ryan—same with the Minnesota Twins and the Vikings. I liked sports—I'd played softball and volleyball through high school and college—but I struggled with the crowds and noise, having grown up in a small town. Books, bikes, board games, and playing ball were my bridge with Ryan. I *played* sports with Ryan. Trent *watched* sports with him.

"That sounds like a good deal for you. And your dad doesn't have to smell that boy sweat." I plugged my nose.

"I don't stink." Ryan furrowed his brow before adding, "Anymore."

Our conversation turned to his Spring Open House at school the following night. He would be at my apartment the night after that. Trent and I typically switched on Sundays, but with Ryan's surgery on Thursday, we agreed to have him stay here ahead of time so that after his surgery, he would already be settled here.

I kept our conversation short so that Ryan would have time for video games before his nine o'clock bedtime. After we said good night, I shot my best friend, Stevie Grace, a text.

Where are you, Waldo? Got time for a call or FT?

Stevie Grace, a flight attendant for Delta, deserted me last year after moving from Minneapolis to Atlanta to work more international flights. We'd grown up together in Grandfield. Once a small town south of the Twin Cities, it had mushroomed into a suburb of the cities over the past twenty years. SG's parents—my parents' best friends—had retired to Orange Beach three years before, giving her, an only child, less of a reason to stay in Minnesota.

Just got home. Give me a min.

I waited a few minutes before hitting the FaceTime button.

Seeing Stevie Grace's smile made me homesick for her. "Hey there, sorry for the delay. I wanted to take off my makeup and put on comfy clothes first," she said, lounging on her patio in Atlanta. Even without makeup, Stevie Grace was stunning. Her thick auburn hair, shades lighter than my dark hair with reddish tints, was pulled into a high ponytail, which accentuated her vivid green eyes. Her lack of a boyfriend at the moment was only because she was picky.

She was named after Stevie Nicks and Grace Slick and was as colorful and dynamic as they were. She was two years younger than me, and I'd known her since the time I remember "helping" potty train her. We had grown up like sisters, living in different homes.

"So, what's up? You look exhausted. Still working a zillion hours at the bank?"

"A little less than a zillion, but not much. I'm trying to work ahead since I'll be off a week for Ryan's appendectomy. One of my coworkers didn't show up at work today, and although he does zero work, I needed his figures from a report for the board meeting this week." I massaged my foot, studying it to make sure I wasn't developing a hammertoe from the despicable high heels, which I wanted to chuck out the window.

"I've said it before, but I'll go ahead and repeat myself." Stevie Grace batted her eyes. "You need a life, and you'll never find it working there. The more you give, the more they expect. And for what? You never spend any of your fortune."

I snorted at her use of "fortune." Yes, I made a good salary, one I worked my butt off for, and yes, I was cautious with my money. I'd been raised to save for a rainy day. In the marrow of my bones, I sensed an imminent downpour coming my way.

"You're not much better: flying all over the place, renting an apartment in Atlanta, keeping your apartment here... which, by the way, says it misses you. Come back to Minneapolis, and I promise to add some pizzazz to my life."

"Ha! Hey, what's with the rash on your neck?" SG pointed at the screen and wrinkled her nose as if I had snot hanging from mine.

"Nothing. It's probably a reaction to laundry detergent or something." *Why am I lying to my best friend?*

"Or stress." SG shook her head. "I know you. You haven't changed detergents or anything else since you moved out of the house." Stevie stopped her lecturing long enough to drain half of her drink, probably vodka lemonade. "Which is another indicator that

I'm right, moneybags. Can you demote yourself at the bank? Go back to mortgage lending? You loved that, right?"

"No. And yes. Our mortgage loans have dropped by thirty percent over the past year, and I'm not going to push someone else out of their job just because I can't stand the boys'-club asshats that have floated to the top with me." I leaned my head back against the recliner. "Scratch that. Only a few of them are jerks. Most of the guys—and Sheila, the lone other woman with me in management—are decent human beings getting the life sucked out of them like I am."

Two in upper management had quit over the past year. Most of our misery stemmed from Dick-dick, my boss.

"Anyway, enough about me. When will you be in Minneapolis again?" After steering our conversation to SG's life, by the time we hung up and I got ready for bed, I was fantasizing that things would look better in the morning.

Chapter 2

We were five minutes into our weekly management meeting before Dick-dick—okay, his name was Richard—casually explained why Gordon, aka Nail Clipper, wasn't at work yesterday or at our management meeting.

"Gordon received some exciting and well-deserved news yesterday and wished for me to share it with you." Dick-dick cleared his fleshy throat. "He has accepted the position of bank president at a small bank near the Minnesota-Iowa border. Per his request, he wished to make a quiet exit without hoopla. He'll use vacation time until he transitions to his new endeavor."

My eyebrows and blood pressure shot up. "Is this a joke?"

Gordon didn't lift a finger in the office other than to clip his fingernails.

"No joke. I wrote a glowing letter of recommendation for Gordon." Dick-dick tapped the notepad in front of him with his designer pen. "Now, let's get down to business."

As Richard droned on, I leaned to my right and whispered to Sheila, "So, if I sit in my office and give myself a manicure every day, I'll get a letter of recommendation for a job I don't deserve?"

"You'd get your butt fired, just like I would," Sheila whispered back. She was a few years away from retirement... less of a threat than I was to Dick-dick. My knee hammered under the board table, bouncing my heel in and out of uncomfortable pumps as Chris, one of my favorite fellow managers, mimicked clipping his fingernails with mock concentration when Dick-dick wasn't looking.

"At any rate," Richard's phlegmy voice cut into my fantasy of flying out the window, "until we find a replacement for Gordon, we'll need everyone here to help pick up the slack."

I choked on his implication that Gordon's absence would leave a hole. *Not your problem, Eden,* I whispered under my breath. Ryan's surgery was in two days. All I needed from absent Gordon were the figures for the board report I needed to complete. My mind wandered to my son's upcoming appendectomy until Dick-dick said my name.

"Excuse me, what did you say?" I asked.

Richard's lips pursed like two squished worms in the middle of his goatee. "I'd like to meet with you in my office." He nodded to the dozen other managers gathered around the board table. "We're finished here. I'll catch up with everyone later to see how we can disperse Gordon's duties for now."

Before he breezed out of the boardroom, Richard turned toward me, handing me his Best Dad Ever coffee mug, which I wanted to puke in. "Please bring me some coffee, two creams and sugars, from the break room."

That wasn't the first time I'd been treated as a server, but it never got any easier to swallow a sarcastic comeback. I stormed down the hall to the break room and refilled my water bottle and Richard's coffee. As I was being tempted to add a little spit to the cream and sugar, someone entered the room behind me. I didn't need to turn around to know it was Carl since I could smell his aftershave a block away. He tied with Dick-dick on my can-barely-tolerate list.

Being in proximity to Carl sent a family of tarantulas in a conga line up my spine. I stepped aside from the coffee bar. That didn't deter him. Carl's protruding stomach pressed into my lower back firmly enough that I felt it under my blazer and skirt, even though there was adequate room between the counter and lunch table.

I whipped around. "Get away from me," I spewed.

Carl gave me heart palpitations—and not in the way he hoped.

Carl waved his hands in the air as if a bank robber had appeared. "I didn't touch you."

Carl—aka Mr. Handsy—had cornered me several times over the years, and I wasn't the only one. But every report to Dick-dick had the same comeback, that the women "misread" Carl. More than one woman had quit over the years because of Carl. He—and Richard—gave the rest of management a bad rap.

After I made a stink about Carl a year before, I was passed over for a promotion that was instead given to a man who "had a family to support," as if I didn't have a child, no husband, and a college degree, along with five more years of experience at the bank than the man they promoted. That episode ended with me wearing a heart monitor for three days to see what the issue was with my erratic heart.

My doctor had given me the same prognosis Stevie Grace had when I went in with chest pains and a racing heart that woke me from a dead sleep during too many nights. I slowed my pace and breathing as I headed down the hall to Dick-dick's office.

He sat at his desk with his fingers pressed together, elbows on the desk, the sunlight from the window behind him highlighting the gray in his goatee. "Have a seat." He held out a hand for his coffee, and I tucked my skirt as I took a seat, wishing for shorts and a T-shirt.

"I'll cut to the chase. We've discovered that the budget Gordon was supposed to have finished for the board meeting tomorrow morning hasn't been done. At all." Dick-dick cleared his throat by gulping coffee. "I need you on it. Pronto. Put everything else aside. I'll email you the info."

I closed my eyes at the bongo drums playing behind them. "Why am I not surprised?" I had my own important to-do items before I took a week off, but arguing was a waste of energy. I left Richard's office and the stench of the onion bagel he had for breakfast every morning.

After closing my office door with more force than needed, I clutched my stomach, briefly wondering if I, too, needed my appendix out. Poor Ryan had been dealing with a tender stomach, loss of appetite, and diarrhea for a couple of weeks before saying something. I should have noticed. Trent should have noticed. But that was another thing on my long "should" list that got kicked aside thanks to work.

Other than taking bathroom breaks and trips to refill my water bottle, I scarcely noticed the sun dipping toward the tree line out my office window. I had Gordon's report done and was finishing mine when I realized how quiet the halls were outside my office.

I stood to stretch and opened the door to see the cleaning team two offices down, the rest of the offices dark. I glanced at my watch: 7:36. My shoulders ached, my stomach growled, and a niggling sense of something missing chewed at me. I double-checked my report, making certain I hadn't left out any figures before sending it to Richard for the board meeting in the morning.

Pulling open the bottom drawer of my credenza, I kicked off my pumps and slipped on my socks and tennis shoes before packing up for the day. The heat of the day had left by the time I walked across the empty bank parking lot to my old Chevy Impala—the only car ever in reserved parking that was more than five years old.

"One more day, Eden. One more day, and you get a break," I said as I cranked the ignition. "And yes, you sound like a selfish mother for banking on your son's surgery to get a break." I had enough vacation time to hand out days like Halloween candy, but finding the time to take them and not regret it when I went back to work was the challenge.

I pulled into a Cub Foods on my way home. Ryan loved Toaster Strudels, and although they were packed with sugar, I wanted him to have a special treat once he could eat after the surgery.

Not until I finished grocery shopping and was back in my car did I remember to take my phone off silent mode. That's when I noticed five missed calls and text messages from Trent. I had missed Ryan's Spring Open House at his grade school.

Chapter 3

"I am so sorry, Ryan!" I said over FaceTime minutes later, after I arrived home.

Ryan's Adam's apple bobbed up and down, and his smile didn't reach his eyes. I'd let him down—again. I had one child, and he was my world. Yet somehow, he'd been placed on the back burner of my priorities. It had to change. It *would* change.

"It's okay, Mom. I brought home my papers that were on the classroom walls, so I can show you tomorrow." Ryan's kindness was a gift I didn't deserve.

"I promise to make it up to you tomorrow. You pick where you want to eat, and we'll go out for dinner. We'll go early so you're done eating by seven for your surgery Thursday morning." I would fly us to the moon if that was where he wanted to go for dinner.

And I would leave work early for it.

We ended our conversation with our signature nightly endearment of GLS, which stood for "Good night. Love you. Sweet dreams." It had begun around the time Ryan was four, and we had kept it going whether Ryan stayed with me or at his dad's. I slept little that night. Shame squished me like a panini press.

The following morning, I held a cold washcloth to my puffy eyes before applying my minimal makeup of eyebrow pencil and tinted lip gloss. Determined to start work early so that I could leave early, I was at my desk by six thirty, a desk that cost the bank more than what I paid for groceries in six months. Over the next hour, coworkers arrived, my closed office door blocking the noise so that I could concentrate on wrapping up my work for the following week.

Midmorning, Dick-dick stepped into my office after the board meeting was over.

"Good morning." Richard pulled at his cuffs as if ready for a slugfest. "I've got another project for you that Gordon left behind." He sauntered to my desk. "The board needs a breakdown of the lending payout report from last month. It seems there are a few discrepancies you'll need to iron out." He ran a hand over his unruly goatee. "I'll email their specifications."

I pushed back my chair. "When do you need it? I'm leaving a little early today, and remember Ryan's surgery is tomorrow. I'm off next week while he is home recovering."

"This can't wait. They need this fixed ASAP. Can't your ex sit with him?" Dick-dick scoffed. "And isn't your son, like, sixteen?"

I crossed my arms and pinched the skin under my forearm to keep from screaming exactly how much time off I had on the books. "Trent will be with our son, and so will I. And for Pete's sake, Ryan was born three years *after* I started fourteen years ago." I took a calming breath. "And that's not the point. I had the time scheduled off long before Gordon's sudden departure, I have the time and the right to take it... and I'm going to." I swallowed the frog hopping up my throat.

Dick-dick leaned over the desk, invading my personal space and bringing his stale coffee breath with him. "So you'll have it back to me before you leave today?"

He was asking for the impossible. I knew it. He knew it. It reminded me of the long list of chores the evil stepmother had given Cinderella before she could attend the ball.

But I wasn't Cinderella. I didn't have mice and birds to help me. I didn't have an eternally optimistic outlook that everyone was kind underneath their nasty veneer, and I sure didn't have the patience anymore for a job that had been financially fulfilling but emotionally draining for too many years.

The snowball of the past several days, months, and years, along with the repercussions to my personal life because of the never-satisfied attitude from the board and Richard, suddenly rolled down the mountain and parted the storm clouds. The solution was as crystal clear as the creek that ran through the hobby farm where I grew up.

"I'm. Not. Doing. It." I stood to my full height of six feet, thanks to the three-inch heels on my pumps. The weight of years layered with demands, sexism, deadlines, constricting pantyhose and toe-numbing high heels was lifted from my shoulders. I felt as light as a bubble.

"In fact, Dick-dick," *Ooh, did I just call him that out loud?* "I suggest you give Gordon's project to someone else because I have to leave. I think I might be sick!" The panic in his eyes as he stepped back made me wish I could make myself throw up. Instead, I yanked off my high heels and packed up for the day. If I stayed one more minute, I was afraid of what I might say or do.

If a Surprise-O-Meter had been sitting in the office, I don't know which one of us would've registered higher on it. Richard blanched as if I'd hurled a banana cream pie at his face. Over the years, I had worked through sickness to the point that I was heaving in my office trash one minute and back at my computer the next. Unless somebody died, I showed up at work—until now.

"What the hell, Eden?" Dick-dick's mouth hung open wide enough for my shoe. "You don't have to get so dramatic. Must be that time of the month." He muttered the last sentence.

His sexist comment wasn't a surprise.

"I'm not kidding. I don't feel well." That was a true statement. I worried that my head was going to explode or, worse yet, that I would erupt into tears. I yanked open my bottom desk drawer and took out the folded gym bag Trent had given me years ago with the insignia of his employer, hoping I would join him in his workouts. I never had. If I was going to work out, it would be in fresh air, not a sweaty gym.

"Damn hotheaded redhead." Dick-dick stormed out of my office, slamming the door with enough force to knock a folder off my desk.

I left the scattered papers. That was not my project anymore, not my monkey, not my circus. My fingers hovered over the idea of adding a password to the work folders on my computer to piss Dick-dick off and justify his redhead comment—which technically was inaccurate. I was one-quarter Korean and had inherited my mom's dark hair with a touch of my paternal grandma's red hair, giving my hair mahogany highlights. I remember Grandma Grady having red hair—and not an ounce of sass in her.

I tossed in my pumps and blazer, laced up my tennis shoes, grabbed the gym bag and my purse, and turned off my office light before leaving for the day—or forever.

Get out before this place swallows you! I hurried down the three flights of stairs to the main floor. My eyes zeroed in on the hallway to human resources, a tempting beacon for me. Sanity told me to shelve that idea until I had time to calm down and think. I had a week off—time enough to organize my thoughts.

I rounded the corner, heading for the main door, and collided with Sheila.

"Hey, are you okay?" She squinted at me with genuine concern. I could be honest with two people in management, Sheila and Chris.

"No." I swallowed back anxiety. "I need to get out of here before I give Richard's head a swirly in the toilet."

"Let me guess: Gordon's unfinished business is being pushed on you."

"You've got that right." Sheila knew of Ryan's upcoming appendectomy, and I gave her a condensed version of Dick-dick's demands.

After a long pause, Sheila asked, "Have you spoken with HR?"

"Not yet." Over the years, Sheila and I had talked of the gender disparity in upper management and, recently, of the Bank of America and Merrill Lynch discrimination lawsuit that had rocked the corporate world.

"He doesn't push me like he does you," Sheila commiserated. "Knows I'll be out of here soon enough. But you? You've got a case, Eden." Her words reaffirmed my thoughts.

"Thank you. I've got a lot to think about next week when I'm off."

Sheila gave me a side hug. "Please shoot me a text and let me know how Ryan's surgery goes tomorrow."

"Will do." I waved goodbye and left the building with a lighter step than I'd had in years.

Chapter 4

I arrived back at my apartment before noon, a rare weekday afternoon placed before me like a gift. Every vacation day I'd ever taken had been for a purpose. A constant gentle rain fell outside, cocooning me indoors with the lunch I'd made that morning for work. *Now what, Eden?* My mind was too unsettled to focus on gathering information for human resources. I needed a mind-numbing project.

After lunch, I walked around the apartment I'd managed to spend little time in over the past two years. I opened the hall closet door where I'd stored boxes after moving in. One contained fiction books I'd read years before, back when I took time to relax. Two others were marked "Eden" in Mom's handwriting. I'd received them from my parents before they moved to Alaska. I'd never bothered to look inside them, never had the time to tiptoe down memory lane—until now.

I turned on an oldies radio station that played songs my parents used to listen to and settled in on the sofa with two boxes. As I dug into the one marked Eden's Childhood first. I sang along with Five Stairsteps to "O-o-h Child" about things getting easier, and to "Rings" by Cymarron as they sang of a couple breaking up and getting back together—something I could never see happening with Trent. Inside the box were notes from school friends, dried-out corsages from high school dances, and sports awards and newspaper articles from the Grandfield newspaper highlighting my sports stats.

I found a letter I'd written to my parents in red crayon when I was about seven years old, asking why they hadn't adopted more siblings for me. Specifically, I wanted twin girls younger than me so I could play with them and boss them around. I hadn't had much luck doing that with my younger brother, Nielson.

The note didn't surprise me. I had always wanted a big family—one of the many differences between me and Trent. And I liked to be the boss, which is perhaps why I hadn't completely hated the challenges of my job at first. I couldn't control where I lived or how many children I had, but I could control a lot of things at work in upper management.

Trent, the youngest of five, grew up with little money and few opportunities to go anywhere. When his dad died in an on-the-job construction accident, Trent was ten and the only child left at home. He'd been raised like an only child, much younger than his four siblings.

His mother, Emily, received a decent insurance settlement and moved the two of them close to the cities, and suddenly, Trent's world changed. I understood his need for living near the interstate, his want for material things, and his insistence on always looking his best. He'd had none of that until fifth grade. And the exchange for that was losing a father he loved.

I set that box aside. Once Ryan was born, Trent never regretted our agreement to try for a baby. Unfortunately, he also hadn't regretted our agreement to have only one child.

Already feeling emotional, when The Moody Blues song "Question" played, I blinked back tears as the words to a song I'd heard many times in my youth resonated with me. When they sang about all the love someone had been giving had really been meant for themselves, Trent came to mind. And when they sang of looking for someone to change their life, it was a kick in the pants.

Nobody can fix your life but you, Eden. We had made so many mistakes in our marriage that when we divorced, I burned the journals I'd kept over the years. Looking back at our years together only reminded me of how much I'd given up on my dreams. I took a ragged breath before picking up the box marked Mom and Dad Stuff. My parents were minimalists, one of the many traits I'd inherited from them. I guessed whatever they had saved was worth keeping.

Inside were framed photos of the home they'd built together, with me as a toddler getting a piggyback ride from my older sister, Ellie. One photo showed the five of us fishing from the dock on Lonesome Lake, my new bike parked near the water's edge. I would have been eight, and Nielson, always big for his size, was nearly as tall as I was. Ellie, around seventeen then, showed nothing of the traumatic childhood she'd had before Mom and Dad adopted her. Ellie was always smiling, and I was certain her cheerful disposition brought smiles to the people she nursed in Guatemala, not to mention the three children she'd adopted with her husband.

Along with the pictures were old letters Mom had kept, from distant relatives in Korea. And underneath those was a small wooden box, one I remembered sitting on Mom's dresser. Mom rarely wore any jewelry besides a watch and her wedding band. I expected the box to be empty.

Inside was a vaguely familiar nickel-plated bracelet, one I remembered Mom wearing when I was young. I picked up the Vietnam Prisoner of War bracelet with the name *Lt. Col. David Carpenter* and the date *10-27-66*.

Tucked inside the jewelry box was a folded note in Mom's handwriting.

I've never been sure what to do with this treasured gift. After catching the opening on branches one too many times as I worked in the woods, I took it off before it broke.

These POW bracelets, the creation of Voices in Vital America (VIVA), came out in 1970. I was home from college in the summer of 1971, waitressing at the Woodland Café, when a group of teenagers on a road trip after their high school graduation came in for lunch.

One of the girls, with long brown hair and eyes that appeared much older than her age, wore this bracelet. When I commented on it, she slid it off her wrist. "You can have it. My dad won't be coming home."

I remember trying to hide my shock. "This is your dad?" My heart ached for her.

"Yes. And I have more bracelets with his name at home, so you can have that one. Mom says the father I knew is gone, but we're still supposed to wear the bracelets."

She had an edge to her words, acting as if she didn't care. I didn't believe it. I knew what it was like to lose a parent... both parents.

When they released the POWs two years later, I kept wearing the bracelet. I'm guessing David never made it home, since that's what his daughter implied. I couldn't bear to get rid of it.

I slid the bracelet onto my wrist, remembering the day Mom removed the bracelet. We had been clearing brush in the field behind our house for our goats and sheep. A stick had maneuvered itself between Mom's hand and the bracelet with such force that it pierced her skin, held tightly by the bracelet.

After cleaning the wound, Mom removed the bracelet for safety reasons. I was around ten and wanted to wear it, but my wrists were too small. Ellie had already left for college.

I was curious if the POW had ever made it home. When I googled "Vietnam POW Lt. Col. David Carpenter," I found an article about him from the previous year, commemorating the fortieth anniversary of his release on March 4, 1973.

Not only was David Carpenter alive as of the year before, but he lived in his hometown of Crimson Creek, Minnesota, a town that—according to Google Maps—was only a couple of hours north of me.

Chapter 5
David

My hand shook as I contemplated whether to reach behind my rocket seat to pull the trigger and eject from the F-105 Thunderbird or to go down with my plane. In that split second, a murky silhouette of Jean and the kids appeared in front of me, her image begging me to eject. I tried to shout our Wild Weasel motto, "First In, Last Out!" but no words came out.

Doesn't she understand that I can't give up the fight?

But I must have ejected because when I parachuted into the jungles of North Vietnam, the scent of my sweat permeated my flight helmet, and pain seared through my limbs as I hit the ground. That time, I managed a scream.

I woke myself up and blinked in the semidarkness, the hall nightlight illuminating my bedroom. Several slow breaths in and out helped calm my racing pulse as torrential rain pummeled the sidewalk outside my bedroom window. "You're safe in Crimson Creek, silly old man," I mumbled.

The clock read 3:08 a.m., and I questioned what had brought on the nightmare. They'd dwindled over the decades, my mind usually able to block out those seven years as a prisoner of war.

I couldn't blame the incessant rain that had begun overnight. Rainy days as a POW were generally peaceful. The Vietnamese guards didn't like to get wet taking us back and forth for interrogations.

I'd spoken with my daughter Louise the day before. With Louise and her family tucked away in Vermont, I could only take her word that she, my son-in-law Jack, and my two grandsons were all happy and healthy.

Perhaps a fellow POW passed away. I made a mental note to check in later with my Wild Weasels and Red River Rats online groups. That probably hadn't triggered the bad dream since other members dying hadn't haunted me in the past.

"Maybe it was the two pieces of cheesecake you had yesterday, you glutton," I reprimanded myself in the empty bedroom. After the "seven-year cleanse" as a POW, I came home with a vicious appetite for sweets. Our minimal prisoner diet had done nothing for our health other than lowering our cholesterol. Back in the States, I eventually tamed my cravings to avoid buying new pants every year.

Jean and her delicious cooking and baking had fed my cravings, two of the million things I'd missed in the fourteen years since she passed away suddenly. The nightmare couldn't have stemmed from grieving the loss of Jean or our son, Lee. The seven years without my family had somewhat prepared me to endure the loss of a loved one. Those years gave me plenty of time alone to tune in and connect with my family thousands of miles away, sensing their emotional highs and lows.

I had sensed traumatic things like Lee's fall from his motorbike, which resulted in a concussion and a broken arm, and when Louise's first serious boyfriend broke her heart when she was sixteen. Same with happier times, like their excitement when they went to Paris with other POW families in 1969. When your world is quiet, it's easier to tune in and *feel*.

I gave up trying to sleep and pulled on my bathrobe before heading to the kitchen. I brewed a small pot of coffee and fired up my laptop, settling in at the kitchen table. After confirming that we hadn't lost another comrade, I pushed away the laptop and sipped my coffee laced with cream.

Closing my eyes, which burned from fatigue, my nightmare came back, the choice I'd had to make in that split second back in 1966. Life was about choices: taking chances, pursuing dreams, living with regrets—everything I'd done, everything I regretted, or so I said.

But I didn't. Over the years, I was often asked if I regretted not leaving the Air Force before the Vietnam War. I usually answered "yes" because I understood that's what they wanted to hear. But it was a lie. Saying I wished I'd never flown a Thud in Vietnam because of the outcome was like saying I wished I had never been born, since I would eventually die.

I stood and walked to the dining room, watching the rain pelt against the window as the wind howled in the raven-black sky. Flying was living to me, fulfilling the dream I'd had since I was ten years old: becoming a fighter pilot. Sometimes, dreams were all we had, worth the risk, just to keep feeling like you had a purpose, no matter the cost.

In those seconds before I ejected, the thing that had gutted me to the core was knowing that even if I survived, it would likely be a long time before I saw Jean and the kids again. I regretted how much of their lives I would miss. But I never once regretted living my dream.

Chapter 6
Eden

I had to put aside the boxes and my trip down memory lane. Ryan would be home from school any minute. I stacked them in my bedroom. I would go through them again after Ryan's surgery, and I wanted to ask Mom questions about that POW bracelet.

The boxes had been a good diversion from the chaos at work. I didn't tell Ryan about my day when he arrived home with a look of surprise that I'd followed through with my promise to be home from work early. Ryan chose his favorite burger joint for his last meal before surgery.

At Big Buster's Burgers, we paired our burgers with malts—chocolate for Ryan and raspberry for me. We made up silly names to call his appendix, designed dream homes on our napkins with a pen, and made it back to the apartment early enough to play catch in the field a block from the apartment.

After we walked back home, Ryan showered before I diffused his nervous energy by beating him in two games of Battleship.

I spent most of that night tossing and turning, thinking of my job and Ryan's upcoming surgery and worrying that my alarm wouldn't go off at 5:45 a.m. By the time I got up, showered, and woke Ryan, emotional and physical exhaustion was making me feel eighty-five instead of thirty-five.

"Come on, buddy, rise and shine." I sat on the edge of Ryan's bed and leaned down to plant a kiss on his warm cheek. Check-in time for surgery was seven thirty.

We were quiet on our drive to Children's Hospital until "Counting Stars" by OneRepublic came on the radio, and I cranked it up, hoping it would diffuse Ryan's anxiety.

Trent arrived at the hospital minutes after we checked in, in time to tousle Ryan's hair. I refrained from smothering Ryan with kisses and reassurances and settled on inhaling his shampoo as I pressed my cheek to his.

Not until after they wheeled Ryan into surgery did Trent and I head to the waiting room. His tall, trim body and blond hair gave him a beach-boy vibe, but with neatly cropped hair. He was as handsome as he'd been the day I'd met him in college at a group winter weekend getaway on the north shore of Lake Superior. I had spent the time snowshoeing, skiing, or hiking with friends, and several of the women discussed the new guy's good looks. One of Trent's friends had invited him, and I hadn't paid attention to how Trent spent his time inside the hotel gym instead of outdoors.

I noticed a few women give him a double take as we passed them in the hospital hall. Trent, at thirty-six, could easily pass for late twenties. We took seats next to each other in the waiting room. Being with Trent without the buffer of Ryan felt weird. He leaned back in his chair, his legs stretched in front, displaying his top-dollar running shoes. He was close enough that I could see tiny blond stubble coating his chin and catch a whiff of a familiar scent resembling vanilla and roses, a scent I'd smelled on him before, and not his cologne.

I guessed it was the "super smiley woman that has a lot of blond curls," according to Ryan. I knew Trent had dated off and on the past two years, but that was the first time I knew of a woman important enough in his life to introduce her to Ryan.

"Ryan can stay with me all next week if that works for you. I know our schedule got thrown off with the surgery." I had planned to return to work once Ryan returned to school—hopefully Tuesday—but I had taken the whole week off, just in case. I planned to use that time to fortify the ammunition I would need to break free from my job.

"Okay. That way, we can get back on schedule," Trent said as he fished his cell phone from his pocket.

I stood. "I'm going to get coffee. Want one?"

"Sure." He didn't bother telling me he wanted two creamers and one sugar substitute. I knew. And I knew if there was a spruced-up coffee shop nearby, he'd want a double-shot espresso with whipped almond milk.

The weight of failure walked alongside me as I headed to the hospital cafeteria. Trent and I knew what each other liked and didn't like, but our mutual love for Ryan was the beginning and the end of our connection. We'd spent most of our time at college hanging out with other couples. Marrying right after college hadn't given us time to see how little our personalities had in common.

Trent's and my "come to Jesus" moment occurred the day he walked in the house, turned off the music I'd been listening to, and turned on the TV without asking, always assuming what he wanted was more important than my wants. I'd been making dinner, Ryan was at a neighbor's house, and that tiny move on Trent's part was what lit the stick of dynamite in me.

What followed was a bare-the-truth conversation, one where Trent expressed his unhappiness right along with mine. He was man enough to utter the "divorce" word, and I didn't squelch it—ironic that it was one of the few things we agreed on. I had pointed out how Trent always assumed he should have the final say on our decisions, and Trent fired back how he'd agreed to have one child. That was the extent of him bowing to my desires. I got off the world-revolves-around-Trent ride when we divorced, but the ties that bound us, aka Ryan, tethered me to Trent's city life until Ryan graduated.

I fixed Trent's coffee, left mine black, and added a cup of water for each of us on a tray. Carrying the tray back to the waiting room reminded me of my youth. My parents had had three businesses. Dad ran Ruby's Restaurant for twenty-plus years, and my mother had turned motel rooms into an apartment complex around the time Dad bought the restaurant. When they sold, they asked me if I was interested in any of the businesses. My sister, Ellie, was a traveling nurse in Guatemala by then, and my brother, Nielson, had left for college in Washington.

I had been interested in Grand Scheme of Things, the business my parents had created when they purchased a few connected buildings in downtown Grandfield. They turned them into an open market for local handmade items, and the second-floor end facing the corner was turned into a coffee bar and bakery.

I stopped in the hallway for a minute and leaned against the wall as that homesick feeling of wanting to step back in time knocked the breath out of me.

I missed the summer crowds filtering in from nearby lakes, escaping the heat of the day to shop and sip on something locally brewed and cold. In winter, the locals and a few tourists, possibly venturing in from the ice-skating and hockey rinks, hunkered down in the coffee shop between shopping, their hands warmed by steaming cups.

If someone had asked younger me what I wanted in life, I would have said a small business in a small town. But city-loving Trent had instantly nixed the idea of us buying the business. It was the summer before we married, and although I had little saved, my parents had assured me they would have done a Contract for Deed with me so that I wouldn't have to come up with a hefty down payment or qualify for a mortgage with a bank. Instead, I deferred to Trent's wishes, the first time of many—too many.

I had loved my upbringing, our hobby farm, the surrounding lakes, the laid-back pace, helping my parents at their businesses, ending every day in happiness and satisfaction.

That's what I had missed over the years—satisfaction and happiness at work. *Suck it up, girl.* I stepped away from the wall with my lips pressed together in determination. *You've got a college degree and years of corporate experience. Don't waste it on a dream like that.*

And, I reminded myself as I stepped back into the waiting room where Trent was focused on his phone, *stop regretting him. You aren't looking for a man. You are looking for a life.*

Chapter 7

Trent gazed at his phone with a lovestruck look I hadn't seen on him since we began dating. I wasn't positive he'd worn it even then.

He slipped his phone back into his pants pocket. "Any news yet?"

I handed him his coffee. "Nope, but it should be soon."

I set the two waters on an end table and paced, sipping my coffee. Laparoscopic surgery was estimated to take around an hour unless they ran into problems. I turned toward Trent, who was smiling at his phone again.

I walked over, thinking it might be adorable photos of Ryan. Instead, I caught a glimpse of a blonde in a black bikini. "I'm guessing that's the woman you introduced to Ryan?"

Trent jumped. "Yes, it's Amber. She manages the LifeJoy gym in Minnetonka."

I sat next to him, swallowing a feeling that I'd been left behind in the dating race. I refused to hop on any of the dating apps, almost every man I worked with was married, and my minimal free time was spent with Ryan.

And I was picky, possibly too picky. I'd dated two men since our divorce, neither for more than a few dates. "I should meet her since Ryan has."

Trent forced a chuckle. "She's not a pedophile. Amber is nice, has no children of her own, and I promise, if Ryan has issues with her, I won't have her over when he stays with me."

Not that I didn't trust Trent or his girlfriend, but it was one more thing in the dynamics of our family life that was changing. Just then, a nurse entered the waiting room.

"Ryan's out of surgery," she said. "I'll take you to his recovery room. They'll wheel him in shortly, and the surgeon will meet with you there." All thoughts of my job and Amber slipped away as Trent and I followed the nurse to a room down the hall.

Minutes after they wheeled Ryan in, the surgeon arrived to let us know that all had gone well and that, per our discretion, Ryan should be able to get back to school in less than a week. But he couldn't exercise other than walking for the first six weeks. Summer baseball practice began in mid-May. He wouldn't be joining his team until late May.

Trent hung around until Ryan, slightly queasy, woke up and became alert enough to give Trent a thumbs-up. Easter was my holiday this year, but Trent and I agreed that if Ryan felt up to it, I would drop him off at Trent's mom's house for Easter dinner.

A few hours later, Ryan was able to keep down apple juice, and his vitals looked good. By four o'clock, I was given the go-ahead to take Ryan home. Tucked in his bed at my apartment, he slept off the anesthesia Thursday night.

While Ryan slept on Friday, I sat on the deck with my computer and documented my research before placing a call to human resources.

I had ignored two calls from Dick-dick after I left work on Wednesday, both voice mails demanding that I call him back once I got over my "hissy fit." I ignored his messages along with the emails he sent. I was off the clock and, for once, refused to work on my time off.

I jotted down notes from the Bank of America lawsuit, printed out emails from Dick-dick that I had forwarded from my work email to my personal one over the years—emails with enough backup information to take to human resources. Richard should have been more careful with the wording he used in his emails and the notes he left on my desk.

Along with the disparity between my salary and most of the other upper management, I had enough ammo to start the war—a war I hoped to win and one that would pad my pockets enough until I could find another job that wouldn't kill me, one that would give me time with Ryan.

Pacing like a tiger waiting to pounce, I about wore a hole in the living room carpet by the time I finished my phone call with HR, nabbing an appointment for ten the following Thursday morning. Ryan would hopefully return to school before then.

The excitement of having an appointment scheduled, something concrete to move my plans forward, was something I itched to share. I peeked in on Ryan, and his soft snoring told me he wouldn't wake soon.

I poured myself an iced tea and sent my sister, Ellie, a text to see if she was available to visit, thankful that Guatemala and Minnesota time zones were similar. Her life, while still crazy busy, had let up a little once her youngest enrolled in pre-*primaria* school. Ellie, now forty-five, and Adan, a doctor from Guatemala, had been married for six years.

Two years after they married, they adopted three sibling orphans, now ages five, seven, and eight, and Ellie's zest for life only increased. So did her hectic schedule, with three young children and her nursing career.

Ellie responded via text to give her ten minutes, then she would call me. I stepped out on my deck and shut the sliding glass door, sitting with my eyes toward the living room so that I would see if Ryan woke up. I didn't want him to hear our conversation, wasn't ready to explain my upcoming meeting with human resources.

I jumped when my phone rang. "Hey, Bits!" I said, reverting to my sister's old nickname, something I tended to do when speaking to her. "Do you have a few minutes for me to vent?" I'd sent her a text after Ryan's surgery yesterday but hadn't mentioned the chaos at work.

"Sure do. I took a quick work break so we could visit," Ellie said. "Ryan doing okay?"

"Yes, he's good. Sleeping right now." I drummed my fingers against my knee, reminding myself that Ellie didn't judge anyone. "It's my work." My voice caught on the last word. "It's pushing me to the limit, Bits. I've got an appointment with HR next week. I need to get out of there..." I swallowed hard. "Before they break me." I barely got the words out before my chin quivered and tears flooded my eyes.

"Oh, Eden, I wish I was there for you!" Ellie's voice was as comforting as a soft blanket. My big sister oozed warmth and compassion, even when I'd tested her patience when I was young. "Give me the details. What was the final blow for you?"

Ellie knew I didn't buckle easily, knew of my stress-related health issues over the years. We might not have been blood related, but I hoped a slice of her grit had rubbed off on me. She'd persevered through horrific situations before our parents adopted her.

I filled her in on Gordon's sudden departure, of his projects dumped on me, of Dick-dick thinking Trent could take my place for Ryan's surgery and recovery, and of me missing Ryan's school's open house.

"When I apologized, again, to Ryan, something broke in me," I said, dabbing at my eyes. "I'd said those words to him too many times. Yet never once did Dick-dick apologize to me. He only expected more." I took a long gulp of iced tea.

"What are you hoping to get out of your meeting with HR?"

"Paid administrative leave. I don't think I can set foot in that place again. I swear my heart and soul are being sliced and diced when I'm there." I leaned back in the patio chair and closed my eyes, tilting my face toward the sun.

"Then what? A severance package?" Ellie asked.

"That's my hope. I've got plenty of documentation to show blatant gender inequality." I hoped I wouldn't have to get into the sexist comments and actions from Carl. Those I had evidence of only in my head. He'd been much more careful than Richard.

"You've got this, Eden. Don't let them get the best of you." Ellie cheered me on. "Your perfect job is waiting for you out there. You deserve it, deserve to be happy."

We spoke a few more minutes before Ellie needed to get back to work, a job she'd chosen well—her perfect job.

Now, I needed to find mine.

Ryan and I spent Saturday playing games, watching movies, and going for short, slow walks. On Easter Sunday, I dropped Ryan off at Trent's mom's house for their Easter meal then hurried home to get outside and bike in the seventy-and-sunny weather. I filled a water bottle, retrieved my bicycle from the tuck-under garage, and headed out.

I spent the next two hours on the paved trail near my home that ran parallel to the interstate Trent embraced. Eventually, the trail veered off through neighborhoods and woods, bringing me to one of my favorite nearby areas—a small beach. The area reminded me of Lonesome Lake, located down the dirt road from where I grew up.

I parked the bike, pulled off my helmet, tennis shoes, and socks, and waded in the frigid lake. The ice had melted two weeks earlier. I closed my eyes and took in the quiet, pretending I was back in Grandfield with my brother and sister.

We would likely never live in the same state again, much less the same area. Ellie—who had insisted we call her Ellie instead of Bits once she hit high school—would never move from Guatemala. And I couldn't imagine Nielson—who worked as a Fish and Wildlife Officer for the WDFW in Olympia, Washington, the area where his great-grandfather had been chief of the Puyallup tribe near Puget Sound—would ever leave Washington.

Mom and Dad loved where they'd lived the past fourteen years. Everyone in my family was where they were meant to be—except me. I was the only one left in Minnesota, living in the heart of the Twin Cities, a place I would have never picked for myself. But Trent had loved it. And because of the much-sought-after school district where we lived, I was stuck until Ryan graduated.

But for right now, this secluded spot, which I hadn't biked to since last fall, was my happy place, a mere thirty-mile round trip on my bike. Music played farther down the beach, and as One Direction sang "Story of My Life," I stood in the cold water and faced the sun with my eyes closed until the cold water no longer numbed my feet, thinking of *my life* and feeling hopeful.

Chapter 8

Back at the apartment, I took out the boxes from my parents, eager to unearth more information about David Carpenter, the Vietnam prisoner of war. I pulled up his name again on Google and opened other articles about David's time in the service. My father had suffered emotional trauma after his tour in Vietnam and rarely talked about it. The same was true with Stevie Grace's dad. His time in Vietnam had landed him in a wheelchair.

Although I had called my parents a few days before to give them an update on Ryan's recovery, I hadn't mentioned finding the bracelet. I retrieved my cell phone from the kitchen counter.

My parents weren't big fans of technology, but after much scolding from us kids, they agreed that keeping their cell phones with them as they wandered all over their rural property was a smart idea. Although they were in great shape for being in their midsixties, and as much as I would put my money on Mom over a bear, it gave me peace of mind to know she would have her cell phone to take a photo of the bear's demise afterward.

Mom's cell rang several times before she answered. "Happy Easter, Eden." Every time I heard Mom's voice, my heart ached. I missed her long hugs—the ones that used to embarrass me as a teen.

"Happy Easter. Are you sitting down? I've got some news." Our phone calls were infrequent only because of the time zone difference and our busy lives. Mom knew I hadn't called to wish them Happy Easter after speaking with them three days before.

"Is Ryan okay?"

"Oh yes, he's recovering fine. He's at Grandma Emily's today for Easter. I forgot to tell you the other day that I dug out the boxes you gave me when you and Dad moved." I paced from the kitchen to the living room. "I found your old jewelry box with the POW bracelet inside."

"Oh yes, I remember I left it in there with a note."

"Yep. And I got to thinking—you took that bracelet off decades ago, before the internet. I googled his name to see if I could find anything on him."

"And…?"

"And he's alive, Mom!" I did a little happy dance as if hearing the news myself for the first time. "He lives in Minnesota, just a couple of hours north of the Twin Cities."

"Minnesota? I don't know why I thought his daughter lived in Missouri," Mom said. "His daughter and her friends had said they'd just graduated from high school and were road-tripping. I assumed they weren't traveling that far." Mom had grown up in rural Missouri. She paused, digesting the good news. "Are you going to mail it to him?"

"I don't know." I ran a hand through my hair. My every-six-week trim was overdue. "I'm thinking of driving to give it back to him in person so I can meet him."

"Well, let me know if you do. And get pictures. I want to see this man who brought your father and me together."

"I will."

We spoke for several more minutes until Mom had to leave to head up an Easter dinner at their local community center.

After we hung up, I trailed my fingers over the bracelet, thinking of the story Mom had told me years before about when she first met Dad in 1977. Mom had "borrowed" Dad's family hunting cabin, got kicked out, and was clearing her own acreage outside Grandfield when Dad confronted her, spitting and sputtering.

Then he caught sight of the bracelet on Mom's wrist, and his anger deflated at the sight of her still wearing a POW bracelet four years after their release. Dad, still troubled by his time in Vietnam, decided Mom couldn't be all bad. That was a story I would tell David if I met him.

I continued to research David and Crimson Creek, learning more about the sleepy town now blossoming thanks to mountain bike trails—the first one opening in 2010. The recent story mentioned that he'd continued serving as a pilot in the Air Force until he retired in 1977 as a colonel. It didn't mention a wife or children, yet he clearly had at least one daughter who would be around sixty now. *Had the war shattered his family along with him?*

I was still in Google mode when Trent texted me that he would drop off Ryan soon, so I set my computer aside and proceeded to make lasagna for supper, taking care to put in extra ricotta cheese for Ryan, per his Easter dinner request.

While I cooked, my mind hashed over the need to leave my job, something as frightening to me as bungee jumping. Dad had steered me toward finance for my major at Winona State University. I'd inherited my parents' money and business sense. He had been vice president of a bank in Mason City, Iowa when he met Mom, and he eventually traded in his suit and tie for a chef's hat when he bought the restaurant in Grandfield.

Dad was right about me going into finance. I liked things black-and-white, had been raised to value a dollar, and enjoyed the challenge of climbing my way from mortgage lender to assistant VP of the secondary market at the second-largest bank in Minnesota. There, I had worked in risk management, central operations, the finance department, and even the information security department. I'd become a jill-of-all-trades at the bank, and for nothing but too many hours and too much stress.

I twitched with the craving to hold a burning ceremony of my pantyhose and high-heeled pumps, but I worried that would bring bad juju. I wanted a jeans-and-sweatshirt kind of job but with a decent salary.

Trent and I had survived three years of marriage before he found "his calling" at LifeJoy. I was the main breadwinner, which pushed me to keep climbing the ladder so that we could purchase a home—the loan based solely on my income—and, hopefully, get pregnant. Trent, one year older than me, had graduated from Winona with the same finance degree. My minor was journalism, and his was health science, the field he wanted to work in. Not exactly high paying, but saying no to Trent was difficult, which meant I allowed him to meander along until he could find his dream job.

When Trent landed a management job at the corporate office of LifeJoy, Minnesota's largest fitness company, five years ago, he also landed decent pay and better health insurance than I had carried for the family. Even at his new position, though, I still earned more than twice what he did, in a job that coiled around me like a python.

When we began divorce proceedings a few years ago, there was no question who would keep the house located near the interstate. Trent wanted it. I didn't. And although I made significantly more than him, we agreed on no alimony or support since we split custody of Ryan. Instead, I made a hefty deposit every month into a savings account for Ryan's college fund and paid for all his school and sports expenses.

That had worked for us in the past. I hoped I could afford it in the future.

After Ryan left for school Thursday morning, I dressed in my navy-blue skirt and blazer and gave myself a million-dollar pep talk as I got ready for my meeting with HR. The day before, I had pulled out the old cassette recorder and player Ryan and I used when he was little. I would record us singing songs, and he loved playing them back.

I had inserted a blank cassette to record myself reciting my evidence. The last thing I wanted was to sound unprepared. I'd done a few recordings and kept the final draft, which I listened to while I got ready for my meeting. My voice was confident, my information detailed—information that paperwork would back up.

At 9:45 a.m., I walked with purpose through the bank's parking lot, avoiding puddles from the overnight rain, for my ten o'clock meeting with human resources.

Two hours later, I left with up to a month of paid administrative leave, depending on how soon they could complete their investigation. Nobody in the room had batted an eye at my documentation or verbal details of blatant discriminatory behavior, which gave me hope that we could come to a mutual agreement on severance pay.

After Ryan went to bed Friday night, my cell phone rang, Dick-dick's name and number showing on the screen. The man had balls, calling me while I was off work, but over the years, he'd thought of me as his twenty-four-hour servant.

Did HR already meet with him? Only one way to find out. I answered the phone and instantly realized he'd been drinking.

"You have some nerve, Eden." Dick-dick's words slurred together.

"Do I?" The less I said, the better. I wasn't sure what he knew yet. I walked down the hall to my bedroom so that Ryan wouldn't hear me. That's when I spotted the tape recorder sitting on my dresser. The blank tape I'd used for my HR speech was still in there.

I sat on my bed, tape recorder in my lap, and pressed Record with one hand and put Richard on speaker phone with my other. I caught him in the middle of a slurred ramble about me being ungrateful. I let him drone on before I cut in.

"So, why did you call me, Richard?" My phone history would show he'd called me, but I wanted backup.

"Cuz you're full of shit! I saw you at work yesterday, heading to HR instead of your office. You should've been working on Gordon's projects instead of bitching to HR…" His words were followed by a lot of mumbling, and it sounded like he dropped the phone.

He was back in a few seconds. "I paid them a little visit after you left. Seems you're unhappy with your job?" His sneer accentuated the slurring. "You might want to quit before I make you regret it." I could almost smell the booze through the phone.

I glanced down at the cassette, reassured to see the tape moving as it recorded. "Don't threaten me."

"It's not a threat. It's a promise!" Dick-dick shouted. "You know what I think? I think…" It sounded like he'd jostled the phone again, and a second later, the call went dead.

I clicked off the tape recorder and took several calming breaths before I hit Rewind then Play. The recording picked up our voices well. *I believe you just nailed your career coffin shut, Dick-dick.*

Chapter 9

On Saturday morning, Ryan and I drove to Brady's house to pick him up. His mother, Gretta, an old friend of mine from college, walked outside with Brady.

"Good morning," Gretta said as she jostled her youngest on her hip. Gretta's long blond hair was pulled back into a ponytail.

Brady was her oldest of five, and she was a high school counselor. Although we'd been casual friends in college, Gretta's and my lives had become so full in different ways since then that we mostly connected via our sons' friendship.

"Hey there," I said, reaching through my open window and tickling her little girl's toes. I envied Gretta and her houseful of children, especially since I was officially in the geriatric pregnancy age bracket, not to mention I had no significant other.

After Trent and I divorced, I'd briefly considered a sperm donor. Practicality stopped me. I had enough to deal with emotionally from a recent divorce and too much stress at work. Any energy I had left needed to be focused on Ryan.

And when I needed a reminder that nobody had it all—including Gretta—while Brady climbed into the back seat with Ryan, she leaned down and whispered, "Thank you for taking Brady overnight. My mother-in-law is staying with us for a few months, so she's not alone during chemo treatments, which means he's been sharing a room with his younger brothers. This is a good break for him."

"That's a lot on your plate," I said. Her father-in-law had died the previous year, and they had helped care for him during his final months.

"It is. But I'm thankful we have the room and that we get quality time with her," Gretta said. "I think she sleeps well at night because our kids wear her out."

I thought of how I would love to have my parents living near me. Connecting by phone never seemed enough. Ryan and I had flown to Anchorage for a week last summer, and every other year, my parents, siblings, and I gathered in Grandfield around Christmas to reconnect.

We visited for a few more minutes before her little girl grew restless. "I'll drop Brady off before noon tomorrow." Their home was on my way to Trent's house.

"Thank you." Gretta leaned in and waved goodbye to a smiling Brady.

That evening, I whipped up a batch of homemade mac and cheese and grilled chicken wrapped in bacon for Ryan, Brady, and me. After we ate, they helped clean up the kitchen before heading for Ryan's bedroom to play video games.

I sat with a mug of lavender tea and my computer, my *Best of Guess Who* CD playing while I scrolled through job listings. As "Undun" played, I thought of Dick-dick possibly coming undone once I turned over the recording of our phone call to HR Monday morning. I would have fourteen years at Minneapolis Trust Corporation in June and hoped to be gone before my anniversary.

"No Time" played while I contemplated the few openings in 3M's finance department. I'd found myself some wings and hoped to be on my way to better things, just as The Guess Who promised. United Health had an opening in finance, and an editorial job was opening at the Minneapolis Tribune, as well as a corporate communications and grant-writer position. I hoped all would have less stress, decent work hours, and benefits. But I wasn't certain that would be enough for me anymore. I had never thought I would be one to sit behind a desk, no matter how expensive the desk, no matter how comfortable the chair.

The following morning, I made French toast and bacon for Ryan and Brady before we dropped Brady off at his house. Instead of heading to Trent's, I took a detour to a small park. Ryan deserved to know what was going on with my job so that he could be prepared on the chance I was out of MTC soon.

"I want to talk to you about something before we go to your dad's," I explained as I drove into the park's lot. I turned off the engine and rolled down the car windows, noticing Ryan's eyes widen.

"I've spoken with human resources at work regarding some problems that I've had with management. There's a good chance I'll be off work for a few weeks until we get things figured out. And"—I reached for his hand, his tan from hours outside already changing his skin tone to resemble mine—"I might be done working there soon. I'd like to look for a job that isn't so stressful."

Ryan tilted his head. "You mean you want a job that makes you happy?"

I chuckled. "Yes, that's the goal. It's probably obvious that I'm not thrilled with my job, especially all the hours I have to work. I hate missing your events."

"You weren't the only mom or dad who couldn't be at the open house. One of the girls in my class has a mom who is in the service overseas somewhere. My teacher said that's what happens when we become adults. We have responsibilities." Ryan picked at a string on his T-shirt. "I don't think I want to be an adult."

"Well, I do want you to become an adult eventually." We sat in silence for a moment, his warm hand in mine.

"My teacher said her husband is gone a lot. He drives a semi to different states," Ryan said.

That surprised me. His teacher had three children in grade school—another example of a woman with plenty on her plate.

"She misses him when he's gone, but she said when he's home, they all spend 'quality time' together and don't waste time watching TV or anything."

I tried to imagine not being able to see Ryan every other week. "Sometimes, I have to remind myself that quality is more important than quantity," I said and pulled him in for a hug, inhaling the scent of pancake syrup.

Leaning back, I ruffled his hair. "Let's get you to your dad's before he worries."

After I dropped Ryan off at Trent's, I drove home, fixed a plate of leftovers and some iced tea, and sent Stevie Grace a text to see if she was available to chat. Settled in at the small table and chair on my deck, I gave SG an update via FaceTime on where things were at with HR and my job searches.

"Did you apply to 3M or United Health?"

"I haven't submitted any applications yet. I'm not sure I can handle sitting in an office again." The idea brought heart palpitations. "I tell myself that if it was a straight forty-hour-a-week job, I could handle it. But that may be a lie."

"And Earth Eden would still be stuck inside and living in the cities." SG reverted to the nickname Trent had called me in our early years, back when I'd hung on to a piece of myself and had a large garden, canned, and scoured the woods outside town for herbs and mushrooms, living a slice of the life I'd had growing up.

I stuck out my tongue. "I could do it. And then I swear I'm going to look for a home on the edge of Ryan's school district."

But homes in the district were overpriced thanks to the in-demand school system. The home Trent and I had bought a dozen years ago was affordable back then due to its size and location right off the interstate.

"You're going to make me get real with you, aren't you?" SG gave a dramatic sigh.

"Have you ever *not* been real with me? Isn't 'blunt' your middle name?"

"Ha ha. Listen, whether it's months from now or a couple of years, you aren't going to be happy with a lower-paying job, no challenges, and no say in how things run," SG continued. "You want what we had growing up. Maybe you can't have exactly that, but I think you need to aim as close as you can. You don't have to live Trent's life anymore." She asked a final question. "What's the number one thing you want for Ryan?"

"Duh. I want him to be happy."

Stevie Grace nodded. "Right. So why don't you want that for yourself?"

"Because I don't think I can make us both happy." I blinked back tears. "Anyway, enough depressing talk. Hey, Trent's serious enough about his girlfriend that she was at his mom's house for Easter dinner."

"Hmmm. That's not depressing for you?"

She knew me too well. "It's been weird to talk about her with Trent. I knew our family dynamics would change eventually, but it feels like I'm stumbling backward and he's jogging forward."

"Don't do it, Eden," SG gritted.

"What? I'm not doing anything." I massaged the base of my neck.

"Don't go down the 'why did we divorce' path."

I chewed my lip. "Sometimes, I can't remember how I got here. I could be living back at our house with Ryan every day." I imagined it all in hues of pink tied up in a lying-to-yourself bow. "Trent wasn't bad. We just wanted different things—"

SG harumphed. "Yeah, he wanted *you* to live *his* life! Can I ask you a few questions?" She didn't wait for my approval. "Where did you go on your honeymoon?"

"Vegas. You know that."

"Where did *you* want to go? The area you talked of for a year before your wedding?"

I rubbed my forehead, feeling a headache spreading like a stain. "I wanted to hike the Appalachian Trail in Vermont." I should have done that before we married, back when I had the freedom to make decisions for myself.

"What did your wedding dress look like?" Stevie Grace pressed on.

"Why are we playing twenty questions? You were there, helping hold it up in the bathroom stall so I didn't pee on it."

"Just answer the question, please."

"Geesh, I feel like I'm on the witness stand." I closed my eyes, remembering the lace that covered the long, sweetheart-necked, snug-fitting sleeveless gown. Gorgeous and flattering, the dress had garnered far more compliments than I would have received if I'd worn the long butter-yellow skirt and wrap top I had picked out. That ensemble was comfortable, classy, more Earth Eden–like... and nixed in a heartbeat by Trent.

The same happened with our wedding cake, which was the next question SG fired.

When she brought up Trent waiting to find the right job while I supported us, I held up my hand. "Fine, I get the message." Trent got what he wanted because I always caved. Demoralizing memories like those were what had inspired me to burn my old journals.

"You didn't split up because of your differences, Eden. You were sick of living Trent's life." Stevie Grace's green eyes shone with clarity.

I cringed at her words. "Remember, he's the one who brought up the split." A subject I'd thought of for months, years.

"Whatever. I'm pointing out the truth, and you're dipping it in sugar."

"That's why I love you. You're a good truth arrow for me." SG being right didn't make it any easier. Until Ryan went off to college, I was stuck here in Trent's world.

"And as long as I'm ranting, remember the flip side." Apparently, SG wasn't finished. "You didn't convey enough to Trent how much living in the country meant to you or how much you hated your job."

"Ugh, you are a soul sucker." I wrinkled my nose at her.

"A truth-spewing, soul-sucking friend who misses you."

"And, despite my better judgment, I miss you too, SG."

We hung up, and I sat there, allowing her words to penetrate, steering me to look forward instead of back.

Chapter 10

After I met again with human resources on the last Monday of April, handing them the recording of Richard's call, they took less than two weeks to call me back in and negotiate a severance agreement, one that included me keeping my new work iPhone. I could have waited for them to can Dick-dick and stayed at my job, but once I'd decided to jump off the roller coaster and explore life, I couldn't make myself step back into that dark, stuffy boxcar.

I received a lump sum of six months' pay in exchange for a nondisparagement clause preventing me from making any negative comments about Richard or any staff or against Minneapolis Trust Corporation in general.

We arranged for me to pick up my personal things after hours on Friday, May 9. That was Ryan's week with me, and his baseball team had a game after school. It was too soon for him to play, so I didn't mind missing the game. I'd spoken with Gretta before arranging to meet HR. Ryan would go home from the game with her, and I'd pick him up afterward.

I'd sent a text to Sheila and Chris about me leaving MTC with a severance package, saying that I would miss working with them and most of management, and that I would clean out my office after hours on Friday.

I'd never made my office my home even though I spent more time there than anywhere else. I boxed up the few photos I had of family, along with a few other personal effects, and was escorted out the door by HR minutes later, with their best wishes.

I was tempted to jog to my car with my shoulder bag of things, but I was wearing flip-flops and didn't want to trip. I hadn't bothered dressing up for my final departure, never wanting to look at high heels or pantyhose again.

When I rounded the corner to my car, one of few left in the parking lot, there stood Sheila, Chris, and two other guys from upper management, men who represented the good side of working there.

"Hey, what are you all still doing here?" I asked.

"We wanted to say goodbye, silly," Sheila said, stepping forward to embrace me.

"We were watching for you." Chris nodded toward a bar and restaurant on the other side of the parking lot. "We couldn't leave without telling you we're happy for you."

I unlocked my door and set my shoulder bag on the passenger seat. "Thank you. I mean it. You were all the best part of my job." I swallowed an egg-sized lump. "But I'm glad to be out of there." My nose tingled, and I was certain the tears would follow. "I couldn't take it anymore." Before I finished speaking, I was pulled in for a group hug.

We visited for a few more minutes before a couple of the men had to hit the road. "Even though the ice is just off Leech Lake, we're heading up tonight for Fishing Opener." The Minnesota Fishing Opener was Saturday, and most people headed north for the big weekend.

I sat in my car after everyone left and called Mom's cell phone. I'd been texting my parents updates on my job situation ever since Ryan's surgery. "I'm officially done, Mom," I said when she answered, my voice a mixture of relief and disbelief.

"How do you feel?" Mom asked as I heard her dicing something for their evening meal.

"A bit shell-shocked. With the six-month salary payout, I can take my time looking for something I want. Not sure I'll know what to do with time on my hands, though." I leaned against the headrest.

"It's exactly what you need, Eden. Your dad and I have seen the toll your job has taken on your health, which says a lot since most of the time we're only seeing you through a screen." I heard the smile in Mom's voice.

"You've got a clean slate in front of you," Mom continued. "According to Charles Dickens, 'We forge the chains we wear in life,' and I think that's what's happened to you over the years. You pushed yourself because you had to. And," she paused as if hesitant to say the words, "you've lowered your expectations for your life."

"What do you mean?" I sat up, anxious to hear where I'd gone wrong.

"There was no ceiling for your dreams when you were growing up. And over the years, you took on the responsibility of yourself and Trent instead of him being responsible. You let him choose your life and convinced yourself it was enough." Mom sighed. "I'm only saying it because I lived it. Remember how I told you I would have settled with my old boyfriend on the hobby farm where I grew up? I didn't love him, but I'd have settled because it was easier than trying to figure out what I wanted in life."

Mom let her words sink in. "You've mentioned over the years how you wish you owned your own small business. Maybe now is the time to research that," she said.

"Maybe. I've got enough saved that I think I could pay cash for a small home or a small business..." My voice trailed off. I hadn't allowed myself to think outside the box for a long time, but I had been wise enough to wait on purchasing a home. Something must've told me to hold out.

After Mom and I hung up, I drove to pick up Ryan from Brady's house. Ryan was aware that I'd gone to pick up my things at work.

Once we arrived back home, I decided that a celebration with root beer floats was in order.

We ate our ice cream on the deck, the air carrying the aroma of nearby lilac bushes. "Are you going to buy a business like Grandma and Grandpa had?" Ryan asked between bites.

I'd filled him in on my job search and the possibility of looking at a small business. "Maybe. I've got a lot to research. But the best part is I'll be home now when you're here, and I won't miss any of your games or school events, at least for a while." Reassuring Ryan calmed me, as if someone had finally turned the dial on my life treadmill from sprinting to a walking pace that allowed me to catch my breath.

I dropped Ryan off at Trent's on Sunday morning and asked Trent if I could speak with him on the front steps.

"Sure," he said and eyed Ryan as he hugged me goodbye and headed into the house. Then he turned toward me. "Something going on with Ryan?"

"He's fine. He already knows what I'm going to tell you." I stated my decision to leave my job in a casual voice, as if the news wasn't a one-eighty of what I would typically do.

Trent waited until I finished. "What the hell, Eden?" He rested his elbows on his knees. "What are you going to do?"

"Look for a different job, preferably one that doesn't feel like a life sentence." I crossed my arms. "Don't worry, I've got plenty saved. I'll still cover Ryan's school and sport expenses and add to his college savings." I wanted to point out that I wasn't like him and wouldn't sit around for months unemployed until I found my "dream job."

"I'm wondering what you're going to find in your field that will challenge you enough without the stress. And... you like to be in charge." He leaned away as if I might punch him.

"Very funny. I was never in charge at the bank. They made sure of that." I could have been the most overqualified person, and it wouldn't have mattered. "The upside is I'm free to adjust my schedule if you need me to take Ryan to activities when he's staying with you."

Trent pursed his lips in thought. "Well, Amber has a class reunion coming up that's on a Friday night when Ryan would be with me. I may take you up on that offer."

I stood. "I'd love it. Just text me the date, and I'll put it on my calendar." After years of hit-and-miss with Ryan's events, I promised myself a much better batting average in the future.

Stevie Grace called me later Sunday afternoon from a hotel in London. "So, how did it go with Trent?" She yawned.

SG knew of my severance package and that I was telling Trent earlier when I dropped Ryan off. "He thinks I'll end up trying to climb the ladder in any other job and that I won't be happy if I'm not pushing myself." I sat outside on the deck, smelling of sunscreen and sweat after an earlier hour-long bike ride.

"Aw, Eden, I hate to say it, but I think he's right. You won't be happy unless you're challenged. And you deserve to do something you actually enjoy."

"Says the woman who told me recently that she would like to settle down yet continues to fly all over the world and keeps apartments in Atlanta and Minneapolis."

"I know. I'm preaching to the choir. But I enjoy my job... I'm just ready to settle down. This may come as a shock to you, but I'd like to have a child or two before my eggs shrivel up and die. Thirty-four is staring me in the face."

"I hear you there." I held up my glass of water, wishing it were a tall vodka something. "Speaking of doing something I'd enjoy, I plan to take a road trip soon. Time to deliver the POW bracelet Mom wore for years."

"I think that's so cool. Hey, maybe that David has a son for you," SG teased.

"Yeah, right. His daughter is around Mom's age, so if he has a son, he's probably too old for me. And remember, I'm not looking for a man. I'm looking for a job."

"You know, Eden"—Stevie Grace's voice turned serious—"you deserve both."

"That may be. Right now, I'm focusing on an upcoming day trip to Crimson Creek. I've got a war hero to find."

Chapter 11

May used to be my favorite month—planting gardens full of the possibility of vegetables and beautiful flowers. As long as I lived in my apartment, a garden was out of the question.

I biked, cleaned out closets, and caught up on my shopping at places like Target and Cub Foods, city conveniences that I appreciated. Early Friday morning, I packed a cooler with water and snacks for my drive to Crimson Creek and had the POW bracelet in a small jewelry box inside my purse.

I didn't have a plan for how I would locate David Carpenter and hadn't found an address for him online, but I guessed he would be well known in town.

After breakfast, I drove the two-plus-hour drive north, the last several miles with my windows down before I pulled into Crimson Creek and parallel parked in front of Mined Your Business Bar. At least one bar patron should know David.

In my research of the town, I'd learned it had been a mining town for decades and that many of the "lakes" in the area—especially around the new mountain bike trails—were mine pits filled with water.

I entered the red brick building on the corner of Main Street and Mining Avenue, blinking several times to adjust from the brightness of the late-morning sunshine.

The walls were weathered brick, and an antique-looking U-shaped bar commanded attention in the center of the room. It split the vibe from party on the left, where bar tables and booths were located, to business on the right, where a handful of tables were lined up for eating.

I'd checked out the bar's website the night before. Their food menu consisted mainly of pizza, burgers, and wings. Trent wouldn't spend a minute in a bar like this, but its simplicity appealed to me. "Mr. Bojangles" played over their sound system, mingling with patrons' voices. The oldie likely catered to the bar crowd, which consisted of retired people drinking coffee and playing cards. Two men sipped on Bloody Marys, and a couple sat at the bar, playing pull tabs.

A man with a long scraggly beard stood behind the bar, stocking bottles of booze. He wore board shorts and a T-shirt with the bar's logo of a man and woman peeking over a fence.

"Howdy," he called as I stepped up to the bar. "What can I get you?"

He appeared around my age, and his facial hair accentuated light-green eyes.

"I'm actually looking for someone. Do you happen to know David Carpenter? He's in his early eighties, was a Prisoner of War in Vietnam..."

The man nodded. "Yes."

"Any chance you can tell me how I could find him?"

"For...?" He folded his arms over his chest.

I expected this. One of the many things I loved about living in a small town was that we all looked out for each other. This guy was protecting David. Maybe I came off as a stalker. I took the small jewelry box out of my shoulder purse and opened it to reveal the POW bracelet. "I'd like to return this to him."

He leaned over the bar enough to read the engraving in the nickel-plated bracelet that read *Lt Col. David Carpenter, 10-27-66.* "What's that mean?" He peered up at me.

"They sold bracelets during the Vietnam War to raise awareness of the POWs. This was one my mom had. I recently found it in her jewelry box, looked up David online, and found out he lived in Crimson Creek, at least as of last year." *There, I shouldn't sound like a stalker now.*

"Wow, that's cool!" He smiled as if we'd become best friends. "David comes in here a lot. Not today, though. Today, he'll be at the seniors' dance at the American Legion. He's usually here Tuesdays and Thursdays for lunch and to play cards with his friends. He rarely comes in on the weekends. Too crowded for him, and he's too busy with Goober."

I chuckled. "I grew up in a small town, and listening to you know Mr. Carpenter's schedule reminds me of my hometown." I didn't want to press this man for David's address—I wouldn't have given it out if I were him—but it pained me to realize he was likely only a few miles away or heading to the seniors' dance, whatever that was.

"Can I ask who Goober is?" The old Andy Griffith show's garage mechanic came to mind, and this town seemed like it could easily have a Goober mechanic here.

"Goober's not a 'who.' It's a 'what.' It's David's party van for bar patrons. If you stop by next Tuesday or Thursday, around noon or so, he can tell you more."

"I don't live around here. I drove up from Minneapolis this morning. I knew it was a long shot that I'd find him, but I didn't know how else to do it since all I could find online was that he lived here as of last year." I'd googled his name with the word 'obituary' too, to make sure he hadn't passed away since then. "Would you do me a favor..."

"Whip."

"Your name is Whip?"

He gave me a wry grin. "Name is William Hipp. My friends shortened it by the time I got to middle school."

"Would you do me a favor, please, Whip? Would you tell Mr. Carpenter that I have his POW bracelet and would like to return it to him?" I pulled a pen from my purse and wrote my name and cell number on a bar napkin. "Can I leave this with you? If he would call or text me, that would be great. Then I can schedule a time to meet with him."

Two men approached the bar, and before they reached it, Whip had poured two draft beers and slid them across the bar to them. He picked up the napkin. "I sure will, Eden." He eyed my tall, athletic frame. "You here to bike the trails?"

"No. I'm only here for the day. But since I won't be meeting Mr. Carpenter today, I would like to check out the area. Where's the best place to walk and see the trails?"

Whip pulled a pen from behind his ear and drew a rough sketch on a napkin, detailing a trailhead parking lot about seven miles away.

"Thanks. I love to bike but have never tried mountain biking. The trails are fairly new?"

"Yep. They've been working on them for years, with plans for more trails in a four-step schedule over the next several years." Whip nodded toward the windows overlooking Main Street. "The town is struggling to keep up with the sudden boost in tourism. We're used to the summer flood of cabin owners, but bikers? They're wanting more than Crimson Creek was prepared for, no matter that the trail organizers told everyone this would happen."

He gestured toward the row of beer taps. "We've expanded our bar selections a lot in the last year, thanks to the younger crowd who are looking for craft beers."

"My parents owned three businesses in the small town where I grew up. I understand the business owners here being leery of overspending and it not paying off." I smiled at Whip. "Thanks for the map. The trails sound like a great economic boost to the area."

"They are. You can't walk on the mountain bike trails—too windy and dangerous to share single lanes with bikers—but you can see a lot on the paved trails and from the parking lot and overlook," Whip said. "I'll give David your info. Hope to see you again soon, Eden."

I stepped out onto the sidewalk and decided to walk the downtown area before venturing out to the mountain bike area. Main Street held as many vacant buildings as businesses. A "gently used" store, a coffee shop/bakery, a dentist's office, an insurance company, and a drugstore lined one side of the street. A bank, a café, another bar, a florist shop, and a gas station lined the other side of Main Street. The grocery store, library, clinic, and hospital followed farther down Main Street with a few other businesses on side streets.

Nothing specifically catered to mountain bikers. A block off Main Street, a large lake, Crow Lake, boasted a cement skateboard park, a huge playground, a parking lot, and a nice sandy beach. I made my way back to the car and took Mining Avenue past the lake, through neighborhoods, and to the adjoining town of Mine Key, a smaller version of Crimson Creek.

Mine Key had Mine & Yours coffee shop, a few other seasonal businesses, an American Legion, and an auto repair garage with a bright sign stating they also worked on mountain bikes.

As Whip mentioned, both towns appeared to be getting a slow start catering to the sudden burst of bike tourism after the mines closed in the 1960s and many families left the area.

Tourism had kept most businesses afloat. Seasonal cabins turned into year-round cabins, and winter activities like snowmobiling and ice fishing kept the area alive during winter months.

Crow Lake meandered toward the town of Mine Key. I drove through the small town, eventually taking another right per Whip's map. The paved road curved like a snake until I hit the dirt road that led to the rec area's parking lot.

As I pulled into the lot, my mood soared. Two mine-pit lakes branched out on either side of the paved lot like two long arms surrounded by red cliffs, thick woods, and open blue sky.

I stepped out of the car and stretched my arms, twirling around. I would have been content to set up a campsite on the edge of the woods overlooking the lake and stay there until the next winter, as long as Ryan was willing to do the same.

That wasn't likely. Ryan leaned more toward Trent in the no-thanks-on-roughing-it department. I spotted kayakers on one of the lakes, two people in a canoe, and several mountain bikers on the red gravel trails near the edge of the woods.

Laughter rang out over sunshine-sparkled water. I filled my lungs with the scent of Mother Nature, and something like home settled comfortably in my soul.

Chapter 12
David

Loud banging and the grating of the heavy steel cell door awoke the taste of panic and the scent of fear in me. They were coming for me again, and I didn't know if I could withstand another beating. When another boom reverberated through my cell, I shot upright with a gasp.

The relief that it was just another nightmare flooded through me, and I held a hand to my chest until my heartbeat slowed. My pajamas were soaked with sweat, sheets twisted around my legs, and my alarm clock radio lay on the bedroom floor.

Untangling my legs, I bent to pick up the alarm clock I'd bought after Jean died. Jean, who would wake me from my horrible dreams when I would thrash and groan in my sleep, enveloping me in a reassuring hug.

I set it on the nightstand, patting the top of it in apology. The time was 8:17 a.m., and I realized the banging in my dream and the rumbling must've come from the garbage truck on the other side of the street.

Rubbing a palm over my face, I tried to shake the fear still niggling at me, as if *this* might be a dream and that horror, reality. *What's up with the nightmares lately?* I winced as I stood. My left knee ached from the senior dance yesterday, just as it did every other Friday when I pretended I was young again. The fact that I could still shuffle around the dance floor with a trick knee paled in comparison to Jitterbug Jim with his wooden leg. Most of the men there had war wounds of one sort or another.

The previous night had been a late one with my Goober shuttle, as many Friday nights were in the spring and summer. Pushing eighty-three, I was used to the fatigue and all too certain that the nightmare was a precursor to something from my POW years resurfacing.

The horrible dreams had come back like a tsunami after Jean's sudden death when a drunk woman plowed into her midday as we walked on a sidewalk on South Padre Island. Once I bought Goober, my fourteen-seat shuttle bus, the nightmares lessened again. I drove the bar crowd, sometimes maxing my capacity of twenty-eight people. It cut down the drunk drivers in our area and filled my too-empty nights.

Leaning on the cane I kept near the bed for occasional use, I stripped the bed and tossed the sheets into the washing machine I'd bought the previous year, replacing the one Jean and I purchased when we settled in St. Paul after I left the Air Force. When I purchased this one, I told the young salesman I didn't need bells and whistles. I needed clean clothes. He told me appliances were now built to last only ten years since technology changed so much. The look he gave me said he figured I wouldn't be around in ten years. Forty-five years ago, I would have agreed with him.

The following Tuesday, I walked into Mined Your Business and was greeted by Whip and The Moody Blues singing "Isn't Life Strange?"—a question I'd asked myself many times over the years.

"Hey there, old man."

Few of us daytime customers were under retirement age, and anyone would seem old to Whip, a youngster in his midthirties, younger than I was when I was shot down. I'd lived a thousand lives since then.

Whip poured a glass of chardonnay and slid it across the bar before I bellied up to enjoy the one drink I allowed myself for the day. "Hey there yourself, whippersnapper."

"Got yourself a young girl asking about you." Whip wiggled his eyebrows.

"Another one?" I took a sip of the wine, waiting for my friends to arrive.

"Ha. You wish." Whip enjoyed picking on me as much as I did him, and it wouldn't be a lie to say I cared about him as if he were family. Whip had a soft spot for veterans. His grandpa had been killed in World War II. He reached under the bar and pulled out a napkin. "She left something for you." Whip slid it over. "She was pretty hot. Around my age. Even the young ones love you."

"I've been telling you that for years. It's a curse I must bear." I pushed aside the glass of wine to read the napkin with a woman's name and phone number written in ink. "Who's she?"

"She's got something for you that she wants to hand deliver."

"And the something is...?" I pictured some Ponzi scheme sending a young woman to prey on a feeble old man.

"Your POW bracelet," Whip announced as if I'd won the lottery. "Eden was in here last Friday, said she found it in her mom's jewelry box. She wants to meet you. Eden lives in the cities, and if you call her, she'll drive here to give it back to you."

I stared at her name and number. *This is why I had that nightmare last weekend.* My brain knew that part of my life was going to be resurrected. I rarely spoke of Vietnam. Nobody wanted to hear about it. We were told to forget about all of it. And we tried. Most of us failed.

Whip left to wait on another customer, and several minutes later, I spotted Hal entering the bar. Hal Grove and his wife, Maudie, had become best buddies with Jean and me when we moved back to

Crimson Creek in 1993. He headed for our usual spot at the table near the front of the bar, overlooking Main Street. I grabbed my wine and met Hal at the table for four. Soon, other friends would join us for lunch and then a few rounds of bridge.

"Look what Whip gave me." I unfolded the napkin to reveal Eden's information.

Hal, two years younger than me, had flown rescue missions in Vietnam.

"Guess she's got one of my POW bracelets." I explained how Eden had found it. Over four million bracelets had been sold, and the college students who'd come up with the idea had accomplished what the government hadn't—raised awareness about us.

"That will be nice to get back, right?" Hal asked.

"Yes. That'll make three." The bracelets that had been returned to me decades ago had been sent to the government to make a statue with everyone's bracelets, but it never happened. The two bracelets I had at present were from people like Eden who'd stumbled across them long after the war ended.

I'd told myself it was just as well. I didn't need reminders of what I'd put Jean and the kids through, especially the eighteen months when she'd heard nothing from me, thanks to solitary confinement. When I came home, it was impossible to pretend nothing had changed. My slight limp, scars, gnarled fingers and toes from the hellacious torture—those were obvious. The wary looks from Louise and Lee, both in their late teens by the time I arrived home, told me they didn't know me anymore. And the nightmares, my volatile emotions, me shutting down emotionally—you don't step back into a life after disappearing for over seven years without experiencing a bit of turbulence. Or a lot.

Chapter 13
Eden

In the two weeks since I received my lump sum severance package, I hadn't had a single panic attack—no rash on my neck, no need for antacids, and no pantyhose or high heels in sight. The freedom from restriction reminded me of late summer nights as a teen when my friends and I would go skinny-dipping.

Ryan had three weeks left of fourth grade, and I would have my first summer off work since I was twelve. Yes, I needed a job, but between my severance pay and the money I'd been socking away since Trent and I divorced—over half of my paycheck each month—the nest egg had plenty of cushion.

I spent the days before Memorial Day weekend biking for an hour or two every day, and the rest of the time, I focused on job hunting and researching small business opportunities in the area. I had two options. I could get a lower-paying, less-stress job and pay cash for a small home—since I wouldn't qualify for a mortgage—and put down roots for the next eight years. Or I could spend my savings on purchasing a small business and continue to live in the apartment. Neither screamed "dream job" to me, but either option would be better than what I'd been living.

I'd sent off a handful of employment applications since my first meeting with HR, and I had a few interviews, all with the same results. I was overqualified for every job I applied for, and they—rightly so—believed I wouldn't be happy long-term in a lower position even though I had stated it was my *choice* to leave the corporate world.

At a recent interview, I'd caught the guarded look in the interviewer's eyes and was tempted to reach across the table and tell her, "Hey, I'm not interested in your job. I just want easy-peasy eight-to-five." She wouldn't have believed me. I didn't believe it myself.

Very few small businesses were for sale in my area, and the ones that listed a sale price I could afford didn't interest me. I didn't want to own a small grocery store, bowling alley, or a corner bar.

I drove by every single business I could afford to buy but never bothered with an appointment with a realtor. If I couldn't get excited, driving by the places, it wasn't worth wasting a realtor's time.

I was out for a walk when Trent called my cell phone on the Friday morning of Memorial Day weekend. "Hey, any chance you can keep Ryan until Monday night? Amber and I have been invited on a friend's boat this Sunday on Lake Minnetonka, and they said to plan on staying overnight."

A little green monster of envy tiptoed across my chest. "Sure, that's fine."

"Great. I'll pick him up before five on Monday," Trent said in a chipper voice before we hung up.

I loved boating, but Lake Minnetonka would be like the Daytona 500 on water this weekend. *So what's eating you, Eden?* I stood tight-mouthed, clutching my phone, knowing the answer. I'd allowed my all-encompassing job to rob me of a social life. I mentally added it on my to-do list.

I thought ahead to my two bonus days with Ryan. As much as I whined about being stuck in the cities, there were plenty of perks I'd enjoyed over the years, like the convenience of nearby shopping, paved bike trails, and beautiful parks, especially Minnehaha Falls—Ryan's and my favorite. I felt the same about attending St. Paul Saints baseball games. They were more my style, less crowded than a Minnesota Twins game. Ryan and I also enjoyed going to the Science Museum of Minnesota, but on a busy weekend, those ideas were out.

On Saturday, Ryan and I headed to the batting cages. He was close enough to six weeks post-surgery, and we decided it would be a good test before he participated in baseball practice later in the week.

After the batting cages, we chose a small mom-and-pop café in the suburbs for lunch, away from the lake-loving holiday weekend crowd. I promised Ryan that I would take him and three of his friends to the beach on Monday, when most people would be heading home. The temperature was supposed to hit ninety, a good lake day.

While we waited for our food, we talked about options for Sunday. "Can we go to the game room in the mall?" Ryan said.

I grimaced. "It's perfect weather this weekend. How about a bike ride?" The last place I wanted to be was inside a mall. That was Trent's area, not mine.

"Naw." Ryan leaned his elbows on the Formica table and gave a dramatic sigh of boredom. Trent hadn't given me much notice of my extra time with Ryan. *And why does Ryan need to be entertained every weekend? Because you're in divorce parenting competition, Eden. Shame on you.*

I'd toyed with buying a two-person kayak. That would be a fun addition to our summer. I mentally added that purchase to my list.

"Hey, how about ziplining?"

Ryan's chin lifted. "Yeah!" He high-fived me.

"There's one about twenty minutes from here." I scrolled through my phone for the website. "They'll allow children six and older, so you're good to go." I checked reservations for Sunday, worried they would be booked. They had a few openings in the afternoon.

I called and made reservations for two o'clock on Sunday, and the anticipation of ziplining put us in a good mood the rest of the day.

After lunch on Sunday, we drove to the zipline, south of the Twin Cities.

"Are you sure you aren't scared to fly through the air like Spiderman?" I gave Ryan a side glance.

"Piece of cake, Mom. I'll go first so you're not scared."

"I sure hope I don't scream and cry all the way down and embarrass you," I said.

Ryan rolled his eyes. My mom was petrified of heights, one of the few things in life that scared her. I, thankfully, wasn't. This had been on my bucket list for a while, a perfect experience to share with Ryan.

Arriving in the parking lot, I could see that two of the five ziplines went over a small river, and my heart lurched—not for myself, but for Ryan.

"Are you sure about this?" We walked to view the first two ziplines. "Once we start, we need to finish."

His smirk tamed my concern.

"Okay, Spiderman, here we go." I paid, and they fitted us with helmets and harnesses as an instructor went over safety precautions.

When Ryan hopped off the first ledge, his small body flew down the line, and his screams of pure joy cut through the warm breeze.

I went next, raising my arms in the air, taking in the thrill of freedom, flying over the river and trees, then onto the ramp where Ryan waited. We never stopped smiling as we zipped down four more lines.

When we finished and walked back to the parking lot, Ryan declared, "This was the best day ever!"

"Every day with you is my best day." I pulled him in for a side hug.

"Ugh, Mom, not in public." Ryan stepped out of my hug with an embarrassed half smile.

Later that night, after Ryan and I took turns reading chapters from *An Elephant in the Garden* until Ryan was doing more yawning than reading, I thought back to my life without him, barely remembering what was important to me before he came along. And although I missed him like a limb when he was at Trent's, the knowledge that he was close by got me through the days.

Buckle down and find yourself a job, Eden. You have a son to support. And he's far more important than you being happy at work.

The Thursday after Memorial Day weekend, I was doing laundry when my cell phone rang.

"Hello?"

"Eden Everson?" The voice was deep and a little shaky.

"Yes, this is she." I tried to remember which jobs I hadn't heard back from yet.

"This is David Carpenter. Sounds like you've got something to give me?" A smile danced with his words.

I set the laundry basket on top of the washing machine. "I sure do, Mr. Carpenter. Thank you so much for calling me." That was what I needed, a face-to-face with a war hero. It would help put things into perspective. "I'd love to meet you if you're willing."

After a short pause, he replied, "First off, no Mr. Carpenter. Makes me sound old. David, please." He chuckled at his joke of sounding old at eighty-two. "And second? Heck yes, I'll meet you. Not a whole lot else going on in my life at this age."

"What works best for you?" I mentally scrolled through my upcoming schedule. Ryan was with me the first week of June but would be in school through June 5. "I can be in Crimson Creek by ten a.m.

"How does next Tuesday sound, about ten fifteen for coffee at Mined Your Business? If I like you, we can stick around, and I'll buy you lunch."

"That's my goal, then, to make it past eleven. And if you decide to let me stick around, it is *I* who will be buying *you* lunch. I owe you that much for your service to our country."

"We'll see about that. I used to win a lot at arm wrestling. Of course, that was a few years ago. See you at Mined Your Business next Tuesday, ten fifteen sharp," David said.

"I find it ironic that we're going to meet at a place with that name when I know I'll be itching to ask you a thousand questions," I said.

David paused. "If I don't want to answer your question, I'll tell you to mind your own business. How's that?"

"Sounds fair to me. See you then, David." After we hung up, I fist-pumped the air.

Chapter 14

As I drove toward Crimson Creek in a gentle rain on Tuesday morning, I cranked up the car radio when "Already Gone" by the Eagles came on, words that resonated with me as I joined in, singing about living our lives in chains even though we hold the key. I thought of Mom's Charles Dickens quote about chains. I held the key to my future. The time had come to unlock those chains.

By the time I arrived in Crimson Creek, the sun shone over Crow Lake. At 10:05 a.m., I walked into the bar, a nervous buzz pulsating through me. A handful of men were in the bar, much like the last time. I searched the faces, comparing them all to the photo of David in last year's article. Thankfully, Whip was bartending again. He would point me in the right direction.

"Hey, Eden. Welcome back," Whip said when I stepped up to the bar.

"Hi, Whip. Is David Carpenter here?"

He nodded toward the table of five men playing cards. I faced the men, and there he was, with wavy white hair, wire-rimmed glasses, rosy cheeks, and a cautious smile. He was watching me. My nose tingled with emotion.

I headed toward their table as David pushed his chair back and stood. "Mr. Carpenter?" I held myself back from running to hug him.

"No, Eden. David." He gave me a bemused look. His buddies had stopped playing cards, all watching me with interest.

David made introductions, saying, "Eden plans to interrogate me. If you see her wrestle me to the ground, come save me."

The men chuckled.

"Am I taking you away from a card game?" David hadn't said anything about that.

David shook his head. "Heck no. I was just bending their ear until you arrived. I play in the afternoon, when these old farts are napping." He gave them all a wave before he nodded toward the other side of the bar. "Let's sit over there so these busybody old coots can't hear us."

"Don't believe a word he says. He's delusional," one of the men at the table said, getting another round of laughter from the group.

David led the way with a slightly uneven gait. I studied him from behind. With freshly pressed khaki pants and a navy polo shirt, his solid frame was an inch or two shorter than mine, possibly due to his slight hunch forward. *What physical injuries did he endure as a POW?* I didn't dare ask.

David pulled out a chair and nodded for me to sit. He took a seat across from me, and within seconds, Whip came over with two coffee cups, a carafe of coffee, and creamers and sugars. I poured our coffee before pulling the small jewelry box from my purse and sliding it across the table to David.

His hand moved slowly to remove the POW bracelet.

"So, what's the history behind this? Your mom used to wear the bracelet?" David's arthritic fingers gently rubbed the engraved words.

"Yes. She eventually took it off and kept it in her jewelry box, which I received," I said, explaining how his daughter gave it to Mom decades before.

"My mom was under the impression you hadn't made it home."

David pressed his lips together and gave a small nod. "Ah yes. Louise—my daughter—had been warned that if I made it home, I'd be a changed man," he said. "I think my son, Lee, took the warning a little better. My late wife, Jean, wanted to prepare them as much as one can prepare a teenager to welcome home a stranger after several years."

His voice went reflective. "Louise had been a daddy's girl, twelve the last time I'd seen her. And I'm guessing this was one of her ways of rebelling, acting as if she didn't care if I came back or not."

I felt David's sorrow across the table. *Have I opened up a painful memory best left forgotten?*

I brought up a good memory from the POW bracelet, telling of how it broke the ice between my parents when they first met. "When Dad spotted the POW bracelet on Mom's wrist, four years after you'd all been released, it diffused his anger toward her for "borrowing" their family cabin, and he decided she couldn't be too awful a person if she was still wearing the bracelet."

"I agree with your father," David said, studying his coffee cup. "Louise and Lee went through hell, like every other POW family did. Lee was ten the last time I'd seen him. I'd missed his formative years. Louise was away at college, and Lee was finishing his senior year when I was released. They didn't know me, sure didn't want to take any direction from me." He drummed his fingers on the table. "Thing is, I don't blame them."

"I'm so sorry. For you, for your family. For all the POWs and their families." I had no words to convey my empathy. There were no winners in war. Dad had told me that.

"Not for you to apologize, Eden. Most of the people to blame are gone now. No sense looking back." He took a long drink from his coffee.

"Where do Louise and Lee live now?" The article I had read said nothing about his family.

"Louise's been in Vermont since she graduated from college. She comes back usually once a year, and I fly out there on occasion." David paused long enough that I wondered if he was done. "Lee was thirty-six when he passed away from skin cancer." He pulled out a white hanky to dab his pale-blue eyes.

I swallowed back shock. *Near my age.*

"He'd been a lifeguard through high school and college. Probably never wore a drop of sunscreen. Louise said teens used to rub baby oil on their skin instead of sunscreen."

I wished to reach for his hand in comfort, but he was a strong man, one who had endured so much. *And then to lose a child!* "I have a feeling I'm going to say 'I'm sorry' a lot, but I mean it. My heart goes out to you. I don't imagine that hurt ever goes away."

"It doesn't." David folded his hanky. "The gut-wrenching loss was worse than the hell of Vietnam." He cleared his throat. "Same with when my wife, Jean, died back in early 2000."

No wonder the article hadn't mentioned his family! David likely wanted his private hell kept private. Whip had placed a carafe of ice water on our table, and I poured us each a glass.

David gave me a brief story of a drunk woman plowing into his wife while they walked on a sidewalk midday on South Padre Island, and I pressed a napkin against my damp eyes.

"Anyway, enough of the bad stuff. Tell me about Eden Everson." David took a drink of water. His stoicism amazed me, but he likely had plenty of practice covering up his emotions, guarding the awful truth.

I took a minute to regroup. I spoke of Dad's time in the Army, my upbringing on a hobby farm, my love of small-town life, meeting Trent at college, our marriage, and a bit about Ryan. I told him of taking a big girl job in Minneapolis that ate up my life then of my divorce and recent walk away from a primo job.

"Guess my story isn't exactly uplifting either." I gave him a wry smile.

"Not so, Eden. Your story is one of trying new things, spreading your wings, and I sense, from your determination to get this bracelet back to me, that you will persevere." David leaned over the table. "Just be sure to make yourself happy. Your son won't be happy if you aren't. I learned that the hard way." He patted my hand.

I stared at his liver-spotted hand, its warmth bringing comfort. "I don't want to live in the cities, but it's the only place Ryan has ever lived. He's finishing fourth grade, so I only have eight more years before he graduates. Then I can move."

"Waiting for the future can stifle the present," David said. "I had too much time to think in solitary, too much time planning a possible future. So many thoughts focus on time. And I had control of none of it." He glanced at his Timex wristwatch. "Speaking of time, it's after eleven already. Guess you're sticking around."

"I passed the test? Even with my doom and gloom?"

"I'm a softie. Plus, a pretty girl like you is always a day brightener." He studied my face. "I'm trying to figure out your nationality. I'm Swedish and Norwegian. I see a little Asian in your eyes—which, by the way, are a lovely golden brown. I detect a hint of red in your hair. Or is that some bottle stuff people put in to jazz things up?"

I touched my pixie cut, recently trimmed. "Dad's family has some redheads. My mom is half Korean but is tall like me. Her father was Irish."

"Well, Miss Eden with the pretty eyes, why don't we step out for a bit and tour the town? Get some fresh air. Then we can come back here, and I'll buy you lunch. Or, better yet, let's hit the American Legion for lunch. You'll spice up those old farts in there."

"I'd love it. I'll go settle our bill."

"Don't bother. Whip already added it to my charge. He may have told you I spend some time in here. Anything else he may have said is no doubt a bald-faced lie. So don't believe him if he told you I'm a crabby, crotchety old fool." David winked.

"I had to beat any information out of Whip. He's good at shielding your privacy." I pushed back my chair. "Thank you for the coffee. Lunch is on me, whether you have a tab at the Legion or not."

David hoisted himself up, and I let him set the pace as we headed outside. He nodded to the right before we walked that way shoulder-to-shoulder down the sidewalk, chatting as if we'd been friends for years.

Chapter 15

David

"Since it's early, we can take a little drive around town," I said, pointing at my silver Ford Edge. "How about I drive since I know where I'm going."

"Okay. I drove around town two weeks ago when I was here, and I walked around downtown. I even checked out the mountain bike area," Eden said.

I hit the fob to unlock the doors, and we settled in. I drove through downtown, consisting of two blocks, and headed past the hospital and around part of Crow Lake. "I grew up in Crimson Creek. My wife, Jean, also grew up here. We moved back when I retired from Control Data and she retired from teaching in 1993." Eden turned from looking out the window to listen as I blabbed on. "Louise was in Vermont, and Lee had recently passed away. We had nobody keeping us in the cities and wanted to move back to our roots, to small-town life."

"I feel that way every time I go back to Grandfield, but it's not the small town it was years ago," Eden said. "And none of my family lives there now." She spoke of her parents in Anchorage, her sister in Guatemala, and her brother in Washington.

"Ah, that makes it hard, then," I said. "I had two brothers still living in this area when we moved back. Both have passed in the last five years, but I'm not leaving. I've got my friends and plenty of good memories here." I turned onto a paved road that led to a forested, hilly area. "This is the future home of more of those darn mountain bike trails." I shook my head. "They're taking over our town, driving everyone nuts."

Eden's eyebrows rose. "You're against the mountain bikers? Aren't they waking up this sleepy little town?"

"Who said the town wants to be woken up? We're all happy with the way things were," I grumbled.

Eden studied me. "Spoken like a true small-town person. But don't the business owners need the influx of outdoorsy-people money in their community?"

I used the words she'd said when she spoke of her job. "Remember, money isn't everything."

Eden nodded. "Touché. I guess it's like me wishing Grandfield had stayed like it was when I was growing up. It's hard to realize we can't get our past back."

I drove us back toward town. "Exactly. Jean and I moved back here because we wanted to step back into the past, into the small-town life we'd enjoyed growing up."

She watched a handful of mountain bikers cross at the street corner. "What don't you like about them? It seems like they're mostly based out of town. Isn't the main parking lot about seven miles from Crimson Creek?"

"Yes, but they bike into town, leaving red dirt on the sidewalks, riding down the sidewalk instead of the streets, and parking along our roads, blocking driveways."

"What do you think the answer is?"

I shook my head. "Heck if I know. I have friends on the city council, including Whip, and they promise that they're working on solutions before they continue with the build-out plan." I took a left into my neighborhood, located between Crimson Creek and Mine Key, and pulled up in front of the home Jean and I had purchased after we retired. The white-sided rambler with black trim and shutters partially blocked my garden in the backyard. I put the vehicle in park.

"This is my home," I said. "Some of the council members said they're working on adding more parking lots outside of town by some of the other mine-pit lakes and are adding another one down the road from the beach. They'll supposedly force the bikers to use the alleys. We'll see." I leaned over the steering wheel.

"You have a nice home, and in a quiet neighborhood." Eden all but said, *"What's your complaint?"* She nodded in the direction of Crimson Creek. "It seems like there aren't many businesses catering to the mountain bikers, kayakers, etc." I curled my upper lip. She held up her hand. "I know. You don't care, but I spotted a lot of empty buildings. New businesses could boost the economy."

I pulled away from the curb and continued through the neighborhood toward Mine Key. "Like what kind of business?" My curiosity was piqued.

"Bike and kayak rentals? Another restaurant or two? Microbrewery..."

I groaned.

"Well, they're just ideas," Eden said as she brushed her side bangs off her forehead. The day had turned warm, and the breeze coming in the windows was welcoming. "People were working on the outside of an empty building a few doors down from the bar. Do you know what's going in there?"

"I think things like those healthy snacks made from tree bark and pinecones."

Eden giggled. "Good idea. People who enjoy the outdoors need energy fuel."

I bit my tongue. Eden was young and might like eating tree bark. I pulled into a parking spot at the American Legion shortly before noon.

We stepped inside, where the vibe was different from Mined Your Business. No big screen TVs waiting to blast sporting events, and music came from a player piano in the corner of the dining area instead of a sound system.

"My parents had a player piano in the hallway of the market building they owned when I was growing up." Eden's eyes lit up. "I haven't seen one in years." She walked to the piano, the white scroll of the music centered in the piano's dark, polished wood, moving along as she gently placed her fingers over some of the keys.

"She's a beauty, isn't she?" I stood beside Eden, watching her fingers caress the ivory keys that bounced up and down as it played "The Good, the Bad, and the Ugly."

"She is. The old one in my parents' marketplace was a lot like this. We kids would spend hours there switching out the scrolls, taking turns using the pedals to pump out the music." Eden's smile was wistful.

I led the way to a table in the back room with a small empty area to the side. "You'll have to come here on a Friday afternoon when we have our senior dances." I pointed toward the open area in back. "That's when the place comes alive."

I pulled out a chair for Eden and took a seat across from her. "On the first and third Friday afternoons, I can almost forget my age." Our server dropped off water and menus. "I don't move at the speed of lightning, mind you, but the will is there. Music kept me somewhat sane in solitary confinement, songs from the nineteen fifties and early sixties." I wrinkled my nose. "Not that psychedelic stuff I came home to."

Eden's eyes lit up again. "I love the music from the late sixties and early seventies. It's what I grew up hearing, my parents' era of music."

"Well, there's something we have in common. Those were the years I missed, and when I drive Goober for the bar crowd, that's the music I play. I didn't get to hear it forty-plus years ago, so I listen to it now."

"The Lonely Bull" by Herb Alpert, another favorite instrumental of mine, began on the player piano.

"Goober sounds like a shuttle bus I'd enjoy."

"It keeps me busy at night and keeps the drinkers from behind the wheel."

After we ordered, Eden spoke of her struggle to decide what she wanted next in her career.

"I remember being in your shoes. After decades in the Air Force, it was like starting life all over. Since I was a kid, I had only ever wanted to fly planes."

"How did you decide?" Eden leaned over the table, intent on any wisdom I might share.

I pushed up my glasses. "Jean helped. Ever since we got married in 1952, our lives had focused on my dreams, my career. Ever hear of Glen Campbell? His song 'Dreams of the Everyday Housewife' came out while I was a POW. It played on the radio one day when Jean and I were trying to sort things out. She confessed that she had dreams too, ones she'd never been able to pursue." I'd been so clueless and selfish. "I felt like a shark devouring her life and shoving it into mine instead of letting her swim on her own."

"What did Jean want to do?"

"Jean had acquired her teaching degree while I was gone and wanted to go back to college to get her special education degree. It would have been difficult to do while the Air Force continued to move us all over. I retired from the Air Force, and we settled in St. Paul. Jean completed her degree, got a job at a nearby grade school, and I went to work for Control Data."

We'd spoken little about my time in Vietnam, but over lunch, Eden asked a few questions about life after I arrived home, nothing that I needed to veto.

After we finished our burgers, Eden asked, "Have I worn out my welcome?"

I'd been watching my friends sitting in the bar section, and Eden probably thought I was bored with her. "Not at all. But if I tell you everything today, you won't come see me again."

"You want me to visit again?"

"Eh, you pass muster."

Eden's cheeks flushed. "My dad said that when I was a kid."

"It's an old military saying." I nodded toward the bar section in the front of the American Legion. "I suppose I can't avoid it any longer. I've been watching those old fools at the bar studying you and me." I grimaced. "Can't walk by those Gladys Gossips without introducing you, or they'll hound me like a pack of wolves next time I come in here."

We walked to the bar, where several of my Veteran friends welcomed Eden while also teasing me about giving her a bad taste of the town. Eden kindly assured them that I had been an excellent tour guide, and I turned around and gave them a "told you so" look before escorting Eden out the door, their guffaws echoing behind us.

I drove around several of the mine-pit lakes, stopping at a few that had lookout points for Eden to get a view of our beautiful community. By the time she left for home later that afternoon, I sensed it wouldn't be the last time I saw her.

Chapter 16
Eden

I endured three more job interviews in early June but got no offers on any of them since—big shocker—I was overqualified. I spent the rest of my time researching real estate listings for homes in Ryan's school district, as well as a few more business listings, even ones located in Grandfield, figuring I could commute and chauffeur Ryan to and from school. But even those empty buildings or existing businesses were expensive now that Grandfield was more of a suburb of Minneapolis.

For the heck of it, I checked on empty buildings for sale or lease in Crimson Creek. The price difference between the buildings in a small Central Minnesota town versus business options around Minneapolis was surprising. Empty downtown buildings in Crimson Creek listed for about one-fourth the price of the Twin Cities buildings.

While Ryan was at Trent's the second week of June, I met with a realtor and checked out two businesses in Ryan's school district. One was a bookstore, the other a gift shop. The bookstore was cute but too small to expand what I could offer customers. The owner had been there for thirty years and likely paid little for the shop compared to the listing price.

As much as I'd hoped to own a business someday, I'd never taken the time to think of what that business might be. I didn't want a restaurant like Dad had run for years or a motel-turned-into-apartments like Mom had run. A business like their Grand Scheme of Things was out of my budget to own several downtown buildings.

I wanted something that challenged me enough to keep me interested but not something that took over my life, something that connected me with the outdoors again. Over the years, my too-much-time-indoors skin leaned more toward the Irish side than my one-quarter Korean heritage.

My favorite shop in Grand Scheme of Things was one owned by a woman who rented ice skates, cross-country skis, and snowshoes, etc. during the winter, along with knitted hats, scarves, and mittens that she made with a knitting machine. In the summer, she sold inner tubes, beach toys, and kids' fishing rods—things that could be used at the beach located near the building. She leased the shop area for several years from my parents, so she must have made a decent living. Although I had ample savings, I needed a business that would provide enough of an income so I wouldn't drain my savings.

In a split-second decision, I called a realtor in Crimson Creek and lined up an appointment to check out three empty downtown buildings, reminding myself it didn't hurt to look. I also called David, who had let me know when we met that he didn't do texting.

On the second Thursday in June, I left my apartment at six in the morning and headed north to Crimson Creek to check out business options and meet David for lunch. I didn't tell him that I was meeting with a realtor, because he would want to know why. And the idea of me being one of "those annoying new yuppie business owners," in his words, wasn't a topic of conversation I wanted to discuss over lunch.

I met with Jenny, a local realtor, at nine o'clock to tour the three empty downtown buildings that I had researched online. All were solid brick buildings with good locations and upstairs apartments, reflecting the one-hundred-year-old era in which the town had been built.

Each place needed interior repairs, mostly cosmetic. But the one that stood out to me was located across the street from the park and Crow Lake. Situated on the corner, one block off Main Street, it had the best location for my business idea.

Jenny, middle-aged, had light-brown hair pulled back into a barrette and smile lines around her eyes. She had been thorough in her information with each location and not pushy, which I appreciated. "I have a feeling this is your favorite," she said as we stood inside and looked toward Crow Lake.

"That obvious, huh?"

Something about the building, the location, reminded me a bit of my youth. The walls whispered, "Possibilities here." Over the past week, I had homed in on just what that possibility was for me.

"Yes. Your eyes are sparkling, and you're bouncing on your toes." Jenny and I headed for the door to the parking lot. "As I mentioned earlier, I think there are two more empty buildings that will be going up for sale in the next few months." We stepped outside, and she locked the door. "With the townspeople finally coming to grips that we are on the edge of a mountain bike boom, I think we're going to see the prices go up over the next few years."

Jenny chuckled. "I sound like a pushy salesman, but I wanted to give you a heads-up. Housing prices have increased over the past year after so many years of declining real estate value. It's a good thing for the community but also a barometer for what I believe will continue to climb as the mountain biking craze increases."

I touched Jenny's shoulder. "I believe you. And that's why I feel like this might be the right time for me to move here." My brain had been calculating figures nonstop over the past week. *Don't get ahead of yourself, Eden. None of this happens without Ryan.*

I thanked Jenny and promised to stay in touch. After she drove away, I drove to the American Legion, where I met David for lunch. Over sloppy joes, David soon asked, "I know I'm irresistible, but what's the real reason you're visiting Crimson Creek again? Not that I'm not happy to see you, but..."

"Well, besides your charm, yes, I also came to look at some real estate here." His eyebrows shot up as he opened his mouth to question me, but I held up a hand. "Nope. That's all I'm telling you for right now because I haven't talked with Ryan about it yet."

David nodded. "Okay, I'll keep pretending it was my charm and good looks that brought you back to visit." He folded his napkin over his clean plate and set it aside. "If you have time, I thought you might like a ride in Goober."

"I'd love it! I was going to drive around the area some more before I headed home. A tour in Goober would be fun." After I paid our tab, getting to the cashier before David could, I followed him in our vehicles to his house, where Goober was parked in his garage.

David opened his oversized garage to reveal a freshly washed white shuttle bus with black lettering on the side that read Goober and crimson music notes painted around the lettering.

"What's with the music reference?" I had expected something referring to him driving bar patrons around.

"Get inside, and you'll see." David opened the passenger door for me before going around to hoist himself into the driver's seat with the help of running boards. He backed Goober out into the alley and put it in park long enough to choose a playlist on his stereo system. "Remember how I told you before that I only play music from 1966 to 1973 in Goober? That's why the notes are painted on. Now, here's one of my favorite playlists."

The speakers located in front and back came alive with a song I remembered from my parents' record stash. "Treat Her like a Lady" was followed by "Sweet City Woman." I found myself singing along as David drove Goober to the outskirts of town.

"I'm surprised you know the lyrics," David said. "You weren't born when these songs were popular."

"No, but it's the music my parents listened to when I was growing up. I remember my dad saying that once disco came onto the music scene, he quit listening, preferring instead the songs from the earlier years." When the next song, "Oh, Babe, What Would You Say?" came on, I questioned David. "These are some unique song choices."

"They are," David agreed. "This is my one-hit-wonder song list, the big hit that changed things for these musicians." He turned Goober onto a dirt road that took us over a small bridge and creek. "It's a list that resonates with me. One hit can change your life. It likely did for these musicians, and one hit to my F-105 Thud certainly changed my life."

We rode for a while as I peered out the passenger window at the luscious woods, imagining what David's years away from his family must have been like for them.

I turned toward David. "Tell me about Louise." I wanted to know about his daughter, whom Mom had met all those years before. David pressed his lips together, thinking. "When I was home on leave, six months before I was captured, Louise had been a sweet, quiet, mindful preteen. When I laid eyes on her again in March of '73, she'd become a spunky, independent, young college woman who wanted to burn her bra! She'd become a stranger to me."

I would have laughed at David's indignation at Louise's behavior if not for the remorse in his eyes.

David swallowed several times. "Just like Lee. Just like Jean." His voice was so soft that I barely heard it over "Everybody Plays the Fool" as The Main Ingredient sang about love running deeper than any ocean.

"I missed so much, and now, we've lived apart for so long that I still miss my little girl. Louise will retire next year from her forty-year career as a high school science teacher. I thought I might see her a bit more after she retires, but my son-in-law, Jack, has been having some troubling health issues lately." David turned Goober around in a deserted parking lot surrounded by woods.

"Do you think they'll move here?" I asked.

"No. Louise has asked me several times to move near her in Bennington, Vermont, but I've got a good support system here. This is home to me," David said. "And they've got two sons in college out there, grandsons that I doubt will ever leave the area."

Heading back toward town, David pointed at a home down a long driveway with a large pond next to it. "That's where my buddy Hal lives with his saint of a wife, Maudie. Summer business with Goober is getting too busy for me to keep up with the bar crowd. It's those darn mountain bikers," he teased. "Hal and I have talked about him buying a used shuttle bus to help me out. But his nights are a lot busier than mine. He's got Maudie, and one of their sons lives nearby, and he has young children."

"Was Hal in the service with you?"

"He was. He flew rescue missions during Vietnam."

I digested that ironic piece of information. His friend had flown rescue missions, and David's plane had been shot down. While David changed his music playlist, I read a list of rules posted above the windshield:

1. No fighting.
2. Singing encouraged and kindness required.
3. Fifteen-mile radius limit.
4. Last call for the bar is last call for Goober.

Service is free, and tips go to help pay for school lunches at our local grade school.

"Daydream Believer" by The Monkees flooded the shuttle bus, playing loud enough to drown out the air-conditioning David had turned on. When he turned Goober into the alley behind his home, Three Dog Night belted out "Celebrate."

"I bet your music puts the bar crowd in an even better mood," I said.

"It does." David pulled into his garage. "I've found that if people are singing, it lessens the chance a fight will break out."

After David walked me to my car, I leaned in and hugged him goodbye, thinking of a fight I was bound to have soon with Trent.

Chapter 17

After my trip to Crimson Creek in mid-June, I stopped wasting my time applying for jobs. I wanted a business that was much needed in Crimson Creek, one that would fulfill the needs of outdoor enthusiasts as well as my own.

Ryan and I filled our days and nights with ball games, beach time, and biking. Trent gifted me more time with Ryan on his scheduled weeks.

Near the end of June, the days turned hotter and muggier, and I swore Ryan grew taller every day. Before one of Ryan's baseball games, I asked Trent if I could speak with him while the team warmed up.

We stood in the shade away from the bleachers. Sweat pooled under Trent's armpits, darkening his white polo shirt. I was sweating like a kid caught shoplifting as I pitched my business idea to Trent.

"Are you out of your bloody mind?" Trent leaned back as if I'd tried to punch him. "Your place is here as long as Ryan is in school."

"It's only an idea right now. I haven't taken Ryan to Crimson Creek yet. I deserve a job I *want* to do. And *you* chose Minneapolis as our place to live. The cities was never *my* choice." *Calm down, Eden. If you get huffy, Trent gets defensive.* "I've looked for work here. I'm overqualified for most of the jobs that are worth pursuing." I swiped my side bangs off my sweaty forehead with my wrist. "Other than Ryan, there's nothing here for me. I miss living in a small town, and Crimson Creek is ripe for new businesses. It's barely over two hours from here." I wouldn't get into the logistics of Ryan being able to live with only one of us most of the time.

"None of this would've happened if you had stayed at your job." Trent took a long swig from his water bottle. "If you want to move, fine. But Ryan stays." He rocked back on the heels of his new Brooks tennis shoes. "You want to see him? As you said, it's only two hours away. You can come visit."

No! I can't just up and leave my son! Yes, he's your son too, but I can't do it. "Ryan is old enough to decide. I checked, and there's no age minimum in Minnesota. But I don't want to force that on him. If I do this, the business wouldn't open until next spring, and by then, he'd be going into sixth grade." I kept an eye on Ryan and his team so we wouldn't miss the game.

"I'm not willing to have Ryan move away just because you don't like the cities and were unhappy with a perfect job. It's *your* problem—not mine and not Ryan's," Trent hissed, a rare show of emotion from him.

"So, if the roles were reversed and you were stuck in a small town with a job you hated, you'd suck it up and continue for another eight years?"

The flash of anger in Trent's eyes at me even *thinking* of him having to endure that way of living gave me my answer.

"We can talk about this another time." I pointed toward Ryan's team heading onto the field. "I haven't talked to Ryan about it yet, so please don't say anything to him." It had been a toss-up whether or not I should speak with Ryan first, but Trent was leaving town for a week, and I didn't want to wait.

I would pick Ryan up on Friday and get two extra days with him. I was more than willing to work with Trent to accommodate his social calendar, but I didn't foresee him budging an inch to accommodate me.

After the game, I high-fived Ryan when he joined us. "Hey, great catch in the fourth inning," I whispered into his ear, inhaling his only-a-mother-could-love sweat.

Ryan mumbled a "thanks." We talked for a few minutes on the way to Trent's car. "I'll pick you up at nine Friday morning."

"Okay. Can we take the kayak out?" Ryan had been itching to try out the two-seater we'd recently purchased.

"Sure, that's a great idea." I pulled him in for a final hug while Trent cranked up the air conditioner in his vehicle. "See you Friday."

At my car, I rolled down the windows and turned on the air before sending a text to SG: *Whenever you get a chance, I need your brain.* Her flight schedule had been hectic lately, and we hadn't connected other than text messages since my last trip to Crimson Creek.

The sun was setting over the strip mall two blocks away as I sat on my deck, wiping the condensation on my insulated cup, thinking. I'd been thinking so much lately that it reminded me of my time at the bank, but this brain drain was for *me*. SG's text message pinged on my cell phone: *Just got home. Call you in ten.*

Stars appeared in the darkening sky as I replayed my conversation with Trent to Stevie Grace. I'd filled her in via texts over the past week about my business idea of opening a bike and kayak rental shop in Crimson Creek.

"Okay, just thinking out loud here," SG said. "If you move, you can always use my apartment when you visit the cities. I'm rarely there... as you well know."

SG had promised me when she moved that it was temporary and that she would eventually relocate back to Minnesota.

"So that's one problem solved *if* it comes to where you move and have to visit Ryan at Trent's place." Trent's home was fifteen minutes from SG's apartment.

"Second, you can delay any decision with Ryan until next spring, so why argue with Trent over it now?"

I stepped inside to avoid the mosquitoes that showed up after dark. "Yes, but what if I go through all of it and Ryan won't move? Then I'm stuck in Crimson Creek with a business and no son."

SG paused in thought. "Let's play worst case and say that happens. But you love your new business, living in a small town... and you're happy. And Ryan? He loves staying where he is, hanging with his friends. Trent's a decent dad, and you'd have a schedule to spend time with him..." Stevie Grace cleared her throat. "Is that such a bad thing?"

I closed my eyes, trying to imagine it. *Is it? Doesn't that make me a bad mom? A selfish mother?* "I don't know, SG. It's a question I keep asking myself." I paced the living room. "Making myself happy means also making myself unhappy if I don't have Ryan. The best thing about the timing is he'll be moving to a new school next year anyway, whether it's a middle school here or in Crimson Creek."

"What if Ryan was a girl? Would you be more inclined to show your daughter that her mother is pursuing her dream?" SG prodded me. "To show her that it's okay for women to put themselves first, just as many men have done for decades?"

"I know, but that doesn't make it any easier. One of the reasons I quit my job was to spend *more* time with Ryan, not less." Ten thirty at night was *not* the time to worry. "I'll let you go and unwind. I'm going to ask Ryan if he wants to take a day trip to Crimson Creek with me before the Fourth of July weekend. Once I get his reaction to the town, it will help me decide what to do." I turned off the living room light. "Thanks for being my voice of reason and sounding board."

Stevie Grace chortled. "Oh yeah, I'm chock-full of reason."

I smiled as we hung up, reassured that she had my back. Too bad she was so far away.

Ryan and I kayaked Lake Harriet on Friday afternoon, the intense heat nearly suffocating us in the nonexistent breeze. We stayed near shore, where the trees provided shade, and took several swimming breaks to cool off.

I waited until we arrived back at the apartment and were sitting at the kitchen table with root beer floats before I brought up Crimson Creek.

"What do you think about taking a day road trip with me on Tuesday? You don't have practice or a game."

"Where?" Ryan focused on his float, unaware of how important this day trip would be.

"To a small town called Crimson Creek. It's a couple of hours north of here." My heartbeat stuttered. "Remember the POW bracelet I showed you and the trip I took to give the Vietnam veteran, David, the bracelet Grandma Joleigh wore? That's where he lives."

"Yep. Isn't that where you said they have mountain bike trails?" Ryan gave me his full attention.

"That's the town." I was relieved that Ryan had been interested enough to remember the bike trails. "I've made a few trips there and thought it would be fun to show you around. They have huge mine-pit lakes, and we could take our kayak there, maybe even meet David if it works for him. What do you think?"

"What's a mine-pit lake?"

"They used to be mines that supported the community for decades. The area had an enormous supply of manganese-rich iron ore, which was used for making steel," I explained. "The mines shut down about forty years ago." I'd been intrigued by the transformation from mining to mountain bikes in the area, but I wasn't sure Ryan would feel the same. "When mining stopped, they removed the pumps that had kept the water out, and eventually the pits filled with clean water. The lakes are clear, which makes them great for paddleboarding and kayaking. One is four hundred fifty feet deep!" I wiggled my eyebrows. "And since they're so deep, a lot of people use them for scuba diving."

"Cool!" Ryan licked the root beer from his straw. "Can we go scuba diving?"

"Maybe when you're older and you've taken scuba diving lessons." I wiped a smudge of ice cream from his chin. "You won't see me in a scuba suit. That's too far down and dark for me," I said. "Some are connected by short portages, so people can access a lot of mine-pit lakes."

Ryan's interest brought me relief. I couldn't wait to share Crimson Creek with him.

After our root beer floats, Ryan and I played three games of Rummikub and had a drawing contest—something I always failed at since Ryan had inherited Grandma Emily's artistic talent. I made tacos for supper so that I wouldn't have to turn on the oven. While the hamburger browned, I called David, asking him about Tuesday.

"That would be wonderful. I'm looking forward to meeting Ryan," David said.

I sensed David would be a check mark in the plus column for Ryan liking the town.

And I needed as many check marks as possible in the plus column because the thought of moving without Ryan was inconceivable.

Ryan and I left early on July 1 in humidity so thick we could chew it. An hour north, we hit a sun shower and rolled down the windows for the rest of the drive. By the time we arrived in Crimson Creek, the drizzle had stopped, and the sun came out, revealing a faint rainbow over Crow Lake. As we drove past the park with the kayak on my car's roof rack, the air carried a damp scent of sand, sunscreen, and lake foliage.

"Hey, there's a skateboard park!" Ryan pointed at the cement park on the other side of the beach, already bustling with activity.

"Yep. We'll check that out later when we come back to meet David for lunch."

Not yet ten o'clock, the day promised to be a scorcher. I wanted us to kayak before it became unbearable. I drove out of town to the main recreational parking lot while Ryan's head moved as if on a swivel, taking in the trails and mine-pit lakes along the road.

"This is so cool!" Ryan had his seat belt off before I even parked in the mostly full lot. His enthusiasm ramped up my hope.

We stepped out of the vehicle, and Ryan's flip-flops splashed through puddles as he ran to the picnic area near the beach. I joined him, and we watched flashes of bikers cycle in and out of the woods.

"That looks a little scary," he whispered.

"I agree. There are different levels of trails, though, and I plan to try out the baby-steps trail first when I visit again."

Ryan giggled. "Is that what it's called?"

"Let's go see." I pointed at the enormous trail map located in the middle of the picnic area. "They ride year-round here. There are mountain bikes called fat-tire bikes. They have good traction and are made to go through snow."

I led the way to the trails map. "They've got another few years of building additional trails planned," I pointed to an area at the top of one of the trails. "They're also building yurts here for the bikers."

"What's a yurt?" Ryan scrunched his face.

"It's like a big circular tent, but these are made from wood, have a wood stove, and are built to be used most of the year. They want to accommodate the growing biking community." I contemplated bringing up my business idea but decided to wait until we went back to town.

"Look, there's some kayakers." Ryan pointed at the kayakers hugging the shoreline to catch the shade.

"Come on, let's unload ours and join them before I melt into the ground."

We made our way to two docks at the boat landing, unloaded our kayak, and tied it to a dock post while we loaded our things into the storage. Wearing life jackets and wide-brimmed hats, Ryan and I settled in the kayak and steered it toward the heavily treed shoreline.

The call of loons echoed over the water, and the distant voices of people on mountain bike trails and bikers on the nearby paved trail created a cheerful melody.

We kayaked on three adjoining mine pit lakes before arriving back at the boat launch. After loading the kayak, we drove up to the nearby summit overlook. The steep, winding road's speed limit was ten miles per hour due to mountain bikers and hikers sharing the road with vehicles. Once we reached the parking lot at the top, Ryan ran to the overlook.

I came up behind him. The view was a breathtaking technicolor of sparkling blue water, vivid green foliage, and deep red cliffs.

"Wow!" Ryan said.

"I know, right?" From the overlook, we could see most of the town of Mine Key, several mine-pit lakes, and Crimson Creek in the distance. "The big mine pit over there is called Mine Key Lake and is the one that's four hundred fifty feet deep."

Ryan started crawling over the waist-high rock wall to get a better view.

I pulled him back. "Careful. Come on, it's time to meet David for lunch."

Chapter 18
David

I sat in my usual spot at the Triple C café, a back booth facing the door, and spotted Eden and her young son heading my way five minutes early.

"Hello, hello!" I reached for the edge of the table to hoist myself up. "Who is that fine-looking young man with you?"

"Some stray I picked up on the street. Said he's hungry." Eden made the introductions before she and Ryan slid into the booth across from me.

Ryan had Eden's eyes but fairer skin and blond hair. He studied me, curious.

"So," I leaned over the table and stage-whispered to Ryan, "tell me what your mother is *really* like. She's been acting so nice every time I meet up with her, but I'm not buying it. I bet she makes you eat vegetables and go to bed at a certain hour, doesn't she?"

Ryan fake pouted. "Yep, she does."

I slapped my hand on the table. "Ha! I knew it. I had a mother who did the same thing to me. Drove me nuts when she'd tell me it was because she loved me." I gave Ryan a wink, and his shoulders relaxed.

"And your mom won't tell you this, but I will." I cast a steely glance at Eden. "They have the best malts here. Build big muscles, they do."

"Quit trying to lead my son astray." Eden fought a smile. "Next thing you know, he'll turn out like you."

"You mean handsome and smart?" I feigned ignorance.

"I mean mischievous."

Conversation flowed, and Ryan was courteous with a good sense of humor. Halfway through our meal, when Ryan had finished his cheeseburger and was working on his chocolate shake, he asked, "Mom said when you were a Prisoner of War, they starved you. You didn't get *any* food?"

Eden blushed. "I'm sorry, David. On our drive here, I explained the reason for the POW bracelet." She turned to her son. "Ryan, please. David doesn't want to talk about that."

I was still working through my meatloaf and mashed potatoes and put my fork down. "It's quite all right, Eden. Ryan is curious, and after forty years, many of us POWs wish we'd spoken of our experiences decades ago." I took a drink of water. "To answer your question, yes, we received food—if you could call it that—in small enough portions to keep us alive. That happened in the earlier years as a prisoner. The last couple of years, things improved enough where we were able to put some weight on before being freed."

War was horrific, and being told not to speak of it was cruel, much like telling an abused victim that nobody wanted to hear about the abuse, and it was better forgotten.

"I'm sorry, David. I shouldn't assume you don't want to talk about any of it. You told me a few things, and I obviously shared them with him. I hope that's okay."

I clasped my hands on the table. "Yes, it's fine. I'm not interested in talking to reporters or anyone in the media because that time has passed, but I think the youth in our country should know this part of history that they'll never read about in school."

I turned back to Ryan. "Those vegetables my mother encouraged me to eat as a kid? I thought of those, along with every other food group, and would have gladly eaten a plate of Brussels sprouts or cauliflower while in captivity. So"—I pointed a finger at Ryan—"make sure to appreciate every bite of food."

I wanted to lighten the mood. "And, speaking from experience, never scrape Brussels sprouts from your plate into your shorts pocket when your mom isn't looking and then hide them in your room, because they'll stink like a dirty, wet sock!"

Eden gasped. "You did that? I can only imagine the stench."

"Maybe." I smiled before changing the subject again. "And one more thing? Don't forget to take care of your teeth," I said to Ryan. "When your mother reminds you to brush twice a day, do it. Most of us needed a lot of dental work when we arrived back in the States."

I could see Ryan was a smart boy, and I sensed my words would stick with him. "Now, on to a more uplifting subject," I said. "You're going into fifth grade, correct?"

Ryan nodded.

"I believe that's the age of Whippersnapper's daughter, Willow. She rides a mountain bike like nobody's business," I said. "If you visit our fine town again, perhaps you can check out the trails with her. With your mother chaperoning, of course."

Eden's eyes widened, likely surprised that I would encourage riding mountain bikes on those hair-raising trails.

"You know a guy named Whippersnapper?" Ryan squinted at me.

"That's my nickname for him. His real name is Will, but he goes by Whip. When I was growing up, that's what young boys were sometimes called, and Whip is young compared to me."

"His daughter rides the trails?" Ryan rested his chin on his fists, finished with his malt.

"She sure does, along with many other youth from our area. They're hoping to get the sport into the school's curriculum eventually, but for now, they've formed a youth riding club."

"I'm surprised you're promoting the mountain bike trails, David." Eden arched an eyebrow.

"Eh, I'm fine with the locals. It's the flood of tourists taking over our town that rubs me the wrong way."

Eden shook her head. I knew what she was thinking, and she was right. I was a stubborn old man who didn't like change. But I would gladly accept her and her son moving to our town. She hadn't yet divulged what was behind her frequent trips, but I was no dummy.

She loved Crimson Creek almost as much as I did.

Chapter 19
Eden

After David left for home, I drove the two blocks to the park's lot directly across from the building I hoped to buy. "How about we walk along the beach to the skate park?" I asked Ryan.

"Sure," Ryan said, taking the water bottle I handed him from the cooler. We kept our sandals on as we walked on the hot pavement until we reached the grass.

We waded up to our knees, the water temperature similar to a bath. "Nice beach, huh?"

"I wish we had a beach like this close to our house," Ryan said, wading in deep enough for the gentle waves to dampen the bottom of his shorts. He'd lost the enthusiasm he'd had during lunch, and I had a feeling he knew something was up.

We cut across the grass to the skate park, where at least a dozen kids on skateboards rode the cement configurations. An indoor skateboard area had been built near Trent's home, and Ryan and his friends frequented it, but nothing could be better than being outdoors right next to a lake.

"Let's sit at a picnic table in the shade. I've got something to talk to you about."

Ryan shot me a sideways glance. "I figured so. It's about this town, isn't it?"

It didn't take a genius to question my trips to Crimson Creek after I'd given David's POW bracelet to him. We found an unoccupied picnic table away from the main beach area, shaded enough to keep us from sweating. "Do you have a boyfriend here?" Ryan hit me with the question before I even sat down.

"What? No!"

"Well then, why are you coming here? Why do you want me to like this town?" Ryan folded his sweaty arms over his damp t-shirt.

"That obvious, huh?" I winced. "No boyfriend... This has to do with me trying to figure out my next job. You know I've been looking in the cities and have even checked out a few business opportunities."

Ryan sat across from me, picking at peeling paint on the corner of the picnic table, keeping his eyes focused on the green paint.

I continued, "I want more than a paycheck. I want a job I look forward to going to, one that challenges me but doesn't break me." I pointed at the empty corner building on the other side of the park. "I want to buy that building. It has a two-bedroom apartment upstairs for living quarters, and on the main floor, I want to rent out mountain bikes, kayaks, canoes... things this growing community needs."

I gave Ryan time to let my news settle. He took forever to answer. "Okay. But I can come visit you, right?"

My eyes widened at his take on what I'd shared with him. "Well... I am hoping that if this move happens—which would be a long process over the coming year—that you might consider moving here with me." I reached for his hand. "You don't need to decide now, and this is all still in the 'maybe' stage, but next year, you'll be changing schools anyway when you start sixth grade." I fought back the panic creeping into my chest.

Ryan pulled his hand away. "But when I go to the middle school in the cities next year, I'll already know some of the kids in my class." He peered around at the bustling park area. "I don't know anyone here."

"I can't argue that. But for right now, I'd like you to think of this as just an option. Nothing is settled yet. Heck, I haven't even made an offer on the building." I peered out at the sun shimmering over Crow Lake, listened to the squeals of laughter from the nearby beach, breathed in the aroma of lake vegetation, freshly cut grass, and someone grilling hot dogs on a charcoal grill, and imagined living with Ryan right across the street.

"Can I show you the place I'm thinking of buying?" I turned back to meet Ryan's eyes and thumbed toward the other side of the park. "I've already been inside."

Ryan nodded. We stood, and I led the way across the park until we crossed the street corner to the building. "Like I said, there's a two-bedroom apartment upstairs." I pointed at the second floor. "It needs work, same with the main floor, but a lot of it is cosmetic. The building itself is solid."

We peered inside one of the two large windows facing the park and lake.

"What do you think?"

Ryan passed his water bottle back and forth between his hands. "I dunno." He turned toward the park. "It'd be cool for you to live across from the lake and skate park."

His word choice of "you" instead of "us" rolled off my back. This was his first trip to Crimson Creek. It was a lot to take in.

"It would. And the bike trails and mine-pit lakes..." I itched to pull him in for a hug and say it would all work out, but it was a promise I couldn't make.

"Come on. I want to show you the back of the building." We rounded the corner to the adjoining empty lot that separated the building from the main street of town. "This lot goes with it. I'd probably offer a shuttle service to the recreation parking lots for kayak and canoe rentals."

"What about the bikers?"

"Some will ride from the shop. The trails begin on the edge of town. Some may want to shuttle. It depends." I chugged my water as sweat trickled down my back. "There're the paved bike trails too, and some families may want to shuttle to those if they have younger kids."

Ryan wiped sweat from his face with the bottom of his T-shirt.

"Okay, enough of this heat." We walked back to the car. "What do you say we hit the ice cream shop?"

"There's an ice cream shop here?" Ryan squinted at me from under his baseball cap.

I chuckled. "Yes, silly. They even have indoor toilets and electricity here." I nudged him. "The town has everything you need, including a nice new middle school and high school."

Ryan refrained from pointing out that the town didn't have two things he needed: his dad and his friends.

Figuring I should wait before approaching Ryan again about Crimson Creek, I was surprised when Ryan and his friend Brady came up to me after their baseball game the week after our road trip. "Hey, Mom, I was telling Brady about that skateboard park in the town we went to. What's the name of that place again?" Ryan shaded his eyes from the sun as he peered up at me.

"Crimson Creek," I said. "It's in the middle of the state." Minnesota boasted thousands of lakes, but in general, Central Minnesota was the booming tourist area with so many lakes that you could practically hop from one to the other.

Brady chimed in with questions about the mountain bike trails. Ryan obviously had been thinking of the town. Maybe it wasn't a closed door after all.

When I picked Ryan up from Trent's the following Sunday, I brought up the idea for my business again. "What do you think about getting a tour of the building with me this week? I can call the realtor. I want to check a few more things on the building," I said.

Ryan fidgeted. "I guess. Can I bring my skateboard?"

"You sure can." I called Jenny, the realtor, a few minutes later. I set up an appointment for us to meet with her on Tuesday, two weeks after Ryan's first trip to Crimson Creek.

David was going to be out of town that day, and I promised Ryan we would do whatever he wanted after we met with Jenny. On Tuesday morning, we packed our swimsuits and towels, Ryan's skateboard, snacks, and a cooler, leaving before nine for our eleven o'clock showing with Jenny.

I parked next to Jenny's vehicle in the store's parking lot, and she met us at the door. I introduced her to Ryan, who shook her hand like a young businessman.

He'd fired off a dozen questions on the drive north, most starting with "What if." I answered as best I could, reminding him that any decision on his part wouldn't happen for months.

Jenny nodded toward the two-story building. "So, Ryan, you're here to help your mom make a decision? Let's step inside, where it's cool." She led the way to the front door, unlocked it, and moved aside for us to enter.

"The previous business sold candy and summer toys. Mostly catered to the beach crowd at the park in the summer," Jenny said. "Before that, it was an antique shop."

Jenny led us past the twelve-foot counter to the back, where a small office and bathroom were tucked in the corner. Stand-alone paneled walls separated the office from the brick-walled store, looking like they would fall if you sneezed on them. They would need to be removed so that when I was alone in the store, I could be at my desk and have a full view of the store.

The bathroom was nothing but a toilet and sink, encased in similar dark paneling with a bare bulb hanging from an electrical cord for light. All of it begged for some TLC.

In the far back was a door leading to the garage. Jenny flipped on the lights. "This was where delivery trucks pulled in to deliver inventory." She smiled at Ryan. "Imagine how fun it would have been to be here when they delivered all that candy."

Ryan's eyes lit up, and he turned to me as if a candy store was an option.

"If I do the rental shop," I said, "this back storage area will be used for rental equipment."

"Let's head upstairs," Jenny said, stepping back inside the shop. "You can access the apartment through this door"—she gestured toward the stairs near the office—"or the door on the west side of the shop."

I appreciated the separate outside door to access the upstairs since I wouldn't want to live in the apartment forever *if* I bought the place. Eventually, renting out the upstairs would help pay the mortgage.

Jenny opened the door leading to the enclosed stairs and flipped on the overhead light, and we followed her up the steep, narrow steps, typical for an old building. When we reached the upstairs, Jenny unlocked another door leading from the stairs to a small kitchen and living room.

The carpet would need to be replaced, walls painted, and new kitchen appliances and a new bathroom sink installed. But the view from the living room, overlooking Crow Lake and the park, was refreshing. I slid open two windows facing the park and lake, and Ryan leaned into the screen to catch the breeze.

I had taken photos and measurements of the rooms when I toured the place with Jenny the first time. The bedrooms were small but large enough for a bed and a dresser. Square footage-wise, it was similar in size to my apartment. And the monthly mortgage for the apartment and shop would be roughly what I paid for rent in the Twin Cities—another benefit to small-town living.

"Come on," I told Ryan. "I want to show you the bedrooms." I led the way to the small second bedroom. "This would be your room whenever you're here." I reinforced that this was a commitment-free tour. "Since it's small, I plan to get bunk beds. That way, if you have a friend visit, there's room for both of you."

"Brady could come visit?" Ryan asked as we joined Jenny in the living room.

"Of course. I'd love that." We spent a few more minutes with Jenny as she pointed out things I'd asked about after my first showing before we went out to the parking lot and Jenny locked the front door.

"Thanks so much for the tour again," I said. "I'll be in touch soon."

I'd already told Jenny that it was my pick from the properties she'd shown me. It had been on the market for eight months, but I had a feeling that once Crimson Creek's soon-to-boom recreational community news spread, other business-savvy people would be hunting for a prime location like this building.

"That sounds good," Jenny said before she slid behind the wheel and drove away.

Ryan and I took a drive outside town, past the main parking lot where we had parked when we went kayaking. The road took us around several other mine-pit lakes, more bike trails, and a rope swing at the end of a sandbar where several teens were splashing and swinging.

Back in town, we ate a picnic lunch in the shade at the beach, and I sat on a picnic table near the lake afterward when Ryan headed to the skateboard park with his skateboard. A handful of other kids were in the park, and they seemed friendly enough to Ryan, who spent an hour skateboarding.

He cooled off in the lake afterward, and by the time we headed south, I would have stamped the day with "approved." So I was a bit blindsided when on our drive home, Ryan casually said, "It's a cool town, but I don't want to live there. I like the cities better." Suddenly, all my hopes exploded like dynamite.

Chapter 20

After Ryan's heart-wrenching declaration, I pivoted my focus to suck it up and stay in Minneapolis. I had a prestigious LinkedIn profile from years in various banking positions. I beefed up my minor in journalism experience and put my knowledge to good use. By the end of July, I had more than enough freelance work as a financial writer.

For long stretches of time, I could ignore my dream of a rental shop in Crimson Creek. I didn't bring it up again to Ryan. *Nobody has it all, Eden. Why should you be any different?*

I spent the next few weeks doing most of my writing when Ryan was at Trent's. And when he was with me, I took him and his friends to the beach, to Valley Fair, the movie theater, and a Saint Paul Saints baseball game. Ryan and I went back-to-school shopping and, at the end of August, attended the state fair—twice. All were benefits of living in Minneapolis.

And I made the phone call I'd avoided for too long. I called Jenny in Crimson Creek to tell her I wouldn't be purchasing the building. "It's perfect for what I have planned, but I can't do it. At least not now."

"I understand," Jenny said. "Do you want me to let you know if they drop the price?"

"The price isn't the issue, but sure. Thank you." With the idea of moving squashed, I focused on using most of my savings to purchase a home again, saving a cushion for emergencies.

Living in a home instead of an apartment would help boost my spirits about staying in the Twin Cities. I needed a yard, room to breathe, a place for Ryan to feel at home.

The first week in September, after Ryan started fifth grade, I made appointments with a realtor. I viewed sixteen houses before I found one that checked most of the boxes, including a decent neighborhood, a fairly maintenance-free house, a manageable yard, and a location in Ryan's school district.

But before I had a chance to show the house to Ryan, another potential buyer offered above the asking price, which I had hoped to lowball.

No mortgage lender would approve a loan for me without a steady income, and I refused to sink all my savings into a home. The price of the business and apartment in Crimson Creek had been less than half what I was going to offer for the tiny home in Ryan's school district.

I felt I'd let Ryan down by not being able to purchase a decent home. He knew I'd been house hunting, and when I broke the news that night over cheeseburgers, he responded, "Oh, okay" between bites.

"That's it? You're not upset?"

Ryan scrunched his face. "Nope. Why would I be?"

"I thought you'd want a home instead of living in an apartment with no yard."

"I've got that at Dad's."

That was another reason I wanted a home. Divorce shouldn't be a game of who can offer the most, but it sure felt like it. Ten years before, I would have never dreamed that Trent would be the one with the steady job, the one with the house. *Happy now, Eden? Still glad you left a lucrative job?*

Ryan had been back in school for two weeks, and during that time, I'd written articles about everything from the rise in the stock market, falling oil prices, and decline in gold, to online data breaches. I was sick of staring at a computer screen—again—for most of my day.

I was on deadline for an article and up early, hunched over my laptop with bleary eyes and an aching back. Ryan's alarm went off in his bedroom, and minutes later, he shuffled into the kitchen as I gulped down coffee without my coveted whipping cream.

Ryan came to stand next to me, and I hugged his warm body to mine, planting a kiss on his forearm. He studied the table and then me. "What's wrong?"

I pasted on a smile. "Nothing. Why?"

Ryan nodded at my coffee cup. "You're drinking plain coffee, and your eyes are red. Plus, you're wearing the same clothes you wore yesterday."

"Well, detective, remind me to hire you next time I need a crime solved."

"Seriously. Were you crying?" Ryan wore that wary look one gets when you aren't sure you want to hear the answer.

I rubbed my eyes. "No. I'm on deadline for this article, so I was up early."

He peered at the article on my computer screen. "You're working a lot of hours again at a job you don't like."

My eyebrows rose. "How do you know I don't like this job?"

"You get those serious lines in your forehead." Ryan took a seat at the table. "Why don't you find a job you want to do, like Dad has?"

Oh, to be young and believe adulting is that simple.

Ryan leaned his elbows on the table and his chin on his hands, peering at me. "What job would you want to do if you could pick one?"

I hesitated, but Ryan deserved an honest answer. "Well, I would open a rental shop in that building in Crimson Creek."

"Why don't you do it?" Ryan rubbed sleep from his eyes. "YOLO, Mom."

I nodded at the acronym. "Yes, we only live once, but that dream job is too far away, and you don't want to move there."

"I'm sorry." His shoulders slumped.

I stood and hugged him from behind his chair. "Don't be. I'll figure this out. We'll figure this out." I kissed the top of his head. "For now, we need you to get ready for school. Eggs and bacon for breakfast?" One benefit of my working from home was that I had time to make him breakfast.

"Sure." Ryan stood, scratched his tummy, and trudged down the hall, looking as if he carried the burden of our future, and I hated that I'd put that on him.

The subject didn't come up again until a few days later, when Ryan and I picked Brady up for a friend's birthday party. Gretta walked out with her son when I pulled into their driveway.

Brady slid in beside Ryan in the back seat, and Gretta crouched down to my open window. "Hey, there. I hear you're moving?"

"What? Nope. I was looking at homes in the area, but that's not going to work right now."

"No, I meant the sports rental business. Ryan told Brady you want to open a business north of here?" Gretta smiled. "It sounds perfect for you with your business and finance background."

"It is, and I'd pursue it if the town wasn't two hours north of here. It's called Crimson Creek, and it's becoming a popular mountain bike area."

"I've heard of the area," Gretta said. "My nephew is into mountain biking, and he's mentioned Crimson Creek."

While Ryan and Brady talked in the back seat, Gretta leaned in to whisper, "I still think you should pursue it. And if you do, Ryan is always welcome here to visit."

"Thank you," I said, surprised at her words. "I better get these two to the party."

"Thanks for driving. We'll pick up the boys at seven." Gretta waved goodbye as I backed out of the driveway. The party was at a place with video games inside and a go-kart trail outside.

After dropping them off at the party, I reflected on Gretta's comment about Ryan coming to visit. Gretta assumed Ryan would live with me. *Did Ryan indicate that to Brady?* I had only one way to find out.

Gretta dropped Ryan off after seven, and I gave him time to tell me all about the party before I broached the subject. We sat side by side on the sofa, Ryan still stuffed from deep-dish pizza and chocolate cake at the birthday party.

"I have a question for you." I faced Ryan, leaning against the edge of the sofa. "Gretta talked to me about the shop in Crimson Creek and said something about if I moved there, you could stay with them when you want to visit Brady..."

"Yeah." Ryan shrugged. "Why? Don't you want me to? Gretta won't care. She said so."

"No, it's not that... I assumed you wanted to live in the cities. That's what you said in July." I placed my hand on his shoulder. "I would love to have you move with me, and if you did, of course you could stay at Brady's once in a while."

Ryan fiddled with a small hole in his jeans, poking his finger in and out. "When I told Brady what you said about the store, he thought that would be so cool. One of the video games he has is a mountain biking game, and he said he'd come visit me if I moved with you."

"You bet, Buddy. It's why I planned to put bunk beds in your room there." I peered at him. "So this decision to rethink moving was based on a video game?" I worried he would change his mind a week later.

"Well, also, I found out from a kid at school who has a brother in seventh grade that he never gets to play on his football or baseball team because the middle school is so big and they have too many kids go out for sports." Ryan chewed on his lip. "I might not get to play baseball, but maybe I could in Crimson Creek if their middle school is smaller."

The tightness in my chest loosened as if it were a bale of hay and someone had finally cut the twine. "Yes, their school is smaller. And we can make a trip there soon so you can look it over." I squeezed his hand. "No commitment and no pressure," I said with a smile, "but you considering it is enough for me."

Lying in bed that night, I thought of the two phone calls I needed to make: one to Trent and one to Jenny about the building.

Mom called the following day. We hadn't spoken for a few weeks. When I voiced my worry about Ryan eventually choosing to stay in the cities, it was met with silence.

"Mom? You still there?" I worried she thought I was a terrible person for even thinking of moving without my child.

"Oh, I'm here. Just reminiscing." Mom sighed. "Got a few minutes to hear a story?"

"Of course." Curiosity had me clasping the cell phone tightly and settling in at the kitchen counter with my coffee. Mom didn't waste time. If she had a story, it mattered.

"You know that your dad was living in Mason City when we got together and that we'd met in Grandfield, where his family cabin was," Mom reminded me. "What I don't think you know is that when I sensed I was pregnant with you, before I told your dad, he had wanted me to move to Mason City, and I refused." Mom cleared her throat. "Even when the pregnancy was confirmed, I wouldn't budge... because I'd already had so many changes in my life and Grandfield had become my home, the place I was meant to be."

Mom's voice turned wistful. "I'd visited Mason City with your father. Although it's a nice area and his family all lived there, I knew that I'd wilt like a flower too long without water."

I scoffed. "Ya think? Geez, I can't imagine you living in a big city."

"My point exactly," Mom said. "I'm not a big city girl. If I'd have moved, I would have been miserable, which would have made your dad and you miserable. It took a lot of convincing myself to realize that I deserved to be happy." Her voice cracked on the last words.

"Mom, are you crying?" Mom rarely cried.

"Oh, maybe." She gave a small chuckle. "I remember how difficult it was to stand up for myself, to not sell myself short and live someone else's life."

I tried to imagine growing up in Mason City without Ellie or Nielson, because they wouldn't have come into our lives if Mom hadn't stayed in Grandfield. I would have never known Stevie Grace.

"It's like that saying, 'Bloom where you are planted,'" Mom said. "Many people thrive on the hustle and bustle of city living. You and I, not so much."

"Not that there's anything wrong with those people." I played devil's advocate. "I mean, look at Dad. He turned out okay."

"Well, I don't know about that," Mom quipped. I couldn't imagine Dad ever living in a big city again. If Dad could change from a city boy after thirty years, maybe Ryan could after eleven.

Chapter 21
David

Eden called on Monday to see if we could meet for lunch on Tuesday. She was coming to town to sign a purchase agreement, and that young woman was excited.

The late-September weather had dipped to near freezing overnight, already turning the maple leaves brilliant colors, decorating my drive to the café.

I was seated in a back booth when Eden arrived, bouncing toward me like Tigger the Tiger. "How did the meeting go with Jenny?" I asked as she slid into the booth across from me.

"Great! We think they'll accept the offer." Eden hung her coat on the booth's hook. "When I called Jenny to see if the building was still available, she said the owners had contacted her after Labor Day about dropping the price since the building hadn't sold over the summer."

I pushed my menu aside, deciding on the pork chop special of the day. "Did you lowball them?"

"I offered ten grand less than the listing price, knowing they'd planned to drop the price soon. And I asked to purchase on a contract for deed, something Jenny said they had mentioned they were willing to do, so I don't have to wait for financing through a bank." Eden scanned her menu. "Jenny expects we'll hear back in a day or two." She closed her menu. "Can I ask you something?"

"Certainly." I folded my hands on the table.

"When you were in the service, even before you became a POW, you went months without seeing your children, right?"

"Yes. We received thirty days' leave each year, so sometimes there were several months between my leaves." I shook my head. "The kids changed so much in those months."

Eden leaned forward. "I think about that. And all the women now who are in the service. I know it's a stigma, that it's acceptable for a man to have a job that takes him from his family, but I feel selfish for even thinking about it."

The server came to take our order, and once she retreated, I addressed Eden's guilt. "Every parent feels that guilt, or at least, they should." I remembered mine well. "Children are self-centered, but they're also aware. It sounds like Ryan noticed your unhappiness, and it may have opened the door to his sharing your dream with his best friend, wanting you to be happy."

"Maybe. And Ryan knows he's not committed to moving with me. But knowing it's a possibility—and that he doesn't have to decide for months—is enough for both of us." Eden chuckled. "My ex-husband isn't thrilled, but he agrees we will figure it out come next spring."

"One day at a time, right?" I smiled at Eden, glad to see her happiness even as I knew her shop would add to what I didn't like about the boom in town—more mountain bikers overtaking our community.

But if I had to choose between nixing bikers from our town and Eden's business success, I would choose her success. She was beginning to feel like family. And I had so little family left.

Thinking of my family, I'd received more phone calls than usual lately from Louise due to her concern over Jack's debilitating—and confounding—health issues. Over the past few months, his energy had dwindled, and his joint pain had become so bad that he often resorted to crawling, something I couldn't comprehend since my son-in-law was a big, sturdy man. And Jack had become depressed to the point that he often stayed in bed on weekends.

That I could relate to. You can't force someone to get back to living when their body tells them to give up. Jack's declining health was taking its toll on him and sapping the life out of Louise.

Jean had been the glue that kept our family—and me—together. When I broke down in gut-wrenching sobs in the privacy of our home, often without warning, Jean was there to comfort me.

In the years since Jean's death, I'd done my best to plug the holes she had left in my life. We'd had each other to lean on as we grieved Lee's death twenty-plus years before. Burying a child, whether they were six or thirty-six—as in Lee's case—was something one never recovered from.

The day after I met Eden for lunch, Louise called me when I was making my bed, while she should have been at work. When I picked up the landline receiver on my nightstand, Louise's crying greeted me, and I braced myself for bad news—again.

"Calm down, Louise. Whatever it is, I'm here for you." Nobody liked to be told to calm down, but that was the best advice I could give her from fourteen hundred miles away.

Louise eked out, "It's... It's..." She mumbled between sobs as I clutched the phone.

Heaven help me, did something happen to one of my grandsons?

"Shhh, Louise. It's going to be okay." *Liar! Why would I think nothing else bad could happen to our family?*

Louise squeaked, "It is! I think Jack is going to be okay. He just got a call from the doctor, and they believe he has chronic Lyme disease."

I closed my eyes in silent gratitude. "So, those were happy tears?" That wasn't the first time I'd read a woman wrong.

"Yes. Happy tears. He's got a long recovery and will still have a lot of ups and downs, but he's not dying." More huffs and puffs followed. "I thought he was dying!"

I sat on the edge of the bed before my trick knee buckled. "Ah, Louise my dear, I had no idea you were that worried."

Somehow, after Jean died, Louise had stepped in as if she could be the buffer between me and bad news. She likely hadn't told me the worst of things regarding Jack's health.

"So, what's next for Jack?"

I hoped for Louise's sake that Jack's recovery would be swift. Yes, I liked my son-in-law, truly a wonderful man. But Louise was my number one concern.

"They're starting him on oral antibiotics but have warned us they may not do the job." Louise blew her nose. "Stubborn man should've gone to the doctor months ago, and the Lyme wouldn't have done so much damage. He's going to feel like crap for quite a while, but at least they know what's wrong now. I still plan to come visit you before Christmas. The boys will be home from college on break then, and they can help Jack."

Louise revealed how Jack had fallen several times and struggled to remember how to do simple things then, a few days later, would seem okay. I hoped that his eventual recovery would enable them to travel after they retired.

Everyone thinks they have time to pursue their dreams. Sometimes, we don't even have tomorrow. I'd been living on borrowed time since my plane was shot down.

After Louise and I hung up, I continued to sit on the edge of my bed, thinking—something I usually did my best to avoid.

Nothing is guaranteed. You, of all people, know that. Every pilot flying an F-105 understood they were the most shot-down plane during the war. Yet every pilot thought it would never happen to them.

When my F-105 was hit, the shell didn't explode. We'd been climbing past 8,500 feet, and the plane continued to climb—until it began plummeting with breakneck speed toward the earth.

Two options flashed before me: stay with the plane and meet certain death or eject once gravity allowed me freedom to move, to parachute into enemy territory and likely captivity.

Jean's voice in my head decided for me. I reached behind me and pulled the trigger on my rocket seat. The instant my body hit the ground in the jungle of North Vietnam, I radioed in that I'd landed safely, not realizing at the time that I'd fractured my back when I bailed out. I destroyed the radio seconds before civilians came and nearly beat me to death.

When the Vietnamese soldiers arrived with their bayonets drawn, shooing off the civilians who had stripped and beaten me, my gut roiled at the knowledge that every plan Jean and I had made would likely never happen.

That was much like what Jack's faltering health could've done for Louise and Jack's plans. Plans, like dreams, could be shattered like glass.

Chapter 22
Eden

When I told David that Trent was less than thrilled about me purchasing the building in Crimson Creek, that had been a colossal understatement. I'd called Trent to let him know I was going to sign a purchase agreement for the building and got an earful in return.

"Really, Eden? Let me tell you, running a business takes a lot of juggling. And you're starting from scratch. You don't know what you're doing."

I'd bit my lip to keep from screaming into the phone. "Yes, Trent. I'm aware. Remember, my parents ran three businesses when I was growing up?"

"I'm not changing my schedule for yours," Trent continued. He wasn't telling me anything I didn't already know. He had no problem asking me to change my schedule for his plans, but not the other way around. The world continued to revolve around Trent. Luckily, he held Ryan close in that world. If he ever adjusted his life for anyone, it would be for Ryan.

Five days after Trent told me what he thought of my plan, the sellers accepted my offer, agreeing to hold a contract for deed on the building.

And on the last day of October, I signed the contract for deed paperwork with the seller at Jenny's real estate office.

I had divided my savings and severance pay into a fifty-percent down payment on the building, roughly the same amount to be kept for inventory and building spruce-up. It left me with a decent amount socked away in an emergency-only account, along with savings and retirement accounts that I didn't plan to touch for years. Thanks to the fifty-percent down payment, the monthly payment would be manageable, I hoped, even in the slower winter months.

I had my work cut out for me over the coming months, with fixing up the shop and apartment when Ryan was at Trent's and researching and purchasing inventory on the weeks Ryan was with me at my apartment in the cities.

My parents and siblings had been kept up to date on my decision and purchase venture, along with Stevie Grace, who had been gone for two weeks in October on a European trip.

After the purchase was completed, I drove from Jenny's office to the building that was my future home and business. Unlocking the front door, I stepped inside, my arms full of household cleaning products. I set them on the counter, stood in the middle of the shop, and repeated, *You are home, Eden. You are home.* The tug that had pulled on me for several years, the restlessness running through me as I hurried through life, was at peace.

I went to the front, where the windows overlooked the park. The overcast day did nothing to dampen my spirits. I pulled my cell from my jacket pocket and called Mom.

"I'm so happy for you, Eden," Mom said after I told her the sale was official. "Glad that you are pursuing your dreams." Mom's voice, always chipper, sounded weary.

Dad had had knee replacement surgery two weeks earlier, and I imagined Mom was trying to do it all with their animals, volunteer work, and playing nurse. "Me too, Mom. Hey, how's Dad doing? Behaving himself?"

"He is. Doing his leg exercises and everything, but he's pretty bummed about one thing."

"What's that?" I rubbed my in-need-of-food stomach.

"He won't be able to go with me to see you and your new place," Mom said. "Surprise!"

My mouth dropped open. "Are you serious?" I did a little happy dance. "When?"

"That depends on your schedule. I'd love to be there for your birthday and to help with cleaning your new shop. Our neighbor said he'd drive your dad to physical therapy."

I hadn't seen my parents since last Christmas, and with everything up in the air, I had skipped my trip with Ryan to visit them last summer. "I'm staying here for the next two days to do some cleaning and then picking Ryan up on Sunday." I could get a lot done before I headed back to the cities. "Any chance you could fly in later next week? Then you could spend some time with Ryan, and you and I could drive to Crimson Creek for a few days after he goes back to Trent's house."

I paced the vinyl-tiled flooring, anticipating Mom's arrival. "I think that would work," Mom said. "Let me check flights, and I'll call or text you the information."

We spoke for a few more minutes, and after I hung up, I spent the next hour unloading my vehicle packed with an air bed, an overnight bag, kitchen items, towels, and cleaning products, along with my vacuum.

After I wolfed down the ham-and-cheese sandwich and apple that I'd packed, I walked to the hardware store to pick up a mop and bucket, along with paint color samples in shades of blue and purple for Ryan to look at for his room. I washed windows, cleaned the floors, and added to my growing list of to-buy items.

The toilet and sink in the shop bathroom needed to be replaced, and the same was true with the apartment bathroom, but the tub and shower were in decent shape. I wanted to paint the room before new fixtures and towel bars were installed.

By six o'clock, I was famished. I washed up, changed into clean jeans and a sweater, ran fingers through my short hair to fluff it up, and stepped into low-rise hiking boots. I zipped up my fall jacket and headed down the apartment steps.

Leaving on the outdoor light facing the parking lot, I walked the two blocks to Mined Your Business. A burger and beer sounded good, plus the local bar was always a good place to learn more about the town and townspeople.

Whip wasn't working behind the bar when I arrived, but two other bartenders were pouring drinks for the Friday-night crowd. Instead of taking up a table, I sat at the bar with a full view of the place. I enjoyed people watching, especially in my new hometown.

By seven thirty, I'd finished my California burger and tap beer, not in any hurry to go back and spend the rest of the night staring at the in-need-of-repainting ceiling. I'd blown up the air mattress earlier so that the mattress wouldn't feel cold when I went to bed.

Someone slid onto the barstool next to me—one of the few open. When the bartender came to take the man's drink order, I asked for another tap beer, and the bartender returned with our drinks a minute later.

The man made small talk with the bartender, discussing the Minnesota Vikings and a new wide receiver from Minnesota. "Let's hope they keep Thielen. We need some local blood," the man sitting next to me said. I wasn't one to listen in on other people's conversations, but Ryan loved the Vikings, and I tried to keep up on the team.

After the bartender left to take other orders, the man next to me asked, "You new here?"

I cast him a sideways glance, unsure if he was speaking to me. Even in the dim bar lighting, his blue eyes stood out under dark eyebrows, framed by dark wavy hair as long as—if not longer than—mine. "Me?"

"Yep, you. I haven't seen you in here before." He gave me a welcoming grin, and my gaze fell to his mouth, white teeth surrounded by a trimmed mustache and beard. He chuckled, "I'm sure that sounds like a pickup line, but it's not. I've lived here all my life, and you don't look familiar." He peered around toward the man on the other side of me, the barstool occupied by a man old enough to be my father, speaking to another man on the other side of him. "And since you're here alone, I'm guessing you aren't a mountain biker."

I couldn't remember the last time I'd been in a bar alone, and technically, I was out for dinner. But instead of feeling wary of this stranger, as I would at a bar in the cities, I was intrigued. The bartender knew him, and he was likely a frequent patron, because he noticed I was new in town.

"Yep, not a biker. Yet." I was here to meet townspeople, so I stuck out my hand. "Eden Everson, the proud new owner of the building on the corner across from the park."

His brows rose at the news. "Good for you! Welcome to Crimson Creek." His grip was firm. "Donovan Crosby, proud owner of several yurts and cabins for the bikers and working on some loft rentals for said bikers."

"Wow. I haven't heard of many people catering to the bikers yet," I said.

"Others have ideas in the works, but the wheel turns slowly in getting a small town to change," Donovan said. "Where did you move from, or haven't you moved here yet?"

"The cities. This is my first day as the official owner. We'll be working on the place over the winter and hope to be open by spring. I plan to do rentals for mountain bikes, kayaks, canoes, that type of thing."

"We?" Donovan took a sip of his drink.

I was careful not to give too much away, local or not. He could be a serial killer recently released from prison. *Okay, probably not, Eden.*

"Yes, Ryan and I. We'll be here part of the time and in the cities part of the time until next spring." I wanted him to think Ryan was a significant other of some sort so that word didn't get out about me staying in the apartment alone.

"It sounds like the perfect business for our community. It's been a bitch to get business owners to change their way of thinking from catering mainly to summer tourists." Donovan rubbed his palm over his short beard. "Not that we shouldn't cater to them. They've been our bread and butter for decades. However, the biking community has other needs, and if we want the industry to grow, we need to provide for them year-round."

I studied his working man's hand, wrapped around his drink. "Like what else besides lodging and rentals?"

"The demographics for this community, for the most part, are people in their twenties to forties. The mountain biking community people have money to spend, want decent places to eat, and like their craft beer."

"Is that happening?"

"There's talk of a microbrewery and another downtown restaurant that has more of a dinner menu than bar food or breakfast," Donovan said. "That's the stuff we need. They're a big leap, though, and I get why people are hesitant to sink large amounts of money and time into something that wouldn't have survived here five years ago."

Our conversation continued through several classic songs blasted loud enough to hear over the crowd, everything from the Doors' "Love Her Madly" to King Harvest's "Dancing in the Moonlight." We ordered another round of drinks, and a mellow buzz flowed through me, enough to admit Donovan exuded charisma and was damn good-looking in a woodsy outdoors sort of way. He wore no wedding ring, but that meant nothing.

After nine, I pushed back my barstool. People dressed up for Halloween were filtering in for a costume contest. "I'd better get back. I've got a lot to get done tomorrow."

I pulled on the jacket I'd been sitting on, and when I turned to face Donovan, he stood to shake my hand again.

"I'm sure I'll see you around," he said.

It was then that I realized I was taller than him. At five feet nine, I had been taller than most boys until well into senior high. Donovan was stocky, broad-shouldered, and muscular—and a couple of inches shorter than me. We said goodbye, and as I walked back to the apartment, I kicked myself for not asking a single thing about him.

Chapter 23

I woke long before the sun rose Saturday morning, and went to work, scrubbing walls with vinegar water and listening to a local radio station. "25 or 6 to 4", an oldie by Chicago, played, and I nodded in understanding when they sang of wondering how much they could take—a sentiment I'd experienced too often at my old job. Later, as I unpacked household items, Alicia Keys belted out "Girl on Fire," and I fist-pumped the air, singing along with Alicia to a song I decided was my new mantra.

If someone had asked me when Trent and I married how I envisioned my future, it wouldn't have involved divorce, leaving a successful career, and moving out of the cities to start a business, possibly without Ryan. But it *would* have included me pursuing my dreams. Somewhere along the line, I'd lost sight of them.

David, who tended to sleep in on Saturdays due to his late hours with his Goober shuttle service, was meeting me at the Triple C for lunch. I arrived before him, and when the hostess led me to a booth near the back, I spotted a familiar face.

Donovan and two other men sat in one of the booths, the plates in front of them nearly empty.

"Hey, Eden. Good to see you again," Donovan said as I neared.

"Hello, Donovan," I said in passing. *Has he been in here before when I've been here?* There was another café near downtown, but the Triple C was twice its size.

As I was hanging up my coat on the hook at the end of the booth, David headed my way.

"I beat you for once," I said, walking toward him.

"Only because I had some ne'er-do-wells on Goober until after one o'clock. Slugs didn't want to leave the 'party bus,' as they called it," David said with a fake yawn.

As we were turning back toward the booth, someone touched David's shoulder. Donovan. *David knows Donovan? Of course he does, silly.*

Donovan eyed David and me. "Hey there, David. How do you know Eden?"

Before I could explain, David said, "Eden is my girlfriend. I met her on a dating website."

Donovan threw his head back in laughter. "Good one!"

"What? You have a problem with our relationship?" I asked.

Donovan's eyebrows rose until he caught my smirk. "Clever, girl." He jammed his hands in his jeans pockets. "Does that mean you're two-timing Ryan?"

David was caught off guard. "You mean her son Ryan?"

My cheeks grew warm, and I focused on the floor tiles. But I couldn't avoid Donovan, who ducked to meet my eyes. "So... Ryan's your *son*?"

I jutted out my chin. "Yes. I never said he wasn't."

"You're right. You didn't." Donovan nodded. "But you implied he bought the business with you." His eyes, I decided, were the color of a cloudless sky on a bright sunny day. "You must've had him when you were a toddler if he's old enough to own a business with you."

"What are you talking about, Hurdy Gurdy?" David took a step between us as if Donovan might throw a punch. "Ryan is in fifth grade. Did you smoke your lunch?" He nudged Donovan.

"Yep, must've." Donovan's eyes never left mine.

"Well, I didn't know if you were a stalker or a serial killer... You didn't tell me you knew David."

Donovan's smile twitched. "I should include that in my introductions to people? 'I'm Donovan Crosby, and I know David Carpenter.'"

David clapped as if witnessing an impressive performance. "Ah, I get it now. You were trying to pick up Eden, and she pretended Ryan was her boyfriend."

"Something like that," I muttered, hooking my arm through David's and steering us back to the booth, leaving Donovan's chuckles behind.

Once we sat, David opened the menu, snickering behind it.

"Don't pretend you don't already know what you're going to order." I pulled the menu away from his face. "Heck, I could order for you. Either roast beef or meatloaf since there's no pork chop special today."

"You don't know. I may have a hankering for spaghetti or perhaps lasagna."

"No, you won't. The sauce gives you heartburn."

David shook his head. "Clearly, I've divulged too much about myself." He set the menu aside. "Now, I am guessing you must've met Donovan at Mined Your Business last night?"

"How'd you know that?"

"He usually heads there after work on Friday and Saturday night. Most locals only stay for a drink or two, home by seven or eight, before the younger crowd goes out for the night."

"And that's where you and Goober come in," I said.

"Yes. By the way, Donovan is a nice man… in case you're looking," David said right before our server stepped in to take our order, preventing me from stating that I wasn't looking for a nice man—or any man, for that matter.

After we ordered, our conversation moved on from Donovan to David's son-in-law and his declining health, now with a confirmed diagnosis.

"I'm glad they got an answer. You said Louise comes back around Christmas?"

"Yes, usually the week before. Jack's from Vermont, and Louise has lived there since college, so they're settled there. I don't make the trip there as much as I used to. Getting too darn old."

We spoke of the upcoming holidays, and David mentioned a veterans' luncheon at the American Legion, which I planned to attend with him on Veterans Day.

After lunch, we parted ways, and I spent the afternoon cleaning the kitchen cupboards inside and out, scrubbing the window blinds, and taking measurements of everything to add to my notebook of information.

And, as tempting as it was to head to Mined Your Business that night, I didn't. *Who cares if Donovan might be there? Not you, Eden.* The benefit was a night of cleaning and organizing, a good night's rest, and a clear head on Sunday morning. Mom had called late Saturday afternoon with her plane reservations. I would pick her up at the Minneapolis airport the following Friday for her week-long stay with me,

During that week, I would get to celebrate my thirty-sixth birthday with Mom, which also happened to be Veterans Day, a coincidence that had thrilled my dad—a Vietnam veteran—when I was born.

Heading back to the cities on Sunday afternoon, I stopped at an unclaimed freight store. I purchased a recliner, a set of bunk beds, a queen bed, new mattresses, and a small kitchen table with four chairs for the apartment. I scheduled the delivery for a week from Monday, when Mom and I would be back in Crimson Creek.

When I picked up Ryan late Sunday afternoon, I told him the good news about Grandma Joleigh's visit the following Friday.

"Cool!" Ryan bounced in the passenger seat, something I'd noticed lately when he would return from Trent's place—too much time sitting playing video games and not enough time outdoors, burning off energy.

Back at the apartment, I showed him the blue and purple paint samples for his bedroom. "How about doing one wall one of these colors and then the other three walls white?"

Ryan shrugged. "I guess so. Probably the purple since when I'm up there, my school colors here won't matter. Do you know what the school colors are in Crimson Creek?"

His question was encouraging. "Yes. they're a crimson—or maroon—color and white." I ruffled his hair. "I'm painting all the walls white for now, and we can add the color later on."

A few nights later, as Ryan worked on homework, I sat at the kitchen table across from him, doing inventory research. Most of the bike shirts, jackets, and backpacks were bright neon colors so that bikers were easy to see on the trails. I watched Ryan doodle on the scratch paper he was using for his math homework. He'd somehow turned a two and a nine into the face of a Viking. It reminded me that I needed a logo for the business and attire I planned to sell. I'd already decided on a name for the business, Fun-Key Monkey, giving a nod to the largest mine in the area, Key Mine, which was how the neighboring town Mine Key got its name.

Something with a monkey. Maybe riding a mountain bike. And I knew who to ask: Ryan.

I waited until he finished his homework to bring it up. "What do you think? I'll pay you, of course, for your artwork, Mr. Everson."

Ryan's grin was so wide I thought his skin would split. "What if you don't like it?"

"We'll go over it together until we've got it right. I'll need a few mockups to choose from, sir," I said in a haughty tone.

Ryan lowered his voice an octave. "Of course, ma'am. I can begin working on them for you tomorrow. I'll need to skip school, but I'm sure that won't be a problem."

"Ha. Fat chance there, dude." I squeezed his shoulder. "I'm not in that big of a hurry."

Ryan gave a dramatic sigh.

Later, after he went to bed, I researched used trucks for sale in the Twin Cities. A truck would come in handy for moving and for the business.

As I lay in bed, unable to sleep, I counted dollar signs instead of sheep, worried I would bury myself in debt. "Stop second-guessing yourself. You've got this," I whispered, adding some sass to my voice so that I sounded like SG, my can-do cheerleader.

Chapter 24

Tears pooled in my eyes when I spotted Mom standing at the curb outside the airport baggage claim. My happiness was something I wouldn't have imagined when I was fourteen and butting heads with her daily, Dad having to step between us and our verbal spats because I wanted to run free and Mom wanted me to be safe.

I parked and ran to hug her, the cold mid-November wind whipping Mom's shoulder-length hair over her cheek.

"Ugh, I missed you," we said in unison.

Mom's dark hair had streaks of silver, the only indication that she was in her sixties instead of her forties. I tossed her bag into the back seat before we pulled out into airport congestion.

Mom eyed me. "Stress isn't etched around your eyes anymore, and"—she touched my cheek—"what do we have here? Could it be a laugh line?"

"Ha ha, very funny." I turned and met Mom's smile before concentrating on the traffic.

We were back at my apartment fifteen minutes later. I had made chicken wild rice soup and beer cheese bread before picking up Mom, and we visited over lunch, sharing details of each other's lives that we rarely got into over the phone.

For the next two days, Mom, Ryan, and I went to the Science Museum and played countless games indoors, thanks to the blustery November weather.

When I pulled into Trent's driveway on Sunday afternoon, Mom and Ryan hugged extra long. "I wish you lived here, Grandma Jo," Ryan said. He'd called Mom Grandma Jo since he was a toddler and had shortened Joleigh.

"Well, maybe you can come visit again next summer and stay longer." Mom eyed me in question. "Even if your mom is too busy at the shop, you'll be twelve—certainly old enough to fly on your own."

"That'd be cool!" Ryan's excitement all but rocketed him up the sidewalk and into Trent's house, where he turned and gave us a final wave goodbye.

Dusk had fallen by the time Mom and I pulled up in front of my Crimson Creek building. She stepped out and stretched, taking a deep breath. "Oh my, I feel like I've stepped back in time to Grandfield when you were young," she said.

"I know, right? I think that's what's pulled me here. And even though I know the town is on the cusp of change, it's so far from the cities that it won't be swallowed up by it."

Mom nodded, understanding the appeal.

"Let's get inside." I gestured toward the front door, ready to get out of the near-freezing dampness.

I gave Mom a quick tour of the building before we headed upstairs to the apartment. "We can unload the car tomorrow," I said, setting the box of food and a cooler on the counter. I had packed my backpack for the week, as Mom had, along with more household items from my other apartment. After we freshened up, we dressed for the cold and walked to Mined Your Business.

Mom had suggested the place, ready to hop right in to get a taste of the town. Sunday night in November meant business was slow. Whip was behind the bar, and I made introductions.

"Pleased to meet you, Joleigh," Whip said as he shook my mom's hand. "I've wondered who raised this determined young woman." He nodded toward me.

"Oh, I could tell you stories about Eden's determination," Mom said, giving me a mischievous grin. "Like the time she chased one of our goats all over our forty acres, trying to tie a bow on its head because she thought the female goats should wear bows."

I tugged on Mom's arm, hoping to lead her to a corner table. "Come on, Whip's too busy to hear those tales."

Whip set down the bar rag he'd dried his hands with and waved toward the nearly empty bar. "Yep, I'm swamped." He winked at Mom. "Tell me more."

I was saved by the bell when a woman around my age literally jogged in the door, her dark-blond hair pulled into a ponytail. "Hey, bro, got my order ready?" the woman said to Whip, who gave her a wave before heading back into the kitchen.

He was back seconds later with two large white to-go bags. "Kids extra hungry tonight, Chase?"

"Aren't they always?" The woman handed Whip her credit card.

I had stopped caring about herding Mom to a table away from Whip. Here was a local woman around my age, and curiosity rooted me.

"I've got an end-of-season cross-country meeting, so this is me cooking tonight," she explained.

Before Whip rang up the woman's order, he turned toward Mom and me. "Chase, meet the new owner of the corner building across from the park. This is Eden Everson and her mom, Joleigh, who is here visiting from Alaska."

"Hi, nice to meet you, Chase," I said, shaking her hand before stepping aside for Mom to do the same.

"Nice to meet you, too. My name is Kelly, but everyone around here still refers to me as Chase, which was my maiden name."

"You grew up here?" Mom asked.

"I did. Went to school with Whip." Kelly nodded toward Whip, who was ringing up her order.

"Did not," Whip said, sliding her credit card through the machine. "I'm six years younger, old lady," he teased. "And the reason we all still call her Chase is because she was fast as hell in school. Set all sorts of records in track and cross country."

My brain struggled to remember if Whip had told me his last name was Chase. "You're brother and sister?" I asked, recalling that Kelly had called him "bro" when she jogged in.

"Nope. In-laws. Chase is my deceased wife's older sister," Whip said, not meeting my eyes.

"Oh my gosh, Whip, I'm so sorry! I didn't know your wife passed away. Didn't even know you were married…" I knew he had a daughter around Ryan's age, but that was it.

"It's okay, Eden. It's not like I advertise it." Whip slid the charge slip to Kelly to sign. "She passed away from a brain aneurysm when Willow was four."

I didn't know what to say. Mom reached over and squeezed Whip's hand.

Kelly signed the slip and picked up the bags. "Well, I better get these burgers home, or I'll have four hangry kids on my hands."

"Before you go, remember I told you someone was thinking of opening a bike rental shop here?" Whip said to Kelly. "That's Eden."

Kelly's mouth and eyes opened wide. "Yay! I'm an avid mountain biker. So are my kids. I think your shop is a great idea, and this town needs it."

"Thank you. That makes me feel better about the business," I said. "I'd love any advice you can give me, whenever you have time."

Kelly tipped her head. "You'll be at your shop tomorrow? I can stop by during the day if you want."

"That would be great." I turned to Mom for affirmation. "I think we planned on painting the apartment tomorrow."

Mom nodded.

"Here, I'll give you my cell number. Please call or text before you stop by, and I'll meet you at the door." I took a napkin and pen that Whip handed me and wrote down my name and number, thinking back to months before, when I did the same for David on my first trip to Crimson Creek.

After Kelly left and business picked up for Whip, Mom and I settled in at a table, taking our time over dinner, making a list of what we hoped to accomplish in the apartment and shop before I drove her to the airport on Friday.

The following morning, Mom and I went to work painting the two bedrooms, oldies music cranked up on the radio. Mom sang along, using her paint roller occasionally as a microphone, her mediocre voice belting out the words to "Up around the Bend," "Knock Three Times," and "Ain't No Mountain," among others as the station took her back to a time when she'd lived on a hobby farm in Missouri and cared for the elderly woman who'd adopted her. Mom was a rock star to me, a woman who'd persisted despite all the shit flung at her. She inspired me to press on.

The used furniture I had ordered the week before was delivered midmorning, and Mom and I had just finished lunch when Kelly texted me. I met her at the shop door a few minutes later.

"I hope you don't mind the smell of paint," I said as I welcomed her into the shop.

Kelly pulled off a knit hat and shook out her shoulder-length hair. "Not at all. It's a smell that permeated our house last summer when I painted my kids' bedrooms."

"How old are your children?" I asked.

"Hadley is seventeen, Quinn, fourteen, Mason, twelve, and Kyra is eight. Do you have any kids?"

"Just one. Ryan is eleven. I bet your kids keep you busy!" I gestured toward the stairs that led to the apartment for Kelly to follow me.

"They do. My husband is a financial auditor and travels a lot. I used to teach but now just coach girls' cross country and track," Kelly said as we walked upstairs. "I hope to get back to teaching one day, but for now, I'm plenty busy."

Mom had been painting Ryan's room and washed up so that she could join us at the newly delivered kitchen table. Over the next hour, I pulled up bike and kayak brands and models that I planned to stock for rentals, and Kelly shared her mountain bike wisdom, steering me away from high-end rentals, at least at first. "The people who are serious die-hard bikers already have their own mountain bikes," Kelly said. "Those same bikers will be the ones willing to shell out money for high-quality clothing and bike equipment. And, with the red dirt here, I wouldn't order any light-colored clothing. I can attest that it does *not* come out in the wash!"

Everything Kelly said made sense, and I thanked her several times as I walked her to the parking lot an hour later.

Mom and I spent the rest of Monday finishing painting my bedroom and Ryan's room.

Later that night as we relaxed in the living room, Mom said, "Good thing I insisted on going to Mined Your Business last night."

"Why is that?" I asked between handfuls of the popcorn we'd popped on the stove.

"You wouldn't have met Kelly otherwise." Mom tossed a piece of popcorn in the air and caught it with her mouth. "It's one of the many things I love about small towns. Connections."

"Very true." I thought for a moment. "Whip had said recently that his daughter, Willow, spends a lot of time at her aunt's house. I bet that's Kelly." Connections also applied to people in a small town who were related in some way.

And although I wasn't related to anyone in Crimson Creek, I already thought of David as a grandpa of sorts.

Chapter 25
David

Every year, the American Legion hosted a free lunch for veterans. Many locals also attended, not only paying for their meal but also donating to offset veterans' meals. I had invited Eden to be my guest before I realized her mother would be visiting from Alaska, but Eden had assured me they would both attend.

I was at the Legion, sitting with Hal and his wife, Maudie, when Eden and her mother walked in. Hal and I stood to greet them.

"Hi, I'm Joleigh. It's so nice to finally meet you," Eden's mother said, shaking my hand. Joleigh stood a little shorter than Eden, and her skin, a shade darker than Eden's, was smooth and unlined. She had the same friendly smile and beautiful eyes, also a shade darker than Eden's.

"I'm honored to meet you, Joleigh. And I'm thankful my daughter gave you that POW bracelet years ago." I'd imagined the scene several times over the past months and couldn't believe the domino effect from Louise's gesture decades before.

I introduced Joleigh to Hal and Maudie and was surprised to hear Hal introduce Maudie to Eden. "I'm glad to finally meet Hal's 'vivacious vixen,'" Eden said. She'd met Hal in October when we had lunch at the American Legion.

That got a chuckle out of Maudie, who was eight years younger than Hal but had the spunk and stamina of a woman much younger. Maudie tucked a strand of her short silver hair behind her ear and patted the chair next to her for Joleigh to sit. I watched these two dark-brown-eyed women chattering like old friends within minutes.

Eden took the seat next to her mother. "Who else is joining us?" She nodded toward the two empty seats at our table.

"Whippersnapper and his daughter, Willow. They should be here any minute."

When Maudie left the table to help set up and cut desserts, Joleigh made small talk with me. "I thought of you all the time after your daughter gave me the bracelet. I was so floored when Eden told me she found you." She smiled. "It's such an honor to meet you in person and thank you for your sacrifice."

"Thank you. I'm glad you kept the bracelet and that Eden looked me up."

Joleigh and I spoke of Eden and her business venture, about what life in rural Anchorage was like, and about Jean and what life had been like for her while I was in Vietnam. When Joleigh excused herself to use the restroom, I turned my attention to Eden and Willow, deep in conversation.

"I've got a son about your age," Eden said. "He's in fifth grade."

Willow, a tomboy in braids, scrunched up her nose. "Here? What's his name?"

"No, Ryan is in the cities. I'm in the process of moving here, so I spend some time in the Twin Cities, and that's where he goes to school for now."

Willow bit into a slice of bread from the bread platter. "Does he like to fish and bike?"

"He loves to bike but has never tried mountain biking," Eden said. "I hope to take him out on the trails next spring. And he's not done much fishing, which is my fault. I grew up fishing year-round and loved it."

"I can go out with him on the trails," Willow offered.

Whip, who'd been conversing with Hal, stepped in. "Oh no you don't, Willow." He turned to Eden. "She's got no fear filter."

Willow crossed her arms in a huff.

"I won't let her go alone. But I will gladly take your son with us next spring." He held up his palm. "Scout's honor that I will take it slow if he goes with. You're welcome to come too."

I nudged Whip's shoulder. "You were never a Scout, you slug."

Whip grinned. "Busted."

"Looks like the line is going down a bit. Let's go. I'm hungry," I announced.

Two buffet lines had been set up, and everyone at our table headed that way. My stomach would be full of delicious food soon, something I never took for granted now. I was eating a meal with friends who felt like family, my heart full of thankfulness that I'd been around for over forty years of Veterans Days when so many others had never made it back.

As I said a silent prayer before digging into the meal of mashed potatoes and broasted chicken, I reminded myself that I was lucky—a luck I drew on in my darkest days.

Those days sometimes still got the best of me.

Chapter 26

Eden

Mom had wanted to invite David over for birthday cake, but I'd told her no, I didn't want my birthday taking away from his Veterans Day, not to mention that David wouldn't make it up the steep stairs to my apartment.

In the end, Mom and I decided chocolate-chip ice cream made more sense than her baking a cake that would take us days to eat. We visited that night between birthday calls from Ryan, my dad, Ellie, and even Nielson, my younger brother, who detested talking on the phone.

The following day, we took a break from painting and drove outside town to hike through the woods, thrilled when we found chaga on some dying birch trees. I had a pocketknife in my backpack, and we cut the chaga to make tea. Chaga tea was one of the many things I'd missed from my youth—bounty from the earth—something I hoped to bring back into my life again.

On Thursday, we drove back to Minneapolis, leaving behind an apartment that had been scrubbed, painted, stocked, and organized. I picked up Ryan at Trent's so that he could see his grandma again before she flew back to Alaska in the morning.

After I dropped Ryan off at school Friday morning and dropped Mom off at the airport, I went back to an empty apartment. I'd spent very little time there without Ryan over the past two-plus years, choosing to catch up on my work overload on the weeks he stayed at Trent's place. The apartment had never felt like home to me, yet I realized how quickly the one in Crimson Creek was working its way into my heart.

I was back in Crimson Creek the Sunday before Thanksgiving after dropping Ryan off at Trent's, my car packed with items I had boxed up the week before. When I made dinner for Ryan and myself over the past week, I'd frozen single-sized portions from the leftovers to bring with me to my new apartment.

After I unpacked, leaving out a serving of chicken pot pie to defrost on the counter, I tugged on my winter coat and boots, gathered canvas shopping bags, and walked the few blocks to the grocery store. Downtown Crimson Creek was quiet. A chilly November Sunday at dusk didn't exactly bring out the locals, and I doubted any tourists were in town.

That was something I'd thought about for my rental shop, the ebb and flow of seasonal life in small-town Minnesota. *That's when you'll have time for yourself and Ryan, Eden.*

At the grocery store, as I was bagging up some Honeycrisp apples, I sensed someone standing behind me.

A deep voice tickled my ear. "So, what do you think of our town so far?"

I spun around and came face-to-face with Donovan. His blue eyes stood out against his rosy cheeks and closely trimmed beard and moustache. I felt the cold from outside lingering on his coat.

"I love it. It reminds me of the small town where I grew up."

"Have you been staying full-time in Crimson Creek?"

"No. Still going back and forth. In fact, I got here an hour ago." I set the apples in my grocery basket.

"Do you have time to break away from your shop this week to check out our town?" Donovan gestured toward the front door with the gallon of milk he was holding.

"David's shown me around the area already."

"Yes, but I bet he stuck to the obvious places. Did he take you to the rope swing at the mine pit lake? Or the waterfall and cross-country trails?"

I tipped my head. "No, but now you've got my interest. I saw the rope swing from the lakeside last summer when I went kayaking."

"You mean my charm and wit didn't hold your interest already?"

"Hah. In answer to your question, yes, I can get away sometime this week. When?"

"Do you have plans for Thanksgiving?" Donovan said.

"No, I planned to work through it."

Donovan blanched. My plans were counterintuitive to my get-a-life goal, but I was new to the area and was giving myself a pass.

"I'm having dinner at Whip's sister-in-law's house. How about joining us? You'd love Chase. She's around your age." Donovan stood mere inches from me, the deep dimple on his cheek beckoning my finger to touch it. His mouth was a couple of inches lower than mine, and barely a tip of my head would bring our lips together.

"Um, hello?" Donovan broke into my traveling thoughts.

I stepped back, mortified that I was even thinking of his mouth. *What the heck, Eden? Is this what happens when you don't have a job? Too much time to fantasize?*

"Sorry." I cleared my throat. "I was just thinking of Chase—I mean Kelly. I've met her."

"You have? Perfect! We eat at one, and I could show you around town later that afternoon," Donovan said. "I'll let her know you'll be with me. They always have a houseful, so one more won't matter." He nodded at the two loaves of bread in his hand. "I'm making stuffing. We always have plenty of food."

We exchanged cell phone numbers. I had Kelly's from her text the other day and would check with her to see what I could bring for Thanksgiving.

On my way home with two bags of produce, a quart of milk, and bagels, I felt energized, not because of the drop in temperature or the sunset casting shades of orange over the town, but because I was taking the first step in getting a life.

Thanksgiving morning, I baked a pumpkin cheesecake to take to Kelly's as the sun—a rarity in November—shone on the newly fallen snow outside, creating tiny sparkles on the ground.

While the cheesecake baked, I called Trent to speak with Ryan before they went to Trent's mom's house for Thanksgiving dinner. When Trent put Ryan on the phone, I asked about his few days at school, and our conversation turned to sports.

"Bummer the Vikings aren't playing today," I said.

"Ugh, Mom, I'm still so mad at them for blowing their lead against the Packers last week. I don't care if I ever watch them again!"

"Yeah, right. The day you quit watching football—or baseball—will be the day I take you to the doctor to make sure you're okay."

After we talked for a few more minutes, I let him go. "Please tell Grandma Emily hello for me." I'd always gotten along well with Trent's mother. That didn't change after the divorce. "And don't eat too much pumpkin pie."

I smiled as we hung up. Ryan would definitely eat too much pumpkin pie.

Donovan picked me up at noon, taking the cheesecake from me to place on the floor of the back seat in his pickup. "You packed warm clothes for later, right?"

I held up my backpack. "Plenty." I set the backpack and my Sorel boots with the cheesecake, next to two 9-by-13-inch pans permeating the air with spices from the stuffing.

On the way to Kelly's, Donovan gave me a little background about some of the people who would be there.

"It sounds like there's a lot more young people around here than I thought," I said.

"A lot of us who grew up here left and came back. Some of us, like Kelly and me, never left—other than when she attended college. And with the start of the mountain biking here, we're getting a trickling of newcomers in," Donovan said.

"I guess I've met more older people because of David."

"Where is that grumpy old man today?" Donovan cast me a glance before turning down a long driveway outside of town, his smile contradicting his description of a man he cherished.

"Last week, David, Hal, and Maudie invited me to one of the area churches for a Thanksgiving meal. I said no because I had planned to work in the shop."

At the end of the tree-lined driveway was a large two-story brick home surrounded by woods, with several vehicles parked in the driveway.

I must have sighed as Donovan and I approached the front door.

He took my elbow and leaned in to whisper, "You'll be fine. None of them bite. Well, other than the kids."

He knocked on the front door, and I was still studying his profile when a young boy answered the door.

The noise and aroma that greeted us beckoned me like a warm hug. Over the next two hours, Kelly or Donovan introduced me to so many people that I struggled to remember names or who was related to whom, and through it all, I thought, *This is what you've been craving. This.* The feeling was similar to the holidays of my youth, when my parents invited employees and friends into our home. The comfort of an extended family—a sense of *belonging*.

Chapter 27

By the time Donovan and I left Kelly's after helping to clean up, my stomach hurt from laughing and from eating too much. I said as much to him as we walked back to his truck.

"Don't worry, we'll walk it off." Donovan gave me a once-over. "You layered up, right?"

"Yes, I've got long underwear under my jeans." Back at his truck, I put on wool socks, my Sorel boots, and a cream-colored Love Your Melon knit hat and mittens to offset the below-zero temps.

"Okay, tour guide, impress me with something I haven't seen before," I said, buckling my seat belt.

Donovan arched an eyebrow. "I've got a hundred comebacks, and none of them have anything to do with the outdoors."

I grimaced. "You know what I mean… sights David didn't show me."

"Tell me the real story of how you two know each other," Donovan said as he drove out of the parking lot and toward the mountain bike trails.

I filled him in on the history of the POW bracelet.

Donovan glanced over at me. "You said your parents moved from…?"

"I grew up in Grandfield, south of the cities, went to college in Winona, and once I got married, I moved to the Twin Cities. After my younger brother left for college, my parents sold their businesses and moved to Alaska."

"You're married?" Donovan's eyes widened.

"Not anymore. Divorced two years ago."

"Kids?"

"One. Ryan, remember? My significant other who is in fifth grade," I said.

Donovan thumped the steering wheel. "Ah yes, your business partner."

"How about you? Married? Kids? According to David, you aren't a wanted man."

"No convictions yet. Never married, one daughter. Cassie lives in Boulder, Colorado."

Donovan drove past open mine-pit lakes, the deep blue accentuated by the snow and ice covering a portion of them. "Right now, these back roads are mostly known only to locals, but this area is part of the build-out plan for future trails."

He turned off the truck at a dead-end gravel road. "Watch your step. Roots are sticking up underneath the snow." He led the way down a narrow tree-lined trail, which helped block the breeze.

After a quarter mile, the trail opened up to a point of land between two vast mine-pit lakes. We stopped, and I could hear Donovan breathing in the stillness. I closed my eyes for several seconds to take in the quiet, the fresh air, the peacefulness.

When I opened my eyes, Donovan stood a foot away, watching me. "Takes your blood pressure down several digits, doesn't it?"

I nodded. "This looks like the rope swing area."

"It is." Donovan gestured for me to follow him toward the end of the strip of land. Two thick trees protruded to the side of each lake. "They cut the ropes down in the fall so no fools come out here in the frigid cold."

"It creeps me out, thinking about how I can never touch the bottom here." I shuddered.

"Yep. A few people have drowned in this area."

"Yikes! What's next on your show-and-tell list?" I rubbed my mittened hands together.

"The waterfall, I'll have to save for another day since we'll need either cross-country skis or snowshoes to get back to that part of the woods. Let's head back," Donovan said.

Back in his truck, we drove through town and headed out to the other side of Crow Lake, an area I'd yet to check out. Donovan pulled into a parking lot.

"They used to hold their annual ice bocce tournament here in the bay until the event got so popular. Now, it's held on a lake outside of town." As we stepped out of the truck, Donovan explained that ice bocce was sort of a cross between the sports of curling and bocce ball. "It's a fundraiser for various charities in the area."

Crow Lake was frozen over, but the ice wasn't thick enough to walk on yet. A paved trail led from the wayside rest area along the shoreline.

"In all my visits to Crimson Creek, I've yet to drive around Crow Lake," I said.

"This paved trail goes all around the lake and connects with the trail that veers past the recreation parking lot," Donovan explained.

"You said you grew up here. Do you still have family around?" I asked as we walked side by side along the trail.

"No family around here." Donovan cleared his throat. "My mom died of breast cancer when I was nine. My brother, Gabriel, was six."

"Oh, Donovan, I'm so sorry!" I touched his shoulder. "I can't imagine how horrible that was." I might not be able to spend every day with Ryan, but I was alive, just a phone call away. Donovan's loss reminded me of my mom losing both her parents when she was a child.

"Gabriel and I were too young to comprehend the permanence of death. Dad never remarried." Donovan shook his head. "He passed away several years ago, and Gabriel moved to Florida the summer after he graduated from high school."

The wind was picking up, blowing cold air from the lake.

"Let's turn around," I said.

Donovan agreed, and we made an abrupt about-face.

"What kept you here?" I asked. "Wasn't it a dying town years ago?"

"It was. But the summer before my senior year in high school, I got a job working construction for a neighbor. He built fancy lake homes around the area. The pay was good, it got me out of the house, and he kept me on after high school."

"That's where you learned the tricks of the trade?"

"Yes. I never went to college and initially regretted it. But I loved my job and learned so much from my neighbor. When I purchased the company from him ten years ago, there were already plans in place for the first build-out of mountain bike trails. I researched affordable shelters and purchased acreage along one of the few mine-pit lakes with property not owned by the Minnesota Department of Natural Resources."

I turned to him. "When do I get to see the yurts? I thought we'd see those today."

"If I show you everything today, you won't be intrigued enough to see me again."

"Oh, you're trying to intrigue me?" I batted my eyes.

"Obviously, it's not working, if I have to tell you." Donovan's eyes focused on mine, tiny flecks of snow landing on his dark, thick eyelashes.

For a second, I thought he might kiss me.

Instead, he turned away and continued down the path, tucking his neck down into the collar of his coat to ward off the wind. I jogged to catch up to him. As I neared him, my right foot caught on a patch of ice, and I reached out for Donovan's arm to steady myself. Catching him off guard, I nearly took him down with me.

"Sorry about that." I straightened, making sure my boots were on solid ground.

Donovan looped my arm through his. "I knew it. A damsel in need of rescuing." His mouth twitched. I didn't pull my arm away until we reached his truck.

By the time he pulled into my parking lot, the sun was setting, pulling the already-cold temperature down with it.

"What's on your agenda this weekend?" Donovan asked as he put the pickup in park.

"I've got a plumber coming to install a new bathroom sink and toilet tomorrow morning."

"I could've helped you with that," Donovan said.

"That's okay. I booked him last month. He's doing the apartment bathroom tomorrow and the store bathroom the next time I'm in town."

"If you have time tomorrow or Saturday, I'd like to take you to the yurts. Two aren't rented this weekend, and each one has an outdoor cooking grate, along with a fire ring." Donovan rested his arm against the back of the pickup seat. "The view is breathtaking. We'll have to use either fat-tire bikes or snowshoes or cross-country skis to get through the snow. There's a dirt road nearby, but it's a hike through the woods on a gravel trail. We bring everything in with backpacks or wide-wheeled carts."

"I've seen some yurt photos online. They were from the summer, though."

"Not much different now," Donovan said. "There's no electricity out there, but I've got plenty of solar lights."

It sounded wonderful. "How about Saturday afternoon?"

"Works for me. I've got extra snowshoes for you if you want to trek in that way."

"I actually have my snowshoes here. Cross-country skis too," I said.

"Sounds like a date, then." Donovan grimaced. "Not a date. I meant it sounds like a plan."

Mumford & Sons' song "I Will Wait" played on the radio, and I fought back a smile at his fluster over labeling it a date. Maybe he'd been burned in a relationship. Maybe that was why he never married.

Maybe you don't need to be dissecting Donovan and his past, Eden. "What time Saturday?"

"I've got construction work I need to do Saturday morning. How about early afternoon?"

I opened the passenger door. "Okay. I can meet you at the recreation parking lot."

"How about I pick you up here at two?"

"All right. See you then." I retrieved my cheesecake pan from the back seat.

Donovan's headlights shone on me as I unlocked the shop's door, the sky painted red and orange over Crow Lake when I turned back and waved goodbye to him.

On Friday, while the plumber worked in the apartment bathroom, I worked on minor repairs in the shop. After a twelve-hour day, I soaked in the bathtub in my newly renovated bathroom, the scent of lavender Dr. Teal's Epsom salts wafting through the air.

I crawled into bed early, exhausted, and doubt I moved a muscle until my cell phone rang at five thirty Saturday morning, the screen lighting up the darkness.

It was Trent. My heart beat in my throat as I fumbled to answer the phone.

"Hello? What's wrong?"

"It's Ryan. He's been up all night, throwing up. He can't keep water down," Trent's voice was ragged. "We're at Children's Hospital, and they've just wheeled him into a room."

"I'm on my way." I hung up, flipped on the bedroom light, and was dressed and out the door in five minutes, heading toward Children's Hospital in Minneapolis with my jaw clenched, my heart regretting the miles between us.

Chapter 28

I arrived at Children's Hospital to find Ryan hooked up with an IV, resting in a hospital room, and diagnosed with food poisoning—a much better diagnosis than the many awful conclusions I'd come up with during my two-hour drive.

"Food poisoning?" I faced Trent in the hallway outside Ryan's room.

"Yep. They gave him something for the nausea, are pumping fluids in him, and it should run its course in a day or two," Trent said.

"Pedialyte, Gatorade, Ritz crackers…" I rattled off the grocery list of necessities, mentally thinking of what I had back at my apartment. "I'll call Mom and have her pick it up for me and drop it off at the house."

"He's going home with you?"

"Why wouldn't he?" Trent's jaw clenched. "I'm perfectly capable of taking care of our son. After all, I got him to the hospital."

"And yet Ryan managed to get food poisoning on your watch." I rubbed my bleary eyes and took a calming breath. "Sorry. People get food poisoning every day."

"Yeah, I don't know how that happened," Trent said, scratching his head. "We pretty much ate the same things at Mom's for Thanksgiving. Ryan was there again yesterday while I was at work. Now that I know what's wrong with him, I'll ask Mom what he ate."

"She'll feel awful," I said. Emily was a wonderful grandma. "Let's ask Ryan when he wakes up."

Ryan's vitals improved, and after he went more than an hour without vomiting, he was given the all-clear.

"If it gets to where he can't keep liquids down, give us a call. I think the antinausea meds will help. Lots of clear liquids, lots of rest," the doctor said.

"I'll follow you to the house," I told Trent after we left Ryan's room.

Back in my car, I remembered I was supposed to meet Donovan that afternoon. I dug out my cell phone and called Donovan to explain Ryan's illness.

"Glad to hear he's recovering," Donovan said. "Thanks for letting me know. We'll plan for another day, okay?"

"That would be great. I'll be back in a little over a week." After we hung up, I drove to Trent's, where Ryan was already settled in his bed. Old memories flooded my brain as I stood in Ryan's bedroom, taking in the blue walls I'd repainted six years ago, now a shade darker than the light blue I'd painted after he was born.

An empty ice cream pail sat on the carpet next to Ryan's bed. "Dad's bringing you in some 7-Up," I said, sitting on the edge of the bed. "I'll run to the grocery store in a minute to pick up Gatorade and other things for you."

When Trent entered with Ryan's 7-Up, I said, "We're wondering what you ate at Grandma's yesterday. The doctor doesn't think it's anything you ate on Thanksgiving since you didn't start getting sick for almost a day after that meal."

Ryan scrunched his face, thinking. "Grandma made French toast and bacon for breakfast yesterday. I had a turkey sandwich and mashed potatoes and gravy for lunch." He made a funny face. "And maybe two pieces of pumpkin pie."

The pie was no surprise. "That's it?" Trent asked.

Ryan paused. "Um, well..."

We leaned toward Ryan as if he might reveal a deep, dark secret. "Yes?"

"When I went out in Grandma's garage, I found a bowl with extra turkey stuff. It looked okay to me, and I ate some." Ryan studied his lap.

The night was cold, but not cold enough to keep the turkey edible a day later. And Emily had a heated garage.

"Why would you eat that?" Trent said.

Ryan peered up at me. "I was thinking of what David said."

"David? Who's that?" Trent almost threw his back out, pivoting to glare at me. Apparently, he couldn't imagine a man in my life.

"He's the Vietnam POW I've become friends with in Crimson Creek. You know, the POW bracelet I'd told you about."

Trent's irritation deflated, and he turned his focus back to Ryan. "What's he got to do with you eating turkey in Grandma's garage?"

"I was thinking about what he said about food," Ryan mumbled, "that we shouldn't waste any. It looked like Grandma was going to throw the turkey away."

"Oh, Ryan!" I shook my head. "I appreciate that you took David's words to heart. But that turkey was in the garage for a reason. The meat was probably the miscellaneous parts that weren't edible. And it had sat out for too long."

I turned to Trent. "I guess we never went over food going bad with him, did we?"

"Yep, buddy, don't do that again. Please." Trent rubbed the back of his neck.

Ryan nodded, blinking back tears. "I'm sorry."

"It's okay," Trent and I said in unison. "Now you know."

After giving my reassurance that I would be there late Sunday morning to pick up Ryan, I stopped at the store for supplies and dropped off enough at Trent's to get Ryan through the next twenty-four hours. When I arrived back at my apartment and unpacked my overnight bag, I thought of the herbal remedies Mom had used on me and my siblings over the years. Laziness on my part had pushed me away from the natural healing I'd learned as a child. I hoped to get that back once I lived full-time in Crimson Creek.

After Ryan endured two days of soft foods, I promised him a "real meal" after school. "How about I grill us cheeseburgers for supper?" I still had my hibachi grill on the deck.

"Deal." Ryan shook my hand. "I get two cheeseburgers, right?"

"Of course. We need to build up those muscles so you can help out at the shop next summer."

"What do I get to do there?" Ryan followed me into the kitchen and helped patty up the burger.

"When the shop opens, I'll need you for several things: unpacking inventory, stocking shelves, and helping customers. And there's that artistic side of you I need." We'd set aside the monkey design, but I decided that while Ryan wasn't back to one hundred percent might be a good time for him to start.

"Can we work on the monkey after supper?"

"Do you have homework?"

Ryan groaned. "Yes. After my homework?"

"Sure."

By the time Ryan finished his homework and I cleaned up the kitchen, we were ready to sit down and brainstorm.

"I was thinking a monkey riding a mountain bike and maybe one paddling a kayak on a lake." I had worked up a rough sketch of my ideas and slid it in front of Ryan. "Mine look too busy, though."

"And like a hangman on a bike and kayak," Ryan quipped.

"I never said I was an artist. That's where you come in, smarty britches." I leaned over and kissed his cheek and was surprised when he didn't wipe it away. "We could have a few design options for shirts, water bottles, coffee cups, stickers for the kayaks and canoes..." I stopped as Ryan's smile widened, sure he was going to pick on me again. "What?"

"I like it when you say 'we.'"

"Heck yeah, it's 'we.' Whether you're there with me or not. Yes, this is my dream, but I hope it will provide you with a summer job you enjoy. The mountain bike trails and the boost of water activity on the lakes are a powerful change for Crimson Creek, and the majority of the people are young."

Yes, problems existed, but I had faith the community would work through the growing pains.

Ryan and I spent every night working on logo ideas after his homework was finished. By the time I took Ryan and Brady bowling on Friday night, Ryan had come up with a few different sketches. My favorite was a monkey with a church key figure for a body, one leg propped over a mountain bike, a figure he replicated in another design of the monkey standing between an upright kayak and paddleboard.

The monkey wore a mischievous grin.

Ryan's joy at my reaction of approval was nothing compared to mine at hearing his excitement about being part of the business.

After dropping Ryan off at Trent's house late Sunday morning, I drove to Crimson Creek, passing trees covered with sparkling snow. I had spoken with Donovan twice during the previous week. We had rescheduled our "nondate" for Sunday afternoon.

Crimson Creek had received several inches of snow in the past week, which helped blanket the trails for cross-country skiing. I arrived in town an hour before Donovan planned to pick me up. Christmas wreaths hung from streetlights, and little twinkle lights had been strung around evergreens in the park across the street.

Ryan and I had decorated a small fake tree for the cities apartment. Christmas was less than three weeks away, and Ryan and I would spend most of Christmas break in Crimson Creek.

I was dressed and ready to go when Donovan pulled into the parking lot at two o'clock.

He approached the front door after I unlocked it. "Good to see you again." His smile beckoned my eyes, and his facial hair had been trimmed to more of a five o'clock shadow, one that all but pointed at his mouth, screaming, "Kiss me!" *You may be imagining that, Eden.* The thought stuck with me as he carried my skis and poles to the truck, and I followed with my ski boots and backpack.

"We've got a perfect day for this." Donovan glanced up at the bright December sun.

"It'll feel good to get out in the woods." I'd spent too much time indoors lately.

"Ryan back to one hundred percent?" Donovan asked, backing out of the parking lot.

"Yes, he's back to his old self and wiser now about what to eat and not eat."

"Always good to learn from our mistakes." Donovan pulled out onto the main road. "God knows I ate plenty I shouldn't have when I was young. Nobody told me otherwise. I remember once, my brother and I puking right alongside each other into the bathtub. We had one bathroom, and the toilet wasn't big enough for both of us."

"Did you have the flu or eat something bad?"

"I'm guessing it was the fish I'd fried up for us. We'd been fishing on the bank of a river, and I did a horrific job of filleting the fish and an even worse job of frying them up in lard. They tasted godawful and were probably undercooked, but it was food in our bellies."

Donovan pulled off the gravel road into a small parking lot with several paths leading through the woods. "This is about as far as we can go on this road in the winter. The yurts are up ahead, and there's another parking lot farther on, but since we're going to ski, this is the best place for groomed trails." He turned off the truck. "Speaking of food—and not undercooked fish—I hope you like campfire quesadillas. I have everything we need stocked in the yurt already since I stopped by a few days ago to check on things."

We laced up our ski boots. "They sound yummy. I've got the wine and butterscotch schnapps in my backpack," I said.

"Sounds like we're set. I've got water and a few snacks in my backpack in case you try to lead me astray and we get lost." Donovan wiggled his eyebrows.

"Ha. You wish." I gave him a playful punch and gestured with my ski pole for him to lead the way. The trail took us through tall pines and alongside a creek, slowly climbing in elevation, widening as three small waterfalls came together to form one partially frozen waterfall. With barely a breeze, the only sound was the trickling of water and my heartbeat thrumming.

We stopped where a small bridge had been built for skiers to cross. The sun painted the pines with golden hues above the vivid blue of the creek, surrounded by pristine snow. "This is so beautiful," I whispered, feeling irreverent for breaking the silence.

"Sure is. Whenever things go south for me or I've got a problem I need to work out, this area of the woods brings me comfort and perspective," Donovan said, gazing down the hill. "I've been coming here since I was a teenager."

We stood in silence for a few minutes until he pulled out a large flask from his backpack.

"Want some water?" He held it out to me. "I'll let you drink first. I don't have any communicable diseases, but you don't know that yet."

"How do you know I don't?" I smiled before taking a long swig of water.

"David would never hang out with a woman with anything but impeccable standards."

I rolled my eyes and handed him the flask, our fingers touching. I had an image flash through my brain of his fingers grazing my face, into my hair, down my lower back—

Donovan's voice interrupted my fantasy. "Are you ready to continue?"

"Um, sure." I followed Donovan down the trail, the heat of my thoughts offsetting the ice-cold air.

Chapter 29

After more than three hours of skiing, Donovan and I were famished when we arrived at the yurts, which were spaced far enough apart with a buffer of trees between them. The occupied yurts' solar lights and muted talking from the renters seemed a world away.

While Donovan fried the burgers, I prepared the rest of the ingredients for the quesadillas, both of us enjoying a glass of ice-cold butterscotch schnapps.

He'd started the campfire when we arrived at the yurt, and we took our plates and drinks outside to sit near the campfire. My face, warmed by the fire and schnapps, only amplified the slow-burning internal heat set by Donovan's closeness. *Do I need my hormone levels checked?*

I told Donovan more about Stevie Grace, how our parents were best friends, and that she planned to visit Crimson Creek in the summer. "Most of my friends were work friends, who changed as my job titles changed. The last few years, when I was going through my divorce, I declined their invitations when they'd go out for drinks after work, choosing to either work late when Ryan was with Trent or go home right after work when Ryan was with me. I gave up the last remnants of my social life."

It sounded more painful than it had been. "If Trent and I did anything with other people, it was usually his friends from LifeJoy. He'd made it clear over the years he didn't like my friends from the bank." I leaned my head back and gazed up at the expansive, starlit sky. "The only couple we could agree on to go out with was my roommate from college and her husband. They moved out of state the year before my divorce. Stevie Grace has always been my best friend, one I hope eventually moves back to Minnesota."

"I heard years ago that many people only have one or two really good friends they can count on in a pickle... and that if you've got that, you're lucky," Donovan said. He finished off the last of his schnapps. "It's one of the best things about living in a small town. People have your back. They may not be your friend, but if there's a crisis, the town will rally. At least, it's that way in Crimson Creek."

"That's how Grandfield was too." I shivered, and Donovan knelt to stoke the campfire. Or so I thought. Instead, he reached to pull me from my chair, and the momentum landed me on top of him in the snow. His chest bounced against mine as we burst out laughing.

"Not my smoothest of moves." Donovan grinned as my face hovered above his.

"You've got to warn a girl if you're going to make a move on her," I whispered.

"I guess that was your warning." The snow beneath his dark hair resembled a halo. When his lips met mine and his hands buried into my hair, our kiss should've melted the snow around us.

I was up early Monday morning and settled in with coffee and my computer in the recliner by the windows overlooking Crow Lake. Reliving Donovan's passionate kiss from the night before, I sent him a text, knowing he'd been at work since six a.m. *You should talk to your boss about the ungodly hours he requires of his employees.* He told me the size of his crew varied, depending on the project and season.

Minutes later, he texted back. *I heard he's a real asshole. Makes everyone start early so those with kids are home when their kids get back from school. Jerk.*

Donovan had explained his hours stemmed from the years he and his brother arrived home from school to an empty house while their dad worked. *Heartless bastard. I'd like to see where he's got you slaving away today,* I replied.

If you're not busy at noon, stop by. We take a quick lunch break. He sent me the address of a building downtown.

See you then, I texted.

Snow fell like cotton balls as I walked to the far end of downtown, where Donovan and his crew were working on lofts above the insurance agency shortly before noon.

Inside, I removed my hat and mittens, brushing snow from my coat. Three men were framing rooms with two-by-fours while a plumber worked in the centralized kitchen, Gotye's "Somebody That I Used to Know" blaring from a radio sitting on a sawhorse. Donovan waved me over, his tool belt slung low on his hips, sawdust dotting his gray T-shirt. "Want a quick tour? These lofts are geared toward bikers. The four bedrooms will each have two sets of bunk beds." He pointed at the middle of the open room. "Community kitchen, living room, two bathrooms. And the lofts will come with locked bike storage on the opposite side of the alley so they keep off Main Street."

"David will be happy," I said. "What was this building before?"

"Apartments. Before that, part of the bank that was downstairs decades ago." Donovan wiped sawdust from his face before he leaned in and kissed me. "Are we still on for tonight?" He had invited me over for dinner.

"Yes. I'll be there about five if that still works for you. I'm making spinach artichoke dip and apple cake with caramel sauce."

"Yum," Donovan said, kissing me again. "I'll have the white chili ready."

I inhaled the scent of freshly cut wood on him, a pleasant reminder of when my family would cut and split wood for our wood-burning stove.

"Barf," a deep voice said from behind us.

We spun around to see one of the young men acting like he was going to vomit.

"Serves you right for being five minutes late this morning." Donovan chucked the guy's shoulder as he walked me to the door. "See you at five."

I spent the day researching outdoor-gear suppliers that would allow my logo on the merchandise before I took a break to bake the dessert and put together the dip for Donovan's.

After a shower, I took extra care primping. I arrived at Donovan's early. The long driveway meandered through the woods, leading me to his secluded home. The light-colored wood siding was topped with a red metal sloped roof. The home, settled in front of a mine-pit lake, stood out against tall evergreens.

When I walked up his shoveled sidewalk, Donovan greeted me at the door. "Look at you, a woman who is early." He stepped aside so that I could enter.

"After you berated that poor young man today for being five minutes late, I wanted to avoid suffering the wrath of Donovan."

He chuckled and took the cake pan and glass bowl of dip from me. I sat on the bench in his entryway and removed my boots.

Donovan set the containers on the kitchen table and came back to take my coat. "I love teasing him. He reminds me of a younger version of myself: hardworking yet pushing the envelope with life." Donovan hung my coat in the hall closet. "He had a shitty home life but has a hunger for something better. That's where I come in, making sure he doesn't screw it all up for himself."

"He's lucky to have you," I said. "You'd make a good parent." As soon as the words slipped out, I remembered. "Duh, Eden." I palmed my forehead. "Cassie. Do you get to see her often?"

His eyebrows rose. "I'm surprised you remembered her name. Guess I made an impression on you."

"Nah, I just have an excellent memory," I joked.

"I usually see Cassie a couple of times a year. Come on, I'll show you the place." He led me to the floor-to-ceiling window overlooking the lake. "I've built a few small rustic cabins on the other side of the driveway for the outdoors enthusiasts and hope to add more in the next few years. There'll be campsites for those who want to tent or bring in a camper." He pointed at the driveway.

"We built this place last summer. Eventually, I plan to build my home farther down this road, where I've got some acreage, off the bike trails and away from this area for privacy."

He gestured to the left of the kitchen. "There's a master bedroom and bath over there. I'll spare you a tour, or we may not get around to dinner," he said playfully.

I scoffed, but secretly voted for the bedroom tour. Donovan was good-looking, and his down-to-earth personality made him easy to be around. I didn't care about the height difference. I was comfortable with him, and there was that physical attraction I could no longer ignore.

The hall led to a guest bedroom and bathroom. The upstairs loft contained two sleeping areas with a view of the lake. "Wow, it's breathtaking."

"Thanks."

I rubbed a hand over the smooth light-oak paneling. "Aren't you going to be competing with yourself between the yurts, lofts, and cabins?"

Donovan laughed. "You'll get your answer this spring. Between the yurts, lofts, and eventual cabins, I'll be lucky to house a couple of hundred bikers. That's not even a drop in the bucket and not including the people coming to kayak, scuba dive..."

His words reassured me that my business idea would work.

As we headed back downstairs, he asked, "Ready to eat?"

"Yes, I'm hungry."

As we ate, we talked of our childhoods—mine far more blessed than Donovan's—and what we thought we would do when we grew up.

"I always wanted to build things," Donovan said. "I remember bugging the heck out of a neighbor who was building a swing set for his young children. He probably got so sick of me asking questions and getting in the way that he put me to work helping him. Mom was very sick then, right before she died, and the power of swinging a hammer felt purposeful." Donovan gripped his hand as if he held a hammer. "It helped me pound out a frustration I couldn't understand at age nine."

He nodded toward me. "How about you?"

"I wanted to be a veterinarian. I loved playing doctor to our donkey, sheep, dogs..." Our poor animals tolerated a lot of bandages from me.

"What changed?" Donovan set his empty bowl aside and scooped some dip with a slice of French bread.

"When I realized that veterinarians often have to put an animal to sleep." I winced.

Donovan nodded. "I get it. So, you said Ryan's been working on a logo for you? I'm glad he's interested in your business." He leaned across the table. "*I'm* interested in your business." His eyes twinkled. "And you. Definitely interested in you."

A bold woman might have answered, "Show me." Instead, I settled on "Back at you, baby." As much as I wanted to dive headfirst into the relationship pool with him, I'd done that before with Trent, and I'd nearly drowned.

Chapter 30
David

Ever since Eden moved to Crimson Creek six weeks ago, she'd been relentless in wanting me to be a part of her new business. I tried explaining that I wasn't against the influx of money coming into our community—heaven knows it is much needed—but instead those dang bikers dirtying up our sidewalks, parking in our neighborhood streets, and blocking our driveways. And the town was often noisy after eight at night now.

You sound like an old codger, David. "Well, I am one," I announced to my empty kitchen. I didn't eat breakfast since Eden connived me into meeting her and Hal for a late breakfast at the café—something about the need to haul her future nature-hugging customers.

Minutes later, I slid into the booth next to Hal, with Eden seated across from us.

"How 'bout I use Goober to shuttle them?" Hal, with his white hair recently trimmed, turned toward me.

"Catch me up on what the hell you're talking about, you old fool. And no, you aren't touching Goober." I gave him the stink eye.

"Fine, then. We'll get you your own shuttle bus, Hal," Eden said as smoothly as if she'd known what my response would be. She proceeded to fill me in on the conversation I'd missed, one she'd already warned me about as the reason for our breakfast meeting.

"I'll name it Grover," Hal said.

"Oh, aren't you the clever one?"

Actually, Hal was a little bit clever since his last name was Grove, but I wouldn't admit it to Hal. He was a traitor, succumbing to the bikers.

"We'll have to paint it royal blue," Eden said, "like Grover from Sesame Street."

"Where did you buy Goober?" Eden asked.

"Got him at a used-car dealership in St. Cloud," I grumbled.

"Used is good. I don't need new, just reliable."

After we placed our orders with the server, Eden continued. "You know, David, the shuttle service will help take some of the bike 'riff-raff,' as you call them, off the sidewalks and neighborhood streets." She leaned over the table. "You driving Goober would help."

I harrumphed and followed it with a gulp of too-hot coffee. "Next thing I know, Hal will have oldies blasting in his shuttle van." I chose crankiness over envy.

Hal chuckled at my accusation. "Yes, I'll play 'Born to be Wild' like you do, only I'll wear a flag motorcycle helmet so I look like Peter Fonda did in *Easy Rider*," Hal taunted.

"You wish," I teased. "You'll have to get a helluva lot better looking first."

"All right, you two. That's enough," Eden scolded as if we were in first grade.

Hal and I grinned at each other, happy to get our jabs in.

Hal addressed Eden. "I'll put the word out to friends. We can shop around for shuttle bus options and then get you involved if you'd like."

"That would be great," Eden said. "I'm also in need of someone who knows their way around mountain bikes, a repairman who can work at least part-time."

Hal and I nodded as that was an area I could help with.

"I'm heading back to the cities tomorrow to shop for a used truck before I pick up Ryan on Sunday. It's time to trade in my old Chevy Impala."

Our talk turned to Christmas, only two weeks away, and family gatherings. Hal's family all lived within a fifty-mile radius, unlike my family and Eden's.

Louise was coming back to visit before Christmas, a better solution than me flying. I'd ended up with a blood clot in my leg after my last flight to Vermont.

I couldn't wait to see Louise again. All those years as a POW, I'd wondered if I would ever see my family again. How quickly we forget that things could be so much worse.

Louise arrived in Crimson Creek on the eighteenth, the anniversary of a day that I—and every other Vietnam Prisoner of War—remembered well. December 18, 1972 was Day One of the "Christmas bombing," as many referred to it. The government called it Operation Linebacker II. We didn't care what it was called. All we cared about was the bombing we heard as the earth shook, and we cheered on the pilots. It had been the beginning of the end of the hellacious war.

I picked Louise up at the local airport, a puddle jumper from the Minneapolis airport. Sleet spat sideways, and my windshield wipers worked with the defroster to keep the windshield clear as I waited in the parking lot for her.

Louise had insisted I stay in the car instead of walking into the small airport. "I sure don't need to be scraping your stubborn butt off the pavement when I arrive," she had said when she called earlier to let me know she'd arrived in Minneapolis.

I watched Louise hurry toward my SUV and got out to open the passenger door for her. After a quick hug, she slid into the passenger seat, shaking the snow from her long chestnut hair, the snow blending in with the slivers of gray.

"Thanks for listening to me and staying in the car," Louise leaned over and planted a kiss on my cheek after I settled in behind the wheel.

"Just so you know, I don't have a stubborn butt. It's adorable. Ask any woman in town over the age of seventy."

I snickered at Louise's grimace, as if the idea of any woman eyeing me up appalled her. Maybe it did. Lord knows I had no intention of shopping for another wife. Jean had been it for me. We'd conquered a lot after I came home in 1973, and I doubt any other woman would have put up with me.

Louise was a lot like her mother, a taller, trimmer version of Jean and with the same take-charge attitude. Relaxing had never been part of their vocabulary.

So it shouldn't have been a surprise that when we arrived at my house and had a late lunch of BLTs, Louise decided to clean out my attic.

"What's wrong with my attic?" I asked as I put away our leftovers and Louise loaded the dishwasher.

"Who knows? I doubt you've been up there in years. You shouldn't attempt to go up there, and once I'm finished, you won't ever have to climb those stairs again." Louise punctuated her words with a slap of the dish towel after she dried her hands.

"There's nothing up there I need." I wasn't sure that was true, but since I couldn't handle the steps and hadn't been in the attic for a decade or more, I decided if I hadn't needed the things in ten years, then I would never need them.

"Perfect. Then I'll clean it out and throw everything away. One less thing for me to clean out when you join Mom and Lee." Louise placed her hands on my shoulders and gave me a gentle squeeze. I was ready to meet my maker at any given moment. Eighty-three wasn't old, but outliving a child can age you. Yet the idea of leaving Louise alone twisted my heart.

Louise has Jack and their sons, David. But her road with Jack's health in the near future would be uncertain. The fact that she didn't buckle under pressure was a good thing. That, I would say, she got from me. Nobody lives through intense wartime interrogation and torture without a lot of gumption.

Minutes later, Louise had stacked several dusty boxes in the corner of the living room while I watched from my comfortable recliner.

"Do you even know what's in these boxes, Dad?"

"Already with the quizzing, as if I've gone feeble." My mind was sharper than it had been as a prisoner, when I would hallucinate that I was playing cards with the rat in my cell—a rat I'd shared some of my precious rice with so that it wouldn't crawl on me when I was shackled. "Yes. Stuff."

"Ha." Louise flashed me her scolding-teacher look.

"Fine. If it will calm your hackles, we'll take a gander at the contents." I was a bit curious, enough to lean forward as she pushed the boxes across the carpet toward me.

She took a seat on the nearby sofa. With the gas fireplace cranking out welcome warmth, we took a walk down memory lane. One box contained childhood memorabilia of Lee and Louise. Lee's brought tears to our eyes.

Louise opened another box after setting their childhood one aside. "Look at this!" She held up a flat white box tucked inside a larger one. It contained a satin garter belt, white lace gloves, and some papers. "I've seen these gloves and garter in your wedding photos." She carefully slipped a hand inside one of the gloves, tears rimming her eyes. "It feels weird to think Mom wore these over sixty years ago." She rubbed her hand reverently over the lace.

I swallowed back the dam of emotion tied to our wedding day—before the war changed us, before demons became shadows in our family. "She was a beaut, that's for sure," I managed.

One of the few remaining boxes had "Vietnam" written on the side in Jean's bold handwriting. The word itself made me break out in a sweat. I turned down the temperature of the fireplace, and Louise slid the box in front of my feet.

"I think you should open this one," Louise said gently.

"No. It's nothing I care to revisit."

"Fine, then. I'll open it."

"Not with me around, you won't." My words came out gruffer than intended. "I'm sorry. Yes, you may open it, but please wait until after I go to bed." I placed a hand on hers.

Louise's chin quivered. "Thank you, Daddy," she whispered.

She hadn't called me Daddy for decades. That, in itself, about undid me. I pushed the lever on the recliner until I stood, then I shuffled to the kitchen for a glass of water and a swallow of regrets.

Chapter 31
Eden

On Christmas Eve Day, I spent so much time on my cell phone between phone calls and FaceTime with my parents, siblings, and SG that I kept it plugged in so that the battery wouldn't die. Stevie Grace was spending the holiday with her parents in Florida, and this was the off year for my family's every-other-Christmas family gathering in Grandfield. Trent and Amber were leaving for a cruise the day after Christmas, so Ryan spent Christmas Eve with Trent, and I picked up Ryan Christmas morning.

Instead of celebrating Christmas at the apartment in the cities, we drove to Crimson Creek for nine days of Ryan's holiday break.

After we unpacked, Ryan opened his Christmas present from me: a video game, three books, and a new ski jacket. His gift to me was a wooden sign he'd designed, which read, "I'm a Fun-Key Monkey" with an image of the monkey on the bike that he'd sketched.

"I love it!" I exclaimed, admiring the quality. "Where did you make this?"

Ryan beamed. "Grandma Emily helped me. She's got a friend who makes signs in his garage."

I beckoned Ryan to follow me downstairs to the store. I held the sign against the wall behind the checkout counter, turning toward Ryan for approval.

"Perfect place for it," he agreed.

The sign warmed my heart, not only because of his clever craftsmanship but also the thought that he'd put behind the gift and his support of my dream.

After supper that night, Ryan and I decorated the small evergreen I'd bought a few days earlier from a local tree farm while we discussed plans for the coming week: sledding, ice-skating, and at some point, ice fishing with Donovan in his fish house.

The day after Christmas was balmy by Minnesota winter's standards: high thirties and sunshine. Ryan and I walked to the grocery store for spaghetti and salad fixings.

I hadn't realized I was humming until Ryan said, "Did you know you sing and hum a lot now?"

"I do?" I used to love to sing when I was growing up, maybe because Mom and Dad had music playing all the time. My voice was average at best, but I didn't care.

"Yep. You never used to sing or hum," Ryan said. "I think it's because you're happier now that you aren't at the bank."

I turned to him. "You think so? I guess I never thought about whether I used to sing because I was happy or that singing made me happy. You know, the whole chicken-or-the-egg thing."

"What was that song you were humming?" Ryan asked as we entered the grocery store.

"'Crystal Blue Persuasion.'"

It was a favorite of my parents, one that played in my head when I took the time to appreciate the beauty of nature: the warmth of the winter sun and the cloudless blue sky. Ryan and I dissected the message of peace and hope in the lyrics while we shopped.

"Another favorite of mine is from an album Grandma Jo played a lot. 'Out in the Country' by Three Dog Night," I said, pausing in the grocery aisle. "The song is about when the world feels like it's closing in on you, that getting out in the country, where there's room to breathe, brings relief."

Ryan studied me before stating, "Like what happened to you at your job."

I nodded. "Exactly." He got it. Three Dog Night got it.

After making our purchases, we headed home down Main Street, and I spotted a familiar man walking half a block in front of us—arm in arm with a woman.

In less than a second, my brain stopped my legs.

"What's wrong, Mom?" Ryan peered at me and shifted his grocery bag from one hand to the other.

My grocery bag suddenly felt as heavy as a ship anchor. The couple continued walking, their backs to us, the man's arm wrapped around the woman's shoulders. Their laughter wafted back to us, and his head dipped to hers as if they were sharing a secret.

Donovan's dark, wavy hair grazed the collar of his black ski jacket, his broad shoulders slightly above hers, a woman who wasn't taller than him.

Ryan tapped my leg with his grocery bag. "Come on. I'm hungry."

I worried Donovan would turn around and see me. *Why do I care?* I wasn't the one doing anything wrong. "Let's take a left here so we can walk back by the park." I turned, and Ryan followed me away from Donovan. I reminded myself that I couldn't accuse Donovan of doing anything wrong. *Are we even dating? How can I not know?*

Fish houses dotted Crow Lake, people ice-skated on the shoveled rink near the park, and a few snowmobiles whizzed down the middle of the lake as we walked toward the apartment. "I should've brought my skateboard." Ryan nodded toward the kids on the skateboard ramp.

"I never thought it would be open in the winter," I said, happy to refocus from Donovan to Ryan's plan of future trips to Crimson Creek. After lunch, I pushed away thoughts of Donovan and the woman as Ryan and I spent the afternoon snowshoeing along Crow Lake's shoreline.

After supper—at which I'd eaten little, thanks to Donovan—he called in the middle of Ryan beating me at Uno. I ignored his call. Twice.

When it rang a third time, Ryan asked, "Why aren't you answering? That's not Dad, is it?"

"No, silly, I'd answer his call."

In less than twenty-four hours, Trent and Amber would board the cruise ship.

Ryan peered at the cell phone screen. "Who is Donovan?"

"Nobody. Your turn."

But Donovan was persistent. When he called again, several minutes later, I'd redeemed myself in a third game and decided to address the issue. I took my cell phone into the bedroom and shut the door.

"What?" Ice encompassed that one word.

After a pause, Donovan answered. "What do you mean, 'What?' Don't you mean, 'Hello, I missed you'?" His voice was teasing and hesitant.

"Sorry. Hello. What's up?" My jaw clenched.

"Uh, is this a bad time? Are you and Ryan in town yet?"

"Yes, we came up yesterday."

Allegedly, Donovan had been spending time with his little girl, Cassie. At least that's what he'd told me days before, the reason we hadn't spoken since before Christmas Eve.

"Let's just get this over with now, so I can sleep tonight."

"Sounds good to me once you give me a heads-up as to what 'this' is." Donovan forced a chuckle. "I need time to call in my defense team."

"I'm not laughing, Donovan. I saw her. And honestly, maybe I'm angry with myself for thinking we had started something." I flopped on the bed and stared at the ceiling.

"You mean like dating?"

"Yes. No. I don't know what to call it..." I blew out a sigh. "Just forget it. I think I've been out of the dating scene too long and have no clue how to read adult relationships anymore."

"I'm not sure what the hell you're talking about." Donovan's voice held a dose of frustration. "I thought we were dating too or whatever you want to call it. We aren't?"

This... this is why you don't date, Eden. You like someone, and they want different things. "Are we? I saw you with that woman this afternoon. It's fine if you want to date others, I don't care"—*Liar, liar*—"but I'd appreciate your honesty so I'm prepared if I come face-to-face with you and another woman."

Donovan burst out laughing, and I held the phone away from my ear, surprised at his warped sense of humor when all I wanted to do was chuck the phone against the wall. "That's what's made you Miss Crabby Pants? Let me guess. Did the woman have long, light-brown hair and was wearing a blue plaid coat?"

His owning up to it only poked the fire. "Yes."

"I suppose we were walking arm in arm downtown? You've got to admit she's a beauty, isn't she?"

"I only saw her from behind, sicko." *What kind of man asks his maybe girlfriend if a woman he was with was beautiful?*

Donovan snorted. "She's my daughter. That was Cassie."

I felt my eyebrows touch my bangs. "What? Isn't Cassie some little pigtailed girl you see a few times a year?"

"She was... about twenty years ago. Cassie's twenty-nine," Donovan clarified.

"*Twenty-nine?* How old are you?" I bolted up on the bed. *Am I dating a man who's had work done to look younger than he is?*

"Isn't that impolite to ask a person?" Donovan deadpanned. "I'm forty-six. And yes, that's about a decade older than you—David coughed up your age—but age is just a number."

I stood and paced my bedroom. "Holy hell, that means you were, what, seventeen, when Cassie was born?"

"Hey, quick on the math. Cassie's mom was also seventeen." His voice grew serious. "We were sixteen when she was conceived, and I had to sell myself like the devil to keep her from having an abortion or putting Cassie up for adoption. I worked my butt off in construction that summer, and when Cassie was born in the fall of our senior year of high school, her mom gave up custody, went back to school, and I officially became the sole parent of Cassie."

"Oh my God, Donovan. How did you do it?" I couldn't imagine the struggle with no mother around and his father emotionally absent.

"The man who hired me on for construction—he was there for me when my dad couldn't be. His wife took care of Cassie during the day, and my last class was done at two o'clock. I took care of her nights, weekends, every waking moment that I wasn't at school. I gave up my senior year of football, dating, anything." Donovan's voice grew soft. "But she was so worth it. And in a way, she brought some joy back to Dad. Having a baby in the house gave him a reason to put one foot in front of another. He helped when he wasn't working. Even Gabriel was a good backup babysitter. We were like *Three Men and a Baby*."

"How did I not know this about you?"

"Obviously, we need to spend more time together," Donovan quipped. "It's not something I lead with when I meet someone. And hey, you thought that Cassie was young and I'd be a slug dad who only saw her a few times a year? Wait, don't answer that." The smile was back in his voice. "Anyway, I dropped Cassie off at the airport a couple of hours ago. I don't want to intrude on your time with Ryan, but I'd love to meet him and take you two fishing, like I'd mentioned." His voice dropped an octave and sent chills from my ear to my neck. "That's if you'll have anything to do with this old man."

His age was nothing but a number to me, much like the small difference in our height. The things that mattered—his sense of humor, work ethic, and calm self-assurance—were all there, qualities important to me after my years with Trent. Although I was treading lightly in this relationship, I wanted Donovan and Ryan to meet.

"After hearing about your devotion to raising Cassie, you've amped up my interest in you," I whispered into the phone.

"Good. All those sleepless nights years ago were worth it, then. Now, what else do you have planned for Ryan?"

"We went snowshoeing earlier. Whip mentioned taking Ryan and Willow sledding over Christmas break, maybe mountain biking too, although that makes me nervous." I shuddered at the idea. "But yes, we'll have plenty of time to go ice fishing. That would be fun."

"The bike trails are safer now than the rest of the year," Donovan said. "The trails aren't well traveled, so you don't have others behind you, pushing you to go fast."

"Okay, we'll see. I want to get out there too so I can experience the trails in the winter." I hadn't ordered any fat-tire bikes yet. "I'll see how Whip does with the sledding first. No injuries for Ryan, and he may get another chance." I smiled. Suddenly, I was famished.

After we hung up, I headed to the kitchen, where Ryan was playing his new video game, and I reheated a heaping plate of spaghetti, tasting relief with every bite.

Ryan and I walked to Mined Your Business for lunch on Saturday to catch up with Whip on the plan for sledding and mountain biking. We found a table in the corner, and Whip sauntered over to take our order. He had the right personality for a bar: laid-back and tolerant.

"Hey there, mister," Whip said to Ryan. "I bet you're Ryan. I'm going to be your tour guide for sledding and possibly mountain biking..." He raised his eyebrows at me. "You could come with so you don't have a heart attack worrying. I bet Chase will loan you her fat-tire bike."

"Believe me, I've already decided, if you go, I'm tagging along," I said. "I'll ask Kelly if I can use her bike. She recommended Trek and Yeti brands. What do you think?"

"I've got two mountain bikes. A Trek and a Rocky Mountain. Both are good brands. Same with Yeti," Whip said.

"I'm on the hunt for at least one bike mechanic, if you know of anyone," I added. Mechanical knowledge was high on my list. I could adjust seats, handlebars, and shocks, but anything above that was out of my wheelhouse. And I couldn't do it all on my own.

Whip nodded. "I'll put the word out." He took our order of cheeseburgers and hot chocolate and was back at our table minutes later with mugs of hot chocolate with whipping cream. "You got a sled for tomorrow, Ryan?"

"Yep. When should I be ready?" Ryan took a drink, and whipped cream stuck to his nose.

"I'll be there around ten. The weather looks warmer tomorrow, but that time of the day will still be cool, so make sure to dress warm," Whip said. "It's Chase's son, Mason, whose fat-tire I'm picking up for Ryan. I invited Mason, who is twelve, along if we go, but the family is out of town at a basketball tournament. I texted Chase a few minutes ago, and she's happy to have you try her fat-tire bike, so I'll pick them up later today."

"Sounds good. Thank you."

"Willow is excited to meet you and show you around 'her town.'" Whip turned back to Ryan. "I'm warning you, though: she's fearless. So if she bugs you to go down a hill that looks a little dicey to you, don't do it."

"Good to know." Ryan cast a sideways glance at me.

"Do I need to tag along for sledding too?" My mothering radar was on high alert.

"Nah, we'll be fine," Whip said. "Nothing bad ever happens on my watch." He winked.

After lunch, Donovan picked us up to show Ryan the yurts. I'd told Ryan ahead of time that Donovan and I had started spending time together but nothing serious. "So, not all mushy like Dad and Amber?"

I refrained from asking what Ryan considered "mushy." "No, nothing like that."

Donovan hopped out of his truck when Ryan and I stepped out of the shop. He stuck out his hand to shake Ryan's. "You can't be Ryan. You're way more handsome than the troll your mom described. And taller too," Donovan said.

Ryan played along. "Oh, I know. I get better looking every day," he said, walking with a swagger and a smile to Donovan's truck.

We spent the afternoon checking out the yurts and trails before swinging by Crow Lake Bay to watch snowmobile racing.

Ryan ran ahead toward the lake, leaving us for a moment of privacy.

"One of the reasons I called you last night—before I had to defend myself from your tongue lashing—was to tell you I'll be out of town the next few days to meet up with high school friends for ice fishing on Red Lake. Will New Year's Eve work for you and Ryan for ice fishing?"

"Sure. I'm bringing him back to Trent's on January second so Ryan can spend time with his friends before school resumes." I snuck a quick kiss since Ryan was fifty feet away. I didn't want him to witness me getting "all mushy" with Donovan.

Chapter 32

The following morning, Whip and Willow met Ryan and me in the shop's parking lot. After introductions, Ryan studied Willow. "You look harmless."

"Did Dad tell you I'm not? He thinks I take too many chances." Willow fisted her hands on her hips. "If I were a boy, he wouldn't say that."

"Oh yes, I would," Whip chimed in. "You scare me, and I don't scare easily. So, I'm reminding you in front of Ryan to behave yourself on the hills. I'll be watching you from the warming house."

Willow gave us a devilish grin and hopped in the back seat of the truck. Ryan shot me a fake "I'm scared" look before joining them in the truck. I headed inside, not worried about Willow's live-on-the-edge motto while sledding, but the biking concerned me a bit.

I had been working on merchandise orders with the Fun-Key Monkey logo: water bottles, T-shirts, socks, and visors for kayakers. Around noon, I prepared tomato soup and grilled cheese sandwiches for when Whip and the kids showed up. Before one o'clock, they arrived at the apartment, Ryan using his key to let them in.

Their cheeks were red, and their eyes bright. "Let me guess, you had fun?" I said as they undressed from their winter wear.

"It's the coolest sledding hills ever, Mom!" Ryan turned to Willow after they stepped out of their snow pants and winter boots. "Come on, I'll show you the video game I was telling you about."

"Thank you so much," I said as Whip joined me in the kitchen, chunks of ice nestled in his long beard.

"You're welcome. And hey, no broken bones. That means it's a go for biking this afternoon, right?"

"For sure. You get an A+ on the sledding. Lunch will be ready in a few minutes."

"Anything I can do to help?" Whip said.

"I'm good. You relax. We need your energy this afternoon." I nodded toward Ryan's bedroom. "They look like they're getting along well."

"They talked the whole way to the sledding hills. And, you'll be happy to know, I watched Willow try to convince Ryan to go down one of the hills that is too steep and has a couple of sled-launching bumps, and I watched him shake his head 'no.'" Whip accepted the glass of water I handed him. "He'll be a good influence on my wild child."

After lunch, Whip, with four fat-tire bikes loaded in the back of his pickup, drove us to the recreational parking lot. We unloaded the bikes and donned helmets, and Whip led the way to the easiest trail. "I think we should go in this order: me, Ryan, Willow, Eden. I'll go slow, I promise. Yell for me to stop, and I'll hear you."

I got butterflies as Whip led us down a trail that veered away from the cliff of one of the mine-pit lakes. After several minutes, my shoulders loosened, and my stomach settled. Ryan would be fine. I breathed in the crisp, earthy scent of fresh pine trees.

We completed the loop in two hours with everyone uninjured. My legs and butt muscles burned, but it was worth it. Ryan had made a new friend and had fun.

The following day, my entire body ached from the previous day's ride. I took Ryan and Willow to the movie theatre twenty miles away then out for pizza, cementing their friendship.

Donovan called when he arrived home late New Year's Eve morning. "I'll pick you and Ryan up about four for fishing."

"I'll pack snacks and drinks for us." Ryan and I ate a late lunch, and I prepared Chex Mix and cooked ham-and-cheese sliders on Hawaiian buns for the fish house.

Donovan picked up bait before collecting us at four. He drove to the lake access, where a road had been cleared on the ice. At his fish house, Donovan lit the propane stove, and Ryan and I cleared ice from the holes. I'd done a lot of ice fishing in my youth and set the line depths using a sinker.

Five-gallon pails were flipped over for seats. "We're each allowed two holes for fishing," Donovan said. "I should've checked before, but you've got your fishing license, Eden, right?"

"Yes."

Ryan was in the clear until he turned sixteen. We went over the basics of setting the hook with Ryan. I'd taken him fishing in the summer but never ice fishing.

Once our lines were baited, Donovan pulled out a cribbage board. "Playing cribbage is a necessary part of ice fishing."

"I don't know how to play," Ryan confessed.

Donovan feigned shock and then turned to me. "Please tell me you know how to play."

"Duh. I grew up fishing, remember? Yes, they play cribbage south of the cities." I jabbed Donovan's shoulder.

"You'll be my helper this first game," Donovan told Ryan. "Watch and learn. And no crying from you, Eden." He pointed at me with the deck of cards.

I smirked. Fifteen minutes later, I'd left their pegs below the skunk line and accepted their challenge for a rematch.

Between cribbage games, Ryan caught a huge northern that scared him when Donovan had to let it squirm around on the fish house floor until he could get the hook out of its mouth. He tossed it back in after I took photos of Donovan holding the fish in front of a smiling Ryan. Northern pike were good for pickling, but canning was something neither Donovan nor I had time for right now.

The fish quit biting by ten o'clock, and we had two walleyes and six crappies out on the ice. We'd played five games of cribbage, and both Donovan and I had yawned several times more than that.

"How about we call it a night before we need Ryan to drive us home?" I said. Ryan's eyes lit up at that idea.

"Good idea," Donovan said. "I promised David I'd take him fishing tomorrow. I'll take the fish home and clean them. We could have a fish fry tomorrow, and I'd like to invite David over too."

"That's a great idea," I said.

We packed up and headed out into air so cold that it froze nose hairs. And after Donovan pulled into the shop's parking lot, he walked to the door with us. "You might want to go inside now, buddy. Nobody wants to see their mom getting kissed." He ruffled Ryan's hair and laughed at Ryan's lip curl.

Ryan turned and ran into the shop after I unlocked the door.

I took a step closer to Donovan. "Thank you. This may be the best New Year's Eve I've ever had, which either means I've led a boring life or that you're fun to be around."

Before his lips touched mine, he muttered, "I'm going with the second choice."

As I floated up the apartment stairs minutes later, I agreed with his pick.

Ryan and I arrived at Donovan's shortly after David on New Year's Day. Ryan looped his arm through David's, and they shuffled ahead of me as Donovan held open his front door.

"Happy 2015! I hear you two fishermen caught plenty of crappies today for the fish fry," I said to David as we shed our winter wear in Donovan's entryway.

"Hurdy Gurdy tell you that? There weren't two fishermen. Just me, only me." David puffed out his chest, stretching the material of his red flannel shirt.

"Hurdy Gurdy?" Ryan asked.

"It's an old song from long before I was born," I explained. "The man who sang that goes by the name Donovan."

Donovan crossed his arms over his chest. "I take offense at that reference. It came out the year I was born. It's the reason I'm named Donovan."

"Just be careful of this Hurdy Gurdy man, Eden," David leaned in and stage whispered. "If you don't watch out, he'll come singing songs of love."

Donovan scoffed at the lyrics quote and led us into his open kitchen. Donovan fried fish, I warmed up the au gratin potatoes and homemade baked beans I'd made, and David unwrapped a vegetable tray he'd brought.

Donovan had a playlist of oldies turned low in the background—songs about love or love lost, a favorite topic in music. After we finished our meal and were visiting at the table, I quietly sang along to "The River Is Wide" with The Grass Roots, and "Baby, I Love You" with Andy Kim—a song David pointed out was on his one-hit-wonder playlist.

Ryan piped up about not wanting to go back to school the following week. "This has been the best Christmas vacation ever," he proclaimed.

"And to think you've got many more years of school ahead." David nudged Ryan, receiving a groan in response.

"So much fun that he hasn't memorized his speech for history class next week," I said.

"What speech is that?" David asked.

"We got our choice. We have to memorize part of either Abraham Lincoln's, Martin Luther King's, President Kennedy's, or President Franklin Roosevelt's speech. Not their whole famous speech, but a few minutes' worth."

"Which one did you choose?" Donovan gave Ryan his full attention.

"I chose Martin Luther King. We're supposed to say why afterward, and I picked his because we all have dreams. Like you're doing your dream with the shop, right, Mom?"

I nodded, warmed by his perceptiveness.

"That's a good choice," David said. "Did your teacher tell you to try putting the speech to music? You don't have to sing it, but music helps us remember things better than words without a melody. It's why I can sing you every word to songs from seventy years ago but can't recite my grocery list from memory." He nodded toward me. "And why your mom can remember words to songs that were popular before she was born."

"Cool. What song should I pick?"

"That's up to you." David drummed his gnarled fingers on the table, studying them as if they'd provide a tune. "Let me tell you a story about a fellow Vietnam POW named Doug Hegdahl. He was one of three prisoners freed in 1969 on a prisoner exchange—something normally frowned upon. We'd all taken an oath that no man would be freed ahead of time." David eyed Ryan. "But Doug was different. And he became a hero."

David cleared his throat. "Doug pretended his thinker didn't work." He tapped the side of his head. "Doug convinced the Vietnamese military that he couldn't read or write and sure as shoot couldn't memorize anything." David said conspiratorially, "But memorize he did. Over two hundred fifty names, capture dates, their hometowns, and other information about his fellow POWs, including the location of our prison in Hanoi."

My eyes widened at this piece of news.

"He memorized it all to the tune of 'Old MacDonald Had a Farm.'"

Ryan's mouth dropped open.

"He took that information back to the government. He also had the freedom to work in the commons area out of our prison cells, and he sabotaged Vietnamese prison trucks by adding dirt in their fuel tanks."

"Holy hell!" Donovan exclaimed. "How have I not heard about this before?"

"Nobody wanted to hear a peep about what happened in Vietnam. Doug has somehow flown under the radar all these years. But we didn't forget him." David shook his head at the memory.

"I'm going to use 'The Ants Go Marching,'" Ryan piped up. "You know, my favorite song from when I was little. Can I try it tonight, Mom?"

"Wow, that's the first time you've begged to do homework." I mouthed a "thank you" to David.

True to his word, Ryan practiced his speech after we arrived home later that night, and that song played like an earworm in my head as I lay in bed afterward, blessed by my time with Ryan and wishing I didn't have to drive him back to Trent's in the morning.

Chapter 33
David

I waited until 2015 was several days old before I caved. I should never have opened the damned box, should have told Louise to throw it away. How silly of me to believe I could just take a peek at what Jean had packed inside. Now, in desperate need of a shower and shave, I sniffed the unwashed pajamas I'd been wearing day and night. They should go in the trash along with the Vietnam box.

As if the devil was hissing in my ear, "Come see me," I had caved.

For three days, I'd played my "sad, sappy songs" playlist, as Hal called it, music Louise had helped me put together years before, when I purchased my song choices from iTunes for Goober. That particular playlist was just for me. The bar crowd would've booed me off the bus for being a wet blanket if I'd played the sappy songs, well, other than The Rolling Stones "Paint it Black." That one resonated with me and would likely be a popular sing-along in Goober.

The playlist included songs released during my time in Vietnam, like "One" and "Precious and Few." Their lyrics reflected the state of our marriage in 1973, a period when we hadn't been on the same page or even in the same book. "If You Could Read My Mind" and "To Love Somebody" resonated with the struggles Jean and I went through, trying to reconnect. Jean had gained the freedom to live her own life, and I was still in love with a woman who no longer existed.

By late 1973, we'd made a promise to commit again to each other, to appreciate each other. We were successful and put the past behind us. And I'd reopened it.

While I sat in my easy chair, listening to "Good Time Charlie's Got the Blues" and nursing lukewarm coffee that gnawed at my too-empty stomach, someone rapped on the front door over and over again. The knocking gained momentum, which I ignored just as I had when the telephone rang like a fire drill for a day until I finally unplugged the damn thing.

"David, I know you're in there. Open up!" Eden shouted through the door, cutting into Bread singing "Make It with You." The living room drapes were closed, but I peeked out the edge and spotted a pickup in the driveway. She must've bought the truck she'd been talking about. I rubbed a hand over the stubble on my cheeks. I smelled like a dead farm animal and likely resembled one.

"Go away. I'm sick!" I shouted from a safe distance, worried Eden would see me through the door window.

"Then let me in so I can take care of you, you stubborn old man!" Eden shouted. "Don't make me get a key from Hal or Donovan. Heck, I can probably go next door. I bet every neighbor of yours has a key."

She was right. We all looked out for each other.

I weighed the odds that Eden would march next door and get a key. She was as stubborn as I was.

"Fine!" I yelled and shuffled to the front door. I unlocked it and stepped aside as she threw the door open. "I'm going to need a little time to get cleaned up before you chew me out."

I was past caring if she saw me in my flannel pajamas, but I stepped away enough that she'd be spared my stench, I hoped.

Eden stomped in like a wild animal, eyeing me up like a meal. "You look awful." She toed off her winter boots.

"Thank you." I folded my arms over my chest. "Nobody asked you to stop by and pay me compliments."

"I was worried about you. Is that a sin?" She tossed her keys from one hand to the other, the jingling adding to my annoyance.

"Stop that." My words came out gruff, making Eden flinch.

I closed my eyes and reminded myself that she was a blessing, not an intrusion. "I'm sorry. Let me get cleaned up." *She doesn't understand the jarring memory of the guard's keys jingling as he approached your cell, David. Stop being such a horse's ass.* Keys rattling and doors squeaking were painful sounds that put us on high alert in our cells.

Eden made her way into the kitchen while I headed down the hall to my bedroom and bathroom. Several minutes later, I walked in on her cleaning up the kitchen.

"You aren't sick, are you?" She turned from the sink, hand on hip.

"I haven't felt like company, yet here you are." I sat at the table and gestured for her to join me. "So, you purchased a truck." *Might as well exchange pleasantries.*

"Yes. After I couldn't find what I was looking for in the cities, Hal set me up with a friend of his son's." She fidgeted in her chair. "No bells or whistles, which is fine with me. A 2010 Ford half-ton pickup with less than forty thousand miles. I put an ad in our newspaper here and the *Minneapolis Tribune* for my car."

A Tupperware container sat in the middle of the table, and my hunger pangs spoke up.

"What's in there?"

"Apple cinnamon muffins. Want one?"

Starving myself for what I'd put my family through had been satisfying. "It would be rude for me to refuse." Eden no doubt heard my stomach rumble.

She retrieved two small plates from the cupboard and served us. "Why didn't you return my phone calls?"

"I've been in a bit of a pissy mood," I grumbled. "When that occurs, I'm better off keeping to myself."

"I'm sorry to hear that." Eden unwrapped the muffin on her plate. "Did something happen?"

"Happen? No." I took a bite, and cinnamon, chunks of apple, and all-around deliciousness hugged my taste buds. "What else is new with you?"

"Mostly ordering stock for the shop. Donovan and I went snowshoeing Tuesday night on a new trail that goes back behind his resort."

"So, you like Mr. Hurdy Gurdy?" My mood softened. "He's a hard worker, that one."

"He is, and yes, I do like him. I haven't dated much since my divorce, and I'm not looking for anything serious—same with him. And he's great with Ryan."

"Speaking of Ryan, how did his rehearsing go for the speech?"

"I spoke with him on the phone yesterday, and he said it went great, thanks to you." Eden stood and filled two glasses of water for us. "When he practiced with me after your tip about putting it to music, he did much better. Although in his case, he kept wanting to sing the speech."

"I'm glad I could be of help. Doug Hegdahl would be proud."

Eden stared at her half-eaten muffin. "I'm worried I might lose him. That I'm making an eleven-year-old choose between his parents because I chose to change careers and move." Her voice dropped to a whisper. "I feel guilty for putting myself first."

I leaned back in my chair, hoping to open my airway, which had constricted at Eden's words as they punctured my regret.

Oh, David. Don't say it. Don't! But I felt as if someone had pulled the pin on the grenade I'd been hiding for decades. "Do you think you're the first person who chose to be away from their child?" I massaged the back of my neck, tense from remorse. It didn't help.

"You think every parent doesn't second-guess if they're doing the right thing for their children?" My voice continued to rise like a volcano ready to erupt. "How about every man and woman who signs up to serve in the armed forces? They know they're leaving their family for several months at a stretch, but they do it." My hands shook. "Are they selfish? Self-centered? Don't care about their children? You tell me!" I shouted.

The terror in Eden's eyes couldn't stop the fire-breathing dragon inside me. "And tell me how you'd feel about someone who knowingly signs up for another tour they don't have to take and then gets themselves shot down so that it's several years before they see their family again!" I slammed my hand on the table, welcoming the sting. "Now *that* is one selfish prick!"

Horror struck Eden, as if I'd pulled a gun on her. As shocked as she likely felt, it was nothing compared to my dismay when I exploded into soul-baring tears.

Chapter 34

Eden

I couldn't move, as if someone had driven a spike through my legs to the chair's wood. But the pain shooting through me wasn't physical. The tears blurring my vision didn't stop me from noticing David struggling to compose himself. He fished out a hanky from his pocket, dabbed at his eyes, and blew his nose.

"Please tell me what's wrong. And I'm sorry, so sorry, for whining to you… of all people." *Sorry* was a pebble of the anguish asteroid inside me.

David's chin wobbled. "Can I trouble you for more water?"

"Of course." I hopped up and filled his empty glass.

David took a long drink, and we sat in silence until he regained composure. "First, I must apologize." He held up a hand to stop me when I opened my mouth.

"It is not acceptable behavior, and I won't tolerate it from myself. You shouldn't either." David fiddled with the cloth napkin in front of him. "As I mentioned earlier, I've been having a bit of a tough go. It's as if when you found the POW bracelet, you dug up the past I'd so carefully buried." His shoulders sagged. "The two other bracelets I have were given to me over twenty years ago, back when Jean was alive and could smooth things over so I didn't self-combust."

"I'm so sorry," I said again, my eyes pleading for his forgiveness. "I am sorry the bracelet has brought back painful memories for you."

"It's okay, Eden. For years, Hal has been telling me to let it all out before I explode. And the older I get, the harder it is to keep it in." David gave a small nod, as if encouraging himself. "Last Saturday night, I had myself a fun group of middle-aged men in Goober who knew the words to oldies like 'Aquarius' and 'Ride Captain Ride.' I enjoyed the night filled with laughter and singing."

David ran a palm over the tablecloth. "But then on Sunday, the devil appeared, enticing me to open up a box with Vietnam memories that Louise had unearthed."

I wished I could have met Louise, who'd been in town while I was in the cities. I squeezed his hand.

"Louise had been hell-bent on cleaning out the attic so I could go through boxes and help declutter. One of the boxes was marked Vietnam—things my wife, Jean, had saved." He cleared his throat. "I didn't know the box contained carbon copies of every letter my family had written to me and every letter Jean had typed to her parents and mine during my captivity."

I could only imagine his agony at reading those letters.

"I'd forgotten how much I missed in their lives. Hearing Louise's solo in her junior year choir concert. Watching Lee win his first swimming medal in high school. Their prom, class trips, meeting their friends..." David stared out the kitchen window. "Now you know the root of my outburst. The match to what fueled my regurgitation of regret."

"Oh, David, you didn't have a choice. You were a prisoner!"

"But I did, Eden. I could have left the Air Force. I'd served for more than a decade. I told myself it was a good career, security for my family." David rubbed a hand over his weary eyes.

"In truth, it was simply because I loved to fly. I craved it like a drug. I loved my comrades, the thrill of flying, and the challenge of a mission accomplished. We all thought we were doing the right thing." His eyes bored into mine. "But is the right thing following your heart or the responsible route that will keep you with your family?"

David sipped his water. "I had the power of knowing. Jean and the kids didn't. Jean didn't hear from me for eighteen months while I was in solitary confinement and had no idea if I was alive. I *knew* what was happening. She didn't. My knowledge gave me control." He shook his head. "Poor Jean—her fears and worries far outweighed the happiness I got from flying. When I wrote home a year before my release, I commented on Louise's short skirt and Lee's long hair in a photo Jean had sent. As if those things were important. Complaining about a family I'd deserted. Shame on me. Shame on me!" He whispered the last words.

Those words amplified my choices. It was too late for David to change his career choice, but it wasn't too late for me.

I arrived back at the apartment before noon and struggled to concentrate on inventory orders for the shop. *Is it worth it? Shouldn't I give up this foolish dream and move back to Minneapolis? Isn't David's regret proof enough?*

Yet my situation was nothing like being a prisoner of war in a faraway country. Feeling unsettled, I set aside my computer, dressed in warm winter wear, and made my way around the walking path that hugged Crow Lake. An hour into my walk, my cell phone rang. I didn't recognize the number on the screen. It could've been one of a dozen suppliers.

"Hello?"

"Hi. Is this Eden Everson?" a woman asked.

"Yes."

"This is Louise, David Carpenter's daughter. I asked for your number, so I hope it's okay that he gave it to me. Well, *asked* might be the wrong word. *Insisted* is more like it."

I stopped walking. "Of course! I missed meeting you when you were here. I hope we can meet next time you're in town."

"I hope so too. You're probably wondering why I'm calling." Louise got right to the point. "I call Dad every few days, and when I spoke with him Monday morning, I could tell he was feeling a bit down, but he wouldn't say why. When I checked in with him a few minutes ago, he said he'd bitten off your head this morning." Louise paused. "I'm so sorry, Eden. Truly, he's rarely like that."

"No need to apologize." I turned around and headed toward home, feeling the chill once I'd stopped walking. "I was whining about my parenting concerns. I had no right to complain to your dad."

"I'm the one who insisted on looking through his box of Vietnam memorabilia and opened up those awful memories for him," Louise berated herself. "I shouldn't have left it where he could look through it.

"I called because Dad told me what he said to you, and I wanted to give you my side of it. Dad shouldn't feel guilty. I get the regret—I do. He missed out on a lot. But being taken prisoner of war wasn't his fault. We're so thankful he survived, that he endured the torture, the horrific conditions. Many didn't. He's a hero in my eyes." Louise's voice quivered, and I could feel the emotion in her words. "My brother Lee felt the same way."

I fished in my coat pocket for a tissue, imagining what it must have been like for Louise and Lee, teenagers who missed their father, wondered if he'd make it back alive, then welcomed back a stranger.

"Did your dad tell you how I came to have his POW bracelet? Do you remember giving it to my mom that day in the café?"

"I do! Your mom's Korean, right? I remember admiring her beautiful skin and hair. We were stationed in Japan before Dad's plane went down, and I grew my hair long and dyed it black because

I envied the pretty teenage girls there." Louise chuckled. "Mom was *not* thrilled when she realized I'd stolen her hair dye."

I smiled at Louise's memory. "Yes, Mom is half Korean. When she told me the story behind the bracelet, she remembered you were all on a road trip."

"I was probably melodramatic, whatever I said to her. But I did know that, assuming Dad survived the rest of his years as a POW, he wouldn't be the same man coming home to us," Louise reminisced.

"So, you're calling to tell me that you don't regret your dad staying in the Air Force, even though it eventually took him away from you for several years?"

"I missed the heck out of him, but we were used to him being gone for several months at a time before his capture. There was never a day that I wasn't proud of him, proud that he did what he loved, flying." Louise coughed back a cry. "Sorry, I get emotional when I think of everything he went through. And yes, my point is don't give up on your dreams. Your son will be proud that you pursued your dreams, and he'll adjust. Heck, we moved all over the place when Dad was in the service."

I'd reached the park and stopped. "Thank you. It helps a lot. My best friend has pointed that out too. Kids move all the time. I don't know how much your dad told you about me, but I'm not a city girl. At all. And the time I've spent here makes me feel like I'm back in Grandfield, the small town where I grew up." Speaking of Grandfield reminded me I owed Stevie Grace a phone call.

"Another positive was Mom got to step up and make decisions for us kids, decisions for her career," Louise said. "That generation, the man made the decisions. When Dad was a POW, Mom took college classes while Lee and I were in school, bought a car... spread her wings. She was proud of herself. We were too."

I recalled David telling me about Jean getting her special ed degree after he left the service. "Thank you, Louise. I mean it. I was having second thoughts before I barged in on your dad this morning, and they only snowballed after speaking with him. It helps to hear your side."

"Most people have at least one epic decision in their life that changes the direction of how things play out," Louise said. "Because of Dad's choice to continue in the Air Force, that trickle-down effect took him from us for years, but it also gave Mom independence and her chance to pursue her dreams... which is what it sounds like you're doing." Louise's voice held warmth.

"It is. Thank you." I stood by the park, my shop in view, and took in Louise's words. I didn't want my one epic choice in life to be that I'd stuck it out at the bank. I wanted it to be that I took a chance and made the leap to own my own business, a choice that resulted in me liking myself again. When we hung up, I sensed I'd made a new friend in Louise. As I climbed the stairs to the apartment, I felt ten pounds lighter than I had when I'd descended them an hour earlier. I spent the rest of the day working on inventory orders with a renewed focus.

Chapter 35

The month of January was bitterly cold, windy, and productive. The weeks that Ryan was with Trent, I spent my days working on shop improvements and ordering inventory, taking breaks either to meet Kelly and a few of her friends for lunch, or, weather permitting, to tag along with them on the fat-tire bike I'd purchased after Christmas. Kelly and the others stuck to the easy trails if I was with them.

Hal had lessened my concern about finding a bike mechanic. "I know my way around bikes and can help out in the fix-it part of the shop when I'm not shuttling people," he had said when I voiced my concerns. I would need another repair person besides Hal but had enough feelers out that I felt confident I would find someone.

During the week, traffic in town was minimal. I knew the real test for my business would hit next winter when it might make more sense to have the shop closed three weekdays.

Donovan visited a high school friend in Montana in late January, which meant I'd only seen him twice in January, but it gave me time to concentrate on the shop and spend more time with the women I'd met through Kelly. Rec volleyball was twice a week at the grade school gym, and I became a sub for Kelly's team. I'd missed the sport and planned to sign up as a regular team member in the fall when they formed teams again.

I spoke with Trent the last Sunday in January when I picked Ryan up, asking Trent if we could meet for coffee during the week to go over our schedules in the coming months.

We decided on Wednesday morning at a coffee shop near his house. Trent arrived in a white polo shirt that accentuated his fake-bake tan, which got darker every week.

"Thanks for going in late this morning," I said after Trent placed his order of a double-shot flat white. I stuck with coffee with whipped cream.

"No problem. You know corporate is flexible with schedules."

Actually, I don't. I don't have male genitals, so corporate wasn't as flexible with me.

I got right to the point. "As I mentioned the other day, my apartment lease is up at the end of March, and I plan to open the shop around April first or shortly thereafter." Voicing it made my heart skip beats.

"With Ryan's baseball practice beginning in April and me getting the shop up and running, what do you think of having him stay with you all of April and May until school is out in early June, and then he could stay with me in Crimson Creek for the summer?"

Trent folded his arms over his chest.

"That's if Ryan is okay with that schedule. He could decide in the summer what he wants to do come fall. Until then, we could enroll him at both schools." My fingers shredded the paper napkin on my lap.

Trent slowly nodded. "That might work, but I've got a life, Eden, and having Ryan full-time wasn't in the plan. Amber and I are flying out this Sunday afternoon for a business trip in Miami."

Aha. That's why the tan. Fake baking ahead for "business at the beach." Our divorce decree stated we had to let the other know ahead of time if we planned to leave the country for anything. Any trip in the US was okay unless Ryan's schedule was affected.

"I'll be closed Tuesday and Wednesday in April and part of May and will stay at Stevie Grace's apartment at least one of those nights each week. She's good with Ryan staying there with me overnight when I visit."

I continued my sales pitch. "And Ryan being with me for the summer would free your mom up from having Ryan every other week."

I'd worried about what to do with Ryan in the summer if I were still working at the bank. He was too old for day care but too young to stay home alone. Trent stretched his legs out to the side of our table, visibly relaxed since he wouldn't have Ryan twenty-four-seven for two months.

"Maybe I can take Ryan every other weekend in the summer," he said. "It'd be nice to have some freedom in the summer so Amber and I can do some things." He swirled his coffee cup. "Speaking of Amber, we've been talking about her moving in."

"It's getting that serious?"

"Yes. She stays with me when Ryan's at your house. Why keep a house she lives in half the time?" Trent said. "Ryan seems to get along with her."

"Did you talk to him about this yet?"

"No. I figured I'd talk to you first. It wouldn't happen until her house sold. She hasn't put it on the market yet but will have it listed by spring."

"Do you think you'll get married?" I didn't know a thing about Amber and had to trust Trent's judgment.

"Neither of us is in a rush. Amber was married briefly in her early twenties, and although they didn't have any kids, she had a traumatic divorce," Trent said.

"You, Ryan, and I need to sit down and discuss the schedule for spring and summer, along with Amber eventually moving in. This is a lot for Ryan to take in, a lot of changes."

Trent arched his groomed eyebrows. "If you weren't moving, Ryan would have minimal changes."

I swallowed words better left unsaid. "We'll just have to be flexible with scheduling." But I knew we couldn't put off a decision for his schooling next fall forever. "Do you have plans this weekend? We could talk to Ryan on Saturday if that works for you." I wanted time with Ryan after we went over the schedule in case he had questions.

"Amber and I have an open house at the new Edina Yacht Club on Saturday." Trent's shoulders tensed as if I might call him out on how ridiculous it was for him to attend a yacht club event when he couldn't afford even the smallest of yachts. He had always been about the illusion of wealth, happiness, and success.

"How about Saturday morning?"

Trent shrugged. "I guess that works. I'll stop by before I pick Amber up at noon."

I left the coffee shop with Trent as he headed off to work, and I drove back to the apartment to work on a budget for the shop. I had to believe the shop would be enough for me—both mentally and financially. I'd had plenty of confidence in the corporate world until I kicked off my high heels.

But the doubt that had crept in was being replaced with a renewed belief in myself. *I'm Earth Eden, dammit, and I belong in a small town surrounded by Mother Nature again.*

Trent arrived at my apartment Saturday morning looking like he was playing dress-up. Even Ryan's eyebrows rose when Trent toed off polished dress shoes.

I'd warned Ryan about our upcoming "family talk," and as we sat at the kitchen table, one Trent and I had picked out when I was pregnant, I noticed the tenseness in Ryan's jaw. Trent and I wouldn't call a family meeting for no reason.

"You know that I've got to be out of here at the end of March and that Stevie Grace offered me the use of her apartment." Then I laid out the schedule Trent and I had discussed for April and May.

"What do you think?" I leaned over the table, trying to read Ryan's eyes. "Instead of seeing you every other week, it will be two nights every week until school is out."

Ryan cast a look at his dad. "I guess that's okay. What about summer?"

I knew that would be the difficult sell, but I painted a hopeful picture of him joining a baseball team in Crimson Creek and helping me in the shop. "Brady or any of your friends can visit as often as they want."

Trent stepped in. "And you can come stay with me when it works out." He cleared his throat before dropping the news that by then, Amber might be living with him.

I sensed Ryan wouldn't be as anxious to stay at Trent's, at least not until they all adjusted. "Flexibility is the key," I said.

We hashed over a few scenarios before Trent glanced at his expensive sports watch, one he'd purchased the year before we split, one that cost as much as the washer and dryer we'd replaced earlier that year.

"I've got to go," Trent said. He stood and leaned over to hug Ryan's shoulders. "See you tomorrow."

Ryan glanced up at his dad and nodded, and a minute later, Trent was gone.

Ryan and I sat in silence, giving him time to digest our tentative plans. I was so lost in my thoughts that I jumped when he spoke.

"I'm hungry."

"What sounds good to you?"

"Homemade waffles and your homemade strawberry syrup?" Ryan batted his eyes.

"Coming right up," I said and pushed back my chair to get to work. I'd make him about anything for lunch, anything to smooth over the bumps we'd created in his life.

A late-January thaw had hit Minnesota the day before I arrived back in Crimson Creek. On Sunday afternoon, Donovan and I hiked through crunchy snow in the woods near his home. I had missed Donovan—a lot. This man I hadn't known four months earlier had wormed his way into my thoughts daily. I didn't know everything about him, but I knew enough to *want* to know him better.

We'd talked on the phone almost every night after he returned from his trip to Montana. When we took a break on a bench along the trail, talk turned to my future employees.

"Hal's wife, Maudie, is interested in part-time help," I said. "Yes, she's seventy-three, but she has the energy of a forty-three-year-old."

"She keeps Hal young," Donovan said, taking my gloveless hand in his.

"Initially, between Maudie and me, I think we'll be fine with the shop until Memorial Day Weekend. I'm closing Tuesdays and Wednesdays until later in May, and if Maudie works every Thursday morning, it will allow me to spend two nights a week with Ryan at SG's apartment." I'd talked to Stevie Grace about the schedule that would end once Ryan was out of school.

"Hal's on board with shuttle service?" he asked.

"Yes, and he'll help out with bike repairs. He's been shopping for a shuttle similar to David's Goober. David's even been helping him." I grinned. "I think he's secretly warming to the idea that if we shuttle the people, there will be less traffic and bikers through town. Being the stubborn man that he is, he won't admit it."

"I'd expect nothing less from him." Donovan offered me a protein bar, which I unwrapped. "Did you hear back from Oliver yet?"

Kelly had connected me with Oliver the previous week. He was a senior in high school and an avid biker, and his dad ran the car repair shop in Mine Key. According to Kelly, Oliver knew his way around a bike.

"I did. He'll bounce between cleaning and repairing rental bikes, helping with shuttles, and filling in at the shop. And he's going to help assemble the bikes when I get inventory. Hal and I practiced with the few bikes I've unpacked, but we were no speed demons."

It would be a skeleton crew, but until business proved otherwise, a skeleton crew was what I could afford.

"Plus, you'll have Ryan to help in the shop this summer," Donovan said.

"Yes. And with my pickup, I can haul kayakers with the small trailer I bought."

"Kelly said you talked to her about her oldest daughter, Hadley, working for you this summer," Donovan said.

"Yes. Hadley's stopping by this week after school."

Donovan and I continued on the trail, making it back to his house as the sun set.

The following afternoon, Hadley—a younger replica of Kelly—stopped by the shop. Hadley was more knowledgeable than I was about biking and the rec area. I hired her before she left, with the agreement that she would start work Memorial Day Weekend—one more step in employee hires, one giant leap into the unknown.

Chapter 36

Donovan had invited me for an early Valentine's Day dinner at his home on Friday since I would be in the cities for Valentine's Day. I arrived late afternoon with twice-baked potatoes to go with the steaks he was grilling. After prepping the steaks, we headed to his secluded patio. His house blocked the wind off the lake, and the late sunshine cast enough warmth that we could sit on a bench he'd carved out of diamond willow branches.

After he got the grill going, I poured wine for us. "Is Gabriel as self-sufficient as you?" I rubbed my hand over the bench he'd created.

"Yes, but I think I protected him too much."

"What do you mean?" I studied the downturn of his mouth.

"It started when I was a young teen. I sensed something was different with Gabriel. I had an inkling, but I didn't have anyone to turn to." Donovan winced at the memory. "I finally talked to Gabriel. He was only eleven, and I would've left it alone if not for some rumors at school." He'd already told me Gabriel was gay and had a long-term partner.

"I waited until we were getting ready for bed to ask Gabriel if he thought he liked boys more than girls. I reassured him I didn't give a shit but just needed to know so I could protect him." Donovan's jaw jutted out as he worked through the memory.

"Poor Gabriel. And poor you." I touched Donovan's shoulder.

"He said he'd been trying not to like boys, and he prayed every night that the next morning he would like girls," Donovan said. "I told him that wasn't how it worked and he could like who he wanted. But living in our small town back then was like walking around with a bullseye on your back."

Donovan shook his head. "It wasn't easy for Gabriel. Two things saved him. Neither of them was me even though I tried."

"What were they?"

"One was that he was a fast-as-hell runner. He ran for the high school track team in eighth grade, and it helped diminish the teasing—enough to make life bearable for him."

"What was the other thing?"

"Chase." Donovan smiled wistfully. "Yes, Kelly. She was popular and kind to everyone, especially Gabriel. They'd been friends since kindergarten, and as her popularity grew, so did her assertiveness at sticking up for Gabriel."

"Every kid needs a friend like that." I wasn't surprised at Kelly befriending Gabriel.

"Okay, enough moping from me. I'm supposed to be wooing you." Donovan leaned in and kissed me, his warm hand caressing my cold cheek.

Eventually, he pulled away to check the steaks. "Let's go in. The steaks are done."

Not until we finished dinner and settled next to each other on his couch did I say, "You carried a lot on your shoulders. When did you finally feel like you could date?"

"I went on my first date when Cassie was three, other than dating her mom in high school." Donovan chuckled. "Being a single dad living with my dad was a real chick deflector in my teens."

"Is that when your dad and Gabriel would watch Cassie?" I thought of so many women in the same situation as Donovan had been.

"Yep. If they were both home, that worked best. They could tag-team Cassie. She knew how to play them both, had them wrapped around her chubby little finger."

"And in all those years, you've never been engaged or married?" I turned to face him. "With all that mojo of yours?"

Donovan pulled me closer, his voice husky. "Mocking me?" He kissed me before settling back into the sofa. "Never married, but I was engaged a few years ago. We'd dated for several years. She wanted to get married even though I'd told her up front I'd never marry."

His face turned serious. "My parents didn't have a happy marriage. Mom had a temper like a trigger, was manipulative, controlling... The one thing Dad had control of was us living in Crimson Creek, and Mom wanted to live in the cities." Donovan's shoulders slumped. "She got her wish two weeks before she died, when she ended up in ICU in Minneapolis." He pinched the bridge of his nose. "After witnessing my parents' marriage, I vowed never to marry. To appease my girlfriend, we got engaged."

"What happened with your engagement?"

"She got sick of waiting for marriage."

I rubbed my fingers along his trimmed beard. "Just so you know, I'm not looking for marriage. Commitment? Yes. But I thought Trent was 'the one' years ago and was wrong. I let him make so many choices for my future. I don't want to ever give up that control again."

"Well then, it sounds like we're on the same page," Donovan whispered before taking me in his arms and laying me back against the couch, the moonlight filtering in the window, the blanket tossed aside.

Teenage hormones crawled inside me as I tugged off his shirt, knowing where it was leading yet yearning for something that scared me. My heart raced, and my fingers trembled, yet nothing was going to stop me.

"This isn't fair," I mumbled against Donovan's lips. His warm hands had just slipped inside my shirt, resting on my lower back.

He pulled back an inch. "What isn't?" His eyes were hooded, his cheeks flushed. "You want me to stop?" His question was followed by a whispered "Please don't ask me to stop."

I chuckled. "No, I don't want you to stop. But I have to warn you: I haven't been with a man since Trent... I'm a little rusty at this."

Donovan sighed in relief. "It's been a while for me too. But I don't think anything has changed in the mechanics of sex." He leaned his forehead on mine. "Just so you know, I had a vasectomy years ago."

I mumbled something about my IUD, one I'd had since Trent and I divorced, on the odd chance I would meet someone I cared about enough. Nearly three years had passed, but I was one-hundred-percent confident the wait had been worth it.

And as our clothing hit the floor, I was reassured that I hadn't forgotten what to do.

Sometime during the night, we made our way to his bed. We didn't wake until well after sunrise.

"Look what you've done to me." Donovan stretched. "I never sleep this late."

"Don't blame me. You're old. Old people sleep." I gave him a playful shove before pulling on my discarded shirt. "And don't you have to get to work?"

Donovan groaned and threw an arm over his eyes. "I wish my boss would fire me."

"You need to misbehave."

He pulled his arm away and yanked me down onto him. "Good idea," he said huskily.

An hour later, as we drove back to town, we spoke of our long-term goals.

"I'd like to find some acreage outside of town and build eventually, when I'm certain I can afford it," I said.

"Hey, I happen to know a builder."

"Hmm, it will depend on how expensive he is." I squinted his way. "And just so you know, my mother helped build our house. I learned a thing or two about building from my parents—not enough to build my own home, but I may be one of those hoverers who annoy the hell out of the contractor."

"I'll file that away for the future." Donovan tapped his head. "I may forgive that hovering if it involves some side perks."

"Eh, we'll see." After he dropped me off, I spent the day stocking the inventory that had arrived for the shop, thinking of all the possibilities in my future.

Every other Friday afternoon, the American Legion held a senior dance. On the third Friday in February, I was David's guest. A three-piece band set up on a small stage in the corner of the back room.

Hal and Maudie met us at the door. She laced her arm through mine and guided me to a large cookie sheet with what looked like cornmeal sprinkled in it.

"This is dance wax." Maudie released my arm and stepped into the granulated wax. "It'll help you glide, but too much and you'll slip-slide away," Maudie said. "You may have to fight all these women for a chance to dance with David. He's a popular partner here."

I voiced my concern about David's trick knee.

"Watch your own bobber," David said, overhearing my comment to Maudie. "They don't call me Fred Astaire for nothing."

Hal guffawed as we picked a table and hung our coats on the chairs. "Oh, please. Nobody calls you that. More like the Tasmanian Devil."

But Maudie was right. David was almost as popular a dance partner as the WWII Veteran, Jitterbug Jim, well into his nineties but not missing a step, even with a wooden leg. As the band played "The

Tennessee Waltz," David guided me around the floor, maneuvering around a dozen or more couples.

Everyone switched partners so that those who showed up without a partner weren't alone. At one point, I found myself guided along by a woman staring ninety in the eye, teaching me Schottische dance steps that seemed easy for her, not so much for me.

The event ended with a formation of veterans holding the American flag in the middle of everyone, as we created a circle around it. We all sang "God Bless America" with the three-piece band, and the patriotic tradition brought tears to my eyes.

As Hal pulled up to my shop, I said, "Thanks for the date," leaning over and kissing David's cheek before I got out.

He blushed. "Don't tell Hurdy Gurdy, or he'll come kick my butt."

"Ha! You've survived much worse than him. I think you can take anyone on," I said before thanking them all and closing the car door.

The following day was the annual snow-bocce tournament. I was taking the place of one of Kelly's friends who had recently had surgery on her foot. Our team consisted of Whip, Donovan, Kelly, and me. Bright and early on Saturday morning, David shuttled the four of us, along with other patrons, to ice bocce. Songs from his one-hit wonder list played: "Vehicle," by The Ides of March—one of David's favorite Goober songs—along with "Incense and Peppermints," and "Nice to Be with You."

The lake was miles from town, large enough for sixty-four teams and patrons. Our first draw was eight thirty in the morning, and we left Goober with a fist bump from David.

Each team of four had "pucks" to slide on sheets of ice, the puck resembling more of a curling stone made from round slices of wood with a handle. We knelt to slide the puck, and I felt like a marshmallow puff, trying to bend at the waist with all my winter wear.

The sun was out, and the air carried tantalizing aromas from the vendor trucks on shore. Little tiki bars were set up along the shoreline, and the food vendors used four-wheelers and sleds to transfer the food to the crowd.

Our team won two and lost two.

"I gotta say, I'm impressed," Whip said to me as we settled on a log on the ice to eat the slices of pizza we'd purchased.

"What? You thought I'd suck?" I elbowed him.

"You're all arms and legs. I thought it'd be like watching Olive Oyl on ice."

"I know how to tuck and roll." I kicked his boot with mine.

As we ate, the four of us lined up like turtles sunning themselves. *This is your happy place, Eden. Good people, good fun, low stress, and lots of laughter.* I could've sat there all day.

Throughout the day, I watched David's Goober dropping spectators off and picking ones up to shuttle back. We stayed until the championship to see who won, and the event, which raised money for childhood cancer, was deemed another huge success.

We caught Goober back to town after sunset. David entertained us with more one-hit-wonders like "How Do You Do?" by Mouth & MacNeal and "Go Back," by Crabby Appleton. When Donovan sang a falsetto harmony with "Tighter, Tighter," by Alive 'N Kickin', I worried I would pee my pants from laughing so hard.

David dropped off Donovan and me at my shop. "I can't believe you're still going strong," I told David before we departed.

He held up a five-hour energy drink. "I don't plan on working too late. Just want to get all the drunk spectators in the parking lot home. Then I'm calling it a night."

"Call me if you get some assholes that won't leave," Donovan said before we stepped out of Goober. After David shut the door, Donovan said, "Some of those spectators should've gone home hours ago."

Donovan left for home shortly afterward, both of us exhausted. I needed to leave by seven the next morning since Trent had plans Sunday afternoon. Ryan's school was closed until Wednesday due to a burst water pipe, so I was bringing him back with me. I hoped the more time Ryan spent in Crimson Creek, the more it would feel like home.

Chapter 37
David

Eden's team was part of the group on my first shuttle run for the ice-bocce tournament. Energized people wearing quirky costumes were packed in Goober, many singing along with the upbeat music I'd chosen, such as "Good Morning Starshine," "I Saw the Light," and the always-popular Goober song, "Hitchin' a Ride."

As the cloudy day turned to dusk, my tip bucket had overflowed more than once. I emptied it into the box I kept under my driver's seat, thinking of all the school lunches the money would buy for the children who never had enough funds in their lunch account.

My body ached, but I could sleep in the next day. Keeping drunks off the road gave me purpose, and pointing to Jean's senseless death as the sole reason I shuttled them was easier than admitting the truth. I saw my younger self in the boisterous drunks, drowning my nightmares after Vietnam, along with many other veterans. We felt we'd earned the right. But right or not, when we got behind the wheel back in the early 1970s, we could have killed someone.

My last run of the night, fifteen hours after I began, included six women and men who were staying at the motel seven miles outside of town. A second group was five men who reeked of booze, men who'd overstayed their time at the ice-bocce tournament.

The windchill had dipped to single digits, and the men had stepped onto Goober with ice hanging from their facial hair or a balaclava pulled over their mouth. They were staying at a cabin nine miles from town, and would be dropped off last.

Most of the side roads in our area had no streetlights. After dropping off the group at the motel, I headed down side roads into the darkness outside town with something niggling at me, a tingle up my spine. For a split second, I was back in the pilot seat of my F-105, on high alert. Sudden movement from behind threw me instantly into military mode, and I understood my premonition.

I had the advantage. Those young pups didn't know the hell I'd been through. They figured I was a tired old man, alone and vulnerable.

I would never be vulnerable again. Slowly, I slid my left hand into my pants pocket, where I kept my Swiss Army knife. The element of surprise would be on my side. Yes, there were five of them, two I sensed had moved up to the seat behind me, but I would not go down without a fight.

It happened a quarter mile before their destination. The gravel road was secluded, not a car or home in sight. When the largest of the men yanked at the wheel, kicking my foot off the gas and shoving his foot onto the brake before thrusting the gearshift into park, I was ready.

With the Swiss army knife tucked in my cupped hand, I waited for the attack. It came from behind. One of the men reached forward and pulled me from the seat, yanking my arms backward, my elbows touching much in the same way as when I was tortured in Vietnam.

That only fueled my anger and determination.

"I'll get the money!" the big guy yelled, cutting the zip ties that held the tip box in place on the floor under my seat. The man behind me, reeking of whiskey, strapped a zip tie around my wrists as I hid the knife in my hands.

"Get the hell out of the way so I can do his legs!" Whiskey Man yelled to Big Guy.

Once the tip box was securely in Big Guy's arms, he stepped aside to allow Whiskey Man to pull me down the aisle, where the other three men stood.

"Just take the money and go." I was smart enough to bet on reasoning instead of unleashing my fury.

"Do we look like idiots to you?" Big Guy said. "You'll come after us." He wore a furry hat, and it was hard to see where his beard ended and the hat began.

Another man with a green balaclava pulled up to his nose came to stand in front of me, holding some large zip ties. Ironically, "I Just Want to Celebrate" was playing, Rare Earth singing about celebrating another day of living. The lyrics fueled me.

With Whiskey Man behind me, I opened the Swiss army knife, placed the handle between my fingers, and leaned back hard enough to dig the knife into the man's leg.

The scream in my ear indicated I'd hit my mark. Whiskey Man's release set two men in motion, one holding my zip-tied arms back after kicking away the Swiss army knife, the other helping hold down my legs so Balaclava Man could tie my legs together as I kicked them like a donkey.

I was back in Vietnam, fighting for my life. I managed to kick the guy in the nuts before one of the other men knelt on my knees, shooting an intense pain down my bum leg that made it nearly impossible to hold back a yelp.

Demons from the past raged through me. As the men flipped me over to face the floor, I bit one of the men's hands when he tried coming at my mouth with a rag. His howl only instigated them to kick the ever-loving shit out of me. I internalized the pain. I'd learned well in Vietnam.

"You stupid old man!" one of them yelled, as if being old was sacrilegious.

"I'm a POW Vietnam veteran, you piece of shit!" My head was turned to the side, and from the back of Goober, I spotted the only man who hadn't touched me, his eyes wide as they met mine.

"Come on, let's go. You've got your money," the man in the back said.

He pushed the four other men toward the door, but not before I received a few more kicks from them, one connecting with my chin. It felt like my teeth had been kicked loose.

Wet warmth trickled down my chin, and sweat from fighting stung my eyes as I tried to see where my Swiss army knife had landed. When the four other men finally stumbled off the bus with the money, the young man who'd shooed them off stepped up with my knife. He quickly cut the zip ties on my feet and hands before rolling me over and placing the Swiss army knife in my hands.

"I'm so sorry! My grandpa served in Vietnam. Honest, I didn't know they'd do this to you." His eyes were filled with terror as he turned and ran off the bus, leaving me bruised, battered, but alive.

I lay there for a moment, unsure I could stand. I pulled myself on my elbows to the driver's seat, where my cell phone sat in its holder. Luckily, a cell tower was nearby. With shaking hands, I tapped on a contact. Several seconds later, a sleepy Donovan answered the phone.

Minutes later, he was crouched by my side, holding a blanket around my shaking body. The ambulance arrived soon after.

The last thing I remember was telling Donovan, "Guess I'm not as young as I thought."

Chapter 38
Eden

The ringing of my cell phone jolted me out of a deep sleep, sending my heart into instant panic. Midnight calls rarely meant good news. I blinked at the screen: Donovan.

"Hey, what's wrong?" I shot up in bed.

"It's David. Some guys attacked him in Goober tonight," Donovan's words rushed out. "I'm at the ER with him. I know you've got to leave early to pick up Ryan, so don't come to the hospital. I called to let you know they're checking him over. I'll stay here with him."

"Oh my God! How bad? I mean..." I struggled to ask, "Will he be okay?" bracing myself for the answer.

"I think so." Donovan relayed the events of the past hour. "They're checking for internal damage. He fought back, of course, but there were five men. Sounds like one of them stayed behind to cut him loose."

"Cut him *loose*?" I had horrible images of David being restrained. Having heard what he'd gone through in Vietnam, I could only guess at what his mind relived during the attack.

"Zip ties on his hands and feet. Anyway, I've got to go. The doctor just came out of the room, and I'm guessing she'll want more info from me. I won't call again unless he takes a turn for the worse."

"Yes, thank you. I'll check with you in the morning." I was sick with worry over what David had gone through. *And for what? Money?* I slept little after we hung up and was on the road early. I hoped

David would be able to identify the men and that they'd be charged and tossed in jail.

I called Donovan when I stopped for gas before picking Ryan up at nine. "He's been sleeping for several hours. He's bruised and battered, and they want to keep him here at least another day," Donovan said, exhaustion dragging his words. "Hal and Maudie are arriving soon to take a shift so I can get some sleep."

"We'll be back by one," I said. With Ryan's school closed until Wednesday, I'd already decided we would spend the time in Crimson Creek. David's attack cemented that decision.

After picking Ryan up at Trent's, I filled him in on what I knew of the attack. We pulled into the hospital parking lot after a quick stop at the apartment for sandwiches.

"We don't want to wake him if he's sleeping," I told Ryan as we walked through the lot.

"Yep," Ryan said as we entered the hospital. "Can David stay with us if he needs help?"

"Oh, sweetie, that's nice of you to think about that. David would struggle with our steps. That's why we haven't invited him to the apartment. We'll figure it all out once we talk to the doctors." I hugged Ryan, appreciative of his kind heart.

Hal and Maudie sat in chairs alongside David's hospital bed and stood when Ryan and I entered, leading us into the hallway to give us an update while David slept. "The doc said David's going to be sore for several days. No internal bleeding, but a bruised spleen, and they had to stitch up his lip and a cut on his forehead." Hal rubbed a hand over his red-rimmed eyes. "His bum knee is puffed up like a hot air balloon, and I'm guessing he'll have bruises everywhere."

"Do you two want to go home? We can stay here with David." Even normally bouncy Maudie had bags under her eyes.

"That'd be nice," Hal said. "We were babysitting two of our little great-grandkids, and between them and Donovan's phone call, well..."

Maudie took over. "We spent the night at our son's house and couldn't leave until they arrived home from the hotel they'd stayed at last night." Maudie covered a yawn. "Those great-grandkids have a way of reminding us we aren't as young as we think we are."

Hal pulled me aside before we opened David's door. "This is going to throw him for a loop—again. David doesn't like his cheese moved. He needs order and control in his life after having zero control in prison." He rubbed his temple. "I'm more worried about his mental health now that I know he will physically recover."

After Hal and Maudie left, Ryan and I sat by David's bed. I studied his stitches, bruises, bandages, and scratched hands and chose to focus on the steady rise and fall of David's chest. He'd recover, at least physically. But, as Hal mentioned, the attack surely resurrected torturous memories.

After a while, a nurse came in to check on David, and shortly after she left, David woke up, his watery eyes struggling to focus on where he was.

"We're here, David. You're in the hospital, but you're going to be alright." I hurried to his side, gently touching his hand resting against the sheet.

David slowly turned his head to me before moving on to Ryan. "Well, look at what the cat dragged in," he said groggily to Ryan, attempting a smile with the uninjured side of his mouth.

"Hi, David." Ryan's fingers grazed David's arm. "We'll take care of you," he promised, sounding very grown up.

"Well, that makes me feel better already." David's words were sluggish.

"The nurse was just in and said the doctor will check in later," I said, wishing I could hug David and make sure he was all in one piece.

"Ah, I may stay here a while longer. That nurse is a looker and could be the next Mrs. Carpenter if I play my cards right."

I snorted, guessing the nurse wasn't all that much older than me, but was relieved to hear David making jokes. "Were you able to identify the men? Had you seen them before?"

"Not locals." David coughed, and I held a glass of water so that he could drink through the straw. "I gave the cops the address of the cabin where they were supposed to be dropped off. Unless the men didn't stay there, I'm guessing they found the buttheads. The cop said someone from the department will follow up with me." He winced.

"Where does it hurt? How can I help?"

"Everywhere. Especially my mouth and gut. But at least one of those men is hurting this morning. I got him with my Swiss army knife," David said with pride.

"Cool!" Ryan piped up. "I knew you'd fight back. You're my hero, David." Then he did what I yearned to do. He stepped forward and placed his head gently on David's chest and gave him a careful hug.

By late Monday morning, David had been approved for release. The doctor went over extended care for David's injuries with Hal, Maudie, and me, and someone from law enforcement had stopped in earlier to speak with David. Five men had been arrested at the address David had given them.

I'd let Ryan sleep in after waking him to tell him I was heading back to the hospital. Donovan had called me twice from his job site, and David looked like he'd fought a battle and lost. But he hadn't.

"Once he leaves here, we'll take turns staying with him," Hal told the doctor.

Louise and I had spoken several times since the attack, and Hal, Donovan, and I assured her we would take care of her dad. She had somehow finagled a promise from David that he would behave. Louise had enough going on with her husband's recent health setback.

"How long do you think before he can be alone?" Maudie said. "He's a stubborn old goat, and if he hears it from you, maybe he'll listen."

The same female doctor who had cared for David the day before eyed him up as he batted his eyes at her. "I'd say at least a few days before David will be able to maneuver around on his own. We need to keep an eye on that knee of yours," she said, pointing a finger at him.

"His lungs are clear, and we want him up and moving around as his pain tolerance will allow," the doctor said. "And I hate to be the one to remind you of this, David, but you are what we consider elderly." Her words were interrupted by his obstinate grunt. "It's going to take you longer to heal. So, despite your protest at four this morning that you were fine and could go home, I want to remind you that if you overdo it, you'll end up back here."

David raised his eyebrows and gave her an innocent look. "You want to see me again, don't you?"

The doctor let out a laugh and shook her head.

"Donovan will stay at David's at night, and we three will take turns with him during the day," Hal said. "We'll make sure he behaves."

"Good luck with that," the doctor said, winking before she turned and left the room.

"Once we bust you out of here, we need to stop by the police station so you can identify the one nice dude for them," Maudie told David.

"All right. Time's a-wasting here. I want to go home and get into my pajamas and have you wait on me hand and foot." Fatigue pulled down David's battered face.

"Ugh, already with the lip." Maudie shook her head. "You get us for the next hour or two, and you know me, David, I like bossing people around."

"Yes, but Hal needs it. Not me—I'm an angel."

"A very battered angel," Maudie said as Hal helped David out of bed with the assistance of a walker. "One I love like chocolate." She planted a kiss on his scruffy cheek.

I had the three-to-eight shift and would drop Ryan off at Whip's to hang out with Willow after school. Kelly was bringing her son Mason over to meet Ryan and spend a few hours with him and Willow.

While Hal and Maudie took David to the police department then brought him home to get him settled, I went back to my apartment and made sweet-and-sour chicken and rice for Ryan and me, along with roasted chicken and dressing to bring to David's—bland and easy to chew. He had told me months before that he despised rice since it had been a staple in the prisoner of war camp. Ryan and I ate an early dinner before I dropped him off and headed to David's.

Ryan and I would take the shift Tuesday morning before we headed back to the cities for Ryan to attend school on Wednesday. In a little over a month, I would be a permanent resident of Crimson Creek. *So many changes.* Yet I couldn't go back to the way life had been. It hadn't felt like *my* life. But it did now.

Chapter 39

I arrived at David's late Monday afternoon to find him shaved, showered, and dressed in pajamas and a bathrobe. Hal was making him tea, and Maudie applied a salve to David's hands and face.

"Ah, this is the life," David quipped, but I caught the haunted look in his eyes.

I placed the casserole dish in his fridge for later and settled in at the end of the sofa near David's recliner. "How did it go at the police department?"

"Got them all identified. Some were easy, with their scratch wounds and whiskey breath's knife wound. The only one I cared to spare was the young man who cut the zip ties and apologized." David's hand shook as he took a drink of water.

After Hal and Maudie left, David napped in his recliner. He woke with a little more color in his cheeks and a few wise comments about not needing a babysitter. When Louise called, we spoke for a few minutes before I handed David his landline phone on speaker, per Louise's request.

"Eden said you're back to your sassy self, so I guess you're well enough for me to say this," Louise huffed into the phone. "This can't happen again, Dad. Time to find a new purpose."

"Maybe now he will finally agree to shuttle bikers and kayakers for me." I eyed David, who scowled before looking away.

"Do it, Dad. Those people won't be three sheets to the wind!"

David refused to look my way, but his shoulders softened, his chin no longer jutting out. I didn't need him to say I was right. I just needed him to be safe.

When he muttered, "We'll see," I considered it a win and thanked Louise.

David was in no shape to shuttle the bar crowd for the next few weeks. The owners of two of the bars had hired a young man who had a taxi service of sorts. Every business in the area was experiencing a slow time, with the weather hovering between winter and spring, a good transition time. David had yet to confirm that he was done with the bar crowd.

While David recovered and our care shifts diminished, I put in twelve-hour days in the shop, stocking inventory and helping Hal and Oliver assemble bikes. Bikes, kayaks, paddleboards, and canoes would be rented by the half day—four hours—or all day—eight hours. I started small with my inventory, one of the many business tips I'd learned from my parents. I'd also promised myself not to extend beyond the one-third of my savings I'd set aside for inventory.

I'd done the calculations for my return on investments. With half-day and full-day rental pricing, I estimated that ten full-day rentals would cover the price of each kayak and paddleboard. Canoes' payback would take longer, and I kept that stock to a minimum. Mountain bike rental rate of return depended on the bike price, but for the most part, the estimated return on investment for both fat-tire bikes and mountain bikes was twenty full-day rentals.

Maudie and I spoke often, between her helping with store inventory so she'd be familiar with stock and our daily chats about David's progress.

"Hal and I have always had David over for dinner on March fourth to celebrate the anniversary of his release from prison in Vietnam," Maudie had told me after David's attack. "We're delaying it this year so David can heal, and we're inviting others over too. We want it to be a celebration of not only that anniversary but also the fact he was a badass and survived the attack by those greedy assholes."

So, on March eleventh, I was welcomed into Hal and Maudie's home, along with several other friends of David. The guest of honor greeted me with a warm hug as if I were family. I missed my scattered family, missed having a grandpa since Mom's parents died when she was seven and Dad's father died when I was a toddler. David had become the grandpa I'd always wanted, a man I'd come to love like family.

"Smells good in here," I said. Maudie took my coat and the bottle of wine I'd brought. I handed Hal a tray of pinwheels I'd made, and he added them to the appetizers table.

"That's me." David raised his hand.

"You smell like pot roast?" I thought of John Travolta in the movie *Michael*, when he smelled like chocolate chip cookies and the women followed him. "I knew there was a reason I liked you."

"Hey, now." Donovan stepped between us and put an arm around David. "Don't be enticing my girlfriend."

"You already know that if David was forty years younger, I'd dump you in a minute."

Maudie laughed at our banter. "Move to Hollywood, Eden, and nobody would blink an eye at you and David. Come on, let's join the rest in the kitchen." She led the way to their kitchen and dining room, where everyone mingled with drinks and appetizers.

Around a dozen of us gathered at the table and center island for a meal of pot roast, potatoes, and carrots as we toasted David.

Everyone left after dinner, leaving Donovan and me alone with the guest of honor and hosts. We'd cleaned up the kitchen, and the five of us settled in their living room, where they had a fire going in the fireplace.

"The doctor suggested David meet with a counselor after the attack a few weeks ago," Hal said and got a steely glare from David in response.

"Only because you pig-prodded her," David accused.

"Eh, maybe. But you agreed to it, so..." Hal took a yellowed newspaper clipping from his desk drawer and handed it to Donovan and me. It was from David's release in March 1973. We sat on the sofa, my eyes darting from the thin, handsome young man in the photo to David, settled in the recliner, imagining his adjustments in life over the past forty-two years.

David's chin wobbled, and he struggled to find his words at first, but with Hal's hand on David's shoulder for encouragement, David took us back to those years when the POWs fought to keep their sanity and then came home to broken families. He spoke of comrades who struggled to mainstream back into society and how they all were required to meet with a psychologist once a month. Everyone pretended to be fine.

"I told the shrink, 'You hold my future in your hands.' I refused to admit to trauma and nightmares so I could keep flying," David said. "None of us was fine. The world had changed while we were gone. I was still back in 1966, in my mind."

He folded his arms across his chest. "The last movie I'd seen before getting shot down was *The Sound of Music*. I came home to *The Exorcist* being the big hit of '73." His words were followed by a harrumph.

"Women's skirts barely covered their butts, men wore their hair long like girls, everyone was talking about sex and thumbing their nose at the world."

I would've laughed at his obvious disgust if not for the reality of how much the world had changed in those years. Those had been years before I was born, but I was well aware of the changes.

"Trying to catch up with it all was as difficult as having to swallow how the things we'd endured had been hidden." David took the shot of bourbon Hal handed him.

"The government had a good idea of what we went through." David scowled. "After capture, before the Vietnamese deemed a prisoner worthy of feeding, we spent a week in the 'fire furnace.' If we survived, we went to the Hanoi Hilton. In that week, we were shackled, tortured, and starved." I held one of the newspaper images of a beaten David after his capture, one that had been purposely leaked by the Vietnamese to the United States government.

Hal stepped in. "The Vietnamese were savvy torturers. They perfected techniques that maximized pain but minimized disfigurement so you'd appear uninjured in front of a camera."

Maudie reached for her husband's hand.

David's nostrils flared. "Have I ever told you about The Lump?" He eyed Donovan, who shook his head.

"Guess I might as well let that demon out too." David winced as if reliving the pain. "He was a commander and interrogator, one of the evilest men ever."

David pointed at his own forehead. "The Lump got his name because he had a large fatty tumor sticking out of his forehead. I got him my first day at Heartbreak Hotel, when they brought me to a small soundproof torture room, bloody rags piled up in the corner."

I leaned forward, bile rising in me at the image David painted.

"The room had medieval contraptions, including a giant meat hook on the ceiling," David said. "They clasped my wrists behind me and into tight cast-metal manacles. When I wouldn't answer The Lump's questions about Air Force targets, they looped a rope around my arms above the elbows and pulled it back."

David absently rubbed his wrists and elbows. "Let me tell you, your elbows are not supposed to touch in the back."

I wanted to fling myself at David and comfort him forty-plus years after the fact. Instead, I let him talk, hoping the toxic cesspool would flow out of his memory and let him heal.

"The Vietnamese were skilled. They knew exactly how far they could go before they completely ripped a limb out of its socket." David worked his jaw, pressing his lips together.

"When I wouldn't give The Lump any info, they connected my ankles to the manacled cuffs to keep my arms up behind my head. My hands and arms would swell to twice their size, my skin turning purplish black." His Adam's apple bounced up and down. "Then he looped a rope around my neck. If I let my arms droop down even a little, the rope would choke me."

The room was silent, other than the crackling of logs burning in the fireplace. I sensed Hal already knew these details since he didn't appear shocked, but pain etched his eyes. Hal likely wished one of the rescue missions he'd flown in Vietnam had been saving David.

David continued, explaining how initially, when the interrogators came back and undid all the ropes, he thought it would be the end of the torture. "Until the nerves in my arms were reconnected with the rest of my system and blood rushed into them. The pain was more severe than anything I'd known before, as if all my nerves had been set on fire."

I didn't realize I was crying until Maudie stood and handed me a box of tissues, taking two herself to mop her tears.

"You okay?" David asked, a look of concern on his face.

I laughed as I cried. "You're asking *me* if I'm okay? I swear, David, I will never whine about anything again." I blew my nose. "Well, I hope I won't."

"I'm writing that down," Donovan murmured.

David continued, pointing at a photo he'd taken from his shirt pocket. His thumb grazed over the faded Polaroid. "This was in the early 1980s. I found it in the Vietnam box," David said. "The three men who were in the cell next to me when I was in solitary. We met again at a reunion. Those men kept me going every day. I wouldn't have made it without their communication."

David gingerly tucked the photo back into his pocket. "We tapped as a way to communicate, but all the prisoners also realized that our tin cup, if held up to the cement block wall, magnified our voice to the cell next door if they held their ear up to their tin cup in the same location on the other side of the wall."

Donovan leaned over and patted David's arm. "Thank you for sharing this. It has to be like reliving a never-ending nightmare, but I hope it helps you in the long run. I'd heard of some of this over the years, but man, I had no idea of the depth of the horror you endured."

"Makes you want to be a little kinder to me, doesn't it, Hurdy Gurdy?" David said.

"Eh, we'll see." Donovan's eyes were damp.

I moved to the other side, leaning my head on David's shoulder. "I never fully realized the reality behind the POW bracelet when I found it. Never grasped what POWs endured."

I pulled back and met David's eyes. "After everything you went through, shuttling harmless outdoor lovers should be easy-peasy." I smiled, and my heart warmed as he reciprocated. "I promise to shoo most of the mountain bikers toward Hal, and you can have the meek and mild kayakers."

"Fine, fine." He eyed Hal. "Guess you and Grover have some shuttle competition."

"Competition, my ass." Hal waved his arm as if shooing a pesky fly. "Goober's got nothing on Grover. I'm painting him bright blue, and Maudie's sewing slipcovers for the seats with outdoorsy material." He folded his hands over his stomach and flashed a grin for his friend, who had finally agreed to join our Fun-Key Monkey employee family.

Chapter 40

The third Friday in March, Donovan and I had our first "fancy date," as he called it—our last weekend together before I opened the shop and moved full-time to Crimson Creek. I had one more week at the apartment in the cities.

The supper club, The Hokey Pokey, was situated outside of town on Key Lake and was known for spectacular food, stunning sunsets, and a spacious dance floor.

I showered, blow-dried my recently trimmed hair, and stood in front of my closet, trying to figure out what to wear, shying away from red so that it wouldn't accentuate my new "flaw." *What the heck, Eden? Why now instead of your teen years?* Just as I slipped on a black-and-white sweater, Donovan knocked on the apartment door—early. I'd given him a key to the store the month before so that I didn't have to keep running downstairs to let him in.

Now, in my fluster, I opened the door with one hand and held the pointer finger of my other hand over the side of my nose. "Hey, you're early." I stepped back to let Donovan in.

Dressed in a pale-blue polo shirt and cream-colored khakis, Donovan looked as snazzy as I'd ever seen him.

"Hubba hubba." I wiggled my eyebrows, keeping my finger on my face as I eyed him up and down and then burst out laughing.

"What?" Donovan said, zeroing in on my face. "Are you going to dance like that tonight?" He pointed at my finger glued to my nose.

"Are you?" I gasped, attempting to talk through my laughter. Seeing Donovan's eyes squint, I pointed at his shoes—platform shoes. "Did you rob the Bee Gees on the way over?"

"Nope. John Travolta. I left him barefoot in the alley."

"You can't be serious about those shoes." The clunky heels were at least three inches high. "You'll twist an ankle."

"I didn't want to be shorter than you when we dance." Donovan pointed at my bare feet. "Unless you're going barefoot."

"I'll wear ballet flats. You are *not* going out in public wearing those. Where'd you get them? Please tell me you haven't had them for decades." I grimaced.

Then Donovan caught me off guard, pulling my finger from my face. "Ah ha! A zit!" he proclaimed with enthusiasm.

"I know, right?" I whined. The pimple was big enough to have its own pulse.

"Don't you have any of that pancake stuff you can put over it, you teenybopper?"

"I don't wear makeup." I headed to the bathroom. "I've got lip gloss and eyebrow pencil, and that's it." My shoulders slumped. "I think it's stress. I haven't had a pimple since I went through my divorce. Should we stay home?"

"Hell no." He came to stand behind me in the bathroom as we stared into the mirror. "We deserve a night out. You're beautiful whether your whole face erupts in craters—oops, I mean tiny imperfections—or not. I don't care." He turned me around for a kiss, wiping out any thoughts about my pimple and his shoes.

Eventually, I pulled away. "I'm not as kind as you are. You're changing those shoes before we go out." I poked him in the chest.

"I've got my shoes in the car. I just wanted to get a reaction out of you."

"It worked. And if you'll give me a minute, I'm going to try and fix this monster on my face." I'd been icing it earlier to lessen the swelling. I dabbed eyebrow pencil on the spot, blending the dark brown with a dab of moisturizer to make it easier to spread. "There. Cinderella is ready for the ball."

I slipped on black ballet shoes and linked my arm through Donovan's, my overnight bag slung on my shoulder. He changed his shoes in his truck.

On the drive to The Hokey Pokey, we talked about Donovan's decision to have a vasectomy when Cassie was a teen. "I didn't want to start over again. I'd been a caregiver for others ever since I came home in first grade and found little Gabriel crying from hunger while Mom was passed out in bed."

"I get it," I said. "As much as I wanted a large family, that ship has sailed." I turned to Donovan. "I guess the Fun-Key Monkey is my new baby."

After we arrived at the restaurant, we feasted on prime rib and shrimp, split a raspberry cheesecake, and were relaxing over drinks when the DJ fired up the music, kicking it off with "Someday" by Green Day.

Slowly, the dance floor filled up, and when "When I Was Your Man" by Bruno Mars began playing, Donovan pushed out his chair and held his hand out to me.

"I'll apologize ahead of time for my less-than-stellar dance moves," Donovan said as he led me onto the dance floor. "Remember, I missed school dances my senior year and all that college fun of hitting nightclubs."

"Your devotion to raising Cassie more than makes up for a lack of dance moves," I murmured before kissing his neck.

"Good. Now, I need to think of how you can make up for that godawful pimple..." Donovan's smile was wicked. "We'll work on that tonight after we go to bed."

I laughed and settled back in his arms, looking forward to our weekend together before I left for the cities for a final move.

On Saturday night, Donovan and I took a road trip north of town toward Duluth with Donovan's Nikon camera and tripod. We set it up in a field surrounded by darkness, donned winter wear, and captured the most colorful northern lights show in years.

Everything in my apartment in the cities had been cleaned or packed by the last Saturday in March. I'd dropped off all my business suits and high heels at a thrift shop, and I whooped for joy as I walked out the door.

Volunteers from the Boys Club arrived Saturday morning to take our beds, kitchen table, and chairs, which I'd donated to the club. With everything packed away, Ryan and I ate out at his favorite pizza place before settling in for the night at our apartment. In the morning, I would drop him off at Trent's and head back to Crimson Creek.

We played cards and cribbage on the living room floor before making our beds with blankets and foam pads.

When we lay side by side on the floor, the light from underneath the microwave casting shadows on the walls, we made up stories. We hadn't done that for more than a year, and it warmed my heart when Ryan suggested it.

The longer we went on, the more creative and outrageous our stories became, bringing us gut-busting laughter that echoed in the nearly empty apartment. That night, our last in the apartment, became my most cherished memory of our time there.

And after I dropped Ryan off at Trent's on Sunday, I went back to the apartment for a final walkthrough, finally collapsing in tears on the living room floor. I called Stevie Grace, Ellie, and my parents. And not a single one told me I was making the wrong decision.

With my plan for The Fun-Key Monkey to be closed Tuesdays and Wednesdays, I decided on a soft open on Thursday, April second. All my employees had been trained on the cash register, the rental schedule on the computer, and the phone system.

Hal and David wouldn't be busy until the lakes opened up enough for the kayaks, canoes, and paddleboards, but both—being pilots—knew their way around equipment. They would help with bike maintenance when Oliver was in school. And Oliver and Hadley would work weekends until school was out for the summer and they went full-time.

Ryan and I set up a schedule for calling every morning around seven while he got ready for school.

"Are you nervous, Mom?" Ryan asked when I called him on Thursday morning.

"A little. If anyone walks into the shop, I'll be shocked. But it will feel good to have the lights on, the Open sign lit up." I sipped my coffee. "Want me to call you tonight?"

"Yep. I'm going to Brady's after school, but Dad's picking me up on his way home from work," Ryan said.

Baseball practice would start soon.

"I'll call you after seven, let you know if I survived. I love you." I said the last words softly, to comfort myself more than Ryan.

"Back at ya, Mom," Ryan said, a smile in his voice.

A little before ten, I flipped on the shop lights, turned on the Open sign, and unlocked the front door. I had plenty of paperwork to keep me busy throughout the day. Any customer would be a bonus.

As it turned out, I had a few bonuses. Shortly after I opened, two young men entered, wearing bike gear.

"Good morning. Can I help you find anything?"

"Yes. Boy, are we glad to see you're open," the taller man said, rubbing his hands together. "I lost my bike gloves last night."

I glanced at his red hands. The temperature was in the high thirties with a projected high later of midforties. "Gloves are over here." I led the way toward some shelving in a corner.

"Thanks."

While he checked out bike gloves, his friend thumbed through the heavier moisture-wicking neon-colored bike jackets.

By the time they left, I had sold a pair of gloves, a lime-green bike jacket, and a neck gaiter. I waved my hands in the air. *Real customers, Eden!*

During the rest of the day, I made two more sales—barely enough to pay the light bill but more than enough to fill my happiness bucket.

Chapter 41

David had invited Donovan and me over for supper that night for a celebration of my first day in the shop. I arrived before Donovan with a bottle of David's favorite chardonnay.

"Welcome, Florence Nightingale," David said when he opened the front door. He'd called me that when I helped him out after he arrived home from the hospital almost six weeks before. He'd been healing, and I'd been busy, so we hadn't seen each other much.

"Hey there, bossy britches." I handed him the wine, knowing he'd drink only one glass.

"Who, me?" David feigned ignorance.

"No cane? You're doing well."

David had been using a walker or a cane after the assault. "Not if I can get by without it. Slow and steady wins the race. Shall I uncork this bad boy?" He pointed at the wine.

"Sure, for yourself. I'm good with water, thanks. My brain is struggling already, and I'll need what few remaining brain cells I've got left for work tomorrow."

David poured himself a glass and another one for Donovan when he showed up minutes later, carrying a cake box from the bakery.

I peeked in the clear cover. "Aww, how sweet. A 'Don't Screw It Up' cake. I suppose you're going to tell me they had a cake that already had that written in icing?"

"Of course." Donovan kissed me.

David turned off the oven and opened it to release the aroma of meat loaf and baked potatoes. "I'm celebrating that it doesn't hurt to chew anymore."

"It's good to see you back to normal," Donovan said. "Or as normal as you get." He gave David a side hug before we helped set out the food.

While we ate, we talked of the forecast projecting warmer temps. "Baseball practice starts next week for Ryan in the cities." I would be able to catch some of his practices and games when I spent Tuesday and Wednesday nights at Stevie Grace's apartment.

"My summer league starts mid-April," Donovan said. "I'm guessing the school leagues start soon."

"Played the sport myself back in the day," David said. "We had a great neighborhood team here when I was growing up." He flexed a muscle under his sweater. "Played in high school and again on our Air Force team the first few years, back in the late 1950s."

"Did you want to play on our team?" Donovan deadpanned.

"Eh, I don't want to show you young'uns up," David said.

"Have you checked into registering Ryan in a summer league here?" Donovan asked.

"I need to do that. His league in the cities ends when school is out, usually around Memorial Day weekend. Is it through a parks-and-rec program?"

"Yep. Ask Chase about it. Mason played the past couple of years. They don't start games until early June, but I'm not sure about practices," Donovan said.

I made a mental note to ask Kelly about summer baseball. A team would be a great way for Ryan to make new friends in town.

After the shop closed the following night, I attended my first Crimson Creek Mountain Bike Crew volunteer meeting with

Kelly. The group worked with the DNR to maintain the trails, things like trimming branches and rerouting water after a hard rain. One of the benefits of the rich iron ore soil was its quick drying.

"Other mountain bike trails may shut down for a day or more after a storm," Kelly explained once the meeting was over. "Here, the trails are usually dry in a couple of hours."

On our walk home through a quiet downtown, I asked, "Have you received information yet on Mason's summer baseball league? I'd like to sign Ryan up if it's not too late."

"Yes, I got an email about it last week. I'll forward it to you when I get home. Practice doesn't start until May, and their first game isn't until early June," Kelly said. "It's a great group of kids. The boys have fun whether they win or lose. Of course, they have a lot more fun if it's a win."

"That's what Ryan needs, less pressure with kids he doesn't know yet," I said.

After Kelly arrived home, she forwarded the email, and I called the contact number listed. I spoke with one of the coaches and explained Ryan's situation. "If he's on a baseball team already, I'm not too worried about him missing our practices in May. We've got a couple of summer-cabin residents who participate in the league too, and they're in the same boat."

"Thank you. I'll register Ryan as soon as I know for sure he's interested." I hung up and immediately called Trent's cell.

Ryan answered. "Hi, Mom. Dad ran to the grocery store to get milk."

I relayed the summer baseball league information.

"Awesome!" Ryan gave a whoop. "I can play even though I'll miss practices in May?"

"Yes. The coach said there are other kids in a similar situation. As long as you're practicing and playing on another team, you're good."

"Okay. And you said Mason is in the summer league?"

"Yes, but since he's a year older, you may be on different teams. Either way, it will be a good opportunity to meet other kids."

"Yeah."

Ryan's enthusiasm dropped a notch, but I couldn't worry. Nobody said everything would be smooth sailing. Yet that night as I lay in bed, I didn't think about the shop. I thought of how one misstep might topple my world with Ryan like a wrong move in Jenga.

When Stevie Grace called me in mid-April and asked if she could visit me in Crimson Creek, I shouted, "Hell-yes-I-miss-you!"

The Fun-Key Monkey had been open for two weeks, business fluctuating from tomb-quiet on a cold Thursday to no-time-to-eat busy on an unusually warm Saturday. So far, things had gone well, thanks to advertising in the local newspaper and a Minnesota bike magazine. We'd rented out several bikes, each one taking roughly ten minutes to adjust the bike and helmet to each rider—a job each employee had been trained in, thanks to Oliver.

Maudie worked Monday afternoons, and I headed to SG's apartment then drove back to Crimson Creek Thursday mornings and took over for Maudie by noon.

SG flew in to Minneapolis on Thursday morning, and I picked her up after dropping Ryan off at school. I bounced like a cheerleader as SG walked toward me outside the terminal gates.

"Ugh, I missed you!" we said at once, squeezing each other after not seeing each other for over a year.

Stevie Grace, a few inches shorter, was looking more like her mom every year, their long auburn hair and green eyes so similar.

We made a pit stop at SG's apartment so that she could go through a few things she'd kept in storage there. "My lease is up in

July, and I think I'm going to cancel it then." She grimaced. "Is that okay with you?"

"Are you kidding? You don't need my approval, silly," I said as we packed up SG's extra dishes. "Ryan will be with me most of the summer, and if—God forbid—he decides to stay in the cities next fall for school, I'll worry about things then. Trent's mom reached out to me last month, saying I'm always welcome at her home."

"That's kind of Emily," Stevie Grace said. "Hopefully, you won't need a place."

"I hope not too, but it's nice to know I've got a room there." I was thankful Emily had room for me and lived close to Trent.

An hour later, we left SG's apartment and headed to Crimson Creek. "Okay, tell me all about him," Stevie Grace said.

"Donovan? You'll meet him tomorrow. He's cute—up-north rugged cute, not GQ cute." I thought of what attracted me to him. "He's funny, smart, not interested in marriage, works hard but knows how to kick back, would rather be outside instead of in a gym or behind a computer, helps people... and is a small-town guy." I would have been interested in Donovan no matter if I'd met him in the cities, but his preference for small-town living was a definite plus. "And don't say you'll live vicariously through me. You've dated a dozen more guys than I have the past few years."

"Yes, but traveling all the time makes getting serious difficult." SG leaned against the headrest. "It's one of the reasons I'm thinking of changing careers."

"Any thoughts on your next career?"

"I'm not sure. Something where I can settle down and see the same people more than a few hours at a time." Stevie Grace gazed out her window. "I don't have to tell you that my biological clock is ticking rather loudly. I'd like a husband, kids, and a community that I'm active in, not just a stopping point until I take off again."

I didn't voice that I thought Crimson Creek would be a good community for Stevie Grace. I would let the town sell itself. The ice had gone off the lakes recently, and as we pulled into town, the sun sent sparkles over Crow Lake.

Stevie Grace rolled down her window. "I love it already. Reminds me of Grandfield when we were growing up." She missed our hometown as much as I did.

I pulled into the shop's back lot, where I'd been parking since the shop opened. "Donovan gave me the keys to his pontoon that he docked at a friend's place down the road from here. We can use it this afternoon if you want."

"Sounds good. Do we need the pontoon for the bar and restaurant you said we're going to tonight?"

"Nope. It's only a couple of blocks away."

We went in through the back of the store and headed up to my apartment before I checked with Maudie in the shop.

"You're staying in my room." I pointed SG toward my bedroom. "I'm taking Ryan's."

"I can sleep in there." SG stood in his doorway next to me. "You've made it home for Ryan, haven't you?" She nodded toward the Vikings throw on a Twins beanbag sitting in the corner.

"I'll do whatever I can to make him feel at home."

SG set her suitcase on a chair in my bedroom. "Mountain biking tomorrow morning and kayaking on the mine-pit lakes in the afternoon, right?" She unpacked her toiletries and set them on a bathroom shelf before I gave her the two-minute tour of the apartment.

"Yes. Saturday looks nice too, but we might as well take advantage of the sunshine and hit the lake this afternoon. We can go on the pontoon again on Saturday." I opened the sliding door to the large deck—four times the size of my old apartment's—which would soon hold several planters with vegetables and flowers.

"You'll meet Donovan and David tomorrow night when we go to Donovan's for dinner, you'll meet Kelly and some of the other biker chicks tomorrow, and I'll introduce you to Maudie in the shop before we head out on the lake." Maudie was working all day until Hadley arrived from school at three, and they would work the same shifts on Friday, with Hal and Oliver taking over on Saturday.

I felt a little guilty for taking days off from the shop after being open only three weeks, but I hadn't seen Stevie Grace for over a year. I missed her, and I wanted her to fall in love with Crimson Creek as much as I had.

Chapter 42

SG and I spent the afternoon cruising the shoreline of Crow Lake on Donovan's pontoon, basking in the warmest day we'd had since last fall. Stevie Grace relaxed on the bench seat across from my captain's chair.

"What's going on there?" She pointed with her margarita glass toward the demolition taking place two blocks from my shop.

"The city is putting in more parking. They tore down three uninhabitable homes." I nodded toward downtown. "They're hoping it will keep the mountain bikers off the main street."

"Will it affect your business?"

"It should help. I only have so much parking space for people who want to use our shuttle service out to the rec area." I took a sip of my margarita. "David was one of the people pushing the City Council to do this. The locals are happy to have the tourists—and their money—but not so happy if they take over downtown and block their driveways."

After three hours of chips, salsa, margaritas, and sunshine, we docked Donovan's pontoon at his friend's place. I'd had one margarita. I couldn't say the same for SG.

Back at the apartment, Stevie Grace showered first, peeking her head out of the bathroom door after toweling off. "Hey, do you have any aloe? I'm a little sunburned on my back."

I rarely got burned, my one-quarter Korean heritage more forgiving than SG's mostly Norwegian blood. "I've got an aloe plant. I'll break off a piece," I said.

"I hope this doesn't mask my natural sexy scent." SG sniffed the aloe piece I handed her to peel open. "You know, in case there's another single guy in town besides Donovan."

"Yes, sassy pants, there are other single men in town."

After I showered, we walked to Mined Your Business wearing sundresses and light button-up sweaters. The bar was busy with regulars who'd finished their workdays.

"How about that table over there?" I pointed at a two-person table tucked in the corner.

Stevie Grace perused the bar. "Or how about up at the bar? I want to be part of the scene, not tucked away as an observer."

"It's louder there. We won't be able to visit as much."

"I've talked to you enough." SG elbowed me. "Now it's time for me to ogle that dude behind the bar."

I about choked. "Whip?" Two other bartenders were in the middle of the U-shaped bar, but I was fairly certain SG wasn't ogling the young woman or the man in his midfifties. "You want me to introduce you?"

"You know him?" Stevie Grace's eyebrows rose.

"You've lived in the big city for too long. Whip's the first person I met. Remember I told you I'd left my info for David with a bartender? That was Whip." I led the way to two empty seats at the bar, several feet away from where Whip was mixing drinks.

"Is he single?" SG sat on the barstool next to me, her eyes focused on Whip. He'd had his sandy-brown hair and long beard trimmed.

"He is. Widowed, actually, with a daughter close to Ryan's age."

SG's jaw dropped. "Why aren't you dating *him*?"

I watched Whip as he expertly made five different cocktails. His green eyes stood out above high cheekbones. Since I'd gotten to know him, his personality added to his attractiveness. Yet from the first time we met, I hadn't felt that vibe.

"Good question," I said. "Maybe I should." I waited for SG's reaction and pulled back from her before she could swat me.

"Ha! You had your chance. So, I assume he's nice?"

"Very. Same with his daughter, Willow. I've asked him why he doesn't have a steady girlfriend, and his answer is always that Willow is his steady," I said. "He's a great dad." I studied Stevie Grace. "You barely set foot in here and zeroed in on him. Why?"

"No clue. I saw him throw his head back in a full belly laugh when he was talking to a customer, and… it made my tummy flip. Isn't that weird?"

I shrugged. "Not weird at all. I guess if everyone was attracted to everybody, it would make dating a real mess. Even more than it already is." Just then, Whip came over and slid coasters and cocktail napkins in front of both of us.

"Let me guess." Whip glanced at me. "Vodka and lemonade because it's finally warm enough out?"

"That's cheating. I told you before that's my go-to drink in the summer." I'd contemplated saying it in a flirty voice just to get SG going.

"And your friend?" Whip eyed Stevie Grace up and down as though he was going to paint her, and her back straightened. "It looks like you've had plenty of sun, possibly a drink or two"—his eyes pierced into SG's soul—"and you look like you want something more exciting than a vodka-something. Maybe…"—he leaned over the bar—"sex on the beach?"

Stevie Grace's body radiated so much sexual heat I expected her barstool to catch fire. "If you insist," she purred.

SG had never been a man hunter, as much of a tomboy as me in our youth. I'd never seen this side of her before.

Whip gave a throaty laugh as he walked back down the bar to make our drinks after sliding a menu toward Stevie Grace.

When Whip was out of earshot, I asked, "What in the hell was that?"

"What? He's the one who suggested the drink," SG said, wide-eyed.

"After you all but gave him the 'Yes, I'll have sex with you on this bar' vibe!"

"Jealous?"

"No. Well, not about him. Maybe about the sex on the bar." I eyed the polished wood. "Ick, how many times do you think that's happened here?" I grimaced.

"I'll let you know if it happens with Whip and me so that you don't ever sit at that part of the bar again." Stevie Grace nudged me.

"Gee, thanks." I stuck my finger in my mouth as if wanting to vomit. SG studied the menu while I looked around. Several other men around our age were in the crowd, and I couldn't help but wonder what attracted humans to one another. It had certainly happened to me when I met Donovan—a first for me since I'd met Trent in college.

Whip arrived with our drinks and took our food order.

"Honey barbeque wings, hush puppies, and coleslaw for me, please." SG leaned her elbows on the bar and rested her chin on her hand, giving Whip her full attention.

"California burger with cheese and sweet potato fries for me, please." I might as well have been talking to myself, for all the reaction I got from Whip. "Um, hello? Earth to Whip?"

"Yep, I heard you," Whip said, finally pulling his eyes from Stevie Grace to head to the kitchen to place our order.

"Geesh, you two. Am I going to have to hose you down?"

Stevie Grace tipped back her tropical drink and took several sips. "I hope so."

By the time we left the bar two hours later, Whip and SG had exchanged phone numbers, along with probably a lot of mental undressing of each other.

Stevie Grace and I walked around downtown and eventually to the beach to catch the sunset over the lake. As the sky darkened, she convinced me to stop at the bar again for one more drink.

"I'm not stupid. You just want one more gawk at Whip," I said, caving.

The bar crowd had thinned by the time we arrived, leaving Whip and SG more time to drool over each other.

"I should've invited Donovan here so I didn't feel like the third wheel that I am," I said.

"You can go home if you want. I'll walk Stevie Grace back." Whip grinned.

"Over my dead body. You two need a chaperone."

Avicii sang "Wake Me Up" while I studied SG and Whip, listening to the lyrics about how life's a game and love is the prize. I wanted to help my friend get one step closer to that prize.

"Hey, Whip, do you work tomorrow night? Donovan is making dinner for us and David so Stevie Grace can meet both of them. Interested in joining us?"

"I work tomorrow at four, but I'll see if I can get someone to cover for me for a few hours since I'm scheduled until closing," he said.

Stevie Grace leaned over and hugged me as though I'd handed her a million dollars. I had hoped to endear SG to Crimson Creek, figuring the lakes and bike trails would draw her in. I had never imagined that a scruffy bartender might be what sealed the deal.

We had a slow start the following morning, neither of us eager to jump on a mountain bike before coating our stomachs with scrambled eggs and toast. Stevie Grace held her glass of cold water to her forehead and whimpered.

"Suffering from pheromone overload?" I teased.

"Very funny. More like mixed-my-booze overload." SG winced.

I mopped up the yolk of an egg with a piece of toast. "That's a side of you I haven't seen before. Please tell me that mile-high-club stuff hasn't rubbed off on you."

She held up a hand. "I swear I've never pledged to that club." She closed one bloodshot eye. "Thanks for inviting Whip to join us tonight."

"I sent Donovan a text last night, and he said he's got enough brats and burgers to feed fifty." Stevie Grace's skin had a tinge of green to it. "You sure you still want to check out the bike trails? We can skip them and just kayak later if you'd like."

"Hell no. I'm going to suck it up and suffer in silence." Stevie Grace rubbed her stomach as it rumbled. "Well, somewhat in silence."

I pushed back my chair and brought our plates to the sink. "I'll shower while you drink a gallon of water."

An hour later, we met Kelly and a few other women at the rec parking lot after I checked in with Maudie in the shop. After introductions, I reminded Kelly that Stevie Grace was a newbie to the trails.

"I promise we'll stick to the easiest trail," Kelly said.

The cool morning breeze offset the sweat already threatening my back and chest.

Stevie Grace whooped for joy as we maneuvered over hills and wound our way through the beauty of the lakes and trees, perma-grins on our faces.

Then SG's back tire caught the edge of a boulder on the trail and catapulted her sideways off the trail forty minutes into our ride.

I was behind her and hit my brakes in time to watch SG narrowly miss hitting a tree with her shoulder before she thumped to the ground. I parked my bike and yelled for Kelly to stop. "Are you alright?" I crouched and unbuckled SG's helmet.

"I think so." Stevie Grace pulled the helmet off her head and took a calming breath. "Damn, I'm not as athletic as I was twenty years ago."

I patted her dirty shoulder. "What hurts the most?" I studied SG's red-dirt-smeared limbs, all attached and not twisted.

"My pride." Stevie Grace sat up and rubbed her hip. "And my right butt cheek." She held out a hand for me to help pull her up as Kelly and the others joined us. Standing, SG turned to Kelly. "Mommy, can we please go home now?" She pouted.

Kelly chuckled. "Yes, daughter, let's head for home." She wiped a smudge of dirt from Stevie Grace's chin as if she were one of her children. "This trail loops around. We'll be back at the parking lot in about half an hour."

The rest of our ride went smoothly. Back at my apartment, SG cleaned up before taking a nap while I checked on things in the shop. Hal was working with Maudie, and Hadley would join them after school. I headed back upstairs and prepared a BLT pasta salad for dinner at Donovan's. The pasta was cooling when SG awoke from her much-needed nap.

"All better?"

SG nodded. "Like a new woman. Where's the tequila?" She winked. "What can I do to help?" She guzzled a large glass of water. "Cut up Roma tomatoes?"

"Sure. Thanks. I'll fry up the bacon after we get back from kayaking."

After grilled-tuna-and-cheese sandwiches for lunch, we took the one o'clock shuttle, with Hal driving us and a few other kayakers in Grover to the rec landing.

I introduced SG to Hal when we met him in the back of the shop. "Welcome to our town. Has Eden convinced you to move here yet?" Hal's brown eyes twinkled.

"After last night, it won't be me convincing her," I said.

Hal cast a side glance at SG. "Was it the town's ambience or a man?"

SG giggled. "What makes you think it isn't just me missing Eden?"

Hal leaned in and said conspiratorially, "I'm giving you an out because I already heard over coffee this morning that Whip was ogling some auburn-haired beauty last night."

SG arched a brow. "Oh yes, the small-town gossip train."

"Quicker than a cheetah," Hal said.

After our kayaks were loaded, Hal transported six of us to the mine-pit landing, where I helped Hal unload the kayaks before the group of four made their way onto the water.

Six of the mine-pit lakes connected there, giving kayakers and canoers plenty of options. Stevie Grace and I paddled through the channel and under a footbridge into one of the larger lakes. A pair of loons swam nearby, making the only noise around us.

"You don't know how much I needed this," SG said as we paddled alongside each other. "My schedule has been crazy, my life too loud." Her mouth turned down. "I've traveled enough, seen every country that I care to see. I'm ready to settle down."

I kept quiet. She had a lot to think about, a feeling I knew all too well.

We arrived at Donovan's home two hours later with the BLT salad and two bottles of wine. Donovan greeted me with a kiss at the door before turning his attention to Stevie Grace. "So you're the she-devil who enticed Whip to take a few hours off from work." He held out his hand to shake SG's.

"Yep, I'm the vixen, here to corrupt Eden and anyone who comes in contact with me." She grinned. "There's your warning."

Donovan chuckled. "Good. I need corruption." He led the way to the kitchen, where David was placing a row of crackers around a port-wine cheese spread. Behind Donovan's back, SG gave me two thumbs-up.

David stepped forward, his hand outstretched to SG when we entered the kitchen. "Miss Stevie Grace, I presume?"

SG bypassed his hand and went straight in for a hug, not worrying whether she was invading his personal space. "David." She sighed over his shoulder before leaning back to look at him. "I feel like I know you already!"

"Thanks to Eden, no doubt." David leaned over and patted my arm. "She's been a good addition to this town. Although she nags me like a daughter, she makes things easier on my daughter since she lives too far away and can now micromanage me through Eden."

When Whip arrived minutes later, Stevie Grace was so engrossed in visiting with David about Vietnam that she barely skipped a beat. "Dad's been in a wheelchair ever since he served. He was wounded four months into his tour in Vietnam and considers himself lucky he got out alive," she told David.

Their conversation continued after SG stopped to squeeze Whip's hand as he walked by to put a pan of brownies on the counter, and I swore sparks flew when their hands touched.

I had a sneaking suspicion that Stevie Grace would be back to visit soon. And by the time the five of us called it a night a few hours later, I was certain of it.

Chapter 43

By early May, I had a routine of sorts. Hal was on call during the week for any scheduled bike or kayak rentals in need of shuttles, a flexibility dependent on the weather. I spent Monday mornings restocking, and after Maudie arrived at noon, I would leave for the cities, arriving at SG's apartment in plenty of time to put a meal together before picking Ryan up at school. While Ryan was in school on Tuesdays and Wednesdays, I worked on bookkeeping and inventory.

Thursday mornings, I headed back home after dropping Ryan off at school, and Thursday nights were dinner with Donovan. Weekends had gotten busy in the shop. Several locals did a sunrise bike ride every morning, and I'd gone with them a few times on Monday and Friday mornings, slowly working my way up from "easiest/adapted" labeled trails to "easy" ones. My goal was to try "more difficult" labeled trails by the fall.

Once the ground warmed, I had cement poured in the back portion of my parking lot, enough to erect a flagpole where both the American flag and the POW flag proudly flew.

Although the shop's business was a mood booster, it would be a long line of balancing inventory and spending. But that worry was set aside for another concern eating away at me.

A few days before Memorial Day weekend, after mini golf, Donovan and I stopped at the new downtown brewery, Crusher.

As we enjoyed Crimson Crusher IPAs at an outdoor table, he broke into my thoughts. "Okay, I've held off asking, but you've been way too quiet. Something bothering you?" He leaned over the small round table, so close I detected gray in his trimmed beard.

I traced the moisture forming on my beer glass. "It's Ryan. I can tell that he doesn't want to come here for the summer. And I get it. He's having fun with his baseball team, kids are making plans to get together this summer, and I'm yanking him away from that fun."

"Did you talk to him about it?"

"I have. But Ryan is a people pleaser. He'd cry himself to sleep every night before he'd admit not wanting to spend the summer here." I pushed my side bangs up. "That didn't sound right. He does want to be here—and there." The problem sat like an elephant on my heart.

Donovan nodded. "Kind of like when I forced Gabriel to ask a girl to prom his senior year. I thought I was doing the right thing, helping him conform... or pretend, whatever you want to call it. Helping him to graduate high school with a fun memory and lessen the teasing."

"And what happened?" I laced my fingers with Donovan's across the table.

"He asked a girl, and she said yes. They had a great time." Donovan gave a small smile.

"So it all worked out?"

"It did, but not the way I'd planned, and that's what I'm trying to tell you." Donovan squeezed my hand. "Gabriel came up with his own answer to his 'problem,' and I bet Ryan will too. Plans aren't set in stone. The girl he asked had her own secret crush: another girl in their class. That girl went to prom with the guy Gabriel was infatuated with. They double-dated and switched partners before they even got to the dance, thumbing their noses up at everyone." His thumb caressed the top of my hand. "This first summer may be a shitshow of you and Trent hauling Ryan back and forth, but you'll all figure it out."

"I hope so. I'll do my best to make that happen. It helps that Trent wants time for himself and Amber this summer. She's moving in, which makes it an even better time for Ryan to get away for a while."

But that night, as my head rested on Donovan's shoulder in bed, I stared at the ceiling, unable to shut off my brain as it recited a hundred different "what if" scenarios.

The high from another busy weekend in the shop deflated when I called Ryan Sunday night and he talked about his team's win at their baseball tournament the day before, along with the fun he'd had with his team after the tournament.

"Brady had us all sleep over last night." Ryan's words tumbled out, fueled by fun with his friends. "We camped out in tents in their yard. It was so cool!" His voice was hoarse. "We played flashlight tag, had a campfire and roasted hot dogs, and told scary stories. Kyle's having a sleepover next weekend after our game, and he has a swimming pool in his backyard!"

The shop was closed, my feet throbbed even as they sat propped up in the recliner, and my head pulsated. "Sounds like fun." I forced enthusiasm into my voice. "You know, when you're here in the summer, we can always have a friend of yours come and visit." I was happy for him yet sad that it was one more thing he would miss while living in Crimson Creek.

"I know. I will." Ryan sounded as somber as if I'd told him he would have homework all summer. "Brady knows about the beach across the street and the skateboard ramp. He's excited to go there with me."

I would let Brady stay all summer if that was what it took for Ryan to be happy in Crimson Creek. Heck, I would invite his whole ball team if needed.

I waited until later, when Ryan was in bed, to call Trent. I explained my concern with the hesitation I sensed in Ryan. "I don't want him sitting here miserable all summer."

"Amber and I already have plans for several weeks in the summer," Trent said. "Don't change your mind now about Ryan." His voice had an edge to it.

"I'm not changing my mind. I want him here, but I'm not certain that's what *he* wants. Right now, all he hears is what he'll miss this summer with his friends from school and the baseball team. I'm hoping that once he's in Crimson Creek, it will feel more like home and he'll meet new kids on the baseball team there."

Trent backtracked. "I'm not saying we don't want him here either, just that we have plans off and on for the summer. Amber's home sold, and she'll move in by the end of June."

"Well, like we've talked about before, we need to be flexible. Even though the shop is open every day now through the summer, I'm still taking Wednesdays off so I can play shuttle driver if needed to bring Ryan to a friend's house or a friend of his to Crimson Creek."

"As long as you don't expect me to change my plans, Eden." Trent's voice was firm.

He loved Ryan and was a great dad to him, but I knew the boundaries with Trent. I'd lived those boundaries for years.

After we hung up, I unwound on the deck. The sun had set over Crow Lake, leaving in its wake a deep-blue sky filling up with stars. Mosquitos would be out soon. The air carried the scent of a campfire nearby, and I took it all in.

I remembered a conversation with Trent's mom, Emily, before our divorce was final. We'd met for lunch, and Emily wanted to make sure I knew our relationship wouldn't change and that she wasn't "one of those mothers who thought their child was perfect."

Emily's reassurance had been comforting. "After Trent's father died and it was just Trent and me in the house, I brought him up to think the world revolved around him, trying to make up for what he'd lost," Emily had explained. "I made a mistake. When everything goes your way, you start believing it always should, making it difficult for those around you as they try to tap-dance to your beat." Emily had shot me an apologetic look. "I set him up for expecting the unattainable. Nobody gets their way all the time."

After I went inside and got ready for bed, I thought about how true her words were. But in most of our marriage, Trent *had* gotten his way.

Chapter 44

Memorial Day weekend was the pivotal change in The Fun-Key Monkey's business. As with most towns, Crimson Creek came alive with the promise of summer vacations, warm weather, and, in our town, the season of full-speed activity on the bike trails and lakes.

Hal and David shuttled more people than I had conceived possible when I opened the shop in early April, and I was proud of the staff choices I'd made. Maudie's gregarious personality was perfect for customer service. Hadley and Oliver used their knowledge of all things bike related and spent much of their workdays adjusting handlebars, seats, shocks, and bike helmets for customers before they headed to the trails, and everyone loved David and Hal and their fun shuttle buses.

The weekend had been an indication of what I needed to tweak in bike and kayak rental inventory. More kayaks and paddleboards were needed, along with sunscreen and water bottles. I had long-sleeved moisture-wicking shirts and heavy bike socks that wouldn't sell until fall. Business was a roller-coaster learning curve, one I intended to ride out for several years.

I'd made sure David and Hal had Memorial Day off so that they could attend the service at the cemetery. Oliver drove Grover, the only shuttle needed since most tourists headed home on Memorial Day.

Donovan and I had planned a relaxing evening for Memorial Day night, and I had to ignore my couch begging me to lounge on it instead. Some mine-pit lakes allowed pontoons, and Key Lake, where The Hokey Pokey restaurant was located, was one of those lakes.

Donovan called after the shop closed. "Let's do takeout. More time on the pontoon instead of sitting lakeside."

"Works for me." I closed out the cash register, cleaned up, and changed into my swimsuit with a T-shirt and shorts, and Donovan picked me up at 6 p.m.

While he drove to the restaurant, I called in our order of prime rib strips, seasoned fries, and coleslaw. After we picked up our order from The Hokey Pokey, Donovan drove to the boat landing on Key Lake.

After we launched the pontoon, Donovan drove while I unpacked our dinner on the small table under the Bimini top. I grabbed two beers from the cooler, slid them into koozies, and handed one to Donovan. With half of the lakeshore owned by the county, we saw little lake activity. Most of the weekenders had headed home.

Key Lake was long and less than a mile wide until the enormous bay with a tiny island in the middle, the bay where we'd played ice bocce. Looking at the lake's shape on a map explained how the lake got its name. It resembled a skeleton key.

Donovan turned off the motor. "The breeze should slowly drift us toward the island." He joined me at the table. As we ate, we talked of his next construction project, another set of lofts for bikers. "The goal by October is to complete the Shred Shed for the new lofts." He had shown me the sheds they'd built for the other lofts, secure storage for bikers' gear and bikes, located across the alley, away from Main Street.

"What does 'shred' refer to? I can't remember."

"They call riding the trails here 'shredding the red,' referring to the red trail dirt," Donovan said. He didn't ride, not wanting to take the chance that he'd get hurt and be out of commission for work.

"How's the booking look for fall?" We'd had little time lately to catch up.

"Good. The larger rooms are renting out more than the two-person rooms, which means I'm going to revise the layout for these next eight rooms. Most people come to bike with a group." Donovan took a swig of beer. "I'd assumed the smaller groups or couples would take the lofts, but that's not the case. The people staying there like the convenience of walking to the bars and restaurants downtown. The families are the ones staying at my campground and cabins."

"You said before that you want to rent out your current home once you move, right?"

"Yes. That's a few years down the road, I think. I like my privacy and don't need to be right there for the rentals. They're like the lofts and yurts, pretty self-sufficient with keyless entry, and I'm only a text or phone call away," Donovan said.

"I hear you. As much as I love the convenience of the apartment, I crave a big yard and privacy like I had growing up. I miss the freedom I had in my childhood to go outside in my underwear if I wanted."

Donovan's eyebrows rose. "You walked around in your undies? As a teen? Why didn't you call me?"

"You know what I mean. I miss our large vegetable garden, our animals, the creek that ran through our property, and yes, the ability to walk outside and have nobody see you other than your family."

"If you play your cards right, I may be convinced eventually to sell you some of my acreage," Donovan said before cutting into another prime rib strip bathed in au jus.

"And I hope to take you up on that in a couple of years."

Every business decision I made was based on money. I expected growing pains with my business in the next few years, much like the town would continue to experience.

Donovan had purchased eighty acres five miles from town. That was close enough for convenience, especially as a business owner, but far enough out of town to have privacy.

"I'm subdividing it into four twenty-acre parcels, hoping that one day, Gabriel will move back here." He frowned. "It's doubtful, but I'm hopeful. I've asked Cassie several times, but she loves where she lives and reminds me that she's got a place to stay already—my home."

"Please don't sell the other parcels before asking me, even if we aren't dating anymore."

"Are you planning on dumping me?" Donovan flinched.

"Eh, hard to say. Depends on whether you behave yourself tonight."

He leaned in, whispering, "Oh, Eden, I definitely do *not* plan on behaving myself."

After we finished eating and drifted down the lake near the island, Donovan fired up the motor and steered the pontoon to shore. I hopped out and guided it onto the sandy shoreline.

I pulled off my shirt, stepped out of my jean shorts, revealing my new red bikini, and set my clothes on the platform of the pontoon.

"Are you joining me for a swim?"

"Duh. You think I'm going to pass up dunking you under?"

I splashed him. "Pretty hard to scare me in water. My parents taught me to swim when I was a toddler."

"You're no fun." Donovan pulled his T-shirt over his head, his words muffled.

"That's what Trent used to say," I quipped. When Donovan tossed his T-shirt next to my clothes, I challenged him. "Last one in has to scrub the other person's back first."

I charged into the lake, Donovan right on my heels. I dove under right when a hand clasped my foot, pulling me back until my knee hit his chest.

I surfaced and splashed his face. "I won," I taunted him.

"Fine with me." Donovan reached for my other leg and wrapped both around his waist. "I'll wash your back. And your front. And those dirty parts that your bikini covers."

As Donovan pulled me closer, I put an elbow between us. "Just remember: I've got a reputation to uphold here. Staunch new businesswoman and all."

"What about me? You could take advantage of me and ruin my stellar reputation." Donovan moved my elbow and looped it around his neck.

"You wish I'd wreck your reputation." I pushed him playfully and broke away to retrieve the soap and shampoo from the front deck of the pontoon. "Come here. It's time to wash my back." I waved the soap at him.

"Give me the shampoo, and I'll wash your hair."

"It takes two seconds to wash my hair." I eyed Donovan's longer curls. "In fact, I'm pretty sure your hair is longer than mine now."

"That's not the point." Donovan took the shampoo from me and squeezed some into his palm. He stood behind me, both of us chest deep in the water, and slowly massaged shampoo into my scalp. His touch sent tingles through my body.

"How have I gone this long and not had you wash my hair?" I closed my eyes to fully enjoy the moment. "It's all I can do to not moan."

"Oh please, don't stifle a moan on my account." After another minute of blissful head massage, he said I could dunk under and rinse.

"You're done?"

"I don't want to spoil you." Donovan kissed my neck.

After the sun set, we lay on a blanket on the pontoon, looking up at the stars, quietly revealing more of our past like offerings of a fruit perfectly ripened.

Donovan spoke of the constant fear for Gabriel's safety. Gabriel, always vulnerable, had found his place and his people in Fort Lauderdale. But he'd been involved in some sketchy relationships and was currently waist-deep in one that concerned Donovan.

"They've been together three years," he said as we watched stars dance in the night sky, "yet I've never met him when I visit. Something feels off, but I need to let Gabriel handle it."

We went on to speak of Donovan's daughter and the unlikely chance that Cassie would ever move back to Minnesota. "That one cuts open my heart," he confided. "When you raise them, you foolishly think they'll be dedicated to you forever." He held my hand, warm under the cooling night. "Which is both selfish and stupid on my part. I want Cassie to have a life of her own, yet I miss the hell out of her."

When we drove home late that night and "Night Changes" by One Direction came on the radio, their words of how fast time flies and of having no regrets reaffirmed to me that I needed to trust my heart. I was in the right place.

Chapter 45

I picked up Ryan and his belongings at Trent's the day after school let out. On our drive to Crimson Creek, I tamped my enthusiasm, still sensing Ryan's desire to stay with his friends in the cities even though he wore a brave smile as we talked baseball. I'm guessing his plan was "fake it 'til you make it."

Already signed up for Crimson Creek summer baseball league, Ryan attended his first practice with his new team two days later. In the following days, he became acclimated to the shop. He learned how to use the cash register and helped stock inventory—including the T-shirts and water bottles with the monkey-on-a-bike or monkey-with-a-kayak design he'd created. Ryan rode along with David and Hal on shuttle runs, helping unload kayaks and coming back after riding with David, belting out butchered lyrics to songs like "In the Summertime" and "Don't Pull Your Love," songs I told him were older than me.

Ryan attended three practices before his team's first game. I sat in the stands with Donovan, certain my stomach had five times the butterflies that Ryan's did. Ryan struck out his first time at bat, but his second at bat nabbed him a double, followed by several more hits. And he'd done well in center field. But what calmed my nerves was watching Ryan and his teammates high-five each other after the game, an enormous smile on his face as he leaned his arms on two teammates' shoulders.

"You okay now?" Donovan patted my shoulder as we left the bleachers.

"Yep." I hadn't mentioned my jitters, but he knew.

Kelly, who'd sat behind us on the bleachers with her husband and children, walked down to the field with me. "Mason's glad Ryan joined the team. It looks like they had fun out there."

"Yes, and I'm relieved. Not that they won, but that Ryan seems comfortable with his new team." I touched Kelly's shoulder. "Thank you, and Mason, for your part in helping Ryan join the team." It had been welcome news to find out Ryan and Mason were on the same team.

"It was nothing," Kelly said with a smile.

Although Mason was a grade above Ryan, he'd already made an effort to introduce Ryan to others in his grade. Between Mason and Willow, Ryan's first two weeks in Crimson Creek had gone well.

We just needed to get through the rest of the summer.

The humid mornings and clear summer June days passed swiftly as Ryan and I fell into a routine. His baseball games were on Tuesday and Thursday nights, and Donovan's baseball team played on Monday and Wednesday nights. For both leagues, the away games were never that far away, usually in one of the several nearby small towns.

I missed Donovan's games on Monday nights because that was my "Babes on Bikes" guided mountain biking night. At 5:30 p.m. every Monday, women met at the shop for our intro-to-biking excursions on the easiest trails. I enjoyed introducing women to the sport, and it got me out on the trails.

On my guided bike nights, Ryan either watched Donovan's game if it was in town or hung out with his new friends.

Although Ryan seemed to enjoy mountain biking, he often chose kayaking or paddleboarding instead. For someone who had previously been content to sit inside and play computer games with his dad, being on the lake seemed to awaken something in Ryan.

I gave not only myself Wednesdays off at the shop, but Ryan as well. On the last Wednesday in June, I drove Ryan and three friends from baseball to a town twenty minutes away, where they practiced at batting cages before moving on to the go-kart racetrack and finishing the afternoon at Ryan's new favorite pizza and sub place, Mickey's Pizza.

We made it back to Crimson Creek in plenty of time to drop Ryan's friends off at their homes and for us to eat supper before biking to the baseball field to catch Donovan's game. We sat with David and several other people Ryan was getting to know, and baseball soon became one of the magnets that connected Ryan with the townspeople.

Whip and Willow invited Ryan to bike the trails with them, followed by dinner at their house, on the last Sunday in June. Donovan and I took the opportunity for some alone time after I closed shop.

I drove to his home with a picnic meal of crab salad and hoagies. We wasted no time in loading his canoe and pushing it off shore. The heat of the day was still with us, and we paddled near shore to make the most of the shade.

Fifteen feet from shore was an endless drop-off, something I tried not to think about in the mine-pit lakes. We paddled to a sand point and docked the canoe. Sitting with our feet in the lake, we ate the picnic meal.

Donovan mowed through his sandwich before resting his elbows on his knees and staring out over the lake. "I used to hate summers when I was young." He turned toward me.

"What kid hates summer?" I'd enjoyed school, but nothing compared to summer as a child.

"I told you before how difficult my mom was. Gabriel and I always felt like we were maneuvering around a time bomb at home. Dad was at work, so in the summers, we were stuck at home with Mom, never knowing if we'd get the fun mom or the erratic woman who could blow up at us and then answer the phone in a sweet voice." Donovan had turned away and clenched his jaw.

I set my sandwich down and reached for his hand, letting silence settle until I could get past the lump in my throat. "How did you get through it?" I'd been very lucky with my upbringing.

"Gabriel and I got through it together. And when Dad was home, he did his best to appease Mom." Donovan gave me a brief half smile. "The thing is, when Mom was happy, it felt like full sunshine after days of rain. And Dad loved her through it all, right to the end. When Mom was diagnosed with cancer and she realized she *needed* Dad, things changed for the better." He grimaced. "Crazy, right?"

"No, not crazy," I reassured him. "Was your mom ever diagnosed with anything?"

"Nope. This was the seventies, when nobody talked about what went on behind closed doors." He shook his head, and droplets of water fell from his hair. "Sorry, I don't know how I went down that path."

"Summer, and how you used to hate it." I rested my head on his warm, bare shoulder, wishing I could take away the pain of Donovan's childhood.

Donovan sighed. "Dad always told us Mom wasn't like that when they first married, which only solidified why I would never marry." He thumbed away a crumb from my cheek. "I don't trust people not to change... or for me not to change."

"Anyway, enough depressing talk." Donovan's eyes focused on mine. "I've missed the hell out of you." He chuckled. "I guess that's kind of depressing too!"

"I've missed you too, and..." I leaned over and kissed him. "I've made some inquiries."

Donovan squinted. "Such as...?"

"As you know, Ryan mows David's lawn once a week and helps in the garden. David, being the wise man that he is, suggested that they could make that a Friday evening event since David is done shuttling midafternoon." I'd been leaving the later shuttle runs for Hal. "David offered to make dinner for him and Ryan, and as long as I picked Ryan up by nine o'clock, he said it would be a gift for him to have Ryan there."

David had helped beckon Ryan outdoors, teaching him about gardening—something I missed.

"And two of Ryan's friends from baseball have invited him to sleepovers in the next couple of weeks. So, I'll be available for a sleepover myself those nights, if they work for you."

"Hell yes. I don't care what nights they are." Donovan pulled me down on top of him on the sand. "I love the boy, but man, I've missed being alone with you."

"Just remember: Stevie Grace is coming to visit again, so I'll be busy those few days."

Donovan nuzzled my neck. "I'll have to count on Whip pulling her away from you for a while."

"I don't think that will be a problem. Every time I talk to her on the phone, she brings up Whip. I think they talk more than she and I do now."

That didn't bother me—quite the opposite. Like Ryan, I hoped SG would settle in Crimson Creek. I would take whatever help I could get for that to happen.

Ryan had spent two days at Trent's in June, and when I dropped Ryan off, Trent and I agreed that we'd give him until August first to decide where he wanted to attend sixth grade. I dreaded that day.

Chapter 46
David

Last night, I dreamt that I was getting debriefed at Clark Air Force Base in the Philippines after our release and was among the POWs who were told that their wives had divorced them during their captivity. I woke to a damp pillow and the reality that Jean was indeed gone.

I took so long to get back to sleep that I ended up oversleeping and missed meeting Hal for morning coffee. I'd been having too many nightmares lately, all because I was finally talking about the monsters I'd blocked out for so long. *Too long, David, or not long enough?*

After Hal's phone call about my standing him up at the café, I invited him over for coffee. I was dressed and shaved by the time he arrived, opening the windows to let in the scent of another beautiful late-June morning.

"What was last night's bad dream about?" Hal asked, following me into the kitchen. He sliced up the blueberry coffee cake he'd picked up at the bakery while I made coffee.

"Jean divorcing me while I was in Vietnam," I said, cleaning my glasses on my cotton shirt. "It's all this talk of Vietnam lately."

Hal knew of the many POWs who came home to divorce or ended up divorced within the first year after the war. At least Jean had known I was alive. Some wives hadn't had that luxury.

"It's like the regret and guilt I repressed are now flooding back through nightmares."

Hal commiserated. "I carried the guilt of that unsuccessful rescue mission on Christmas Eve of '65 with me for decades. The one I told you about where we searched for two days for the downed six-man crew of an AC-47 'Spooky' gunship over the south end of Laos before they called the rescue mission off." He drummed his coffee cup.

Hal had never spoken of that failed rescue until the men's remains were found in 2011, well north of where they'd been told to search. "I worried for years that we'd missed them in the search," Hal murmured.

Worry was something Eden and I spoke of, a fuel for questioning the decisions we make in life and the things we can't control. I could only look back with regret, and Eden could only be hopeful she wouldn't regret her decisions in the future.

I stared into my mug. "The older I get, the harder it is to forget it all." I nodded toward the shadow box hanging in the hallway between the kitchen and living room. "That damn thing doesn't help." It contained fourteen medals I'd received for things I'd done selfishly, just to keep myself alive with a somewhat clean conscience.

"I see you gave up taking it down, knowing Louise would hang it up again when she came to visit." Hal raised his coffee cup to me as if offering a cheer. "You've got a lot to be proud of in there. A Silver Star and a Distinguished Flying Cross are nothing to keep hidden."

"I've got too much time to think at night now." Driving Goober for Eden freed up my nights, a downside to giving up the nightly bar run.

"Sometimes, I feel like David Carpenter's soul seeped into the earth of Hanoi," I said, "as if I never really came home."

Many days, I'd wished I hadn't ejected from the plane. My family could've gone on with their lives. I wouldn't have had to grieve Lee's death and Jean's death—both a thousand times worse than any pain I'd experienced in Vietnam. Like the lyrics from the song "Conquistador" that came out while I was a POW, I did not conquer, only died—at least metaphorically.

Hal leaned over the table and met my eyes. "You served your country. If not you, someone else would've taken your place. We do what we can. Sometimes, it's the wrong thing, sometimes it's right." He clinked my coffee cup with his. "You're human, like the rest of us. We stumble and struggle, we sail and succeed... we try. And that's all we can do."

I nodded, and we sat in comfortable silence as our coffee grew cold.

Eden watched me like a hawk at the shop, worried I'd keel over at any given moment if I worked too many hours. But she gave me a gift: Ryan. I'd missed most of my grandsons' teen years once I quit traveling to Vermont. Louise's family had visited a few times in the years since Jean's death, but never long enough for me to really know my grandsons as adults.

Ryan was a fine young man, one I hoped would stay in Crimson Creek. Every Friday, after I finished work at three, Ryan rode home with me to mow my lawn and stay for dinner.

On the last Friday in June, the temperature hit ninety by noon. Too hot for mowing, I gave Ryan the option of skipping his Friday evening with me as he folded T-shirts and I wiped down mountain bikes in the back of the shop.

Ryan frowned. "You don't want me to go to your house today?"

"I do, but it's too hot now to mow the lawn." Although I enjoyed our time together, I tried to put myself in his shoes. I didn't know if I'd have wanted to hang out with an old man. "Guess I could kick your butt in backgammon or cribbage until after dinner, then we could either work in the garden, or you could mow the lawn if it cools off." My backyard was mostly shade, other than the garden area.

"You're on, grandpa." Ryan flashed me a grin full of mostly permanent teeth. I loved that he'd taken to calling me grandpa even though in reality I was more the age his great-grandpa would be.

After work, Ryan and I settled in at my kitchen table, an oscillating fan helping keep things cool along with the wall air conditioner. Eden had sent along sloppy joe meat and bakery buns, and I nuked the meat in the microwave.

While we ate an early dinner, Ryan talked about a secret handshake his baseball team had back in the cities. "Miss those friends?" I asked.

Ryan shrugged.

"It's okay to say you do. You can have friends in more than one place." I sensed the boy was under pressure to decide where he would go for sixth grade—no reason to add to it.

"I made many lifelong friends when I was in the POW camp. They live all over the United States."

"Wow." Ryan's mouth hung open. "Do you still talk to them?"

"Many of the roughly six hundred prisoners have died in the past forty years. I'm in an online group with my Wild Weasel pilot friends, another online group with my Red River Valley Fighter pilots, and we surviving POWs have an email group," I said. "Over one hundred of us met at the White House two years ago." Catching up with fellow survivors brought a level of comfort, surrounded by those who understood each other's pain.

"We didn't have a special handshake like your baseball team, but we did have a secret knock code. Kept us all connected."

"Cool. Can you show me?" Ryan wiped his hands on a napkin.

Ryan's curiosity smoothed out the jagged edges of the painful memories. Once we finished our sloppy joes, I grabbed a pencil and paper. I wrote out our five-by-five code. "We used K and C as one letter," I explained as I drew the twenty-five boxes. A, F, L, Q, and V went down the left side, and A, B, C/K, D, and E went across the top.

"You tap the left number first and then the top," I numbered one through five on the left and the top and went on to demonstrate the knocks on the table.

"We signed off with GBU, which stood for God Bless You." Just saying it still brought a lump to my throat.

"Mom and I say GLS to each other. It's our code for 'good night, love you, sweet dreams.'" Ryan blushed. "Can I try it?" He pointed at the diagram.

"Sure. Hit me with GBU." I folded my hands on the table in anticipation.

Ryan took his time, slowly tapping out the message: two then two, one then two, four then five.

"Excellent!" I clapped.

"What else did you learn in the prison camp?" Ryan was like a sponge.

"We taught each other things. If someone knew French and someone else wanted to learn the language, we taught through taps. Some of those men I never met in person. First, we had to make sure it was an American on the other side and that we could communicate."

I rapped on the kitchen table five times with one hand and rapped twice with the other, explaining the "shave and a haircut, two bits" rap that we used. "One man rapped the five-syllable rhythm to 'shave and a haircut,' and the person on the other side of the wall rapped twice in answer with 'two bits.' All communication took place when the guards took a siesta at noon," I explained.

Ryan mimicked my tap example.

"I knew about cars and engines, and one of the men on the other side of the wall asked how you changed oil in a car." I smiled at the memory. "I thought, 'Are you kidding? How do you not know that?' I changed my tune when I found out how much this man knew about building homes—and how little I knew." That had been one of many lessons learned.

"Did he tap how to build a home to you?" Ryan guzzled his milk.

"No, but I knew men who kept their minds busy by building a home in their head in great detail. Anything to keep sharp—make the days pass."

I didn't tell Ryan about how you couldn't focus on time passing, or you'd lose your mind.

"What did you think of when you were alone?" Ryan bit at his nail.

"I memorized fellow prisoner's names, where they were from, anything I knew about them." And I avoided thinking about my family. You had to forget anybody you loved.

"The important thing was keeping expectations low. If we thought about getting out or going home, it only made us depressed. We focused on the small positives, a joke someone tapped, a GBU tapped after a beating, shared information and inspiration to get through the day."

"So... my lesson is?" Ryan rested his chin on his hands, grinning at me.

I high-fived Ryan. "Boy howdy, you know me, don't you? I guess your lesson is if things seem too much, break them down. Things often seem worse than they are. Appreciate the small things. They're usually what's important." I thought of my wife's goofy laugh and my son's mischievous smirk, two little things I missed every damn day.

Chapter 47
Eden

I braced myself for the tsunami of outdoor enthusiasts sure to arrive Fourth of July weekend by prepping meals ahead of time for myself and employees. Bookings for rental equipment were full from Thursday through the weekend.

Ryan mowed David's grass on Wednesday since I would need his help at the shop on Friday, and he stayed to help David pick raspberries. The man had a garden twice the size he needed and gave most of his bounty away.

Oldies played while I had the apartment to myself on Wednesday, and I sang along to "Sooner or Later" and "Too Late to Turn Back Now," songs whose lyrics resonated with how I'd fallen for Donovan. I couldn't stop it. I didn't want to.

I prepared barbecue pulled pork for sandwiches and shredded chicken for salads and wraps. If I expected my employees to work their butts off all weekend, I figured I'd better feed them well. When David dropped Ryan off late Wednesday afternoon with a five-quart pail of raspberries, I ran to the grocery store and picked up two angel food cakes and whipped cream.

Thursday and Friday were hectic in the shop, with Oliver and his new sidekick, Ryan, working on bike maintenance and adjustments. Hal and David shuttled, and Maudie and Hadley worked alongside me in the shop. Occasionally, we had time to breathe.

Saturday's Fourth of July parade marched past The Fun-Key Monkey, several of Oliver and Hadley's high school friends more than willing to ride mountain bikes while wearing our logo on their T-shirts and hats and tossing out koozies with our logo.

Ryan beamed with pride, knowing his design was all over town. After the parade, our routine resumed much as it had the previous two chaotic days. Our sales included a lot of sunscreen and snacks, thanks to the influx of beachgoers in the park. The radio played in the back of the shop where Ryan and Oliver worked, and I heard the oldie "Snoopy vs the Red Baron" play with Ryan singing along. Clearly, David had played it for him. It had been a favorite of David's kids when he was a pilot.

By the time I locked the door at seven in the evening, I wanted to collapse. Exhaustion coated my body and mind, accompanied by pride. I was finally doing what I was meant to do.

When Ryan and I climbed the stairs to the apartment, my legs wobbled as if I'd biked a thousand miles. "Can we go to the park now?" Ryan asked, jogging up the steps.

"Oof. Can't you see that I've been beaten down?"

Ryan opened the apartment door for me. "More like dragged behind a horse."

"Very funny." I set the cash drawer on the table, debating whether to count it that night or toss the whole thing into my small safe.

My mother's words rang in my ear: *"Don't delay the inevitable."*

I showered first and insisted Ryan shower after me. "You can't go to the park smelling like a dead animal." Preteen hormones had kicked in. He was in full deodorant-age mode.

While he showered, I closed out the cash drawer and filled out the deposit, and before dusk, Ryan and I walked to the park, where concession stands, games, and later, fireworks awaited us.

Donovan greeted me at the beer gardens with an ice-cold tap beer after I left Ryan with his friends at the tug-of-war. I held the plastic cup to my forehead to cool a brewing headache.

"Where's the nearest chair?"

"That bad?" Donovan raised an eyebrow. His weekend helping campers and cabin renters hadn't been as chaotic. "I've got folding chairs in the back of my pickup. You don't want to walk around? Did you and Ryan eat?"

"Oh, I forgot all about eating. No wonder I have a headache!" We'd all taken turns eating the lunch I'd prepared, but that had been hours before. "I can't believe Ryan didn't say anything. He's got to be hungry too."

"Does he have money?" Donovan asked.

"Yes." The shop had been a windfall for Ryan, especially the tips when he helped shuttle.

"Then he's fine. Now, what do you want to eat?"

I eyed the many vendors. "How about a walking taco? I'll get our food while you get the chairs. Do you want one or something else?"

"I ate already, so I'm good for now." Donovan pointed at an open spot near the bandstand. "I'll put our chairs over there."

I joined him several minutes later, holding two walking tacos.

Donovan's brow furrowed. "I didn't need one."

"Nope, but I needed two." I plopped down on one of the lawn chairs.

"One more day, and then you'll get a reprieve." Donovan gave me a shoulder rub.

"Mmm... you can do that the rest of the night if you want," I said. "And I only have Monday as a reprieve. Remember SG flies in Tuesday." She was staying Tuesday through Friday, not only to visit but to check out downtown buildings for a possible business. I tried not to get my hopes up, but I knew her well enough to see she was ready for a change in her life. "It sounds like Whip will drive her to the airport on Friday."

"Crazy how they connected so fast," Donovan mused.

"I agree. But SG went all psychological reasoning on me, pointing out that a lot of relationships happen that way if you're willing to follow through on your gut instinct, especially when we're older and wiser. She said it would've been different if I didn't already know Whip and could verify that he didn't have a warrant for his arrest."

Donovan laughed. "And you verified that?"

"To the best of my knowledge." I dug into my meal.

After I ate, we relaxed in the chairs with another beer before walking around the crowded park. We spotted Ryan and his friends a few times, playing games and shoveling food into their ever-growing bodies, and the sight of him having fun was the best part of my weekend.

As much as I wanted to go home and sleep, the fireworks over Crow Lake at dusk would keep me awake, so I stuck it out, mosquitoes and all. Donovan walked Ryan and me home after the grand finale.

I barely remembered the minutes between kissing Donovan good night and my head hitting the pillow.

"Holy Hannah, SG! Did you fly here on your own?" An electricity of excitement radiated off Stevie Grace to the point she could have fueled the plane with her energy.

"What did you expect? I haven't seen Whip for ten weeks!"

"Or me," I chided her as we hugged.

"I always miss you, silly," SG said.

We crawled inside the truck, and I cranked up the air-conditioning.

"How many buildings are we looking at tomorrow? And when are you going to tell me your 'bright idea'?"

"Two properties for sure, possibly three, and I'm thinking of a yoga studio. If the tree-hugging-bark-eating-love-earth people are flooding to Crimson Creek, it only stands to reason that they may like yoga too... and a juice bar." SG was one of the few people I knew in high school who had done yoga. She got her instructor's license and supported her college years by teaching classes. "It's a start until I branch out with a few other ideas."

"I don't care if you open a strip joint. I just want you in town," I said.

"Oh, so you know about the side business I planned?" Stevie Grace wiggled her eyebrows as I pulled onto the main road to Crimson Creek.

I took Tuesday afternoon off from the shop, and Hadley and Maudie held down the fort. Ryan was at a friend's house for the afternoon, and after their away baseball game—the first game I would miss—was staying overnight at that friend's home. After a late breakfast at my apartment, SG and I headed down to the shop, where I'd set aside kayaks for us.

We took David's eleven o'clock shuttle with a handful of other kayakers heading to the rec parking lot. SG and I were getting dropped off at a small lake access at one of the few mine-pit lakes I hadn't been on yet. Grace Slick belted out "Somebody to Love" on Goober's sound system. "Picked this one out for you, Stevie Grace," David said. "I'd play a Stevie Nicks song too, but she didn't have a hit before 1973."

"That's quite all right. I—and Grace Slick—appreciate the nod."

When The Supremes sang "Stoned Love," one of my parents' favorite songs, a middle-aged woman sitting behind us harmonized as they sang about the unwavering bond of love.

At the boat access, we unloaded the kayaks, gave David a peck on each cheek, and stashed our gear in the kayak's cubby hole before donning life jackets. "I'll be back around three to pick you up," David said before crawling behind the wheel of Goober.

For the next several hours, we explored the shoreline of the three mine-pit lakes. "There's the waterfall Donovan and I cross-country skied past last winter." I pointed at the creek dropping a hundred feet, the force of the water less in midsummer.

"It's beautiful." Stevie Grace took a deep breath. "Man, I've craved this peacefulness."

"You know I'll be the first to welcome you here," I said. "Well, I'd have to push Whip out of the way." I paddled next to Stevie Grace.

SG looked at her watch. "Only four more hours, and I'll see him."

"It says a lot that he switched his schedule today for you. Tips are much better at night."

"Guess I'm worth missing out on some cash." SG grinned.

Back at the apartment, we got cleaned up and walked to Mined Your Business shortly after five o'clock.

"Slow down!" I tugged at SG, who managed a speed walk with high-heeled sandals.

"What? You've got those long legs," She pointed at my legs peeking out from under my lime-green sundress. "Now you know what it feels like to walk with you all the time."

"You know, if you act too excited, Whip's going to think you like him." I elbowed her.

"I'm guessing this whole town knows how I feel about him." Stevie Grace yanked open the bar's door.

Whip's shift had ended at five, and he and Donovan were sitting at a table in the corner, waiting for us.

SG ran ahead of me, and Whip stood to meet her in an embrace followed by a long kiss.

"Get a room!" one of the bartenders shouted to Whip, who flipped him the finger and a smile.

Donovan welcomed me with a kiss. "Boring, I know, compared to the steam coming off them." He nodded toward Whip and SG.

"We haven't had to go so long without seeing each other."

"Let's hope that doesn't happen." His calloused hand against my bare shoulder was as reassuring as his words.

After dinner and drinks, the four of us took Donovan's pontoon out on Crow Lake, a relaxing end to a perfect night. The following morning, Stevie Grace and I walked uptown to meet with Jenny, the realtor who'd sold me my property, at the first building SG wanted to tour.

"Good morning." Jenny unlocked the door to the corner building about three blocks from mine, on Main Street, where an antique shop used to be.

The building was one of the handful of locations Jenny had shown me the previous year. The business next door was a coffee shop, a quieter part of town, at least for now.

"I've toured this place," I told Stevie Grace. "It's nice. Not big enough for what I needed, and I needed the traffic area by the main road and park."

The main floor, empty of everything but one retaining wall, was long and narrow. The upstairs was also empty, another old apartment in need of updating, much as mine had been.

Back downstairs, SG slowly ran her hand along the brick wall adjoining the coffee shop, and I sensed the wheels turning in her head. Jenny and I gave her space until Stevie Grace turned to face us, beaming.

"I can picture it. Yoga studio in back, possibly a juice bar and a small travel agency area in front."

"A travel agency?" That part was news to me.

"One geared toward retreats in this area. What better way to recharge than reconnecting with nature here? It would be a landing point for walk-ins since most would be done online."

"That's a great idea," Jenny said.

"Thanks. I've traveled the world in the past fifteen years and want to focus on simple retreats. This area has so much to offer." SG's green eyes shone with excitement.

Jenny showed us two more places that I hadn't seen, one next to Crushers, the new IPA brewery, a location too loud and busy for a yoga studio.

SG thanked Jenny for her time and promised to get back to her soon. After leaving the realtor's office, we stopped at the coffee shop to get iced coffees to go then walked to a quiet picnic area in the park. Shaded under an oak tree, we sat across from each other at a picnic table.

"One of the things I've had to ask myself is whether this would look as appealing to me without Whip in the picture. Even I know things could go south as quickly as they heated up."

"What was your answer?" I gulped my coffee before the ice melted.

"Yes. Even besides you being here, which is another great plus, I didn't want to move based on people. I stripped all that away and thought of the peace and the vibe here, the outdoor recreation that no other place offers." Stevie Grace gazed at the sun sparkling over Crow Lake. "I don't know how to explain the pull..."

"You don't have to explain it to me," I said. "I felt it too that first day I came here to find David. The town has energy, yet it also has a calming balance."

SG turned to me and smiled. "Which is why I'm going to make an offer on the place tomorrow." She blew out a long breath. "Oh, and I'm going to have to talk to Donovan about renovating the apartment."

That night, Whip picked up SG and her overnight bag for a "sleepover" at his place. Willow was spending the night at Kelly's.

"You behave yourselves." I wagged a finger at the two of them.

Whip leaned forward and chucked my chin. "Why would I want to do that?" he said with a wink. Then they were off, my best friend and her Prince Charming.

Chapter 48

Ryan's school decision deadline of August first was fast approaching. Ryan had spent a total of five days with Trent since he finished fifth grade, and I'd sensed Trent and Amber were enjoying their freedom since there had been no pushback from Trent—and no driving on his part to pick up Ryan or meet me halfway.

A week before Ryan's big decision for sixth grade, Donovan and I sat by the lake at his home, nursing a drink, our feet up after a hectic Friday at work. After the sun began its descent, I stood to leave and pick up Ryan from David's right as Donovan's cell phone rang.

Seconds into the conversation, Donovan began pacing. "Shit, shit, shit!" he said through gritted teeth after he hung up the phone. "There's been a mass shooting at a gay nightclub in Fort Lauderdale, with several injuries and deaths. Gabriel and his partner were there." He fired the information toward me like bullets from a machine gun. "I've got to get to Florida!"

"Oh no! Was Gabriel hurt?" I ran alongside him back to the house.

"Yes, shot in the chest," Donovan said, his hand cupping his mouth as if to shove the horrifying words back inside. "That was the hospital calling. They're wheeling him into surgery."

He blinked back tears, and I pulled him in for a quick hug. "What can I do to help?"

"Make coffee, please," Donovan said before heading to the bathroom to pack his shaving kit. "And see what you can throw in a cooler for snacks."

I questioned the sensibility of his driving to Florida instead of trying to get a flight.

"It's a twenty-four-plus-hour drive without stops if I push it. I'll be there at the crack of dawn Sunday. Trying to finagle a flight out from here or the cities would take as long."

I didn't voice my concern about him driving, overcome with emotion, sensing that nothing would stop Donovan. I found a small cooler in his pantry and packed bottled water, Gatorade, and ice packs from his freezer. I grabbed granola bars, a jar of cashews, and a couple of apples from his fridge.

Minutes later, Donovan kissed me goodbye at our vehicles. "I'll keep you updated."

"Please pull over if you're tired. Promise?"

"I promise, but I'm so amped up now, adrenaline will keep me going." He opened the truck door and tossed his things inside, setting his coffee in the cup holder. "Thanks for packing the snacks and cooler."

"Of course." After he slid behind the wheel, I leaned in for a kiss. "He's going to be okay." I had no clue, but optimism was everything at that point.

Donovan had told me the nurse who had called said the bullet had missed Gabriel's heart. He was alive. So many others were not. I watched him drive away before I headed to David's to pick up Ryan.

Donovan called around seven Saturday morning. "I just drove through St. Louis." He yawned. "I called the hospital, and Gabriel's in stable condition. The bullet missed any main arteries. Lucky son of a bitch." His voice cracked. "He'll recover physically, but mentally? He's going to be a wreck. I heard from his partner's father. Gabriel's partner died in the shooting."

I gasped. "That's so awful!"

Donovan had recently told me about Gabriel's delicate emotional balance. After the loss of his partner, he would need Donovan more than ever.

"I won't bother you at work but will call you tonight, okay?"

"Yes, please do. I hope you get some rest."

Saturday's chaos helped keep my worry at bay.

Kelly texted me midafternoon. *Up for a bike and beer after you close?*

Word must've gotten out about Gabriel. *Yes! Thank you.*

Great. I'll be there a little after 6.

I'd given Ryan the weekend off from the shop so that he could hang out at a friend's lake home. He wouldn't be home until Sunday. We had recently booked his flight to visit my parents in mid-August, his first solo flight. By then, he would've chosen where he would live come fall.

After we closed for the day, I changed into bike shorts and a moisture-wicking shirt, chugged a large glass of chocolate milk mixed with protein powder, and packed a bike jacket, water bottle, and protein bar in my bike pack.

Minutes later, Kelly met me outside the shop. "Thought you might need to get away."

"You got that right."

I buckled my bike helmet, and we were off, saving our words for later. Endorphins pulsated through me as Kelly led us down less busy trails, guiding us back toward town before the sun began to set.

"Feel up to a beer? We could sit outside at Crushers," Kelly suggested.

"That sounds good."

At Crushers, we locked our bikes in the back-alley rack, placed our IPA orders, and found a table outside. We spoke of Donovan's update on Gabriel and the others in the nightclub.

"It's going to be difficult for Donovan to leave Florida," Kelly said, "no matter how well Gabriel recovers physically."

"He's told me a bit about Gabriel's emotional vulnerability over the years. I'm surprised Donovan didn't move to Florida years ago to keep an eye on him," I said.

"Believe me, he talked about it." Kelly took a swig of her beer. "But his business is here. And at that time, Cassie was still living with him. He didn't want to pull her out of this school and town. He tried like the dickens to get Gabriel to move home." Kelly wiped the condensation from her beer glass. "But it was a struggle for Gabriel here years ago."

"It seems better now. Maybe because of the younger generation finding their way into the community?"

"I think so," Kelly said.

As I biked home an hour later, I wondered if Gabriel would be willing to move now with his partner gone—and whether Donovan could handle it if he didn't.

Forty-nine deaths and over fifty more with injuries—that was how quickly the gunman mowed down his victims, all because of hate. Sometimes, I found it hard to remember that overall, the world had far more kindness than evil in it.

Tragedies like that one peppered the news all too often, but that was the first time I knew one of the victims—because yes, Gabriel was a victim of the hate crime, albeit one of the lucky victims who lived.

While I was talking with Donovan on Sunday after the shop closed, Ryan arrived home from his friend's house and made a beeline to the kitchen for a snack.

"Gabriel should be released tomorrow," Donovan said. "I'm not sure how long I'll stay. It's his right shoulder and chest area, so he's going to be struggling to do much for himself since he's right-handed. I told him I draw the line at wiping his ass, though."

I laughed. "It's good to hear you joke again."

"I'm so relieved that he's going to be okay. I'm too young to be the last person left in my family."

After we hung up, Ryan came to sit next to me on the sofa, clutching a large bowl of Cheerios and milk.

"Did you have a fun day?" I ruffled his long, dirty hair.

"We did!" Ryan shoved a spoonful of cereal into his mouth and used his wrist to wipe off the milk dribbling down his chin, happiness oozing from his smelly pores.

"Ooh, you need a shower before bed."

"Why? I'm just gonna get dirty again. Plus, I have to tell you something." The sparkle in Ryan's eyes was the balm I needed to soothe my concern for Donovan and Gabriel.

"Sure. What's up?"

Ryan cleared his throat. "I made my decision. I want to go to school here this fall."

I quit breathing, not wanting to make a sound in case he changed his mind. After a few seconds, I couldn't stand it; I had to know. "That's great! Are you sure?" I didn't want to get my hopes up, just to have them shot back down.

"I am. I like my friends here, and they said I'll probably have a better chance of making the team here in high school. Plus"—Ryan shot me a mischievous grin—"I figure you made a big change in your old age, so I can probably handle one too."

I pulled him in so quickly for a hug that the cereal bowl and remaining milk went flying onto the floor.

I didn't care. What mattered was that I would have my son with me. I let the tears of joy fall. We had peeked in the Crimson Creek middle school windows the month before, but I hadn't scheduled a tour of the school yet, not wanting to jinx it. I promised to call next week.

Chapter 49

David

I hadn't been sleeping well since Hurdy Gurdy Man's brother was shot. *Such senseless killing!* I couldn't dwell on another war against mankind, or my thoughts would succumb to a dark place.

On the last Wednesday of July, business was steady. I chose a happy playlist for Goober to lighten my mood: songs like "Wake Up Sunshine," "Montego Bay," and "No Matter What." I couldn't change the hatred in the world, but I could spread positive thoughts to those around me.

Things were winding down in the shop when I arrived after my one o'clock shuttle run. Hal and Maudie had the day off for the birthday party of one of their grandkids, so Oliver was driving Grover to haul customers, and Eden worked the store.

When I was in the back of the shop, waiting for my next group of shuttle customers to arrive, the phone rang. I had a bird's-eye view of Eden and Hadley busy with customers, so I took the call. "Fun-Key Monkey, this is David speaking."

"David! Where's Eden? She didn't answer her cell." The words tumbled over each other, and I needed a second to recognize Whip's voice.

"Everything okay? She's with a customer. I can interrupt her—"

"Yes!" Whip shouted.

I set the phone down, the normally easygoing Whip's anxiety fueling mine. He had stopped in before lunch to pick up Ryan and take him mountain biking with Willow.

I hustled as fast as I could to the front of the store as Eden finished ringing up a sale. "Excuse me. Eden, Whip's on the phone." Over the years, I'd been disciplined to hide my emotions, but I couldn't control my shaking hand as I pointed at the phone behind the counter.

Eden picked up the phone and, seconds later, let out a cry muffled by her hand just as an ambulance siren cut through the town, speeding toward the rec area parking lot. After that, everything seemed to happen in slow motion. Hadley stepped behind the counter to replace Eden as I struggled to keep up with Eden, who ran toward the stairs to her apartment.

I'd caught enough of Whip's first words, shouted through the phone before the ambulance went by. Ryan had had a bad accident on the bike trails.

Dear God, please watch over Ryan, I prayed as Eden flew up the stairs, and I heard her running around in her apartment.

"Eden? How can I help?" I shouted from the bottom of the steps.

"I'm meeting them at the hospital. Ryan crashed on the trail." She huffed sobs between words. "But I can't find my keys! Where're my damn keys?"

She went back inside her apartment, and I headed behind the counter, where I'd spotted her cell phone on top of her small strap purse, and her keys were there.

I carried everything to the bottom of the steps and called up to Eden, "They're here with your phone."

Seconds later, Eden flew down the steps and took everything I held out.

I put my hands on her shoulders. "Let's take a few calming breaths." I put my face close to hers and nodded for her to follow my slow inhalation and exhalation. "I know this is scary, but you'll be no good to Ryan if you don't keep a cool head."

I didn't let go of Eden until the caged look diminished in her eyes. The hospital was four blocks away, and I changed my prayer to include her safety.

The siren blaring toward the rec area reassured me that Ryan was alive. Within an hour, Oliver had shuttled the people I was supposed to and was back in the shop with Hadley and me.

I manned the phone and would stay until closing now. Suddenly, Whip burst into the shop, his face as pale as winter. "Did Eden tell you?" Blood was smeared on his shirt and forearm.

I led him to the back of the shop, away from the customers. Hadley and Oliver would take care of them.

"Only that she was heading to the hospital because Ryan was hurt," I said.

"I just left the hospital." Whip rubbed dirty palms through his hair, blinking back tears. "It was awful! Willow was first on the trail, and I followed behind Ryan. He was struggling to keep up with her, and although I yelled for Ryan to ride at his speed, you know how boys are…"

"Didn't want a girl to outride him." I rubbed my palm down my face.

Whip nodded. "Ryan took a corner too fast, his front tire hitting a boulder, and he went sailing over the handlebars. We were on a decline, he landed on his back, and… he didn't move." He held a fist to his mouth until he composed himself. "Luckily, we weren't far from the main parking lot, so the paramedics were able to reach us fairly quickly."

I retrieved a glass of water from the break room. "It's okay, Whip. It was an accident. You got the ambulance there right away." I rubbed his back, much as I used to do when Louise and Lee were young and woke with a bad dream, back when I'd been there for my family.

"Willow feels awful. She'd seen Ryan behind her, last time she checked, but he fell behind when we hit a couple of steep hills. I think he figured he could catch up on the down curve." Whip chugged the glass of water.

"What do they think is wrong with Ryan?"

"It's his spine." Whip's fingers drummed his crossed arms. "Ryan could move his hands but said he couldn't feel his legs. I stabilized his neck and head until the paramedics arrived."

Whip paced. My stomach roiled with nausea at the grim possibility of spinal damage. "Eden promised to keep us updated. I'm sure she'll do the same with you."

"They did a CT scan when I was there. Eden was waiting for the results once the radiologist reviews the CT." He ran a hand through his beard. "I'm going to see Willow. Kelly picked her up. I need to reassure Willow that, that..." Whip's chin quivered.

"It will be okay," I said as if I could predict the future. "Willow needs you now."

"I'm going back to sit with Eden once I know Willow's okay. It sounds like they might do a spine reconstruction on Ryan," Whip said.

"What the hell is that?" It didn't sound good to me.

"I guess they use a special computer that generates a three-dimensional reconstruction of the spine so the surgeon can see what's going on," Whip explained.

He left a few minutes later to check on Willow, and I attempted to keep my mind occupied in the shop until Hadley told me Eden was on the phone for me.

"Whip said he stopped by and talked with you." Eden's voice was calmer than I expected. "Whip's back with me, and the surgeon just spoke with us. He's connected with a neurosurgeon at Children's Hospital in Minneapolis and has scheduled an airlift transfer with them."

I sat at the break room table, taking it all in, and sensed this levelheaded Eden speaking with me was the same one who'd navigated her way up the banking ladder.

"The chopper should be here soon. The CT scan shows pressure on his spinal cord and injury to his T8 vertebra. They'll do some sort of decompression surgery and spine fusion at Children's," Eden said. "I'm leaving from here. I've got my travel bag." With all the trips to and from the cities over the past several months, Eden was keeping a packed bag in her truck.

"Drive safe, Eden. Ryan's in good hands. And we've got everything covered here."

"Thank you," Eden whispered before hanging up.

I stood next to the wall in the back and softly rapped out the POW tap code for GBU, hoping Ryan and Eden could feel the blessing in their hearts.

Chapter 50
Eden

My first call had been to the last person I wanted to tell—Trent. I'd arrived at our local hospital with little knowledge other than of Ryan's back injury. I called Trent's cell while I waited for the ambulance, my words stumbling out, unable to find a way to explain what I'd yet to see, something my brain wanted to block out.

"Are you freaking kidding me, Eden? Ryan doesn't even like to mountain bike! Why do you push him to do stupid shit like that?" Trent's accusation zapped me.

Have I been pushing Ryan? "I didn't *make* him. I wasn't even there. Ryan went with a friend of mine and his daughter, who is a friend of Ryan's. And that's not the issue here. Our son has a possible spinal injury!" I refrained from adding *"You pompous jerk!"*

"Are they going to be able to help Ryan at that country bumpkin hospital?" Trent's question was one I'd asked myself.

"They're a good hospital, well equipped. I'll know more soon, and I'll call you back then." I hung up to avoid questions I had no answers for yet.

When Whip rejoined me after checking on Willow, the ER doctor explained Ryan's diagnosis and the need to airlift him to Children's Hospital for back surgery.

"Ryan's left ankle is swollen, but for now, his spine is the main concern. There's pressure on his spinal cord, and his T8 vertebra has a compression fracture that will need to be fused. They're going to do surgery to remove bone fragments and do a fusion to stabilize the traumatized area."

I functioned like a robot on autopilot, nodding along with the doctor's words. After he left, I called Trent again, thankful Whip was there to help me relay everything the ER doctor had said. "The surgery will remove the pressure on his spine, and then Ryan should start getting some feeling back in his legs."

"I'll head to Children's now," Trent said before mumbling something to someone at work.

It hadn't registered with me that Trent would be at work. For me, all time had stopped once I got Whip's call. After we hung up, I was able to briefly see Ryan, kiss his forehead, and reassure him that Trent and I would see him at the hospital.

Back on the road, I focused my concentration on getting to the hospital safely. I would call my parents and Donovan later—same with Stevie Grace. Thinking of SG also brought her father, Moe, to mind—Moe, who had been paralyzed at the waist since his injury in Vietnam.

It was early evening when I joined Trent in the waiting room at Children's Hospital. We agreed our focus would be on doing whatever it took to help Ryan recover, a pendulum of promises and fear swinging between us.

When Ryan was in surgery, Trent had already alerted his mother, so I left the waiting room to make phone calls. I called my parents, who promised to call Ellie and Nielson for me, then I called Donovan and left a message for Stevie Grace, who must've been flying somewhere.

And when I returned to sit by Trent, I silently bartered with God for the surgery to go well so that Ryan would regain feeling and walk again. I would sell the shop, move back to the cities, go back to a corporate job—anything, anything at all. No bribe was off the table.

"I'm sorry about what I said earlier." Trent's words cut into my bartering thoughts.

"What?" I turned and saw fear etched on Trent's face.

"When I accused you of making Ryan ride the trails." Trent cleared his throat. "He did tell me a couple of months ago that the trails scared him and that he'd rather go to the skateboard park or kayak. But that was before he moved in with you for the summer."

Trent's words "for the summer" reminded me I'd yet to tell him about Ryan's decision to attend sixth grade in Crimson Creek. I'd planned to wait until August first in case Ryan changed his mind. It didn't matter now. He could move to Alaska with my parents and attend school there if he wanted. I just wanted him okay again. Thinking of Alaska reminded me of his upcoming trip, one I would need to cancel. It didn't matter. Nothing mattered other than Ryan's recovery.

It's funny how tragedy rearranges our focus on what is truly important. Jobs, where we live, vacations, who likes us and who doesn't—none of that's important. When you're backed into a corner and trying to cut a deal with God, it is never for any of that. The bartering with God is for the people you love. When it's all said and done, they're what matters.

I pinched the bottom of my nose, tingling from unshed tears. "I think Ryan's new friends have been the encouragement for him to keep trying the trails. He's stuck with the easy trails, but today, he rode too fast for his experience."

We'd gone through two cups of coffee each, waiting for an update on the surgery that could take four hours or more. Sitting next to Trent, I thought back to when Ryan had his appendectomy. That seemed like a lifetime ago, back when my life was corporate work, stress, and dissatisfaction. I would gladly embrace that life again if it meant Ryan would recover.

After eight o'clock, the surgeon came out to give us an update. "Surgery went well, and Ryan will be wheeled into a recovery room soon." The surgeon's shoulders sagged a little, and I wondered how many hours he'd put in already on this never-ending day.

"Ryan's got a bad left ankle sprain, so we'll need him to not put any weight on it for around six weeks. After crutches, we'll put a walking boot on until he's fully recovered." The surgeon took off his glasses and rubbed his eyes. "With his back injury, even at six weeks, he won't be hopping up or down steps."

His comment brought my mind to the many steep steps to my apartment, and I voiced my concern.

"Once he can bear weight on his left foot—usually around three months—then he can tackle steps like the ones you mentioned," the surgeon said. "Ryan will need to wear a TLSO brace, also called a clamshell, that will cover his thoracic and lumbar spine area and sacrum. He'll need to wear that for four to six weeks."

I struggled to focus on all the time frames, so fixated on the news that Ryan would walk again.

"The combination of his back injury and ankle sprain will mean Ryan needs to be extra careful even after his ankle heals. We need that spine to heal."

Trent and I nodded like obedient children, trying to take in all the information.

By the time we finished with the surgeon and were led into Ryan's recovery room, I knew this much: Ryan would not be staying with me in the near future.

He would be in the hospital for a few days with outpatient physical therapy after that and checkups over the coming weeks. His PT would be in the cities. His follow-up appointments would be in the cities. I had all those steep steps to the apartment, impossible for Ryan to tackle without hopping.

Remembering my barter promises, I took my emotions out of the equation. "We need to discuss possible options for the next several weeks," I said.

"When I called Mom to tell her what happened, she offered for Ryan to stay there," Trent said. "She can take care of him during the day. I'll stay there at night."

Emily's rambler-style home had no steps and three bedrooms. "That's a good option. If she doesn't mind, I can stay with her Tuesdays and Wednesdays, give her a break."

I refrained from telling Trent how I'd bartered everything, including my soul, and would walk away from the shop if needed. He'd likely made similar bargains.

Trent went home late that night. I stayed in Ryan's room, weighed down with worry.

David answered when I called the shop the next morning. After receiving confirmation that they had things under control, I unloaded on him.

"Ryan will need to be in the cities another couple of months, which means he won't go to school in Crimson Creek, which makes me question why I should stay there..." I paced the sidewalk outside the hospital, trees shading me from the sultry late-July morning.

"One thing at a time, Eden," David said. "The best thing you can do right now is to be there with Ryan, and save the worrying for later. We've got the work schedules figured out, and Maudie said you've gone over ordering with her before. When you're ready, give her a call."

I rubbed my eyes coated with sandpaper, unsure I'd slept at all the previous night. "I will. Thank you."

"Just so you know, Hal and I are working eight-hour days, and there's not a damn thing you can do about it," David continued with sass. "You aren't the boss of us right now."

I scoffed. "Don't I know that."

Not having to think of the shop was a relief, not worrying about anything other than Ryan. He'd regained a prickly feeling in his legs, a feeling that should continue to improve with extensive physical therapy.

Ryan was released from Children's Hospital on Monday, and we'd all agreed with Emily that her home would be the recovery camp for the next couple of weeks.

I stayed at Emily's until Thursday before driving back to Crimson Creek, feeling like I'd been gone a month instead of a week.

Trent would stay at his mom's and help for the weekend, and I would be back at Emily's on Monday. None of us spoke of school, which would start in five weeks. We only focused on getting through each day. I bypassed the shop when I arrived in Crimson Creek, instead heading to my apartment.

I'd spoken with Donovan almost every day, and he estimated it would be another week or more before he returned to Minnesota. He refused to leave Gabriel until he was emotionally on the way to recovery. I called him after I unpacked and showered.

"Gabriel spoke with a counselor today, one who specializes in grief therapy," Donovan said. "It helps that others from the nightclub are going through similar emotions, knowing they aren't alone in their trauma and grief."

"I love you even more for being there to make sure your brother's okay," I said, reclining on the sofa. I had zero energy.

Donovan was no doubt beat, and I guessed that my employees—whom I would check on soon—were worn out.

"Well, I feel awful for not being there for you," Donovan said.

"I'm doing fine other than I miss you. A lot."

After we hung up, I thought of the past week of our lives. It seemed like forever since I'd seen Donovan. I pushed myself up from the couch and headed down to the shop to touch base with my employees—my wonderful, big-hearted, couldn't-do-it-without-them employees.

I was back in the cities the following week, taking Ryan to outpatient physical therapy and a follow-up doctor appointment. If he was careful, he could be done wearing the clamshell before school began and would only need crutches for that first week of school.

Although Ryan and I hadn't talked about it, any fool could see it made sense for Ryan to start school in the cities, not Crimson Creek. And I was no fool.

Chapter 51

The next few weeks blurred together. I focused on the shop's needs Fridays through Mondays. The rest of the time, I focused on Ryan at Emily's home. Ryan, who had moved back to Trent's at night after the first two weeks, would stay with Emily during the day until school began. And other than playing video games with Brady, Ryan was bored—no baseball, no skateboarding, no fun. We played a lot of board games and cards between physical therapy.

Donovan and I had spent little time together since he arrived home from Florida the second week of August. He spent every moment playing catch-up with his construction business.

We had a rare night together one Saturday night, both of us feeling a decade older than we had in July.

"I don't let my guard down with Gabriel," Donovan said over fish kebabs he'd made on the grill. We sat by the lake in front of his house, enjoying the cool breeze after another sultry August day.

"I can't control his life," Donovan continued, "but I don't know how to quit worrying."

"I don't think we ever quit worrying about people we love..." I leaned my head back against the beach chair.

"So, how are you handling the school decision? I imagine it's bothering you more than you're letting on," Donovan said.

"I'm putting on a pretty good act in front of Ryan. I think it's been a big adjustment in Trent's life with Amber. We're all struggling."

"Emily told me I can stay there every Tuesday and Wednesday for as long as I want. But with Ryan attending school in the cities..." I paused to swallow the cry-ball forming in my throat, "I will need to find a permanent solution. I got spoiled having SG's apartment available."

"Speaking of Stevie Grace, what's the latest on her move?"

"She made an offer on the building last week. If it goes through, she's putting her notice in with the airlines." The excitement of SG living in Crimson Creek was a bright spot that helped offset Ryan's attending middle school in the cities. Trent and I had agreed to table any long-term plans with Ryan. The accident had changed our perspective on a lot of things.

The sun had set, chilling the air. Donovan pulled me in for a hug. "Stevie Grace moving here is proof that we never know what the future will bring." He brushed back my bangs, his thumb massaging my temple. "Things will work out, Eden. It's not always what we want, but it's what we get, and we make the best of it."

His other hand caressed the back of my head, and as the stress headache of the past few weeks lessened, I could only hope he was right.

I took Ryan back-to-school-clothes shopping the week before school began, the first day he took off his back brace, something he'd negotiated with the doctor. When Ryan started school, he would be able to take the brace off for those seven hours, a victory in Ryan's eyes.

"The crutches are kind of cool. A back brace... not so much," Ryan said. "Do you think middle school kids wear shorts to school? I don't want to look like a nerd." Jeans were still uncomfortable for him.

"I'd think so. And if you find that you're the only one, maybe you'll start a trend."

Ryan squinted as if I said Martians attended middle school. "I'm glad I'm going to school here. I bet the kids at Crimson Creek's school wear clothes stained from the red dirt."

I stopped looking through the clothes rack of shorts. "Ryan! Why would you say that? They're no different from you or your friends here in the cities."

Ryan blinked at the floor. After I waited out the long silence hanging between us, he said quietly, "Do you think they're making fun of me?"

I leaned down to meet his eyes, realizing how little I had to crouch. He would be as tall as me in a couple of years. "Who? The kids in Crimson Creek?"

Ryan nodded.

I made a decision. "Let's skip shopping for now. How about an early lunch?" I received another nod, and we turned to walk out of the store, Ryan clipping alongside me with his crutches. We headed for the food court, placed our orders, and found an empty table.

As we ate, I unwrapped the topic we'd avoided for weeks, thinking I was helping Ryan by not talking about the accident. "I read the card Willow made for you, read the card your summer baseball team sent with all their get-well wishes. Do you honestly think they're making fun of you getting in an accident?" I kept my voice low. "They like you, Ryan. And guess what? There are a lot of kids your age who live there and haven't dared to try the trails yet. Adults have accidents on those trails too. Unfortunately, it happens a lot."

Ryan pushed his sesame chicken around with a fork. "They don't think I'm a wimp?"

I shook my head. "You're a badass for trying. Remember when we went on that class trip two years ago and you had the chance to try rock wall climbing?"

Ryan's brow furrowed, likely confused as to where I was going with the memory. "You chose not to do it but were impressed by your friends who did try. Remember Brady losing his grip near the top?"

Ryan's eyes widened. "I remember. Brady's harness kept him suspended up at the top!"

"Did you think he was a wimp?"

Ryan grimaced. "Heck no!"

"Okay, then. Case closed. Now, let's talk about the decision for you to stay here in the cities. I didn't want to add to the stress in your life already, but although I'm supportive of you staying to attend sixth grade here, I want you to know that I will always want you to be with me in Crimson Creek," I worked at keeping the pleading out of my voice.

"I know, Mom."

Lately, I'd been struggling—again—to remember to be grateful he was alive and would be okay. The greed of wanting Ryan with me was seeping back in, and I had to build a mental dam to stop it. "I'll be here every Tuesday and Wednesday night, staying at Grandma Emily's until I can figure something else out." I'd looked into an Airbnb room as an option.

When I dropped him off at Trent's, I hugged his shoulders. "I'll be at Grandma Emily's next Monday night and will drive here Tuesday morning so I can see you before you get on the bus."

He surprised me with a kiss on the cheek, and my knees about buckled in gratitude.

I arrived at Trent's on Tuesday morning after Amber left for work. Trent greeted me at the door as Ryan finished his breakfast. I'd offered to drop him off at school and had been reminded that would make him look like a baby. He would always be my baby.

"I'll be here when you get home from school," I said, gently hugging Ryan before he hobbled to the bus stop on his crutches.

Trent and Amber would still be at work when Ryan got off the bus. He could've been home alone, but I wanted to be there for his first day.

While he was at school, I checked several Airbnb listings and found an elderly woman who lived a handful of miles from Trent with a small mother-in-law apartment above her detached garage. I couldn't impose on Emily forever.

I didn't feel comfortable going inside Trent's house when nobody was home, so I sat on the front steps and waited for Ryan. Fifteen minutes after I arrived, he hobbled up the driveway, wearing a wide grin. That was the happiest I'd seen Ryan since his accident.

I stood. "School went well?"

"Yeah. I've got some cool teachers, and I met some new kids." Ryan unlocked the front door, and I followed him inside as he maneuvered the two front steps. He set his backpack down on a recliner and leaned his crutches against the wall. After six more days, he could ditch them for a walking boot.

"How's your back feeling?"

The day before, Ryan had taken the brace off for six hours, but he hadn't been maneuvering crutches down a school hallway off and on.

"It's kind of sore. I'll put my brace on in a minute."

I sat with Ryan at the kitchen table while he made himself a snack, and we visited. I told him of the Airbnb place and that beginning the following week, I'd rent the place every Tuesday and Wednesday night. It would give us time together and give Trent and Amber time for themselves. I would take whatever I could get.

But can you do this for the next seven years, Eden?

I saw no point in staying at Emily's another night, so I drove home Wednesday night, the oldies station cranked up in my pickup. I tapped the steering wheel in time with the drums in "Indian Reservation" by Paul Revere & the Raiders, butchered the heck out of the lyrics to "We've Got to Get It On Again" by the Addrisi Brothers, and sang at the top of my lungs to "Never Ending Song of Love" with Delaney & Bonnie. The music helped lift my mood.

Back home, I unpacked before stepping onto the deck. I picked at the dead leaves on my tomato and pepper plants, all in sore need of TLC.

Mom and I had kept in touch after Ryan's accident, mostly sticking to Ryan's recovery updates. As I sat on the deck, the park illuminated by streetlights, I called my parents' landline, and Dad answered. After giving him an update on Ryan, I let out the worry I'd been holding in.

"Please tell me this will all work out," I begged. "I know in my heart I won't leave this town or my shop, but I am still struggling to wrap my head around this being our future." I hugged myself, wishing for a sweatshirt. "I don't know what to do."

"I can't make that decision for you, Eden." Dad's voice, always so reassuring and comforting in person, had the same effect over the phone. "Listen, I can only tell you that I watched my mom live her life for everyone but herself. Yes, she was content, but you know when she was happiest?" He answered his question. "After my dad died. Mom finally had a chance to pursue her dreams. She took history and art classes at a local college, traveled outside of Iowa with some of my sisters, even went on a cruise!"

I remembered Grandma Grady, the woman from whom I'd inherited the red tinge in my hair. She was a sweet grandma who'd died when I was in grade school.

"That's so sad. Poor Grandma!"

"The point is my siblings and I were so happy for our mom when she finally got to do things she should have been able to do before she was in her seventies," Dad said. "If you move back to the cities, I'm afraid you'll regret it, and Ryan will feel that regret."

I heard Mom enter the room and Dad fill her in on our conversation before handing Mom the phone.

"I wish we were there for you, Eden," Mom said.

I felt the same, yet I also knew my parents were thriving in their slice of heaven outside Anchorage. *How would you feel, Eden, if they moved back to Minnesota just to make you happy?* I knew the answer.

"I've told you about Unity over the years," Mom said, referring to the elderly woman who adopted her after her parents died. "In her last few years of life, when I was taking care of her, she kept making me promise that I wouldn't settle for things in life when she was gone." Mom's voice took on a wistful tone. "She worried I'd stay living at her old hobby farm in Missouri, worried I'd settle with never leaving to pursue my own life..."

Mom had told me the story of how she'd ended up in Grandfield all those years before, but I never thought of the courage she'd needed to step out of her comfort zone and pursue her own life. Now, it hit home.

"Nothing is forever, Eden. You know that life is a constant change of highs and lows, dreams and despair. It's *life*." Mom's words were slow and measured. "Accept the present. Hope for the future."

I reminded myself that the most important thing was that Ryan was healthy.

We talked for several more minutes, and after we hung up, I counted the weeks until I would meet up with my parents and siblings in Grandfield for Christmas. Once every two years wasn't enough. I recited a phrase Ryan had learned at school years before: *You get what you get, and you don't get upset, Eden.*

I met David and Donovan at the Triple C for supper on the Thursday after Labor Day. I was back to closing at five during the week and closing on Wednesdays.

While we ate, David mentioned a mountain biker who'd ended up getting airlifted to a hospital in the cities after a nasty crash on the trail over the holiday weekend.

"He didn't brake on a curve," David said, shaking his head.

His comment brought Ryan's accident to mind.

"Makes me wonder why Ryan didn't brake." I knew he'd been taught not to override the trails, no matter how fast the person in front was going.

"Do you mean brake as in slowing his bike or break as in not more broken bones?" Donovan asked.

"Like brakes on the bike. I feel like *I'm* the one who's broken." My voice caught. "Someone should write a manual on how we move on after we break."

David reached across the table and patted my hand, and Donovan put his arm around my shoulders.

"How we move on after we break is by accepting the brutal reality that the world keeps moving forward, no matter the pain of the past," David said.

"Speaking from experience?" I held David's hand.

"It's how we got through the days in prison." David paused, likely reflecting on the unbearable pain that came later, when his son and wife died.

"After we feel broken is when we're given the chance to rearrange the broken pieces," David continued. "For me, when I came home from Vietnam, I focused on my marriage and being a father with an intensity I didn't have before I became a POW. I'd taken my family and marriage for granted before then."

I thought of how my dad said he struggled after coming home from Vietnam, how my mom struggled after losing her parents when she was young and during her years in foster care.

My life had been easy, with minimal bumps along the way. I laid my head on Donovan's shoulder, thinking of all he'd lost, all the challenges he'd endured. I vowed not to focus on *where* Ryan lived but *how* we lived our lives.

Chapter 52

My first autumn in the shop was unpredictable, with some weekends warm enough for lake activities and others so blustery cold that nobody wanted to venture outdoors. During the week, I headed to the Airbnb in the cities to spend Tuesday and Wednesday nights with Ryan. While he was in school those days, I worked on various financial writing projects again, the flexible income helping to offset the slower business days at the shop. Every Thursday morning, I drove to Crimson Creek to open the shop and played volleyball Thursday nights—a weekly activity that had expanded my social circle.

Ryan had worked his way through physical therapy to almost one-hundred-percent recovery. Gone were the walking boot and the clamshell back brace, and by the end of October, he was able to slowly maneuver the apartment steps to spend the weekend with me. He'd spent two weekends in Crimson Creek before then but had stayed at Kelly's house, bunking with Mason, his bedroom located on the main level of their home.

The week of Thanksgiving, I skipped my trip to the cities since I would get Ryan for the long weekend when I picked him up Friday morning. Donovan insisted on hosting Thanksgiving at his house, and although I had offered to cohost, he'd refused. He'd been acting a little aloof lately, unavailable at times, and I put it down to his concerns about Gabriel's emotional recovery.

Stevie Grace, proud owner of a building downtown, had quit her job and had been spending the past month "prettying up" her apartment on the second floor while Donovan and his crew were redoing the ground floor for her future yoga studio.

SG, Whip, Willow, David, Hal, and Maudie were all attending Thanksgiving at Donovan's. His daughter, Cassie, would be home before New Year's Eve; David's daughter, Louise, would visit David the week before Christmas... and Donovan, Ryan, and I would meet my parents and siblings in Grandfield the week of Christmas.

Thanksgiving dinner was set for noon at Donovan's, and I arrived early to help. Donovan, usually as cool as a cucumber, seemed a little flustered. I wanted to point out that was what he got for trying to do it all.

"Want me to pour you a glass of wine?" I asked as I set the appetizers I'd made on the kitchen counter. I dug his corkscrew out of a drawer and waved the bottle at him.

"Um, sure." He basted the turkey and checked the dressing. Everything else would be brought by guests.

As I unwrapped the dip and crackers I'd brought, I swore a dog barked outside. "Do you have people at the cabins?" We typically couldn't hear anything from his cabin rentals.

Car doors slammed, and I assumed some of the others were showing up. The only one I knew of who had a dog was Whip. I couldn't imagine they'd brought their dog. I set my wine glass down and noted that Donovan had pretty much guzzled his. The barking was getting closer. I opened the front door to find David and a golden retriever puppy with a leash dragging behind him. It zipped right past me and into the house.

"You got a dog?" I had talked to David yesterday, and he'd said nothing about a dog.

Before he could answer, I heard a voice that my heart would recognize anywhere, even though its timbre was changing by the week. Ryan appeared around the corner from Donovan's parking area with a smile bright enough to power the whole town.

"How did *you* get here?" My joy at seeing Ryan a day early was thwarted by a what-the-heck-is-going-on question boomeranging in my head.

"Stevie Grace picked me up this morning," Ryan explained before he ran for the dog.

Behind Ryan were Whip, Willow, and SG. I turned to them, confused. Donovan called from behind me, "Why don't you come back inside, where the cold won't shock you with a heart attack."

Stevie Grace stepped inside with me and looped her arm through mine as Whip closed the door behind us. Another car pulled up, likely Hal and Maudie, but the chaos in front of me couldn't wait for them. Ryan and Willow were chasing David's puppy all over the living room. I worried they'd add to Donovan's stress, and I worried that Ryan would trip and hurt himself.

But Donovan didn't appear anxious. In fact, the stress of minutes earlier seemed to have evaporated. Maybe the wine had kicked in.

"Why do I feel like I'm out of the loop here?" I asked.

Donovan threw an arm around Ryan with the caught puppy tucked in his arm like a football. "You going to tell her?" he asked Ryan.

"Um, Mom, meet our dog." Ryan batted his eyes as though that would lessen the shock.

"Glass of wine?" David handed me my glass from the counter with a twinkle in his eyes.

I decided David was the guilty party. "Did *you* get Ryan the dog?"

His words were drawn out. "Not exactly."

I turned my steely gaze toward Donovan.

He held up his hands. "Hey, I'm innocent in all of this." He pointed at the puppy. "Well, at least this."

"What else is there?" I sat on the nearest chair, feeling like Alice in Wonderland.

Ryan and the puppy came to stand in front of me. "We've got it worked out about where March will live and stuff like that."

"March?" I asked as Ryan nuzzled the puppy's neck.

"Yep. David and I decided on the name. The owner sent videos, and it looked like the puppy was marching when he walked. Plus, David said it's a good month. It's when a lot of the POWs were released from Vietnam."

I gave up and collapsed against the back of the chair as Hal and Maudie entered the scene.

"There's the culprit." David pointed at Hal. "Blame Hal. His son's golden retriever had pups a couple of months ago, and they had three left from the litter. Ryan told me last summer that he wished he had a dog. Be lucky I didn't buy all three of them for him," David said.

"Does your dad know about this?" Trent was *not* a fan of pets.

Ryan met Donovan's eyes. "Um, I think so." He nodded toward me as if he thought Donovan should step in and explain.

"You *think* so?" I took a long drink of wine, feeling a headache brewing. Ryan's happiness would soon be wiped out when Trent told him no to March.

Donovan shook his head and mouthed "you" to Ryan, who cleared his voice like a man about to come clean.

"Um, Dad doesn't have to know about March. David's agreed to take care of him—with my help—until March can live with me." Ryan's mouth twitched. "Until you and I move out of the apartment and into a house with a yard, David and I will... What's it called? Co-parent?"

I leaned forward, certain I'd heard wrong. But the joy in Ryan's eyes—and everyone else's—reaffirmed I'd heard right. "You're moving in with me?"

Ryan nodded. "During Christmas break. Dad knows about *that*. He and Donovan have been talking and making sure my records get transferred to the school here."

I leapt out of the chair, engulfing Ryan and March in a fierce hug, the puppy licking my neck. "Oh, Ryan, I am so, so happy!" I cried into Ryan's shoulder and eventually pulled away. "Why? I mean, what made you change your mind?"

Ryan's face scrunched in thought. "A lot of things. My middle school is so big. Too big. I didn't have Brady in any classes. And I missed everyone here. Mason and Willow have been calling me in between my weekends here." His eyes met Willow's before turning to me. "And I missed you." His chin quivered.

Christmas had come early, giving me the best gift ever.

I was no longer broken. I had never felt more whole.

Epilogue
End of May 2022

My cell phone read 7:09 a.m. when I dragged myself out of bed. A slight headache thrummed like a drumming grouse. I liked to wake with the sun, get outdoors on our acreage, and breathe in the fresh air, enjoying the quiet before I drove to the shop. But I had the day off.

The day before had been a long one. Ryan's high school grad party could've been given an A+ for success. Now, the house was quiet, thanks to the majority of the partiers staying at Donovan's place next door. "Next door" was a loose term, given that our homes each sat on twenty acres. Even March had stayed at Donovan's, sleeping in Ryan's tent.

Sunshine filtered into the kitchen through open windows as I brewed a small pot of coffee. I set out David's mug and spoon at his spot at the kitchen table alongside a canister of herbal tea. Even David had stayed at Ryan's grad party for a few hours, watching the adults and teens play volleyball, the little kids playing tag and blowing bubbles, a few of them, including Whip and SG's six-year-old daughter, snuggling up to David as he sat in the shade.

Tiring David out didn't take much, ever since his stroke two years before. It had happened as he drove customers in Goober to the rec parking lot. A young nurse sitting up front near David had watched it all play out and stepped in to take control of Goober, pulling the shuttle bus to the side of the road before she attended to David.

He'd recovered enough over the past two years, his slurred speech transitioning back to a slower version of his old speech, and the need for a wheelchair transitioned to using a walker after extensive physical therapy. David would never fully recover at ninety, but he was a fighter, the best fighter I ever knew.

After his stroke, and much pig-prodding on Louise's part, she had convinced David to sell his home. That was when Ryan and I insisted he move in with us. No steps, no lawn care, no worries—and plenty of love from us and Donovan next door. Donovan's home wasn't an option for David since Cassie, her husband, and her two young sons had moved from Colorado to a suburb of the Twin Cities a few years before. They were frequent visitors, and the little boys kept us all entertained and exhausted.

I thought of Louise as I sat on the deck with my coffee, listening to the birds. Her husband had made a long recovery from Lyme disease but still tired easily and had some memory issues. "Post-treatment Lyme Disease Syndrome," they called it. Their sons had finished college, and one had married. He and his wife had had a baby girl the week before, and when Louise called to tell David the news, he'd given a nod to lyrics from an old Blood, Sweat & Tears favorite of his. "There. Now when I die, there's been one child born to carry on." Louise poo-pooed him and reminded David she would be visiting us in a few weeks, bearing photos of his first great-grandchild.

David, Ryan, and I had flown to Vermont a few times over the years until David's stroke, visiting Louise and her family and taking in the beauty of the area. Ryan had fallen in love with their town and the University of Vermont in Burlington, two hours from where Louise and Jack lived, the same college their sons had attended.

The year after we moved out of the apartment and into our home that Donovan had built, Donovan took me and Ryan to Vermont to hike part of the Appalachian Trail. He'd known of my hope to hike it years before, on my honeymoon with Trent. Ours hadn't been a honeymoon trip, but Donovan and I celebrated our commitment to each other, a commitment that became stronger with each passing year.

I might have tested Donovan's love for me with a yard full of teens at his place. He'd insisted, though, so that David could rest. I finished my coffee, went back inside, and dressed in jean shorts and a tank top. Not yet June, the morning held enough humidity to curl the short hairs on my neck.

I opened David's bedroom door to check on him and watched the slow rise and fall of his chest under the sheet and blanket, and it reminded me of the countless times I would check on Ryan when he was a baby.

Ryan, fully recovered from his biking accident, had gotten back on the horse—so to speak—the following summer, riding the mountain bike trails at a much more cautious pace. Those trails had added fifty miles in the seven years since I'd opened for business.

Donovan and I had joined our local Lions Club a few years earlier, giving back to the community we loved so much. I still volunteered with the mountain bike group that maintained the trails in our town, which had found a balance of growth and small-town living.

I filled my water bottle and headed out the door and down the dirt road that led to Donovan's place, humming the tune "Beautiful Sunday" from David's old playlist, agreeing that it truly was a beautiful Sunday. All was quiet, his yard dotted with tents of sleeping teens. I found Donovan sitting on his back deck, which had a view of one of the mine-pit lakes, with March curled up at his feet.

"Good morning," Donovan said before I leaned down and kissed him.

"Did you get any sleep?"

"A few hours. I told them at two o'clock that I was calling it a night, and that if they didn't behave themselves, I'd put them all to work today." Donovan nodded toward his home. "I've got all their car keys in my bedroom."

"Smart move." I eyed his freshly mowed lawn—Ryan's part of the party planning—and Donovan's apple trees filling out with small apples.

We'd had to manually pollinate them in the spring, as the bees hadn't shown up in time. We each had a large garden, apple trees, a raspberry patch, and a creek that ran through the south end of our properties, the type of place I'd hoped for as an adult.

I took a seat next to Donovan. "Isn't it crazy to think I moved to Crimson Creek less than ten years ago? It's one of the best decisions I've ever made."

"It's all worked out, hasn't it? You got Trent to move from the cities, and your best friend moved here," Donovan reached for my hand.

Trent and Amber's move five years ago had surprised me. A new LifeJoy gym had opened in a city an hour from Crimson Creek, and Trent took the management position. Amber switched to corporate work for LifeJoy and could work from home. For Ryan, it gave him his two parents back.

"Speaking of Stevie Grace, Whip said he wants to surprise her with an anniversary getaway to the Boundary Waters in June," I said. Suddenly, a wave of nausea hit me, and I clutched my stomach, the pain radiating to my chest. I rarely got sick. Something felt wrong.

"Oh boy, I don't feel well." I went through everything I'd eaten and drunk the night before—nothing unusual.

And the nausea didn't make me feel like I wanted to throw up. It made me feel like I wanted to cry. "I'm going to head home." I stood.

"You sure? You can lie down here if you want." Donovan stood and rubbed my back.

"That's okay. I'm sure it's nothing. I'll call you later." On the short walk home, I felt as if I were walking through a distorted maze.

But everything became clear when I opened the screen door and entered my kitchen. The silence carried a weight now, a void as if the world had been tipped too far on its axle.

When I entered David's room and saw his chest no longer rose and fell, reality slammed me. *No. No. No!* I dropped to my knees by his bedside, frantically searching for a pulse.

David had left the world the same way he'd lived—without fanfare, seeking only freedom and peace. As I clutched David's still-warm hand, his voice came to me, a memory from the days after Ryan's accident. *"We all break, Eden. And then we put ourselves together again. Maybe not the same as we were before, but we rebuild and move on. It's what we have to do, or we'll never survive."*

I thought of all his loved ones who didn't know—people I would have to tell. I'd wanted David to live forever and felt cheated that I hadn't met him until he was eighty-two. It hadn't been enough time for me and certainly not enough time for Ryan.

David's recent singing of "And When I Die" resonated now—lyrics about how all he'd asked was to have no chains on him and to die naturally. The physical chains for David had been gone for decades, and he'd died a peaceful death, something that would bring comfort to Louise.

Louise. Did she sense his leaving? I wondered if she had suddenly felt, as I had, that something was horribly wrong. She would be my first call after I texted Donovan. Pulling my cell phone from my shorts pocket, I typed, *"David passed away. Please wake Ryan and bring him here with you. I'm calling Louise."*

Forcing myself to stand, I leaned over and placed a gentle kiss on the man who'd brought so much happiness to those who'd loved him. Those lives would be broken for a while, but they would slowly mend with treasured memories and the resolution to move on.

Because that's what we do after we break.

Acknowledgments

Every book I've written has brought me to this story—the one I feel I was meant to write. A few years ago, I found the Vietnam POW bracelet my mom had worn during the war. I Googled "Lt. Col. David Everson" and found out he'd survived and lived just a few hours away. David agreed to meet with me so I could give him the POW bracelet bearing his name. Meeting David was an honor, and over the next several months, we—and his daughter, DeAnn—continued to meet. I realized I was hearing pieces of history that few had the privilege of hearing. David knew I was writing a fictional character based on him. (Sadly, he passed away in early 2024.) During this time, I was in the final-draft stage of *Closer to Home* and added a POW bracelet in the story, an appropriate addition, since that story took place in the 1970s and featured three Vietnam veterans.

While this is Eden's story (loosely tied to *Closer to Home*), it's also David's. Although David's story here isn't David Everson's story, it's based on some of his experiences as a prisoner of war. I'm thankful for books like Kristin Hannah's, *The Women*, that are shining a light on the Vietnam War and its aftereffects, something I touched on in *Closer to Home*.

I worked in the loan department of a bank in the 1980s and loved it—and my coworkers! Eden's work experience is not mine, but it's still all too familiar to women in the workforce. Things have improved over the decades, but we have a long way to go.

The mountain biking town of Crimson Creek is loosely based on the small towns that make up the Cuyuna Country State Recreation

Area (CCSRA) in Minnesota, which has transformed from a mining community decades ago to a thriving outdoor rec community. This story takes place in the early stages of that transformation.

I appreciate the wisdom these people shared with me: Jenny Smith, owner of Cycle Path & Paddle—a store similar to Eden's, which opened at the cusp of the community change—kindly shared her business experience with me. To Dr. Shawn Roberts for sharing his medical wisdom with me again (he also was a major contributor to getting the rec area started). To the many small-business owners in the CCSRA area, like Red Raven's bike repair shop, who helped in my research, thank you for your part in growing the CCSRA community. And to all the trail maintenance volunteers, people like Nick Statzs, who was so dedicated to creating the CCSRA that he went to school to work for the DNR. Any research errors are mine.

To Lynn McNamee, owner of Red Adept Publishing, for bringing this story to readers, to content editor Diane Byington and line editor Kelly Reed, for helping make Eden and David's story shine, and to Streetlight Graphics for designing the perfect cover!

A heartfelt thank you goes to DeAnn (Everson) Opheim, David's daughter. If not for her paving the way for me to meet with David, this story would never have been written. DeAnn's input on what it was like for her family while her father was a prisoner of war helped paint a picture of what he missed in his family's lives. DeAnn and her husband, Doug, have been so welcoming to me.

The character Hal, David's buddy and fellow air force pilot, is loosely based on my dad, Hal, who flew rescue missions in the Vietnam War. Thank you, Dad, and every other veteran, for your service.

Kelly Chase won the bid to have a character named after her, and her last name worked perfectly for the character! I appreciate Gary Jensen and the seniors at the Deerwood American Legion for welcoming me to their bi-monthly dances (featured in the book). Thank you to the anonymous human resources person who helped me solve

Eden's work nightmare, and to the WFWA (Women's Fiction Writers Association) Zoom crew, who kept me accountable in my writing. Books that helped round out my research: *The League of Wives*, by Heath Hardage Lee, and *A P.O.W.'s Story: 2801 Days in Hanoi*, by David's fellow prisoner friend, Col. Larry Guarino.

There are many songs mentioned in the story, popular during David's captivity. Those songs reflect happy memories of my youth, but since I met David, those same songs now remind me of what he—and roughly seven hundred other men—endured as POWs while those songs were popular. (The Spotify song list is on my website.)

A special thank you to my husband, Don, who has been so supportive of my writing. A final thanks to you, the reader, for spending your time with my stories. Reading, recommending, and reviewing books you enjoy helps both the author and fellow book lovers.

About the Author

Jill writes about women determined to reclaim their lives—stories of family, friendship, forgiveness, and fortitude.

She lives with her husband on a lake in central Minnesota, where they enjoy visits from their adult children and their many grandchildren. When Jill isn't writing or reading, she enjoys the outdoors, curling, pickleball, and time with family and friends. She is an active member of her local Lions Club.

Read more at www.jillhannahanderson.com.

About the Publisher

Dear Reader,

We hope you enjoyed this book. Please consider leaving a review on your favorite book site.

Visit our site to find more quality books!

Read more at https://RedAdeptPublishing.com.

www.ingramcontent.com/pod-product-compliance
Lightning Source LLC
LaVergne TN
LVHW040039080526
838202LV00045B/3409